Jeremy Noble

Jeremy Noble read English at Magdalene College, Cambridge, where he won a half-blue for polo, saved a princess from a raging fire, and drove a black Ferrari.

In the traditional way, he has made and lost several fortunes, and now writes for a living.

Visit www.jeremynoble.com to learn more.

Villa Eilenroc

Jeremy Noble

EGRET PRESS

The right of Jeremy Noble to be identified as the Author of the Work has been asserted by him in accordance with the Copyright, Designs and Patents Act 1988.

First published in paperback in Great Britain in 2015 by
EGRET PRESS

Cataloguing in Publication data is available from the British Library

ISBN 978-0-9933869-0-9

Cover design by Stuart Bache

Typeset by Geoff Fisher in Dante MT 11.5/14pt

Printed and bound in Great Britain by
CPI Group (UK), Croydon CR4 4YY

This book is a work of fiction. Any resemblance to actual persons, living or dead, or actual events, is entirely coincidental. Names, characters, businesses, organisations, places, events, and situations are the product of the author's imagination or are used fictitiously.

All rights reserved. Apart from any use permitted by UK copyright law, no parts of this book may be reproduced in any form or by any means without written consent from the publishers or, in the case of reprographic production, in accordance with the terms of licences issued by the Copyright Licensing Agency.

Egret's policy is to use papers that are natural, renewable and recyclable products, made from wood grown in sustainable forests. The logging and manufacturing processes are expected to conform to the environmental regulations of the country of origin.

EGRET PRESS
London

For D

About the four-letter words. I write what I hear people speak, and how I imagine they are thinking. Defenders of the right to be vulgar, profane or obscene, like to bring in Shakespeare as their witness: look at *King Lear*, they say. But, for me, that is just cussing and swearing – a surface emotion. A better example, I think, is Sonnet 135, where Will makes such a vicious use of "will" that he seems to have lost the will to live.

I will never forget my 4th Form English master reading with us Chaucer's Prologue, from *The Canterbury Tales*, and asking me what I thought these lines meant? You need to know that I was sitting next to the only girl in the class.

> "We wommen han, if that I shall nat lye,
> In this matere a queynte fantasye."

I'm with Cole Porter on this one.

"Good authors, too, who once knew better words / Now only use four-letter words / Writing prose. Anything goes."

Prologue
Convent of the Sacred Heart, Manhattan   xiii

Fatty
The Catering Countess	1
Fatty	12
Claudia and *Claudia*	20
St-Trop	32
Chanel	38
Dishing the Dirt	41
Les voiles	52
Les people	53
Menu du jour	72
Marcus Gavius Apicius	74
Montrachet	78
Chablis	84
1961	90
Romanée-Conti	96
Haute chocolaterie	104

Thinspiration
Thinspiration	121
A Hothouse Atmosphere	137
The Gardens of Queen Elena	146
The *Belle Époque* Railway Station Scene	161
Versace Romance	171

Lose Weight through Sex
A Totally Fat Wardrobe	181
A Fuck Me Lunch	190
The Plot Thickens	211
Left Bank v Right Bank	214
Montecatini Terme	220
Fat Girl Rodeo	224
Kind of Blue	237
Lucca	246
Figgy-Dowdy	263
Moscow-on-Sea	269
Lose Weight through Sex	281

Rubenesque

Pierre Marcolini	297
A Woman Scorned	304
Pros and Cons	310
Cherchez la femme	311
Rubenesque	322
Combattente	327
Kompromat	330
A Balanced Diet	340
Pros and Cons (again)	343
Thigh Gap	344

Food For Thought

La Croisette	351
Oh! s'io potessi dissipare le nubi	354
Culoni	358
À la carte	363
Size matters	368
Pelmeni	375
Caviare to the General	386
Escoffier	392
Truffle Hunting	395
Le déjeuner	408
Boeuf en daube	416
Food for Thought	421
Bombe Néro	426

Villa Eilenroc

"Nothing tastes as good as skinny feels"	437
Le Numéro Cinq	445
Cooked English	454
Comfort Food	459
The Tale of a Fairy	467
Villa Eilenroc	470
Myth-making	483

Epilogue

Sur la plage	489

"The chauffeur, a Russian Czar of the period of Ivan the Terrible, was a self-appointed guide, and the resplendent names -- Cannes, Nice, Monte Carlo -- began to glow through their torpid camouflage, whispering of old kings come here to dine or die, of rajahs tossing Buddha's eyes to English ballerinas, of Russian princes turning the weeks into Baltic twilights in the lost caviare days."

Tender is the Night (1934)
F. Scott Fitzgerald

Prologue

Convent of the Sacred Heart, Manhattan

SISTER URSULA RAISED her eyes heavenwards. "Gluttony, Miss Imogen O'Rorke, is one of the seven deadly sins."

"But Sister Ursula, you're always telling us that we shouldn't be vain. We have to eat and not think about being pretty."

"Don't be clever, Imogen. Men don't like clever women. Try to be more like Claudia with all her gold stars. You don't see her stuffing her face with ... with ..." Sister Ursula extended her goose-like neck and sniffed.

"It's *jalousie* of crab and spinach wrapped in puff pastry, Sister, and these are veal cheeks braised in red wine, served with dumplings, and this is *bavaroise* with pears and chocolate sauce."

"Foreign muck, Imogen. The kitchen is not for cooking in, the kitchen is out of bounds."

"Oh, but I haven't been cooking, Sister Ursula. I can't cook. I'm not allowed in the kitchen at home, either. Too much temptation, my father says. Well-brought-up young ladies like me don't cook. I ordered it from Lutèce. It's my father's favourite restaurant. I've been eating and reading. Is that a terrible sin, Sister?"

"And the book, Imogen, show me the cover."

"It's a book of Mediterranean food, Sister."

Judging by the cover – a Dionysian still-life of a wrought iron round table dressed with a white tablecloth, bearing a red cruciform lobster; a bottle of olive oil; sinful oysters nestling in their shells; a kaleidoscope of soft Southern fruit; a fresh fish; a wedge of golden melon; a blue ceramic bowl piled high with green tagliatelle; the table attended by amphorae; and everything artfully arranged *en plein air* against a refulgent seascape – Sister Ursula would have recommended that the book immediately be added to the *Index Librorum Prohibitorum*.

"Imogen O'Rorke, for the love of God, haven't I said to you till I'm quite blue in the face that food has nothing to do with pleasure?"

"But Sister Ursula, the Archbishop, before he sat down for dinner, I heard him say, 'It is not what goes into the mouth that defiles a person, but what comes out of the mouth; this defiles a person.'"

Sister Ursula wrestled with her rosary. "Now, will you be listening to me very carefully, young lady." She paused for greater dramatic effect. "Fat girls don't get married, Imogen. Fat girls aren't happy. But for the truly penitent there is salvation because, Imogen, buried deep inside every fat girl, a thin girl is desperately trying to get out."

Fatty

The Catering Countess

THE RED VESPA sagged, like a pack mule, as Imogen O'Rorke nestled her big behind on to the seat. She hitched up her brightly coloured floral caftan, revealing meaty thighs that gripped the quivering machine like a gaucho on a polo pony. A masculine pose; and yet her yellow ballet pumps were feminine and delicate, with telltale Chanel golden bows; and completely at odds with the aggression with which she manhandled the Vespa around the gravelled driveway.

On both sides of the fuel tank, painted in large gold script were the words *The Catering Countess*. A large wicker picnic basket was strapped to the passenger seat, and on all sides, *The Catering Countess* was sploshed in bright red. Imogen wore a safety helmet, in the same bright red, with her advertising slogan painted in gold around the rim, like something out of the circus.

The mechanised gates swung open, and the Catering Countess set off on her daily commute.

It was a quite fantastical sight, and sound: there was a small radio fixed to the handlebars, with speakers on either side, and she had earphones fitted inside her helmet. This morning, because she was in a good mood, she was listening to her late grandmother's favourite upbeat music: Bing Crosby singing Cole Porter's *Let's Do It, Let's Fall In Love*; the original recording from 1928, with the Dorsey Brothers and their Orchestra.

Recherché stuff – very Cap d'Antibes – but there was a family connection. In the summer of 1922, Cole and Linda had invited Gerald and Sarah Murphy to stay with them at Château de la Garoupe; Imogen's newly married paternal grandparents were living close by. Imogen could still hear her grandmother's mock horror at the new neighbours: "They spent the day on the beach! In July! They were black!" They were tanned, impossible to ignore, and jolly good fun. Once, sporting only an all-over tan, her grandmother, Marie-Hélène, had danced an impromptu Dance of the Seven Veils to *Let's Do It*, with Cole at the piano. Marie-Hélène had danced it in front of Imogen a thousand times.

Yes, Imogen made for a very strange sight, the "fat woman of Antibes", as all the book-reading locals called her – a nod to Somerset Maugham – seated astride what looked like a motorised butcher's bike, buzzing down the Boulevard John F Kennedy, past the 'billionaires' bungalows' skirting the fabled Villa Eilenroc, where Marie-Hélène had danced her flawless nights away, burning through her youth. There wasn't a day that Imogen didn't pass the villa, expecting the ghosts of Mrs Beaumont's guests to step out into the road – crinolined queens and cruel kings, Romanov Grand Dukes and Spanish grandees, the Fitzgeralds, Carnegie, Garbo, and Valentino. Imogen zipped along the Boulevard de la Garoupe, hugging the coastline and sweeping down the Boulevard du Bacon, with her horsey Hermès scarf whipping in the wind.

There had been no rain for months, and the ground was parched and cracked. Behind the high walls, however, all was lush and wet and fragrant: there were parasol and marine pines,

Arabian maples, cypress trees, oaks, olive trees, arbutus, bougainvillea, lavender, laurel, heliotrope, eucalyptus, mimosa, ficus, and clipped pittosporum hedges. Inside these perfumed walls live some of the richest people on the planet; the 92,000 who make up the world's super-rich.

Imogen knew this world well; she had grown up with it, its glamorous echoes and memories. This had once been Scott Fitzgerald's South of France. He had called it "the nearest thing to paradise." Even before people had understood that they were living a legend, Diaghilev had premiered *Le train bleu* in 1924, with Anton Dolin, dressed by Chanel, performing acrobatics in the Parisian sand (designed to mimic the Murphys' beach at La Garoupe); a world immortalised in that iconic photograph by Robert Capa of Picasso and Françoise Gilot walking on the beach at Golfe-Juan, with a chivalrous Picasso holding a parasol. Only it doesn't exist any more, mysterious Provence, not because the property developers have overbuilt, and concreted over all the trees, as people love to moan – the Romans started that – no, the myth has lost its potency. Brigitte Bardot is the last mythical creature to inhabit the Côte d'Azur. Yes, the Russians have returned, after an absence of a hundred years, but this is not *Sleeping Beauty*; these Russians are newly minted, loud and vulgar; Kschessinskaya and her Grand Dukes would never have entertained them. Imogen cooked for them, the super-rich, catered their parties. As she saw it, however, while they could afford to live the life, few of them knew how to live it.

A herd of cyclists swarmed behind Imogen, their tyres kissing the tarmac. Imogen steered into the side, and a mass of tight bums packaged in neon lycra flashed past her. Familiar words floated back – *"Grognasse!" "Y'a du monde au balcon!" "Grosse vache!" "Tonneau!"* Imogen ignored them; she was used to it. One man, at least, was more appreciative. *"Bien roulée!"* he shouted. And he waved.

There was not a moneyed person in sight; it was too early for the rich to be awake in Cap d'Antibes. Here, even the sun rises late. But along the Boulevard James Wyllie, down by the public beach, the rest of Antibes was up and about – joggers, dog walkers, driftwood collectors, camper-van residents, and an army of municipal workers; hosing the pavements, pruning the palm trees, prettifying the roundabouts, and raking the beach. None of these people matters; they are supporting players. Antibes is manicured for manicured people.

The bay was waking up with the chugging sound of the fishermen's *pointues*. They moved around the bay, hauling in their pots and nets, bringing their catch – *fruits de mer* still flapping and crawling – into the market.

Around the bay, the southern Alps were framed in the far distance, like a slice of bourgeois wedding cake with icing plastered on top. All the houses so many crumbs clinging to the coast, thought Imogen – her images were always of food. Food was why she was here; she made her living out of it.

Her route into Old Town took her past at least a dozen open-air cafés. It was 8.30 am, and the continental breakfasts were out on the tables – brioches, croissants, *café crème,* hot chocolate; and *Nice Matin.*

Imogen swooped into the Cours Masséna, and bagged a parking spot for the Vespa. She unstrapped the picnic basket and walked the few steps to the covered Marché Provençal, in the middle of the square. It was already filling up with locals, eager to get in and get out before the tourists finished their breakfasts and swarmed in with their cameras; and not enough money to be of any interest to the stallholders.

For Imogen, this was a sacred place, the scene where the uncooked Elizabeth David had met the aged Norman Douglas – writer, bon viveur, gastronome, and pederast, talking about tarragon. That was what the Côte d'Azur meant for Imogen: where people had eaten, and what; not a place of literary pilgrimage, or beautiful people, or painters, or topless starlets. Right around the corner from where she was elbowing her way to the butchers' stalls, Graham Greene had eaten a "frugal lunch" every day in Café Felix. That word "frugal" had always fascinated Imogen: how could you be frugal about food? Food was something to worship, not to ration.

It was the height of high season, not a day to dawdle. This was work, and today she had competition: the superyacht chefs. In the market they were the best customers. Money was no object and, for as long as Imogen had been living here, money talked louder than anything else on the French Riviera.

To be in the market was to feel the pulse of the town, the eternal appeal of Provence, all mixed up in people's minds like ratatouille: they were all looking for the symbols of a successful jet-set holiday to take home in a suitcase – *herbes de Provence*, olive oil, tinned tapenade, lavender bags ...

"Don't be such a snob," Imogen told herself for the umpteenth time. "They have as much right to be here as anybody else."

Still, today, there was nothing romantic about fighting for the best peaches. This wasn't shopping; this was a plan of campaign. She had to get the ingredients for the lunch tomorrow: the appetisers, the meat, fish, truffles, cheese, herbs, spices, fruit, tea, and pasta. Being in the market was the second movement in the symphonic, creative process that thrilled her no matter how many times she did it: thinking about and planning the menu, buying what was needed, the alchemy of cooking, and finally, the dramatic presentation on a perfectly laid table; all this was as uplifting as taking the sacrament.

Claudia had given her clear yet mysterious instructions about the lunch she was holding at their villa in Saint-Tropez during the regatta. "Mo, I want the women to be green with envy when they see what's on the plate, and I don't want the men to be hungry when they stand up, and whatever you do, don't forget the chocolate 'cos Frank says there's another fortune riding on the success of this."

Frank was Claudia's husband, older than Claudia, as nice as pie – well, he acted nice – and rich as Croesus. Imogen usually only cooked for people with money. Worrying about a pile of dough 'at stake' had never yet bothered her enough to spoil a soufflé. But cooking for well-heeled men and women was tricky; the women were always on a diet, and the men just wanted to tuck in.

"The way to a man's heart is through his stomach and his cock," was Claudia's favourite saying, and that was how she had caught Frank. The day after leaving Brillantmont finishing school in Lausanne, Claudia had gone looking for a husband. She had found Frank in the pages of *Paris Match*; one of those articles about "rich and unmarried." Frank had been way down the list of the top one hundred, but Claudia had said that he had "potential."

"How can you be so mercenary?" asked Imogen. "And how can you know that he has potential?"

"I'm not going to even answer the first question. And you'll see about the second. Men are such mutts."

Engineering a 'chance' meeting with Frank had taken Claudia all of a week. Her doting father – the archetypal Swiss banker, discreet and amoral – had given her the office address. A few days later Claudia fell over in stiletto heels, right in front of Frank as he left the building.

Claudia had marketed herself as a rich man's daughter who just wanted to be 'normal', to be a good wife and mother – cooking, washing and cleaning.

But Claudia couldn't cook. Cue Imogen who did the ghost-cooking for Claudia's nightly dinners *à deux* with Frank, in the apartment she shared with Imogen in Geneva. As soon as dinner was ready, Imogen made herself scarce, leaving Claudia to entertain Frank, and amaze him with her talents. Claudia had looked after the cock part herself; she had had lots of practice with her father's chauffeur.

It was a successful campaign – Claudia had a ring on her finger less than six months later. And she had been right about the potential: Frank was running a new type of investment business called a hedge fund; in the early days, when he had told people what he did, he was mistaken for a landscape gardener. Not now.

As she walked around the market, Imogen ticked off in her mind the ingredients she needed for each course. They were going to eat outside on the terrace. Saint-Tropez at the end of September would be warm and windy; that was why they held the yachting week when they did – the season for sunglasses.

Foodwise, you had to hedge your bets. First, trays of little appetisers that you could pick up with your fingers – miniature *burek*, filled with lamb, and cheese and spinach (for picky vegetarians); warm foie gras glazed with wild strawberries, on Melba toast; and *anchoïade*, because you had to have something Provençal.

A dozen wild partridges, expertly dressed, were waiting for her at Henri's stand; she had ordered them a few days ago. Imogen was fond of the corpulent, ruddy Henri; there was something arousing about a man who always had blood on his hands.

"I could have sold them three times over," laughed Henri, handing over the birds, "to the yacht chefs."

Using her weight to force a path through the crowd, Imogen crossed over to the other side of the market. Her favourite fisherman, Julien, dressed as always in gumboots and a stiff blood-stained plastic apron, and smelling of gutted fish, presented her with a dozen white fillets of Saint Pierre.

"I've packed them in ice to keep them fresh. There won't be a fridge on that speedboat you're taking to St-Trop."

"Oh Julien, *merci mille fois.*"

"Don't get seasick!"

At the Roche truffle stand Imogen waited while an English chef accompanied by a Russian bagman bought three kilos of black truffles – that came to just over ten thousand euro!

"Have them delivered to the port, will you?" demanded the chef.

"Yes, of course, *monsieur*, which boat?"

"*Billionaire's Row*. The biggest one."

As the chef and his bagman turned away, Gilbert shrugged at Imogen, as if to say, "What can you do with such people?"

"You wanted two-hundred-fifty grammes, *non*, Madame Imogène? I saved it for you."

Claudia had told her not to think about the cost of anything. But that was not Imogen's style: she liked her clients, especially her best friend, to think that they were being treated fairly. With truffles, though, it was difficult to watch the pennies; the price had skyrocketed in recent years, and still the Russians kept on buying.

Imogen had been around money all her life, but these Russians were something else: "oligarch" was a word everybody in the market knew; a buzz would go around the market whenever an oligarch's yacht dropped anchor.

It wasn't only oligarchs; ordinary Russians spent money like water. At the cheese stand Imogen waited while a badly dressed couple – cheap shoes, she noticed, and a tacky handbag – bought two whole wheels of aged Parmesan; that was more than a thousand euro. They weren't interested in any other type of cheese. Parmesan had become a status symbol, for God's sake. Imogen bought a small slice of Parmesan, aged twenty-four months; it was for the *hors d'oeuvre*, and with it eight other cheeses for the cheeseboard, one from each of *les huit familles de fromage*, as she would carefully describe them on the menu – gastronomic detail always went down well with her status-conscious clients.

The central line of the market was all home-grown fruit and vegetables. Organic produce was still fashionable – clients liked her to emphasise the word on the printed menu cards – but Imogen didn't see the point in buying organic if you could buy from an old lady; they never used chemicals. Imogen had a horror of those waxed apples and perfectly formed plump and tasteless tomatoes they sold in supermarkets. She liked her fruit and veg misshapen; leeks, celeriac, spinach, potatoes, juniper berries, chestnuts, horseradish, and walnuts all went into her canvas bags, now that the basket was full. She was tiring; that was why she kept the most enjoyable things for last.

At Olives Pellegrino, Pierre scooped out shining black La Nyons and green Lucques olives; they were for the stuffing to go inside the partridges.

A few stalls down, Madeleine looked harassed, standing in front of her mosaic of herbs and spices. It was the most gorgeous sight in the market, a cornucopia of colours and smells: sand dunes of green, orange, crystal pinks, pale greens, dark reds ... Every tourist wanted to take a photo, and only a few of them were gracious enough to buy a bag of something. This was definitely not a day for chit-chat. Imogen knew exactly what she wanted, and just saying the words gave her an exquisite pleasure – the language of the Silk Route: *"Saffron, ciboulette, sel rose de l'Himalaya, flocons de sel de mer de Chypre, poivre blanc de Malabar, poivre noir de Sarawak, et nigelle, s'il vous plaît,* Madeleine."

Next door, at Hélène's stand, full of teas and infusions, Imogen experienced that tingling glow, which comes from the commingling of an aesthetic pleasure, and a craftsman's appreciation of the impression she would make when she presented these teas at the end of lunch tomorrow: *rose bouton, badiane chinoise, tilleul,* and *verveine citronelle*.

She was exhausted. She lumbered the few steps away from the market, to the rue Sade. In La Boîte à Pâtes she bought *lune Provençale* pasta.

The sun was high, stoking and intensifying the heat that radiated through, deep within, under and around Antibes, soaking up and sweeping away the monastic shadows of the Old Town.

Everybody without money in Provence feels the heat; they wipe salty droplets off the brow, dab away the perspiration forming above the top lip, surreptitiously sniff and inspect under the arms to make sure that the chemical deodorants have blocked up the sweat glands; and they slip and trip, in their greasy, cheap flip-flops.

Money doesn't feel the heat on the Côte d'Azur; it lives in an air-conditioned postcard environment. Outings in the sun are always protected by café blinds, cooled by close proximity to the sea breeze, and refreshed by glistening ice buckets.

Fat people suffer in the heat; sweat lingers and congeals in the cracks – between the buttocks, the genitalia, the swamp under the armpits. The suffering is tortuous: the sun's morning tendrils lick around the ankles, wreathing the legs, attacking the flesh, like burning faggots scorching a prisoner tied at the stake. For the poor and the fat, heat in Provence is pitiless.

Imogen rubbed the back of her kaftan just where the knicker elastic was sticky. It was 10.15, the shopping was finished; she had everything she needed for the lunch. Time to meet Claudia in L'Enoteca on the edge of the square.

Fatty

L'ENOTECA WAS NOT Imogen's favourite bar, not because she didn't like the place – they had a wine list that was always food for thought – but because of the barstools ...

Imogen was too big for them. She tried to squeeze her whole ass on to the seat, without her butt cheeks flopping over on either side; no, they wouldn't both fit, so it would have to be that familiar game of hide the fat. Like a secret agent who works out where is the safest place to sit in any room, she figured that Claudia would make her grand entrance for maximum male impact: she would get the driver to stop on the far side of the market, and walk right through the centre – a showstopper.

Being at the centre of anything for Imogen was torture, she always had to sit at an angle or else she looked like an elephant perched on a bucket in a circus. She had chosen a barstool at the far end of the bar, beside a vase of overblown white roses and floppy green fronds – good camouflage. No, the angle was wrong, face-on she looked like a jumbo jet. She lowered herself, not in one go, that was too risky and much too noticeable, but in orchestrated movements: first the right leg, a horse rider's leg – a thick calf and brawny thigh; whoops! The heel of her ballet pump slammed into the parquet floor, like an asteroid pitting the surface of the moon. Next, the right ass cheek plopped down, so far, so good. Now the left side; she was almost up, but her left breast somehow refused to smoothly follow the beautiful ballet movement she had fixed in her mind, and it dragged and slid a little across the bar. Surreptitiously raising her left arm – "God, please," she prayed, "not like a shot putter" – she scooped it up and let it balance like a blancmange until she was standing on the floor.

She turned the barstool at an angle, and now she had to manoeuvre her bulk back to where she had been a few minutes ago. "It takes a super tanker two days to turn around," she said to herself, "and that's me, Imogen O'Rorke, super tanker, super cook."

She ordered a gin and tonic. Sitting next to her was the type of woman she most disliked: a sporty-looking blonde of about thirty-five, who looked as if she had just left the gym – pony-tail, pink sweatband and matching trainers, black leggings, and a black T-shirt with the zig-zag coordinates in white of a bobsleigh run in Switzerland coursing down her spine, designed to show, no, *announcing* the fact that this woman had no fear. Certainly, she had no fear of talking on her mobile loud enough for all the bar to hear. The voice was very Holland Park.

"It's really good news. I was two-fifty-three, now I'm one-sixty. My tummy was forty and now it's twenty-three. It's like a miracle: a whole new me to look at. And he says that I'm burning fat, and that's much better than carbs. Sixteen hundred calories is the absolute maximum. And my shape is better. My shape is much better, isn't it? He did say it wouldn't all happen at once, don't you remember? Actually, I was feeling a little bit depressed about how long it was taking. I mean, he said I can't expect to lose it all overnight. But now I can see the difference so I'm really motivated. And he's charging by the hour so the sooner the better."

Imogen had long ago painfully learned to accept that she was living in a thin world, with a lot of fat talking; the ritualised conversation that she knew by heart: "You've lost weight! You look so well! What are you on?" What made these women feel entitled to talk about things they knew nothing about? Had they ever really been fat? But she listened; she even joined in, like a gay man engaging in blokey banter, all the time feeling a fraud.

There was a shift in the atmosphere. "Fuck!" Claudia was making her way towards her, and Imogen was not in position. There was a little stirring amongst the men, sly knowing glances, a frisson. Imogen had seen it all before, always when Claudia made an entrance.

"Why can't I do that?" Imogen asked herself. "Why can't I ever have that effect on men?"

Claudia wasn't wearing much: a sand-coloured cashmere shift dress that barely covered her thighs, gold Roman sandals, and her hair was a mass of the finest blonde highlights that money could buy. Not a designer label in sight, not even on the sunglasses that she pushed nonchalantly to the crown of her head, in that "look-at-me-but-don't-look at-me" style Imogen always associated with rich women.

"*Salut.*" Claudia kissed her on both cheeks – her skin was cool to the touch – and elegantly sat down on the barstool. As always, all her thoughts came out in one go: "You look hot, fatty. Did you buy that kaftan in the kasbah? It's been bothering me all the way here."

Imogen bristled. "*T'est une vraie pute,* Clod. I'm hot because I've spent all morning buying your lunch for tomorrow, thank you very much. What's been bothering you? And what's wrong with a kaftan?"

"It looks like something nomads live in, in Mongolia. Why did you get me to order a dozen small teapots?"

"For tea."

Villa Eilenroc

"Must be some tea. What are we drinking?"

Without waiting for Imogen to reply, Claudia ordered *sirop de menthe* and chilled San Pellegrino.

They spoke in *Fritanglais*, a mixture of French, Italian and English. Claudia was her usual charming self. *"Eh bien*, you're not fucking anybody, Mo, I can see 'cos your skin is all tense."

"Grazie tesoro. Tell me about the lunch. Who's coming?"

"Il est ni flash, ni russe, ni riff-raff. Les people will be there. What are we having for lunch?"

"Oh, Clod! I sent you the menu for approval, and you said it was okay. You didn't look at it, did you?"

"I trust you. Don't make such a big thing about it. I've been really busy, you have no idea, organising this marathon of entertaining. Frank gave me a list of nearly a hundred people he wants to invite during the week, plus our friends. *Tu n'as aucune idée* how hard my life is. *Les voiles de Saint Tropez* really take the wind out of my sails."

"Who did you steal that *bon mot* from?"

"Quel bon mot?" asked Claudia, *faux-naïf*.

"Come on, Clod, you're not that clever. But it's good. Just don't use it too many times this week."

"I hate you."

"That's what best friends are for."

"Lunch! Details!"

Imogen lovingly described the menu she had been thinking about for weeks: "The appetisers on trays are a surprise; then, at table, to start, there's chilled leek and celeriac soup; then scrambled eggs with grated aged Parmesan and black Périgord truffles; followed by a tiny plate of pasta because you've got Italian guests. There's a fish course of fillet of Saint Pierre, with sauce Escoffier, and partridge for the meat course because it's just come into season, with Italian stuffing, served on a bed of potatoes with juniper berries, and a side dish of sweet-sour red cabbage and devilled chestnuts."

Imogen could tell Claudia wasn't listening. She was checking out the handbags artfully displayed on any available chair by all of the other women sitting in the bar. Good, nobody else had a Barneys alligator tote bag. Antibes is a very competitive place.

"Sounds amazing, what's sauce Escoffier?"

"I made it up, the name I mean. Escoffier gives the recipe for it at a shooting party in nineteen-twelve. I'm trying the sauce out for the first time."

"You're using my guests as guinea pigs?"

"Well, it tasted nice at home. Horseradish and walnut. I'm sure it'll go down well."

It's yachting not shooting, Mo. And don't roll your eyes like that. I know you know. What are you making that's Russian?"

"Nothing. *Tu m'as dit que c'était une fête sans Russes.*"

"I meant none of those horribly vulgar Russians who wear high heels on deck."

"Clod, you didn't specify anything Russian in particular."

"Don't get on your high horse. You said you're making Italian because I have Italians coming, so you must be cooking something Russian. I was sure you would."

"I was just saying that, and anyway I can't cook Russian!"

"It's easy, must be."

"Clod, you can't cook, so what makes you think it's easy?"

"It's just peasant food, and spoonfuls of caviare."

"So, then we'll have caviare."

"People eat caviare every day. You have to make something special."

"Does it really matter?"

"It's for Andrei."

"Who's Andrei?"

"Andrei Volkov. I even know how to pronounce it properly. He's Russian."

"I worked that out for myself. I saw his name on the guest list. I meant how does he fit into the picture?"

"Something to do with Frank's deal. He mentioned something about people lurking around in the shadows. Andrei is the gamekeeper, apparently."

"That makes sense, it's the season for game. They were in the market this morning, lots of them."

"Not that type of gamekeeper, stupid!"

Claudia never gave up, not when she really wanted something. "You'll have to download a Russian recipe this evening. You didn't forget about the chocolates, did you? It's really important, for Frank's deal."

Imogen was beginning to feel petulant; Claudia always made her feel like she was a schoolgirl. "Does my food really matter? They're all going to be talking about money anyway, not looking at what's on the plate."

"Don't be so naïve. Some catering countess you are. Did you get the chocolates or not? Shouldn't be difficult for you ... I mean, it's your ..."

Imogen was needled. "Go on, say it, it's my what? My weakness? My speciality? No, I didn't forget. I called every *chocolatier* I know in Brussels. The fridge has been full of truffles and *ganaches* for days.

"I hope you put a padlock on it. I know what you're like."

"I can be strong when I have to."

"Good. You have no idea how important chocolate's become in our lives."

"You look good on a diet of chocolate."

"Don't be silly, I don't eat the stuff. We'd better go. The car's here."

"That open-topped big thing sitting outside blocking the traffic?"

"It's a Maserati."

"I have to get the Vespa."

"It's already on the boat. I told them to find it and pick it up."

"You and your money Clod."

"I saved you the parking fine, you might say thank you."

"Thank you. How did they know which one's mine?"

"Are you kidding, that mobile sandwich-board you whizz around on?"

"Don't look at me when I try to get off this barstool."

Claudia suppressed a giggle. "I'm trying not to."

"And before you ask, don't ask me what size I am."

"I wasn't going to ask, fatty. You're my best friend."

Only Claudia could get away with calling her "fatty."

A uniformed chauffeur – he looked like a model for Dolce&Gabbana – was standing by a blinding white Maserati. He opened the door for Claudia, closed it; calmly did the same for Imogen, then nonchalantly walked around to the driver's seat, ignoring the honking of outraged horns, and drove them the half-kilometre to Port Vauban.

Imogen had calmed down in the bar, but now she was keyed up all over again, going over in her mind what she would have to do the moment they arrived at Claudia's villa. She knew the kitchen well, but Claudia couldn't cook, and didn't have any idea about what might be needed.

"Did the wine arrive? Frank thought the Burgundy in his cellar didn't make a perfect fit with the menu."

Claudia rolled her eyes melodramatically. "You two together are something else, you know that. Relax, it's fine, some chinless wonder from Berry Brothers delivered it a few days ago. Told Frank he had good taste."

"He spent a small fortune."

"There's no such thing as a small fortune. Anyway, you know what Frank's like when it comes to wine."

Imogen looked around at the thousands of boats crowded into the harbour. "How do you ever find a little boat in this crowd?

"Like a homing pigeon. It's over there."

Claudia pointed to an arrow-like superyacht, with navy-blue hull paint and a shining white superstructure. The design reminded Imogen of a shark – predatory with a raked bow and louvred gills set in the flanks.

"*Mon Dieu*! Claudia, what is it?"

"It's the new boat, the new *Claudia*, do you like it?"

"It's very big. Where did you get it?"

"Mo, you know full well you don't get a boat like this off the shelf. Frank ordered it from a shipyard in Italy."

"Right, like couture. When I said it'd be easier to just come and pick up the stuff we need for lunch I meant bring the launch, not this, this monster ... you only had to come from Saint-Tropez. And where's the old boat? This must be twice the size."

"Oh, the old boat's been sold, too small. This one's more than sixty-five metres. Frank loves telling people. You know what men are like, size matters, right? And I didn't know how much you'd be bringing with you."

"Claudia, I'm catering for twelve people, not twelve hundred!"

"Well, the partridges won't get seasick. It doesn't roll at all, you'd hardly know you're on a boat."

"Clod, the partridges stopped flying days ago."

Claudia always had to have the last word.

"Anyway, I just hope they're well hung."

Claudia and *Claudia*

THE MASERATI STOPPED right by the swimming platform at the rear of the boat; and Claudia, in three graceful steps, was on board.

"Come on, Mo, you're going to love it! And it's all thanks to chocolate."

Imogen stepped on to the platform, which moved a lot more than it had beneath Claudia's dainty movements. She obediently followed Claudia up the few steps that led to the aft deck in front of the *salon*. "What do you mean, chocolate? You're not making sense. Even less than usual."

A young crew member was standing to attention, holding a bottle of pink champagne and two champagne flutes. He had a crew-cut of Neapolitan black hair, liquid brown eyes – the Latin-lover type – and was smartly dressed in pale blue shorts, with a matching polo shirt, embroidered with the logotype of the *Claudia*. Imogen gave him the once-over. "A bit too handsome," she thought, and then inspected the label on the bottle: Bollinger *La Grande Année Rosé*. Claudia, however, hardly gave him, or the champagne, a look; and Imogen cottoned on at once. "She's fucking him, I know it. It's written all over her face. Keep quiet, Imogen."

Claudia wet her lips a little with the champagne, and this time she looked at the waiter. Imogen saw his nostrils flare for a split second, like a stallion picking up a mare's scent.

"Frank put money into a chocolate business and it's doing really well. He's coming to the lunch, Nick Austin, the chocolate guy; he and his wife, she's called Cassandra."

"Makes her sound like bad news."

"Why?"

"Did we really go to school together?"

"You got the education, Mo, I got the man."

Imogen pursed her lips. Claudia leaned over and kissed her.

"Mo, that was mean of me, I'm sorry."

"It's okay. It's true."

The horny waiter spoke. "Do you want to watch as we leave the harbour, *madame*, or you want to sit down?"

An image of Claudia sitting on his hard cock flashed into Imogen's mind. Why was it that when she and Claudia were together, she most felt the weight of her body, fat, unloved, and unfucked.

"I have to sit down, Clod."

"Well, let's do both. We'll go up to the sundeck."

"Lift or staircase, *madame*?"

"Oh, the view's much better from the staircase." Claudia made a face at Imogen that she recognised from when they were schoolgirls – it had always meant fun and trouble.

Claudia smiled wickedly. "Just follow him, I'm right behind. Then I'll show you around."

As the waiter climbed the spiral stairs to the sundeck Imogen was uncomfortably conscious of her eyes following the line of his underwear etched beneath his shorts.

"Bikkembergs – he looks good in them, doesn't he?" Claudia half giggled, half whispered. "*Vraiment très mignon*. Massimo by name, and Massimo by nature. He gives a whole new meaning to a 'pleasure boat.'"

Up on the top deck, Claudia waved the Latin Lover away with

a dismissive gesture, and threw herself onto an over-stuffed ottoman sofa. Imogen lowered herself a few kilos at a time.

They were seated beside an infinity pool that somehow remained motionless, even as the yacht got up speed leaving the harbour.

"How does it stay still like that?"

"It was Frank's idea, something to do with a drain and jet-spray nozzles. And it's contraflow."

"What's that mean?"

"So you can swim for as long as you want without actually going anywhere."

"Right. Mmm, Clod, isn't this the champagne I asked Frank to buy for lunch tomorrow?"

"I don't know. What, you don't like it?"

"No, I mean it has a lovely golden-copper colour, but it's a bit too powerful to drink on its own. It's much better with food. And are you sure we should be drinking it? Will we have enough for tomorrow?"

"Oh Mo, I do love you! You're such a puritan! You sound like a fuckin' wine bore, just like Frank in full flow – 'Must've been grown on the right bank of the vineyard' bullshit. It's only bubbly for crissakes. Anyway, Frank bought three times what you asked for. Let's have lunch now, if it makes you happy, or you want me to show you around? I thought you'd like to see my new toy."

"I've seen him," said Imogen, archly. "Don't play the innocent with me. I'm not Sister Ursula."

"Sister Ursula's dead so just relax and let's have fun."

Imogen crossed herself. "May she rest in eternal peace, the old dragon. Sorry but I just want it to go perfectly, that's all."

"It will. You're a perfectionist, and I'm the perfect hostess."

There was silence for a few moments. Imogen knew what was coming – the 'lecture.'

"If you were to just . . ."

Imogen cut her off. "Do you think you could stop sizing me up? You're unbelievable, Clod. I know you mean well but you never learn, do you?"

Claudia abruptly changed the subject, as one can with somebody you've grown up with. "Cassandra's lovely to look at but a bit neurotic, never eats anything; you know the type."

"That's meant to make me feel better is it? I get it, her character's made out of bitter chocolate. Trophy wife."

"But Nick's completely yummy."

Imogen merely raised her eyebrows.

"What! And to answer your question, no, I haven't. Not yet."

They again sat in silence for a while, both of them looking out at the sea as the yacht carved its way through the swell. Imogen liked that about Claudia; she could be horrible sometimes but she knew when to shut up, and let the moment go where it would.

She looked at Claudia, so at ease and happy. Was she, Imogen, less happy than Claudia? Did she want to be Claudia, was it as simple as that – fat girl secretly envies her beautiful thin friend? Claudia loved herself so much; she was always looking in the mirror, making meaningless adjustments. Imogen tried not to look at herself, the fat got in the way of her willingness to examine her grossness.

Claudia was living exactly the life that she had planned, in rooms full of money. The new yacht *Claudia* suited Claudia; they were made for each other, both with a hard-edged beauty. Imogen didn't think of herself as a sleek yacht, not like Claudia; she saw herself as a tugboat.

Did she want to be Claudia? Not really. Claudia's single-minded pursuit of a 'top one-hundred husband' had never appealed to her. "Oh, stop lying to yourself, Imogen O'Rorke, it was never an option, period."

Fat was an obstacle to happiness. That was what she had heard ever since she had started to fatten up at eight years old, the year her mother had died, of a broken heart according to Mrs Cross, her nanny. Her mother had, in fact, died of cancer, but Mrs Cross preferred to blame the "floozies, fancy women and ladies of the night" who had kept her father company while her mother waited for him patiently at home.

Imogen's mother had never talked about her daughter's fatness. Perhaps she had thought that being fat would keep her away from faithless men. Imogen's grandmother, however, Marie-Hélène, had talked about it every day, or it had seemed that way. Imogen looked out at the waves swelling up, cresting and falling, and she thought about what her grandmother had said to her over and over again: "*Tu sais*, Imogène, *ma petite*, being fat is being rude. You're offending other people's vision."

Marie-Hélène had been like Claudia would be when she faded past fifty: living on past glories. Hers had been a very glamorous life, the life that she had planned for her grand-daughter. Coming out of nowhere – she liked to claim that she was an orphan – and with only her beauty to get her anywhere in life, she had sensibly married into an Anglo-Irish banking family, the O'Rorkes; and then had abandoned being sensible for the rest of her life. Edward, Imogen's paternal grandfather, had inherited good looks, a sizeable fortune, and a talent for doing not very much – he was often pictured behind the wheel of a racing car.

As a child, Imogen had loved to turn the pages of the family photo album: leather-bound volumes of the 'in-crowd', in the days when it was still possible to know everybody who was worth knowing. If there was one photograph that said it all to Imogen, it was the one of Marie-Hélène dressed in a *redingote* – a costume copied from a portrait of Marie Antoinette – with Edward cavalier as Axel Fersen. They were at a masquerade ball in the Villa Eilenroc, the most magnificent residence on the Riviera, and only a short distance from Imogen's modest villa. Scott Fitzgerald was standing at her grandmother's side, and her grandfather had his arm around Zelda. That was glamour. Nowadays, only Brangelina come close.

Edward had died young, in a collision at Brooklands. Marie-Hélène lived into her nineties, fading away, as the fortune dwindled. Imogen had kept all of her clothes, wrapped in tissue paper, and stored in huge Vuitton trunks – tea gowns, ball gowns, feather boas, long kid gloves, silk corsets and hats galore. Imogen had never been able to fit into any of her grandmother's clothes. The shoes fitted perfectly, but what was the point of shoeing a carthorse? That was how she saw herself; unable to fit into a world that she had grown up in, and could only observe from the sidelines, dressed in an apron.

Vintage clothes and sepia photographs; that was about all Imogen had inherited of the O'Rorke money. Oisin, her father, had been Marie-Hélène and Edward's only child, and the attention had not been good for his character. He did have considerable charm but he was not particularly clever, and, unlike his mother, he had not been sensible enough to marry for money. Charm does not always beget a charmed life, and Oisin, despite his name, was not blessed with the fabled luck of the Irish.

For Imogen, what was left of the O'Rorke money had been just enough for an education: St Mary's Ascot – that was where she had made friends with Claudia; the Convent of the Sacred Heart; and then Brillantmont. What did that expensive education amount to? A highly developed sense of guilt; a habit of using English phrases; a passionate dislike of over-cooked English food; an undying love of cheeseburgers; and a Swiss way with money.

Imogen looked across at Claudia, and asked herself for the umpteenth time how on earth could they have ever become – still be – friends? Why hadn't Claudia chosen to go around with somebody almost as beautiful as she was?

Claudia caught the look. "*Comment?* Oh, that. Easy. Beauty and the Beast."

"*Salope*. Tell me why."

"Again? Because opposites attract. And you're not afraid of me. You're not even in awe of me. And you keep me sane."

"Right. I'm the one who must be insane to put up with you."

Claudia just smiled. She was one of life's winners.

Imogen remembered how single-minded she had been in her pursuit of Frank. In an unguarded moment, Claudia had once summed it all up: "The trick in life is to land a good catch, and never let anybody see the sleight of hand." That was too hard-nosed for Imogen; she liked the romance of being rich, but not the mercenary reality.

No, she knew that she didn't want to be Claudia because Claudia couldn't cook, and that was all Imogen had ever wanted to do, from the moment her father, and then her grandmother had banned her from the kitchen. At first, cooking had been an act of defiance; she had been a secret cook, experimenting when there was nobody at home, first in St Jean Cap Ferrat where they had lived until her father went bankrupt, after one too many get-rich-quick-schemes; and afterwards in her grandparents' kitchen, when they moved in poverty to Cap d'Antibes. Imogen had methodically made every recipe in every Elizabeth David book, and then eaten the whole lot, dish after dish, even if it "serves eight;" no wonder she had put on weight. At finishing school, she had been top of the cordon bleu class, where cooking a few select dishes with lots of red meat and heavy sauces was the "way to a man's heart;" that was what they had been told by Mademoiselle Beauclerc – spinster. "Cooking and cock" was Claudia's interpretation of *mademoiselle's* maxim.

After Brillantmont she had lived in Geneva, sharing with Claudia, for a year and a bit, where she had tried to become what her father and grandmother had pushed her to be – a rich man's wife. She wasn't as big then as she was now, and a few 'eligible' men had squired her to wherever Claudia and Frank were going – hangouts of the *jeunesse dorée*. In honour of Mademoiselle Beauclerc, the second date was always supper at home. Imogen's food was much admired, and there was never anything left on her beau's plate, but when it came to bedtime, he always "had to be somewhere." Of course, even rhinos fuck, and she had lost her virginity; only, as Claudia brutally said, it had been a "mercy fuck." It was a boy whose name she tried not to remember – Anatole – but for certain she had made Chicken Marengo. First, he had made her bleed, and then he had made her cry.

Claudia had comforted her. "Men just see what they want to see, Mo, so you only let them look at what they want to grab hold of. You have such a pretty face, and lovely hair, so why don't you just lose some weight?"

It took a long time before the pain went away. After that, Imogen wrapped herself up in loose fitting 'tents', and made cooking the love of her life.

The day after Claudia married Frank, Imogen flew to Paris, and into an apprenticeship at a restaurant owned by a friend of her father's, the only time she had asked him to help her.

It was a legendary Michelin-starred restaurant, with a menu that hadn't changed since Paris was liberated, and run by a tyrant who didn't believe that women had a place in the kitchen. But Imogen had stuck it out, and taken from it what she knew she needed, before setting up on her own as *The Catering Countess*.

That had been a jump off a cliff top. Opening her own

business so early in her career, and hoping with clenched fists that a parachute would open before she hit the ground, and went bust like her father. It had been Frank who pushed her into it. After six years in Paris, stirring sauces and slicing vegetables, Imogen had sensed that the world of food was changing. Cream in every dish, presented in a stuffy and over-decorated restaurant was going out, and lighter dishes were the coming thing, served in a more dressed-down, relaxed atmosphere. She knew that it was time to move to another restaurant with a less classical kitchen, more *nouvelle cuisine*. But she was not happy working in a team. Insults about elephants getting in the way didn't bother her, but she didn't take orders well, a trait she had inherited from her grandmother. Frank had put it bluntly: "In life, Mo, you can either be a slave or an overseer, so now it's make-your-mind-up time."

Imogen had served a good cooking apprenticeship, but actually running a restaurant or any type of business was not a part of that learning. She had listened to Frank's one-line advice about how "snobbery sells Mo, every time," and that was how she had come up with the name of *The Catering Countess*. The title was all that her mother's family had been left with after they fled Czechoslovakia, leaving a mining fortune behind the Iron Curtain.

"Breeding will out," they say, and the catering countess had traded on her connections, hustling for lunches, suppers, and celebrations, all along the French Riviera; funerals were a good money-spinner – so many old *roués* and raddled beauties shrivelling under the Provençal sunlight.

Frank had once said to her, "We buy lots of things Mo, but we have no idea what, or why we're buying; think about it." He was fond of these cryptic, loaded phrases. After thinking about it for a while, Imogen understood what he had meant. The catering countess would sell food snobbism, wrapped up in the history of *haute cuisine*; and that was why her menus always presented signature dishes created by the great chefs of yesteryear – Carême, Cubat, Dubois, Escoffier, all the way back to La Varenne – but without the heavy cream. It was a winning formula.

So, here she was, Imogen O'Rorke, a cook – oh, all right, a caterer, as if that enhanced her status. She would never be rich, not the owner of a yacht like this, anyway. When her father had died, he had left her only the house on Cap d'Antibes. Indulged by his mother, Oisin had run through his money in casinos all along the French Riviera, all the while bemoaning the "luck of the Irish;" and had been bailed out far too many times by Marie-Hélène, ever to become independent. The fear of failure was what drove Imogen to cook.

Claudia abruptly stood up. "Stop day-dreaming, Mo. Time for the tour. Follow me."

A glass lift took them to all four floors, and on each floor Claudia led Imogen about like a carefree wench pulling a bull by a ring in its nose. They visited the bridge deck aft, the touch-and-go helipad, the lower deck, the staterooms, master suite, VIP suite, the four lower-deck cabins ... All the while Claudia talked non-stop like a tour guide:

"The whole décor is inspired by the Exposition Internationale des Arts Décoratifs et Industriel Modernes, held in Paris in 1925. All the carpets were hand-loomed in Tibet, and delivered in single pieces."

Claudia knew the name of every fabric, inlay, and curlicue. "There's watered silk, plush velvet, mother-of-pearl ... that's Makassar ebony ... Siena marble ... Calcutta marble ... Swarovski crystals, of course. This is *Jatoba* parquet ... *amboyna* burr ... and those are called Vitruvian scrolls ..." On and on until Imogen's head was crammed with a surfeit of luxury.

She stared at the grand piano in the stateroom. "You can't play the piano!"

Claudia was unfazed. "It plays itself. I thought of everything, don't you think? Look at these copper fixtures, much warmer than stainless steel."

Claudia was so confident of herself and her terrible taste, thought Imogen; that was why she and Frank made such a good team. Yes, Claudia fucked around, perhaps Frank did too, but they believed in the two of them together.

Claudia left, as she put it, "The best to last." The two women walked down a short passageway, hung with pictures of tranquil seascapes – "Much too good for Claudia to have chosen," thought Imogen.

"This is just ours, the owner's deck, nobody's allowed here," announced Claudia. "Isn't that the most enormous bed you've ever seen? And there's a study for Frank and a sitting-room for me, and how about this!" Claudia flung open a heavy, lacquered wooden door to reveal a cavernous bathroom that was swimming in cream onyx, cherry-wood cabinets and gold taps.

Imogen thought that it was hideous, and tried to find something to like: "Lovely towels."

Claudia gave her a look. "That's a nice Matisse," Imogen said, admiringly, as they walked into the cinema room, thinking how soothing it was to look at something that didn't glare in her eyes.

Claudia pressed a button, and the Matisse disappeared, becoming a TV screen.

"Neat, huh?"

"I like the Matisse better. What about the kitchen?"

Claudia shrugged. "I don't know where it is."

They found it, after Claudia rang for help, and Massimo the

toy boy came running. Imogen admired the stainless steel appliances and prep surfaces that looked as if they had never been used.

The kitchen was empty, not a chef in sight.

"How are we going to have lunch here, without a cook? Where's Marcus?"

Claudia smiled sweetly. "I gave him the day off. Poor boy's been slaving away. But he'll be helping tomorrow at the villa, I promise."

"Oh no, Clod! I said that I would cook lunch tomorrow, not all weekend!"

"Stop going on so much, Mo. Anyway, it'll do you good to go without lunch occasionally."

"Thanks a lot."

"Well?" asked Claudia eagerly. "What do you think?"

"It's a nice kitchen."

"The boat!"

Imogen didn't hesitate. "It's vulgar and revolting."

Claudia wasn't at all put out. In spite of what Imogen had said, she was smiling. "You're a fat cow, you know that, Imogen O'Rorke."

St-Trop

*I*T SEEMS EXACTLY right that Saint-Tropez should be named after a Christian martyr whose life story is the stuff of legend, and so completely unreliable. All we know for certain about Saint Torpes of Pisa is that he died in Rome in AD 65 during the reign of Nero. He must have come to a bad end because otherwise he wouldn't have become a martyr, would he?

Nothing much happened in Saint-Tropez for another thousand years or more. They built a fortress at the top of the hill; and fish must have been an important part of the diet.

12 April 1887, and Guy de Maupassant sails into this fishing village. He's on a small sailboat called the Bel-Ami; it has a two-man crew that does the hard work and the cooking while the boss steers and communes with nature – that's very Saint-Tropez.

Maupassant is on a nine-day cruise, sailing along the Riviera coast between Saint-Tropez and Monaco. Sur l'eau, the published account of his trip, is a little gem. He describes Saint-Tropez as "one of those charming and simple daughters of the sea, one of those lovely modest and tiny villages, pushed into the water like a shell, feeding on fish and nourished by the sea air, and giving birth to sailors."

Lovely, only the book is a beautiful lie: Maupassant cut and pasted together all sorts of bits and pieces from articles he had already written. The nearest he comes to the truth is when he admires a stretch of unspoiled coastline, which hasn't yet been "desecrated" by the

Villa Eilenroc

"Parisians and the English and Americans." Between Saint-Raphaël and Saint-Tropez, however, the virgin forest is being felled for winter resorts; proof that property developers have always been with us.

Next, it is the turn of Paul Signac to sail into Saint-Tropez in 1892 on Olympia. He likes the place so much that he buys a house and a studio here; and keeps his boat in the port. He liked to paint views of the harbour and the town, in ravishing colours – lemon, lilac, azure, burnt umber, fuchsia, and cerise, so luminous they seem to give off their own heat haze. Signac created the postcard images of Saint-Tropez.

The French like to sit in cafés that have a literary association, and that is why Sénéquier and Gorille are still the most fashionable places to watch the world go by in the old port because this is where Jean-Paul Sartre, Simone de Beauvoir, and Jacques Prévert used to sit.

People say that the Russians have ruined St-Trop but it was a Russian (by way of Ukraine ...) who put the place on the jet set map. In 1956, Roger Vladimir Plemiannikov made film history, and fuelled millions of masturbatory fantasies, when he displayed almost all of Brigitte Bardot's charms, stretched out on Pampelonne beach.

For fifteen years, from 1956 to 1971 Saint-Tropez was Saint-Tropez. You can pinpoint the day when it started to become a parody of itself: May 12 1971, when Mick Jagger married Bianca in St Anne's chapel. The bride wore an Yves St Laurent white trouser suit (no bra underneath), and the wild party was held at the Byblos. The image of the topless jet setter was forever fixed in the public mind.

That's the history of Saint-Tropez, and it takes a lot of living up to. Only Karl Lagerfeld understands this. In 2010, when the House of Chanel opened its new palace of fashion at 25 Rue François Sibilli, Lagerfeld made a short film called Remember Now.

It's a pretty confection: the women are beautiful and unmemorable, and only Lagerfeld's 'muse', Baptiste Giabiconi, stays in the mind – he gets to be topless. It's a film populated by ghosts of people who used to inhabit Saint-Tropez – Coco Chanel, Alain Delon, Jane Birkin,

Mick and Bianca, Bébé, Colette, and Karl Lagerfeld …

Lagerfeld is saying that nowadays in Saint-Tropez you can only look backwards. He's right: 'Les beautiful people' come to Saint-Tropez to dance on tables on Plage Pampelonne, and wait in vain for a Russian tycoon to spray them with jeroboams of Cristal champagne.

The rich and famous come to Saint-Tropez to confirm that they are rich and famous.

Everybody else comes to Saint-Tropez to say that they've been to Saint-Tropez.

Imogen felt it very keenly, these expectations. She could feel a hundred pairs of eyes looking at her as they waited for the Maserati to be lifted out of the hold of the *Claudia*. Claudia was used to it, the stares of the envious, the ones that took the boat trips advertising "Villas des célébrités," but Imogen felt uncomfortable. She imagined that everybody was saying, "You'd think that if she could afford to be on that boat she'd go on a diet." This was one of the moments when she most wanted to be thin and glamorous.

When they stepped off the boat and into the car, Imogen felt the stares even more, and the accusing looks of the salaried poor, disappointed that she and Claudia were not magazine celebrities; as if the day-trippers had been short-changed.

In St-Trop the traffic jams are even worse than in Moscow, and, although, you could fit a good part of the world's most glam fishing village into Red Square, the rich don't like to walk much farther than the length of a catwalk.

They were soon stuck in the world's most expensive traffic jam – open-top Bentleys, Ferraris, Porsches, and Maseratis not going anywhere fast. They were moving so slowly that the strolling tourists were overtaking them. Imogen hated being in this goldfish bowl.

"Welcome to Toytown," she muttered.

Claudia was annoyed. "What's wrong with you? You know what your problem is?" Claudia didn't wait for an answer. "You're always trying to bite the hand that feeds you."

"I'm fat in a town full of thin people."

"So go on a diet."

"In my life I've lost two hundred kilos."

"I remember your diets. You put a box of biscuits right at the back of the cupboard because 'Out of sight is out of mind,' you said. Two days later you ate a quarter of the first layer because 'They go stale after too long.' Then you ate the rest of the top layer because you felt guilty about eating the first ones and couldn't bear to look at the rest lying there accusing you. Then you ate the second half of the second layer, and a week later you bought a new box to cover up the fact that you'd scoffed the first box."

Imogen was heating up. "*Casse-toi*. Are you just trying to get at me or something? What do you know about being me? You can eat anything you like, and you never put on weight. I just have to look at food and it tips the scales."

Claudia was in a schoolgirl, baiting mood. "When a fat woman steps on the scale it says, 'One at a time please.'"

"You can be such a bitch when you want to be."

Claudia shrugged. "That's just what they call friendly fire. You know I don't mean it. I've always been this size. Always will be."

"Don't be so smug. You know what's it like to wake up every morning and pray that you haven't added any pounds while you've been asleep?"

"*Tu me gonfles*. If you're not happy with your life then do something about it. Don't you like cooking?"

"What makes you say that?"

"You're the fucking catering countess, for God's sake, you

have more clients than you can handle, you live in Cap d'Antibes, and I haven't seen you smile once all morning."

"So, now you're going to tell me all I need is a good fucking, is that it?"

"If it puts a smile on your face, yes."

It was no use. Imogen changed the subject. "How do you tell if a man in St-Trop has money when all the rich men dress as if they haven't a bean?"

Claudia, of course, knew the answer – the rich have a keen nose for modern anthropology. "If he looks in the window he doesn't have any."

"Rich men just walk right in, is that it? They don't plan their pleasures, they just go and get them."

"Yah. That's why rich men are no good in bed."

"Does Frank know that?"

"If he does, I haven't told him."

"And the poor ones pouring the champagne?"

"Don't, Mo, please, or I might start squirming. Massimo – massimo in everything."

Imogen gave her another look.

Not for the first time that morning, Claudia gave her best friend a critical top-to-toe. "What are you wearing tomorrow? Not another one of those tents?"

"Don't worry, I'll stay out of sight. I'm the caterer not the eye candy. What's it matter?"

"Because, *ma chérie*, as you know very well, during *les voiles* there's as much competition in the villas as there is on the boats, and I need you to look as good as your food."

"Right, so then I should have made toad-in-the-hole, shepherd's pie, and rice pudding."

Claudia pulled a face. "Ugh, and spotted dick!"

"You've got dick on the brain, Clod."

Claudia suddenly laughed. "Oh Mo, you are your own worst enemy! We have to do something with you." Suddenly, from out of nowhere, at parade ground volume, she addressed the gorgeous driver. "Stop the car, Perry! *Grouille-toi* fatty. Let's get the fuck out of here, and go shopping."

Imogen wanted to be angry, but how could you be angry at a gadfly? For form's sake she tried. "If you call me that one more time …" But she did as she was told, and stepped out of the car, instantly aware of the surrounding envy, in a way that Claudia never would be. "That's your answer to everything is it, shopping?"

"You have a better idea?"

"What are we going shopping for?" asked Imogen, warily.

"Something for you to wear tomorrow under your apron."

"We're wasting our time. The only thing they'll have in my size are shoes and handbags, and I have a wardrobe full of them."

"Exactly, you have nothing to wear. Come on, fatty."

Chanel

Shopping in St-Trop is the Holy Grail of spending. But you have to shop right. The true St-Trop celebrity is always papped laden down with shopping bags, holding the hand of a designer toddler, in the company of two men: a rather ordinary looking man in T-shirt, shorts and Tod's – he's the one with the money – and a nice looking one, much better dressed – he's the bodyguard. The 'St-Trop look' is actually quite easy to get right, if you practise it enough times before you leave the villa; you simply have to act as if you are unaware that everybody is staring at you. Karl Lagerfeld, by the way, does it a little bit differently: Google "Karl Lagerfeld with Baptiste Giabiconi in Saint-Tropez" and you get the picture …

For most women shopping is a pleasure much more enjoyable than sex because you don't need a man to enjoy it; and so it's never a disappointment. But for Imogen, shopping was not an out-of-body experience, and most of all in Saint-Tropez where she couldn't hide. In the triangle between Place des Lices, rue Gambetta and rue Allard there is such a concentration of designer shops that Imogen felt like a lab rat in a cage. Claudia, of course, was in her element but not even Claudia's enthusiasm could change the facts of shopping life: money cannot buy you everything, not in a size twenty-two. Wherever they went the story was the same:

Dior: "Not in your size, *madame*."

Dolce&Gabbana: "Not in your size, *madame*."

Louis Vuitton: "Not in your size, *madame*."

Brunello Cucinelli: "Definitely not in your size, *madame*."

They were standing in rue François Sibilli, bagless; for Claudia that was a shameful admission of failure.

"Gucci?" asked Imogen, wanting to be helpful.

Claudia couldn't help herself. "Do you know, there are still people who think that Gucci is a luxury label."

Imogen knew better than to answer back.

Claudia was suddenly blessed with an idea. "Chanel, of course! Come on!" she shouted. "You'll love it! It's like a chocolate shop!"

"No, please Clod, not Chanel." How could she explain to Claudia what Chanel meant to her? For Imogen, trying to fit herself into a Chanel would be sacrilege.

Chanel in Saint-Tropez is not a shop; it's a temple – sort of Counter-Reformation Baroque, a place for swooning not communing. With its playfully stencilled walls matching Karl's whimsical fashion fantasies, there is, however, nothing Coco-esque about it – she spent her life mocking woman as *poupée*.

Claudia entered like a true believer, reverently pulling out armfuls of dresses that would have fitted her perfectly. In solidarity with her best friend's mission, however, she only tried on one: a long, flowing chiffon *djellaba*, pale blue with a pastel floral print, cinched below the breasts with jewellery, like a Moorish breastplate.

Chanel loves Claudia. "*C'est magnifique, non?*" oozed the *vendeuse*. "From the new resort collection, *madame*. So many, how you say, beachy vibes."

"You don't think that it makes me look fat?" Claudia asked Imogen – perfectly seriously. "No, I musn't, not today. I must be strong."

Imogen had undressed down to her support bra and lacrosse knickers. She felt exposed, for all the world to see, like Marie Antoinette, leaving Austria behind her, and stepping naked into France: to be dressed for a new role in life. Claudia looked at her, like a farmer sizing up a prized dairy cow. Imogen hated these moments. "What? No, I mean, say it. Say what you were going to say! You're admiring my toned, hourglass-shaped figure, is that it?"

"What I was actually going to say, fatty, is that if you could ever find a man to fuck you, he'd have a lot of fun. You're super-sized but it's all firm."

"Ferme ta gueule!" Imogen stood in the changing-room, thinking that it reminded her of going to confession at school: Claudia was the one having had all the fun, and Imogen felt guilty. There was nothing in her size. She admitted her sins to the *vendeuse*. "Forgive me, I think that I'm too big for Chanel."

"Mais non, madame! Madame is, *comment dire en anglais?* Rubenesque."

Suddenly, Imogen snapped. She had had enough of worshipping; she hated all designers. She exploded: "I'm not Rubenesque! I'm not full-figured! I'm not queen-sized! I'm not plus-sized! I am not a big beautiful woman! I am not overweight! I am fat!"

Dishing the Dirt

IMOGEN AND CLAUDIA had driven to the villa in total silence. Imogen wanted to say sorry, but she couldn't. She knew that she had committed a *faux pas* that would be gossiped all around the regatta by tomorrow afternoon, and in Claudia's book that was a mortal sin. But Imogen so wanted Claudia to understand the extremity of her frustration, and that was why she stayed silent, apparently unapologetic. She had never expected to find anything in her size, that wasn't what was bugging her; and it wasn't envy of Claudia's money; and it had nothing to do with any dissatisfaction with her career – she loved catering. No, she didn't want to admit it to herself but it was the waiter on the *Claudia*: Massimo, in Bikkembergs; Claudia had chosen them for him, no doubt with lascivious pleasure, caressing them and him when they came together. Women have 'dirty' thoughts, and Imogen's thoughts about men were pressing too hard into her consciousness. Imogen wanted to be a man's plaything; she wanted to cavort and quiver in front of him, vamp it up, gorge herself on him.

Claudia might have been vapid on the surface but she wasn't blind. She had made only one passing remark to her husband when they came back from their shopping expedition, empty-handed: "We have to find Mo a man."

"Don't you have a spare one?" Frank had remarked, deadpan. He knew his wife; and he still loved her.

"Would he paint it today, do you think? It doesn't look much like this now, does it?" Imogen was looking at a very pretty view by Signac, of a *tartane* moored in Saint-Tropez port, another iconic picture hanging in Claudia and Frank's open-plan *salon*, a 'casual' room over-decorated by somebody else with quite good taste, and with panoramic picture-perfect views over the Golfe.

"Why wouldn't he?" asked Frank, coming up behind her. "He'd still have painted the boats in the harbour."

"There's nothing colourful about a superyacht, they're all white and blue," objected Imogen.

"So, then, he would have painted the supersailers here for the regatta," countered Frank, good-naturedly. "The sails are all in different colours."

"*Peut-être.*" Imogen didn't want to push it. They were picking their words carefully, treading on eggshells, trying not to let Imogen's paddywhack in Chanel spoil a weekend that they had been so looking forward to, for they really were the best of friends, the three of them.

"I've always wondered if it's really by Signac, or if I was done. I suppose it doesn't really matter. Fake is fine by me."

Imogen searched Frank's face for some clue as to how serious he was being. Frank liked to play these games, to see if you could play along, and pick your way through the maze. You could never be sure where you were with Frank; nothing was ever what it seemed. If a man could be said to have a *provenance*, Frank's background was a little sketchy. She knew that he had been to M.I.T.; in his study on the *Claudia*, there were photos of a long-haired Frank in a mortar board and gown, clutching a diploma, in mathematics. Before that date, Frank said only that he was "from Oklahoma." Imogen had asked him, on their very first meeting, "What do your parents do?" She was checking him out to make sure that Claudia wasn't making a mistake. "They grow wheat, red winter," Frank said. If that were true, he didn't look like a Middle American. Nobody could ever describe Frank as clean cut, or built like a quarterback; he was tall but not tall enough for a basketball player; he had been a rower – another photo in his study, muscular at Henley in a rowing eight. He had fine, olive-skinned features that must have seemed out of place in Oklahoma; Imogen decided that there was Mediterranean blood in him somewhere.

His parents had not come to the wedding in Geneva, a lavish society affair; nobody from his family had been there. Imogen had asked Claudia if she weren't bothered that she didn't know who Frank really was. Didn't she want to run a check on him, "Just in case?" Claudia was adamant. "I don't need to find out that I love him. And the money's real. What else do I need to know?"

Frank disproved every cliché about Americans: he didn't live in America (except for business nights at a townhouse on the Upper East Side, and three weeks of ocean-front simplicity in the Hamptons); he didn't celebrate Thanksgiving; he didn't do high fives; and he spoke a foreign language with a good accent. Frank Schulte had been transplanted, and taken root as a European.

The maths education and the rowing pointed to an obsessive personality; and Frank was obsessed about making money, in the same way that he lived his life – against the grain. When Imogen had asked him the secret of his success, he had been frank: "Very simple: if everybody else is doing it, I'm not."

Coming upon them in the *salon*, after a shower, Thai massage, and meditation, Claudia tried to repair the atmosphere. "And the weather's exactly the same now as in the picture," she offered, breaking into Imogen's thoughts. "Look at that heat haze."

Imogen was still on edge. "More likely exhaust fumes."

Only best friends could be this hateful, and Claudia looked hurt. Imogen checked herself; she was spoiling everything.

"Clod, I'm sorry. It was all my fault."

"It was unforgiveable. But I forgive you."

Frank knew nothing about the fracas in Chanel, and was nonplussed by this *froideur*. Claudia had been excited as anything before she left for Antibes in the morning, and now she looked ready to spit blood.

"Andrei isn't coming, by the way, darling. He called earlier to say that something's come up."

"That man is so inconsiderate." Claudia pouted.

"That man, as you call him, is so useful."

Imogen knew that she had to repair the damage. "Children, don't fight, I've only just got here. Let's sit out on the terrace and catch up. Then, if Marcus isn't here, I'll make something special for supper." That was Imogen's olive branch.

Claudia loosened up. "Mo's happy now, 'cos she doesn't have to cook anything Russian."

Frank laughed. "We could just have given them caviare and a bowl of *borsch*. Frozen margaritas everybody?"

They were friends again, and happily walked out on to the terrace.

Imogen sniffed the air. "Mmm, how lovely, honeysuckle, lavender, and thyme."

Frank laughed. "That's so you, Mo: most people smell the roses, you pick out the herbs."

The semi-circular upper terrace was bounded by a low stone wall; on both sides, a row of steps led down to the swimming pool, and then to the sea. Frank employed a full-time local gardener who had no liking for fancy designer horticulture – no statuary or water features. There were just a few large terracotta pots filled with red geraniums and giant cacti; aromatic and alpine plants sheltered beneath artfully placed heavy boulders; and climbing roses and espalier fruit trees that caught the eye and perfumed the air. The estate was bordered on all sides by clusters of fig, cypress, and olive trees; they gave the villa the privacy that Frank and Claudia valued so highly.

Within moments, the margaritas had appeared; the staff Claudia and Frank employed was always close at hand. Imogen, who was neither a master or a servant, and yet belonged in both camps, had a lot of time for Bill, the English major domo who ran their seven households worldwide – Saint-Tropez, Paris, St. Moritz, London, Wiltshire, Upper East Side, East Hampton – like an old school butler, but with much less formality. Frank addressed him as "Bill," and Imogen had always thought that was a mark of the highest breeding. Bill had been with them for years. Marcus the chef, as well; that was also a good sign – Imogen didn't like to think of her friends as 'monster' employers.

Frank had found Bill in the direct, cut-price way that he relished: Bill had been serving Frank at a state banquet in Buckingham Palace, for President Bush; Frank had given Bill his card, and said, "Call me, I'll pay you twice what Her Majesty is giving you."

"Are we all set for tomorrow, Bill?"

"Yes, sir."

Frank was grinning. "What do you think of the menu?"

"I think that it should do the trick, sir."

"You hear that Mo? Praise indeed. I'll decant the wine myself, Bill. Just put the bottles out on the sideboard an hour before we sit down, please. The white in coolers."

"Very good, sir."

Bill withdrew as unobtrusively as he had materialised.

Frank was scanning the Golfe with a pair of Swarovski binoculars, zooming in on the multi-coloured mass of sailing yachts preparing for tomorrow's race.

The racing fleet was sailing downwind, sails billowing, tacking this way and that, heeling at crazy angles, at any moment seemingly about to keel over, but at the last possible moment righting themselves and sailing on; jibbing round the buoy, and heading for home.

Imogen was back in working mode. "Tell me about the guests tomorrow."

"Who's sleeping with whom, or who hates whom?" asked Frank, not really concentrating, but with typical grammatical exactitude.

"Frank!" exclaimed Claudia. "She meant vegetarians and picky eaters. And I told her ages ago."

"Good. Come here, Mo. I'll find our boat for you."

Imogen leaned over the wall of the terrace, trying to make figurative sense of the yachts as they manoeuvred for position. They were strung out in a line, and from far away, with the naked eye, barely seemed to be moving.

"I meant why have they been invited? They're not really friends, are they? What's the deal?"

Frank smiled, and talked behind his binoculars. "You've become such a businesswoman, Mo. If you ever give up catering, how about coming to work with me? The guests, if you add them all up, come to eighteen and a half per cent of a company that's in play." He handed Imogen the binoculars. "Straight ahead. We're sponsoring the boat with the orange sails."

Imogen put the binoculars up to her eyes, and searched for the orange sails. "Eighteen and a half per cent of a chocolate company?"

"That's a good guess. But please don't buy the shares on Monday, and move the price. See it?"

"Yes. Skimming over the waves as if she's about to take off."

"It's the perfect wind. Hope it'll be like this tomorrow. Now, show me the seating plan."

Imogen put down the binoculars, fished out of her pocket a creased sheet of paper, and gave it to Frank. He scanned it rapidly as he walked around the teak table and chairs that were used for sitting outside. "Claudia at one end, me at the other, fine ... No, this isn't right. You have to put Casimir between Ray and Baroness Sophie."

"I was going for balance," said Imogen.

"This isn't a boy, girl, boy, girl lunch, Mo."

Claudia showed off her liberal values. "You have to have a gay couple or a gay single at lunch nowadays, or else people think you're small-minded."

"This is not about being open-minded, darling. Casimir is the bait. He's there to butter up both of them. Ray's an old queen, and the Baroness likes a beautiful smile."

"He's a gigolo?" asked Imogen, following Frank around the table, memorising the change in seating.

"No, he works for me. Twenty-five. Polish background. Oxford. Drop-dead gorgeous, even I can see that. He's very hungry. A real operator."

"He's gay?"

"Don't know, haven't asked him."

"How ruthless he is," thought Imogen, "wringing what he can out of people." Frank looked at her – Imogen's thoughts were easy to read.

"Don't feel sorry for him, Mo, you make a career in any way you can. It's a two-way street: you give way, they give in. I don't think Nick and Cassandra should be sitting together. Put Nick next to Galia sitting on my right, and Cassie on my left. Papoche has to sit next to Jade because that's why she's been invited."

"More bait?" asked Imogen.

"Yes, the poisonous type," remarked Claudia, quite viciously.

Imogen hurriedly moved on. "Who's going to sit in the empty place, now that your Russian isn't coming?"

"Why not you, Mo?"

"She'll be busy in the kitchen!" objected Claudia.

Frank showed his good side. "Mo's a friend, darling, your best friend, remember? Not the *bonne*. Besides, tomorrow she'll have Marcus to help."

"What Clod really means, Frank, is that I don't have anything to wear."

"I don't care what you wear, Mo. As far as I'm concerned you have real class, you make people laugh, and you know things."

Claudia kept quiet. When it came to it, Frank had the final word.

Imogen steered a middle course. "Honestly, I really will be frantic in the kitchen, but I could probably join you at the end for the chocolate."

"Well, that's a surprise!" laughed Claudia, not unkindly.

Frank put his foot down. "Stop it you two! Worse than schoolgirls." Without waiting for any sign of acquiescence, he put a stop to the squabbling. "Good, that's settled." The squall had passed.

"Only, I'm still lost," said Imogen, "I get the seating but who are they?"

Frank sat down, and took a sip of his margarita. "Papoche is Paolo Lascari, an old Italian guy who owns a big slab of a chocolate business. Classic rags to riches story. Knows everything there is to know about chocolate but still wants to run the place the same way he did thirty years ago. They're way behind the times, been losing market share for years."

"Which is where you come in?"

"You're learning fast. Cassie – Cassandra – his daughter, hates chocolate, can't stand the sight of it. Absolutely no interest in the business. That's where Nick comes in. Same classic story – he married the boss's daughter, and now he works in the chocolate business."

"Good at it?"

"Brilliant, and that's the problem. He wants to bring the company up to date, and the old man's putting the brakes on."

"Happy marriage?"

"They make the perfect couple: money, looks, position, everything ..."

"Children?"

"Two, a boy and a girl."

"Perfect in every way."

"He was the gardener," said Claudia. "She saw him mowing the lawn without his shirt on, and that was it."

Frank looked surprised. "How do you know that?"

"Don't look surprised. I do know some things. Cassie told me."

"You mean he married for money?" asked Imogen.

Claudia was eager to put the case for romance: "Well, he's very nice looking, and Cassie's very beautiful, so there must have been love somewhere."

Frank laughed. "Yes, in the safe with the share certificates!"

Claudia was riled. "Don't! You can have love and money, look at us."

"And there I was thinking that you only married me for love, darling."

Imogen was again thinking that with Frank, you could never tell when he was joking, or being serious. Either way, the conversation was moving too close to home. She brought it back into safer territory. "Ray?"

"Don't be fooled by Ray's fluttering, or all the talk of colour schemes and terrible dresses. People think he's just a Palm Beach queen, but if we're talking about really successful gold-diggers, Ray outranks them all. You'd be surprised where Ray started out."

There was something menacing about Frank. He was like a hungry cheetah lying hidden in the long grass, poised to sprint and kill. To hear him talk, Imogen's elegant lunch seemed to her now more like a sacrificial offering than a social occasion. She had an image of Frank tearing apart tomorrow's partridge, leaving his knife and fork untouched.

"How do you always know all these things about people?"

"Andrei. The man who knows everything, and never gives anything away." Claudia shivered. "He gives me the creeps."

"You win when you know more than anybody else. And winning pays for your wardrobe."

"Don't preach at me."

Imogen stepped in, to break them up. "Honestly, you two! Who else is there? Charles and Galia. Is that the English couple that live in Beaulieu? She was a ballerina. Aren't they friendly with the Grimaldis?"

Claudia snorted. "They like to say that they're friendly with the Grimaldis but that's not what the Grimaldis say."

"But she really was a dancer?"

Frank was enjoying himself. "Oh yes, and her husband's led her a merry dance too."

"Is it my imagination, or is small talk getting smaller nowadays?"

Claudia was quite elated. "But Mo, scandal-mongering is such fun!"

Frank was topping up the margaritas. "This is small talk about a very big deal, Mo. And anyway, you were brought up on small talk. Marie-Hélène made it her life's work."

"I thought you liked my grandmother, rest her soul."

"I did," replied Frank, benignly, "but this is your world as much as ours, saucepans or no saucepans."

"I think I like it better by the stove. Who does that leave to dish the dirt on? Baroness Sophie?"

"The title is real, if that's what you mean," was Frank's only comment.

"Jade?"

"She and Casimir would make a good couple if you ask me."

Claudia's tone was again quite vicious, although she didn't elaborate.

Frank was having none of it. "You can be so wrong about people, you know that, darling?"

Imogen switched to a jolly tone, to head them off. "Well, I have to say that I love the idea of cooking up an intrigue. I mean, you've gone to all this trouble but does everybody know why they've been invited?"

"Some yes, some no. The holdings are tied up in family trusts, and hidden away offshore, so they might not know the why and wherefore."

"But they are going to find out tomorrow? You're going to make an announcement? Like Inspector Poirot?"

"In a way, yeah. But that's down to you, Mo, s'all in your hands. Right, I'm famished. Didn't you promise us supper?"

"Yes, yes, of course, mmm … I'm still mystified. Why am I so important?"

Frank finished his margarita, and grinned, full beam. "You'll see. That's why we're finishing the lunch with chocolate."

Les voiles

THE NEXT DAY, just as the guests were arriving at Frank and Claudia's villa, and once the easterly breeze had filled in to about five knots, the race committee of Les voiles managed to find enough wind in the starting area to send the fleet on a short nine-nautical-mile coastal race.

The largest group proved intent on the favoured committee boat end. Alone towards the pin end was the Gazprom boat, which found more pressure on the northern side of the gulf. The lone Russian contender was safely just behind the first starters, but her towering sail plan made the most of the challenging conditions and allowed her to quickly gain on the others.

Most boats, having left the gulf and cleared the Porte Seiche mark, found the breeze clocking towards the south, which allowed a mix of running sails to be set: spinnakers, fishermen, topsails. Further along the coast, the wind went painfully light, and the fleet compressed around the leeward mark off the town of Issambres. From there it was a beat upwind until they could lay the mark of Porte Seiche, and then ease sheets for a reach towards the finish in a slighter, fresher breeze.

On the terrace of Frank and Claudia's villa, nobody took much notice of the yachts, except to remark that they made "a pretty sight" – a nice backdrop for lunch.

Les people

CHARLES HELD THE terrace. "Queen Victoria invented the Côte d'Azur, and Scott Fitzgerald made it glamorous."

"What do the Russians make it?" asked Ray.

"Dangerous!"

Everybody laughed at Charles's quip. Imogen heard the laughter but she was too busy in the kitchen to catch much more than snippets of the conversation, relayed from the terrace via the intercom system. Its main purpose was to let the chef know when to serve the next course, but it also meant that being in the kitchen was much like eavesdropping – cooking and listening to a play on the radio where you know some of the actors.

Imogen had stepped out on to the terrace a couple of times to say hello and help pass around the trays of appetisers. Bill and his staff didn't really need her help, but she liked to show her face, and get a feel for what was going on.

Marcus was helping her in the kitchen. 'Helping' was not quite the word that Imogen liked to use about Marcus because it was 'his' kitchen. He was twenty-six, baby-faced, spoke terrible French with a Yorkshire accent, and, outside of the kitchen, still had the nervous manner of a first-day *commis*, although he had been executive chef with Frank and Claudia for nearly five years. Imogen thought that he was brimming with talent – he was adventurous with his tastes and textures – and she was always telling him, quietly, that he needed to get his own restaurant. "Get Frank to back you. Only, make sure you find him a replacement."

"I can't, Mo. If it wasn't for Frank, I'd still be gutting fish, and Gordon getting all the glory. This way, I get some recognition."

"You need a wider audience. You can always cook for billionaires in your own place."

Frank had found Marcus in the same cut-out-the-middleman way that he had found Bill: he had been having dinner in a Mayfair restaurant, owned by a celebrity chef who put his name on the door but was not often in the kitchen. After the main course had been served, Frank told the *maitre d'* that he wanted to know who was doing the cooking. A young chef – flustered, cheeks flushed beetroot, capsized toque – came to the table, clasping his hands in prayer – "Looked like he'd only just started masturbating," Frank liked to joke, retelling the story.

"You cooked this?"

"Yes."

"You think it's any good?"

The boy found his courage. "I know what I'm doing."

Frank nodded, and, a little too loudly, said: "It's the last meal you're going to cook in this restaurant."

A tremor of social unease ricocheted around the dining-room. Frank gave the chef his card, and smiled. "Tell Gordon from me, when you quit tomorrow, that you found somebody who really appreciates your cooking, and is going to pay you five times what he does."

Marcus never minded Imogen taking over his kitchen; she had asked him yet again if he really didn't mind.

"Are you kidding, Mo? I never thought I'd say it, but it's nice to take a back seat. Do you know how many guests we have coming the rest of the week? It'll be like feeding the fucking five thousand. Only, I'm going to steal that Escoffier sauce from you. What does it look like upstairs?"

"Like a photo shoot for *Vogue*, with text by Marcel Proust."

Before the guests had arrived, Imogen had complimented Frank on his clothes. Frank was decanting the wine, and concentrating on the job in hand. "Tom Ford. I bought the look, number twenty-six, I think it was. Let me see if I can remember." He pointed to his shirt. "Violet cotton grand degrade check." Then to his trousers. "Tailored sport pant in warm grey silk fourteen gg – whatever that means." Then at his shoes. "White suede Kevin moccasins. Have no idea who Kevin is. Don't you just love fashion language?"

"I knew it!"

"What? Even geeks wear Tom Ford?"

"You're not a geek Frank, you're a gem."

That was so Frank: no interest in fashion, spend as little time as possible shopping – buy the whole lot in one go – and, yet, still know, with mathematical precision, exactly what he was wearing.

Ray was sixty-four going on twenty-two, to judge by his boyish charm, a charm that, no doubt, had always been used with steely purpose. In his teens Ray would have been what gay men call a "twink;" and, if they find the right sponsor, twinks can have brilliant, albeit generally short careers – Mapplethorpe had been a twink. Ray's career had gone on and on, a measure of his gritty determination to escape from the trailer park, hard by the Texas Motor Speedway – Ray would never totally remove that engine roar out of his head. Over time, as the sugar daddies came and went, perhaps that sunny charm had become shaded with petulance, and the occasional tantrum; you can only give yourself to a man so many times before he becomes bored with your perfect ass. Ray was well preserved – a man who had used moisturiser all his life. No crows' feet had ever alighted on Ray's face or if they had, they had been instantly snared and buried on Harley Street. He had a luxurious mane of auburn hair, more coiffured than cut; on Venice Beach, once, in the days when he was on the look-out, it must have been tousled, surf-wet and salty; now it hardly moved.

Ray and Charles were the only men in jackets, but colour-wise there was a world of difference between them: Ray was colour-coordinated, head-to-toe, in flamboyant Italian. Brioni, most likely, or Canali – a fuchsia silk jacket over a rose linen shirt, and cream cotton/silk trousers. Around his throat he had draped a silk scarf in shades of raspberry and gold. He looked like a raspberry ripple ice cream. But he wore oddly conservative shoes – tan calfskin lace-ups; only the shoes hinted at a 'grounded' inner self.

He had arrived wearing a Panama, and when he first saw Imogen, hovering in her 'Mongolian tent' and apron, he had given it to her, with the instruction to "Put it in a bathroom, won't you. Panama needs a damp climate to keep its shape. Thank you so much." Imogen had done as he asked. When she was introduced to Ray, by Claudia, a few moments later as 'the catering countess,' Ray blithely ignored the fact that he had thought Imogen was a servant, and said, "My, isn't that lovely. Well, I can't cook, but I can shop."

Ray was talking with Charles and Galia, trotting out his edited history: "I've been a bit of a nomad, followed the sun, like a crocodile. California, Tangier, Marrakesh, Palm Beach, I've been in Monaco for nine years, much longer than anywhere else. Monaco is a good last haven for a nomad."

Charles looked like a merchant banker even at the weekend: a white shirt and dark jacquard silk tie, cream flannels, topped with a well-cut navy blazer – Savile Row, no doubt. The only splash of colour Charles allowed himself was a yellow polka dot pocket-handkerchief. An Establishment look. But Charles was not old school, he was a 'grammar grub.' What does it matter, where you come from? If you think that it doesn't matter then you know very little about English society, and you quite clearly don't have your clothes made on the Row.

It certainly mattered to Charles who liked to be buttoned up even on a Sunday. It was a very understated, avuncular, top-drawer style – Cazenove, Hoare, Pearson ... only Charles didn't belong in any one of those closed worlds; he described himself as a 'financier;' for an old-school Englishman that is rather a dodgy word. In bastion England, the right clothes can only get you so far; Charles had got into Annabel's, yes, but he would never make it into White's. In the 1970s he had overstated the non-existent profits of a property company he had asset-stripped. Charles's name was mud in every boardroom in the City; tellingly, there had been very little about it in the FT, and even now you won't find the scandal anywhere online; that tells you how serious it was, and how much money Charles did them for – enough to keep him and Galia living in style in the South of France for decades. Frank, of course, knew all there was to know about Charles's history.

Galia, the retired prima ballerina, was on her grape diet; she had brought them with her, and had asked Imogen to wash them in mineral water. She was not really Russian – she came from Basingstoke. Massine, who had been Diaghilev's lover, and then Galia's, said that everybody in the company had to have a Russian name, and he had christened her Galia – Doris was her real name. Imogen did the maths, and worked out that Galia must have been eighty odd; there was something in those grapes.

Galia, theatrical as always, was dressed in a black, felted wool dinner jacket, embroidered with gold-sequin palm trees, and gold *paillettes*; worn over a pair of black tailored wool trousers. She was extravagantly bejewelled: around her head she had wrapped a black silk scarf into a turban, pinned at the front with an art deco diamond brooch. In her right hand, she carried a black clutch bag, collet-set with cabochon rubies; on her left, the wrist was weighed down with a de Grisogono Allegra watch, red and black, set with spinels. The look said 'prima ballerina', and her sculpted face, with its cigarette-smoker's cheeks, glowed exactly as it must have done the thousand times she had sat in front of a theatre dressing-room mirror – shocking pink lipstick, exaggerated eyebrows, dramatic eyeliner.

Claudia went into raptures when Galia stepped on to the terrace, making an entrance like Kitri in the *pas de deux* from *Don Q* – head held high, erect, disciplined, coquettish. "That's so Marlene Dietrich! I love it!"

Galia acknowledged Claudia's full-throated enthusiasm with a *ronde de jambe*. "Schiaparelli. Marlene bought one as well but after me."

"Vintage is so chic now, honestly, one shouldn't wear anything new."

"Mmm, I like that idea, darling," said Frank. "We can turn your wardrobe into a wine cellar."

"Yes, sweetheart, only we'll lay down hundreds of Prada, and I'll bring them out in twenty years' time."

For the record, Claudia was wearing the Chanel *djellaba* that she had tried on the day before. Yesterday, she had been able to resist it; today, she had called Karl on his mobile, and asked him ever so sweetly if there was any way she could have it before midday? It arrived at 11.55.

Galia brought out the theatrical in everybody: with her arrival, the terrace had become a stage in glorious Cote d'Azur technicolour. Everybody had dressed the part, and the dialogue and repartee tripped off the tongue, polished and deadly, after so many outings between Marseilles and Monaco. Forty years after she had retired, there was still something of Kitri in Galia's pose – hand on hip, quaffing champagne, popping a grape whenever 'her' tray was brought to her.

Charles was giving Ray his version of history. "I was in property in the 1960s. I was in residential; they call it buy to let now. I left the UK when I thought that it was going to just float off into the North Sea. I stopped believing in us; that was a mistake as it turned out. I should have persuaded the sheikhs to buy up all those office blocks that were going for a song."

"Oh, I have such a thing for real estate!" exclaimed Ray – just occasionally a shrill treble gave the game away. "I've always told everyone I've ever been with, 'Let's buy a house.' Then I gut it, and I completely rebuild. It's such a challenge!"

A screaming teenage queen is to be laughed at; a middle-aged queen to be pitied; an old rich queen is to be admired.

Imogen was double-checking the table when a confident-looking man, who could have been anywhere between sixty-five and eighty, accompanied by a couple in their early thirties, was shepherded on to the terrace by a very solicitous Claudia. Imogen understood that this must be Paulo Lascari – Papoche – with his daughter and son-in-law. She lingered.

Nick Austin, she decided within seconds, was too perfect to be interesting – he was that brooding, broad-shouldered specimen they always put on the covers of books to sell to women.

Cassandra was so thin her clothes looked as if the hanger had been left inside them – famine breasts, incorporeal. Imogen recognised the outfit; she had seen it in Brunello Cucinelli yesterday: a cream silk-linen cardigan that fell to below the knees, over a beige suede T-shirt. Bored or nonchalant – Imogen couldn't decide which – Cassandra kept her hands buried in the pockets of her ivory silk satin trousers. As with all thin women, Imogen hated her on sight. Cassandra had everything: size eight, husband to-die-for, money, and a Pre-Raphaelite face, framed by long dark hair. Why, then, did she look so tense? Rossetti's women have that faraway look in their eyes, remembering something too painful to reveal.

Stepping on to the terrace, Cassandra seemed disconnected from the party eddying around her, moving only in her own space. She smiled, said exactly the right thing, and offered nothing in return. She sought out the shade offered by the fruit trees; it was her father who shone.

Paulo Lascari was not tall, barely one-seventy centimetres, bronzed, toned, white hair – everything in good condition, like a well-serviced vintage car. He was an Italian comfortable in expensive Italian: Zegna lemon polo shirt, ivory silk trousers – keeping faith with his daughter – lizard belt, tan Tod's. More dapper than dandy, it was the wardrobe of a man at ease with his success.

Frank welcomed his guests of honour: "Nick, nice to see you; it's been too long"(it had been two days ago ...). "Cassie, you look beautiful, as always, very chic."

Imogen had no interest in these perfect people; time to go back to the kitchen. Passing him, close enough to recognise his aftershave, she saw that Nick Austin, of course, had a firm handshake.

"Hello, Frank. This is my father-in-law, Paolo. By the way, you should tell your gardener that he's overwatering the roses."

Imogen thought that this was a very odd thing to say, not at all high society. She stole a glance at his hands – they were manicured office hands. Some gardener.

The remark, however, had apparently sailed past Frank: "Mr

Lascari, Paolo, perfect timing! The race is on, only we're not winning this one!"

"Mr Schulte, so nice of you to invite us. Please call me Papoche, or my daughter will wonder who you are talking to."

Papoche spoke grammatical, very correct English, carefully enunciated, with a slight Italian-American accent.

"Papoche it is. Please call me Frank. How about some bubbly everybody?"

Imogen would have loved to watch more of the show that was beginning on the terrace, but lunch was scheduled to start in thirty minutes, and preparing scrambled eggs demanded her full attention – a cook who cannot prepare perfect scrambled eggs is not a cook.

Bill served the champagne; Claudia introduced Nick and Cassandra to Charles and Galia; and Papoche wanted to know how much Frank had spent on sponsoring the boat with the orange sails that was not winning.

"It's a six-figure sponsorship with a seven-figure return."

"How can you be so exact? Sponsorship is just guesswork, and, as I see, you are not winning."

"Not winning *this* race, Papoche. You don't get more high profile than this, in our market that is. Three hundred boats owned by some of the richest people on earth, all in one port during one week. That's a lot of money concentrated in one place. All looking at the name of my company."

When she came back out on to the terrace, following Bill bearing the soup tureen, Imogen's eye was drawn to a dramatic-looking young man with slicked-back jet-black hair, skin a walnut hue, and features so perfect he looked as if he belonged on a Roman coin. He reminded her of Rudolph Valentino (there was a photo of "Rudy," as Marie-Hélène had always called him, in the O'Rorke family album). This must be Casimir, she thought. He didn't look Polish, much more exotic – Tartar blood perhaps. He was dressed in that upper-class English way, neat and askew: tapered white jeans; a pale blue dress shirt, cuffs casually pulled back – not rolled – and unbuttoned low to reveal the most magnificent chest: defined pecs, and matted with dark hairs like a finely woven rug. Unlike everybody else, he had no status wristwatch, just a brightly coloured, knotted bracelet. His clothes were not new – jeans ragged at the edges, frayed shirt collar; his alligator belt was well worn, and his electric blue suede driver shoes looked as if he had walked a long way in them. He spoke animatedly, and moved around a lot – too much coke the night before – and every few moments he flicked back a lock of stray hair that had fallen on to his forehead.

Imogen watched him with interest because she knew why he was there. He knew that he was good looking – even without his parading it, that was easy to see – but he was not too self-conscious about it. She was not the only one who seemed to have been transfixed by him: Ray, she noticed, had been unable to keep away from his side, since he first arrived. Frank had chosen well.

"Small cock," said Claudia, in passing, *sotto voce*, and went to greet Baroness Sophie.

Well, that was one unanswered question out of the way.

"You have bought a new boat, I hear," said Papoche.

"Mega big, must be making mega bucks, Frank," said Charles.

"Mega? The *Claudia* doesn't come even near to making the list of the top one hundred."

"Are you going to take her far?" asked Nick.

"She can do twenty-one knots, but if we keep it down to ten, she's a range of five thousand nautical miles, enough to get us to St Bart's."

"Are you going to charter her? Even Abramovich, I hear, has the *Eclipse* advertised."

"Yeah, I thought about it, only I hate anybody else sleeping in my bed."

Nick liked talking money. "It's an expensive toy."

"Too right it is. I tell myself I use her like an office but I'm just bullshitting it. I mean, it's not just the buying; it's the fuel, crew, mooring fees, maintenance, just never ends."

"What do you think she's costing you?"

"My wife or the boat?" All the men laughed. "You can figure on annual operating costs running at about ten to fifteen per cent of the value, so a fifty-million yacht is costing you about five to six million a year."

"What's she costing to fill up?"

"Not so bad, about thirty-three thousand. At cruising speed, she's burning four hundred bucks an hour. Claudia took her to Antibes yesterday to pick up the partridges for lunch. Fucking expensive birds they turned out to be!"

Again, all the men laughed. Imogen was on her way back to the kitchen. She had only a few seconds to collect and filter her first impressions of the Baroness, and she decided, again irrationally, that she liked her. The Baroness had arrived without any fanfare. She was in her seventies – the neck gave her age away, and the mottled hands. Her face had been worked on but she could still smile; not a dazzling laser-white statement but almost demure, as if she were waiting in line to curtsey at court. Her *maquillage* had been expertly applied – it didn't draw attention to itself. Her raven hair, cut in a bob, was streaked with silver highlights; a hairstyle she had probably sported decades ago, when cut by Vidal Sassoon. She was flat chested; her cream silk shift dress fell in a straight line to her knees. Chiffon would have made her seem ancient: *crêpe de chine* made her look chic. Her jewellery was striking – an antique amethyst and diamond necklace, with matching cluster brooch *en suite*. They were not big stones – no gewgaws or sparklers for the Baroness – but they were perfectly matched and graduated. She was wearing cream court shoes, and carried a cream, quilted silk clutch bag.

It was a style that would have found favour with Chanel; it was a style that Imogen recognised from snapshots of Marie-Hélène and her friends, pasted into the O'Rorke family album. Chanel, in 1959, when the Baroness would have been at the height of fashion, mischievously said that fashion goes out of fashion after it has been worn for just a few days – *"elle est déjà démodée, elle a une semaine"* – only style has longevity. In such a way had the Baroness outlived fashion; she was a classic.

The impossibly handsome Nick was talking in a low voice with Frank.

"I talked to the old man, like you suggested. Told him that if we didn't come up with something new we'd be swallowed up by Nestlé or Kraft."

"Did he listen?"

"Oh yeah, he heard me out, then he blew me out, like always. Said that he'd built up the company from nothing, all the usual crap about how we'd been making chocolates the same way for decades, and that was the way it was always going to be. Said sugar-free chocolates were the work of the devil."

"He's old, just wait your time. Cassandra inherits the lot, then you can do what you like."

"He'll go on for ever. I can't wait that long."

"Look, Nick, the fund will support you, you've done wonders with the share price, and the dividend helped pay for the new boat. But whatever you're planning, remember, that without your wife's shares you'll lose a boardroom showdown. If Cassie has to choose between her father and her husband, do you know which way she'll jump?"

"No, I don't, to be honest. And how do you think that makes me feel?"

"Like a man with only two per cent of the company he runs."

"Trying to run."

"Still makes you a very rich man."

"I'd like to be richer."

"By the way, check your share register. You've had some unwelcome visitors. Offshore, but I can tell you they're Russians."

"Fuck. What do they want?"

"You'll have to find out. I can put you in touch with a good investigator. If you want to find out a secret, he's the best. In Zurich."

Cassandra came up behind them, attracted by conspiracy.

"What's this about secrets? Aah! My husband has a secret mistress!" she said playfully. "A private detective in Zurich? I'll shoot them both dead!"

Frank laughed. "Hell hath no fury like a woman scorned."

Imogen brought them the last tray of appetisers; and complimented Cassandra on her outfit. "That really is so elegant. It's Brunello Cucinelli, isn't it? I saw it in their window yesterday. I love the way they have such wonderful soft fabrics." Cassandra smiled, sweetly. "But they didn't have it in your size, right?"

Imogen dug deep down into her reserves of politeness.

"Appetiser? They're fat-free."

Cassandra shook her head. Imogen retired to the kitchen.

Frank spoke with Bill. "Let's give it another ten minutes, for our missing guest. Then we'll start, either way."

Bill nodded, and withdrew.

A few moments later, the 'heartbreaker' walked in to the kitchen.

"The party's that way," said Imogen.

"Yes, I know. I'm Nick. I'm married to the hard woman in the wonderful soft fabrics. I came to apologise."

"Right. I'm Imogen. Stir this, will you. Slowly."

"I can't cook."

"And your wife doesn't eat."

"She was rude."

"You think that I haven't heard it before? Isn't that right, Marcus?"

Marcus was busy with the fish. "Sure thing, Mo. Rolla Bowla knows all the jokes. 'How easy is it to get a fat woman into bed?'"

"Piece of cake," said Imogen.

"Yo momma, she was so fat I had to roll her in flour ... "

" ... and find the wet spot."

"When a fat woman goes to a restaurant ..."

"They give her the menu and ..."

Nick cut her off. "She says, 'Yes please.'"

"Wow! I'm impressed," said Imogen. "How come you know fat woman jokes?"

"Doesn't everybody? The appetisers were very good. I liked that red sauce."

"It was strawberries. You didn't notice?"

"Funny really, I spend a fortune in restaurants but I never take any notice of what I'm eating. Too busy talking business, I guess. Didn't you ever want to open a restaurant?"

"No. Too many jokes."

"Interesting what you call yourself."

"It's for real."

"The catering? Well, it's good to know that you can cook."

"The title, I mean. I'm a Czech, Irish Catholic countess."

"Just catering countess is probably easier to sell to clients."

"Hold the handle, and stir slowly, it's béchamel, you're not mixing concrete."

"Yes, miss. Do you have to bow to a countess?"

"Don't be silly."

"I remember going for dinner in Menton, at the villa of Princess Marisol de Baviera Bourbon, with Princess Antoinette of Monaco, and she curtseyed when we arrived. A Royal Highness outranks a Serene Highness."

"You sound like a *parvenu*."

"I didn't used to be rich."

"I was always a countess."

"I came to apologise."

"I accept. Sorry, but I have to work."

"Yes," said Marcus, "or you'll get me the sack."

"Sounds like a Yorkshire accent to me," said Nick.

"Huddersfield. You?"

"Ripon."

Imogen took hold of Nick's stirring hand, to slow it down – "Slowly. Like this." She could feel the soft hairs on the back of his hand, beneath her palm. "You're both from Yorkshire?"

Nick was enjoying himself. "Never ask a man if he's a Yorkshireman, because if he is, he'll have told you already …"

Marcus finished the line: "… and if he isn't, why embarrass him?"

The two men laughed.

Imogen still had her hand over Nick's hand, dreamily stirring. He gave her the faintest of smiles. "I always thought I was pretty good with my hands."

She quickly took her hand away. "How's that?"

"How's what?" He was smiling broadly – was he playing with her? "Oh, that. I was a gardener."

"Must have been a long time ago. Those aren't gardener's hands."

"A lifetime ago. You're an expert in hands are you?"

Imogen said nothing. She didn't know what to say. She liked this man much more than she thought she would. "Right, take it off the heat."

Nick did as he was told, and put his hands in his pockets, leaning back lazily against a counter top. He seemed in no hurry to go.

"Standing in your kitchen, it's like standing in a kitchen garden or a perfume shop full of exotic, foreign smells. What's that, a perfume bottle?"

"No. *Confiture abricots façon Nougat*. But you don't dab it on your neck; it's sweet and slightly tart. I serve it in little dishes, with black tea, Russian-style, instead of *petit fours*."

"Might be more interesting to eat it off the back of the neck."

The frisson was there; Imogen felt it. Marcus rescued her.

"Not in my kitchen."

"Right, I, um ... thought."

"No, I don't do the washing up," said Marcus, tartly.

"Sorry."

"Don't mind Marcus, he's not really as cutting as he sounds. He just trained with a monster."

"I get it! You're the chef Frank stole from Gordon?"

"I am."

"I'd like to try your food someday. Frank rates you very highly. I'm a gourmet too."

"We'll see. You know what that is?" asked Imogen.

"Now, that I know. Foie gras."

"Why am I not surprised?"

"Isn't that what a gourmet eats?"

"How can you call yourself a gourmet when you don't know anything about food? Here, close your eyes, can you tell me what this is?"

Nick obediently allowed Imogen to spoon-feed him a dark paste.

"Olives?"

"*Polpa di Olive*, but they're Ligurian olives. I buy them in the market in San Remo."

"Know it well. I'll have to look out for you."

"It's quite a drive from Cap d'Antibes."

"You go to Italy to buy mashed olives? They're delicious. Damn!"

Drops of olive paste had fallen on to Nick's white linen shirt.

Imogen was horrified. "Oh God! I'm sorry! It'll wash out if we do it now. Go stand by the sink."

"*Figurati*. It's only clothes."

"They look expensive."

Nick was unconcerned – that was money for you. "Who cares what they cost or where they came from? You can always buy more."

"I don't think so. Your wife doesn't like me already."

Imogen pumped a blob of liquid soap onto her middle finger, and rubbed hard at the olive stain on his chest – she realised that she was stroking his nipple. She diluted the stain with water, and it spread, making the fabric transparent. She was standing very close to him, could feel his breath. She took in everything about him: she smelled the lemon-scented soap that he had used in the shower; and the aroma of coconut shampoo in his dark brown hair. He wore it short, but she noticed a slight wave that must have been very pronounced if he ever grew it long. For certain, he had been a very pretty boy. She imagined that he stepped out of the shower, and just ran his fingers through his hair, no comb.

"What are you thinking?" he asked, softly.

"That you were teased at school."

"Yeah, only sweet wasn't the look that I was going for."

Through the intercom the terrace transmitted a scene by Noël Coward.

Nick cocked his ear. "Sounds like a good play."

"Murder or farce?" asked Imogen.

She could sense that he was watching her, not what she was doing. For a very long minute, neither of them said anything. She concentrated on rubbing out the stain, and her line of vision hit the kissing point on his neck where the collar of his shirt rose to expose his collarbone. He was a fair-skinned Anglo-Saxon, almost untanned – a man who spent his days in the office, not on the beach. Up close, his skin had a glazed clear texture – no blackheads in his pores; a man who looked after himself. His face and neck had been smoothed with a fine moisturiser, and she could trace the dark outlines of where he had shaved. His aftershave enveloped her.

"Green Irish Tweed."

"You have a good nose."

"My father."

The stain had gone. She tried to smooth out the wrinkles in the linen; his nipple was erect.

She hurriedly took a step back. "There, as good as new. Stay here, let it dry. It's sort of obvious at the moment."

She turned her head to look at Marcus. He looked up from dressing the plates, and opened his eyes very wide, raising his eyebrows, half-laughing, half gob-smacked. She had been spotted.

She said the first thing to Nick that came into her head. "I have to grate the truffles. You see? You can't keep me away from food. Don't you have an obsession about something?"

"I don't talk about it in the kitchen."

The frisson fizzled again, like a *sauté*. She was flushing. It didn't matter what the hell she said, but she had to keep on talking.

"What do you do?" She knew what he did.

"I'm in chocolate."

"That's good because I'm a chocoholic."

"I can satisfy that desire very easily. That's what made you want to cook?"

"No, I used to read cookery books."

"Now you have something in common with my wife. She's always reading about food."

"She doesn't eat."

"Dieting books."

"Elizabeth David was my bible growing up."

"Never heard of her."

"Philistine. *A Book of Mediterranean Food* changed the way people ate, and she had a great sex life."

"She cooked breakfast in bed?"

Imogen was sure she heard Marcus stifle a laugh.

Bill could be heard announcing, "Ladies and gentlemen, luncheon is served."

"You'd better go and sit down," said Imogen.

"Right. Nice talking to you."

"You're in there," said Marcus, the moment Nick was out of earshot.

"Don't be silly. He's married, and he's way out of my league. Did you get a good look at him? He could melt chocolate."

"Sister, so, what's not to like? You go, girl. P'raps he's a chubby chaser."

"*Mais oui.*"

Menu du jour

"Les voiles"

Le déjeuner chez Frank et Claudia

Miniature burek, filled with lamb, cheese, spinach
Warm foie gras glazed with wild strawberries, on Melba toast
Anchoïade
***
Chilled leek and celeriac soup
***
Scrambled goose eggs, aged Parmesan, black Périgord truffles
***
Pasta lune Provençale
***
Poached fillet of Saint Pierre, sauce Escoffier
***
Partridge with Italian stuffing, served on a bed of potatoes with juniper berries, and a side dish of sweet-sour red cabbage and devilled chestnuts
***
Les huit familles de fromage
Exotic fruits
***

Villa Eilenroc

Haute chocolaterie
★★★

1999 Bollinger La Grande Année Rosé
1978 Montrachet, Domaine de la Romanée-Conti
1990 La Moutonne, Chablis Grand Cru, Domaine Long-Depaquit
1961 Jaboulet Hermitage La Chapelle
1964 Romanée-Conti, Domaine de la Romanée-Conti

Marcus Gavius Apicius

IMOGEN HAD PLACED on the table, at every place setting, printed menu cards in specially made terracotta holders. All of the guests sat down, and glanced at the menu.

"That's quite a spread, Frank," said Charles. "You've really gone to town. What have we done to deserve this? Must be a very special occasion."

"Just *Les voiles*, Charles; and we eat like this every day, don't we, darling?"

"If I ate like this every day I'd be as big as …" Claudia almost said "Imogen," but opted for "too big for a bikini."

"An all Burgundy wine list, very interesting, Frank," said Papoche.

"Nick told me how much you appreciate a good wine, so I thought we'd just give these a test drive."

"You could buy a Ferrari with these wines," said Nick.

"Men," said Claudia.

"Oh, dear." What Cassandra meant by this – men, food, wine – perhaps nobody understood, and didn't ask.

Galia lit a cigarette. "So, ladies, the men are going to be talking about what they always talk about. What are we going to bore them with?"

Claudia had a suggestion. "Let's talk about something we know nothing about, and then they'll feel they have to talk to us to put us right."

"Nobody minds if I smoke?" asked Galia. "How about starting with the male ego?"

"Much too big to dissect," said the Baroness, to laughter. She was a woman who knew exactly how to pitch and lob her *bon mots* so that they brought up chalk – witty, but rarely cutting. Seated beside her, Casimir tried a little too hard.

"There are some men who understand women, Baroness."

"Yes, and a little bit of understanding goes a long way."

Bill and his staff served the soup course.

"Such a pretty table decoration," commented the Baroness, appreciatively.

"*Les sept grains,*" explained Claudia. "It's an old peasant tradition, apparently, to do with keeping bread on the table every day of the week."

"How nice to see something simple, and so perfect for sitting outside," said the Baroness. "In Palm Beach they do so love their larger-than-life bouquets, it's overpowering."

"Oh, I miss Palm Beach!" said Ray.

"Do you? I don't. Sometimes, I long for a street with litter on it."

Jade arrived, very late. Adroitly, she neither apologised directly for being late, and yet did so. "Well! That was good timing! I'm positively starving. Am I terribly late?"

Frank kissed her warmly. "Yes, but I forgive you."

Jade kissed Claudia. "You look lovely, Claudia. Karl said that if you want something else for tomorrow, he'll play postman."

"Isn't that sweet of him. Did he tell you he'll be here for lunch?"

"Yes, that's what I meant."

Out in the Golfe, the boat with the orange sails was not in serious contention; here, on the terrace, however, Frank was bidding for supremacy – his chosen arena, Saint-Tropez, the ideal site for a feast harking back to Marcus Gavius Apicius, lover of flamingo's tongues.

Frank made the introductions, going round the table. Instead of sitting down and politely nodding as Frank put a name to a face, Jade shook hands with the men and air-kissed the women. She had force of personality, but there was nothing else outwardly colourful about her – no bright clothes, no jewellery. Unlike the other guests, she was not immaculately turned out (Casimir was immaculate in a shabby sort of way). Either she had got ready in a hurry, or she cared little about her appearance; or was it an anti-fashion look worn by an arch *fashionista*? Every 'look,' studied or not, is exactly that – a 'look.' She was wearing an off-white vintage tennis dress – sleeveless, round neck, pleated skirt to below the knees; white Converse sneakers without laces, white half socks, and carrying an anonymous canvas holdall with bamboo handles. When she burst on to the terrace, she waltzed in with a free and easy manner, like Suzanne Lenglen striding on to the court at the Carlton Club in Cannes, in 1926, to play Helen Wills in the 'Match of the Century.'

She was in her mid-twenties; her nondescript brown hair was pulled back into a pony tail, secured with a white band; she wore little or no make-up. Looking at her, and listening to her – a lot of women are designed only to be looked at – you didn't get the idea that she had arranged herself in any deliberate way, like a calculating wannabe – the type favoured by Tyler Shields; as if, in dressing down, ready for tennis, at a high society luncheon party on the French Riviera, she might increase her rating on the social scale, from a C to a B. No, there was nothing artful about her simplicity, nothing affected. It was a look that suited her – she had presence, and presence of mind.

She was tall, with clear skin, no tan (that was about all that was physically remarkable about her); her teeth were small, a natural pearly white; tangerine-shaped breasts, not melons or pineapples. She was not beautiful in that immediately noticeable, turn-around-in-the-street-and-lust-after-her way (that action, which men perform when they want to show that they're definitely straight); and she was not overtly sexy in that starlet grab-your-balls way that arouses builders on scaffolding. Her features were so regular and bland that she was exactly what you need to make it as a model – a perfectly blank canvas on to which you could paint whatever colours you wanted. In short, she was casually upper crust. Sargent would have painted her; today, you see her in a Ralph Lauren campaign.

Jade was a woman to appeal to a connoisseur; forget about any well-used chat-up lines – she would incinerate them. A man would have to be very sure of himself to try his luck with her; not cocksure like Casimir; perhaps an old-fashioned and chivalrous lady-killer like George Clooney might have a chance; a man like Frank, more dangerous, would probably get better odds.

It was *de rigueur* on these occasions to compliment a woman on her wonderful clothes sense, and the exorbitant cost. Cassandra got in first.

"Is that a vintage Jean Patou? I do so love retro."

"This old thing? I bought it in a charity shop in Notting Hill."

Montrachet

THE INTRODUCTIONS OUT of the way, Jade sat down, glanced through the menu, and immediately set about establishing her dominance of the table.

"You have pulled out all the stops, Frank. Bill, is there anything left of that champagne?"

"Yes, that was a very nice champagne, Frank," said Casimir, winningly. "Big mouth-feel, woodsy, and aromatic."

"Cook's recommendation."

"Really? I would have thought that a woman would have gone for something pretty like Perrier Jouet."

Jade skewered her first victim. "Do you always treat women like you treat champagne?"

In the kitchen, Imogen and Marcus could hear every word of this exchange.

"Who is that Jade?" asked Imogen. "That's not a guest, that's a tornado."

"Jade? Oh, she'll eat him for breakfast. You just listen."

"Who is she?"

"Have no idea. She's a model or something. I think Frank's fucking her, in revenge for Massimo."

"Oh, thanks for that. I can always rely on you to give me the lowdown on what's going on upstairs."

"It's one of the perks of the job. Saves buying *Hello!* magazine."

"And who are you fucking, Marcus?"

"Massimo."

Bill brought Jade her champagne. She didn't drink it immediately: she held it up to the light; brought it down to her nose, breathed in; and drank a large gulp. She had everybody's attention.

"Peasant flowers, pink champagne, nicely individual. Must be a woman in the kitchen, or gay."

Nobody said anything – not a good sign. "I meant it as a compliment."

"Oh, I always accept a compliment," said Ray.

"Where did you buy this Montrachet, Frank?" asked Papoche, adroitly.

"It's exquisite, isn't it? Sotheby's, in two thousand and one. Seven bottles. We're drinking most of them today."

"I'm not a wine person, is it something special?" asked Ray.

"It's a Burgundy," said Casimir, helpfully.

"Were they expensive?" asked Galia.

"Came to twenty-three thousand nine hundred twenty-nine bucks a bottle."

"My God! That comes to ..." Galia couldn't do the maths.

Frank laughed. "A hundred and sixty seven thousand, five hundred and three dollars."

"And he complains about how much money I spend on clothes!" exclaimed Claudia.

"Wasn't it the most expensive bottle of wine ever sold?" asked Nick. "I'm doing rather well with my wine investments."

"Most expensive that you can actually drink, yes."

"With scrambled eggs," remarked Charles.

"They make a perfect match, if you ask me," said Jade, tucking in. "Truffles are absolutely delish."

"Breakfast on the terrace, how lovely," said Ray.

"You could buy an eighteenth-century Lafite, cost you four times what I paid for this Montrachet."

Jade had strong opinions about everything. "It'd taste like vinegar. No wine can live much beyond fifty."

"In general, I'd agree," said Frank, "but there are the rare exceptions. I drank a nineteen-twenty-one d'Yquem not so long ago. Tasted pretty good."

"Do you know anything about wine, young lady?" asked Papoche.

"Do you?" retorted Jade.

"I have a very good cellar."

"Really? That doesn't mean you know anything about wine."

The table was very quiet. "Little madam," thought Imogen. She had come out on to the terrace to take back two glasses of the Montrachet, for her and Marcus, to see how it paired with the truffled eggs. She was surprised to see that Frank seemed to be delighted with this display of flashing venom; the smile on his face was one of wide-mouthed enjoyment, not a nervous social veneer. She didn't understand why Frank would let a guest sit at his table like a loose cannon on deck. The guests had chosen themselves, as it were, but Frank never left anything to chance; and he would never let a guest upset his plans, even if he was fucking her. No, she was sure that he was playing a careful hand, but she failed to see where it was going.

Papoche had been stung by Jade's stiletto. "Well, *mademoiselle*, perhaps you would like to give us your expert opinion about this wine."

"*Mais oui*, I'm sure that we would all love to hear your verdict," said Galia. The implication was clear to everybody sitting around the table – let's defrock the fraudster.

"If you like," was Jade's breezy reply. All of the women –

except for the Baroness, who seemed, like Frank, to find it all amusing – hated her; and she didn't care.

Jade held the glass of Montrachet to the light; swirled it around, let it settle. Again, just as she had done with the Bollinger, she breathed in the aromas, unhurriedly – once, twice, a third time; and only then took a swig – not a ladylike sip. It was an erotic show, near to pornographic; the slow, luxurious, lascivious and caressing way she left the wine lying in her mouth, her lips still glossy with the liquid, letting it develop on the tongue, at the back of the throat, in every one of her senses. She was concentrating, not play-acting; wine tasting is not about drama – that is for vine whores. Jade was searching for the essence of a great wine; if she made it look like a sexual act, that is because she understood how closely they are allied, in the mouth of a knowledgeable, experienced woman. The straight men at the table were imagining what it would be like to be licked and loved by her – Casimir put it better than he knew when he used the expression "mouth-feel"; the women were thinking, "slut." Finally, slowly, and deliberately, she spoke, keeping the glass close to her nose, and drinking between phrases.

"Aromas of hot, roasted, buttered popcorn, the sweetcorn present right from the start. Notes of gunflint signalling a classic crisp Chardonnay with a nice toast and a smoky sex appeal. The nose is long, smooth, pure and deep. Incredibly complex, with big-time minerals balanced with sweet tones – layers of skin, nuts, palm ... exotic fruits and honey. Lots of personality. Developing a big powerful bouquet, rich and concentrated with plenty of spice and fat, perfumes of rich musk, and buttery flavours. The palate is mouth-filling, and still amazingly young. Great earth flavours making the *terroir* very noticeable – *évidemment terroir du Montrachet*; just a hint of root vegetable. Very nice match, Frank; the eggs and the truffles make the acidity stand out even more – and a wonderful long finish."

She had triumphed.

"Bravo," said Frank, clapping, like a teacher applauding his most talented pupil.

Claudia, Cassandra and Galia said nothing.

The Baroness liked to give praise where praise was due. "How different." Different from what she didn't say.

"My, my," was Ray's reaction.

"Class in a glass," said Nick.

"I'm impressed by you, young lady," said Papoche, smiling at her for the first time.

"I'm sure you have a talent for something," Jade answered, wiping the smile off his face.

"You make it sound very sexy," said Charles.

"That's why they call your men's pleasures 'wine, women and song,'" said the Baroness.

"You have a nice French accent. I thought you were American?" said Cassandra, finding something to say at last.

"*Non, je suis française,*" said Jade.

"*D'où êtes-vous?*"

"*De* Beaune."

"Well, that explains a lot," said Nick.

"Does it?" asked Ray, bewildered.

"It's the capital of Burgundy, Ray," said Casimir, making himself useful. "She's a Burgundian." He made it sound like she was a cunt.

"Right. Not just a pretty face then."

"If you like the gypsy type," remarked Casimir, viciously.

Jade let the slur pass.

"I was referring to you." Ray liked to lace his sweet talk with an acidic putdown. He was having fun; in his flirtatious relationship with Casimir, he was the one with the money. He had been in this market many times – from the selling side; now, he was mastering the business of ass, from the buyer's side.

"I'm starting to understand the game he's playing," said Imogen. She was straining the pasta.

"What game is that, then?" asked Marcus.

"Snakes and Ladders."

"She's a bitch, but she's right about those eggs matching the wine. You got it exactly right, Mo. I've never seen them made in a *bain-marie* before. Gordon makes them in a saucepan."

"Yes, like a housewife. Takes ages this way, but it gets the best results. Time to serve the pasta."

Chablis

JADE SEEMED TO enjoy baiting Casimir most of all. When he surreptitiously checked his BlackBerry, during the pasta course, she brought it to everybody's attention. "Are we keeping you from something more enjoyable?"

Casimir tried to fight back. "The world's a twenty-four place."

"Yes, that's probably how you'll describe this luncheon to your friends, and put it on your Facebook page. A one-of-a kind opportunity to advance your lifestyle."

"Ouch!" said Imogen, in the kitchen.

"I told you, she bites, that one."

"And what do you do, Jade?" asked the Baroness.

Casimir couldn't resist the gambit. "Pole dancing, prancing down a catwalk?"

"I've done some shows, yes. A few covers. Girly stuff."

"I couldn't have put it better. What do you do when nobody looks at you?"

"I look at myself in the mirror."

"I thought as much."

Casimir should have left well alone; for he had fallen into the trap set for him.

"What I really do is run a charity for the child victims of violence in Africa."

"How very noble of you," said Casimir, chastened and yet still childishly defiant.

"Yes, that's exactly what it is, young man," said the Baroness – the first sharp words she had uttered. She seemed immune to Casimir's charms; he had several times tried to chat with her, dazzle her, but she had responded off-handedly, though always politely.

"Have you actually been to Africa?" asked Cassandra.

"Yes, many times," said Jade.

"We went on safari, didn't we, Nick, do you remember? All those lovely wild animals. We watched a lion attack a ... what was it?"

"Gazelle."

"Why do they need your help?" asked Galia.

"Soldiers chop the limbs off children, to demoralise the parents. It works."

Frank signalled an end to the hostilities. "Shall we move on to the next wine?"

"That's our signal, Mo. Fish time," said Marcus.

"Why Burgundy, Frank, and not Bordeaux?" asked Charles.

Frank answered with the fluent and carefully articulated logic employed by a man who has thought about this question a great deal. "Like everybody, I suppose, I started off with Bordeaux. My cellars are full of it, and I still like to drink it. But I fell in love with Burgundy."

"Nice," said Claudia, rolling her eyes.

"Claudia's my wife, and Burgundy's my mistress."

Papoche made his entrance into the conversation. "It's a game of chance with Burgundy."

"Yes, exactly, Papoche, I agree, that's the thrill. There are so many more variables to go wrong; the odds are longer, the rewards much bigger."

"Do you buy it as an investment?" asked Charles. "Prices have gone crazy."

"Best return on anything in my portfolio," said Nick.

Frank shook his head. "Never. If I'm not going to drink it, I'm not going to buy it. I'm happy to lay it down, but not because I'm waiting for it to go up in price. I'm not interested in making money out of wine."

"Hear, hear!" cheered Charles. "It's about understanding the finer things in life. Money isn't everything."

Galia looked as if she were about to say something, but didn't.

"People who enjoy fine wine have some understanding about what it means to be a human being." That was Casimir's pennyworth.

"How very profound," Jade fired back.

"A pearl beyond any price." There was no doubt that Papoche was aiming at Nick.

Nick was irked. "Aren't we all forgetting something?"

Frank had been expecting this. "You want to say, Nick, that you have to have lots of money to be able to enjoy wine like this?"

"Exactly."

"But it's people like you, Nick, who have put it out of the range of people like them."

Bill and his staff served the fish.

"Why are they ganging up on him?" Imogen asked Marcus.

"Same reason why you're so much on his side, darling. This Escoffier sauce: I grate the horseradish; mix with the same quantity of skinned and chopped walnuts, right? Then add sugar, salt, juice of two lemons, and just stir in the cream? That's it?"

"Ouais, c'est tout simple."

Ray had a good appetite, his appreciation always peppered – he couldn't help it – with added bite. "This fish is divine. She looks as if she shops in WalMart, but she sure can cook."

"I'll be sure to pass on your compliments to the chef," said Frank.

"Perhaps not all of them," suggested Nick.

"Nick, care to try to talk us through this Chablis?"

"Oh God, that's putting me on the spot. I'm really not qualified for this."

Jade dispatched him with a single thrust. "But you said that you buy wine as an investment. Do you actually know what you're buying?"

Cassandra was always awake when her husband was the subject. "Nick has good taste in everything, don't you darling?"

Claudia volunteered the obvious. "He married you Cassie – of course he has!"

"Okay, here goes." Nick made a good masculine show of holding up the wine to the light; letting it swirl and settle in the glass; sniffing, and waiting a few moments. "Sorry, Frank, but I think the nose is a little off? Is it just me?"

"Skunky," was Jade's opinion.

The guests all grimaced.

"Let it be skunky." Nick drank a good mouthful. "Anyway, it's quite nutty … citrus fruits, and a little spice?" Nick was finding his confidence. "A bit too thin for me. Not at all like the Montrachet, is it? This is very austere, as if it's been made by Jesuit priests. It's almost steely in character, like opening a safe deposit box and finding the contents of a Caribbean island. Aah! The skunk's going away, and now you get that lovely clean Chablis taste; lots of minerals coming through. Does it sound silly to say it reminds me of the landscape where it comes from? Limestone rock? It's not as voluptuous as the Montrachet, which I liked much more, but it's still a beautiful wine."

Frank held the table together. "There you are, you see! That's the thing about Chardonnay. It's quite a boring grape, not much character; it's a nerd, not a school hero. But it loves to learn; it likes to soak up everything it can find in the soil, and hand it in for a gold star."

"You've missed your calling, Frank, you should have been a wine grower," said Galia.

"Or a wine critic," chipped in Charles.

"Who's to say I won't?"

"Oh no!" exclaimed Claudia.

Imogen had been listening, minding the vegetables. "He didn't do too badly, did he?"

"You like him, don't you?" said Marcus.

This was not a question that Imogen was willing to answer.

"Do you think they've finished the fish? Are those partridges ready to fly?"

"Yes, they are. And you're very good at avoiding the subject of men."

Upstairs, the Noël Coward luncheon continued.

"This wine is an outsider," said Papoche, "and I think that is why you chose it, no, Frank?"

"I hear you."

"How can a wine be an outsider?" asked Ray.

"I'll let Papoche provide the explanation, seeing how he's divined the meaning."

Papoche spoke in measured phrases; like Frank he valued accuracy. "La Moutonne is a white wine from the far north of Burgundy. Chablis is a little unfashionable, it does not have the reputation of the Montrachet from Côte de Beaune, where *Mademoiselle* Jade I think for certain grew up."

Evidently, Papoche was warming to her. "Officially, Chablis has seven *Grand Cru* wines, the highest quality. This is the unofficial eighth."

"Exactly," said Frank.

"So, it's not really the best?" Ray liked to nail down a point, once he had bitten into it.

Papoche smiled. "La Moutonne is a perfect paradox. Because the wine is so good, the Burgundy wine authority says that, yes, they can put the words 'Grand Cru' on the bottles, but no, it's not official."

"There they are behind us," said Frank, pointing to the sidetable, with the empty bottles. Says it's *Grand Cru*."

Nick was pleased with himself. "Well, I wasn't so far out. Does what it says on the label."

"How very French," remarked Galia.

"How fascinating," said the Baroness.

"It's a wine that comes from behind," said Casimir.

Ray waved his hand at Bill. "I like that idea. Let me have a top-up."

"Somebody doesn't like your food," said Marcus, as Bill brought back a plate of untouched fish.

"Cassandra doesn't like any food, period." Imogen set about eating Cassandra's fish. "That charming American gentleman is right, it is delicious."

"He only said he didn't like your clothes sense, Mo; and he does have a point."

Imogen gave Marcus one of her fiercest looks.

"Sorry! Anyways, it's good to like your own food. I see you polished off what she left before."

"Good food shouldn't go to waste."

1961

THE PARTRIDGE WAS served, and both the birds and the plates caused a stir.

"Wow!" from Jade.

"*C'est magnifique, non?*" from Galia.

"Awesome," from Casimir.

"Oh my!" from Ray, followed by a squeal of delight, as he read the quotation, hand-painted in bright red script, running around the rim of the over-sized white Limoges plate: "'A princess never cooks.' That is *so* true! What does everybody else have?"

"I think this one is meant for me," said Galia, "'A woman can never be …'"

"Be what?" asked Claudia.

"Whatever you want her to be," said Frank, "I have 'Today's Menu – Take it or Leave it.' Thank you, countess! What does my wife have?"

"'*Jamais economiser sur le luxe.*'"

"She certainly got that one right."

"What do you have, Cassie?" asked Claudia.

"'Nothing chocolate, nothing gained.'"

"But you can't stand chocolate!" exclaimed Nick.

"What do you have, darling?" Cassandra spoke to her husband with love and respect, submissively, as if she worshipped the ground he walked on.

"'Highly fed and lowly taught.' Haven't a clue what it means. Does she mean me? She's very clever, your countess."

"Oh, she was like that at school. I was chasing boys and she was reading books!"

"That explains a lot!" Frank was laughing.

"But what does it mean?" asked Ray.

"It's the clown in *All's Well that Ends Well*." Casimir put on his best theatrical voice: 'I will show myself highly fed and lowly taught.'"

Ray clapped. "Well done you!"

"Sort of, I played the clown."

"Nice, she thinks I'm a clown!" Nick was only half-joking.

Downstairs, hearing this, Imogen scalded her finger on a saucepan handle. "*Merde*! I messed up there, didn't I? How was I to know he'd get that plate."

"I told you, one day you'd get in trouble with that painting lark."

"It's meant to make them laugh!"

"It did. Except him. Why's it matter?"

"I didn't think that I was going to like him. There, I've said it. Happy now?"

"Sister, I worked that one out when you were stirring the sauce with him, hand in hand, and massaging his nipple."

"I didn't mean to!"

"I thought that Catholic girls weren't meant to lie?"

Upstairs, Charles stood up, and his honeyed words gave some clue as to how, all those years ago, he had conned so many people out of so much money: "What can I say, Frank? This is a feast. The food of the gods. I feel as if we should be lounging on divans. I'd like to propose a toast to the most magnificent, most generous hosts on the Côte d'Azur, to Frank and Claudia."

All of the guests raised their glasses: "To Frank and Claudia!"

Galia was re-reading the menu. "Nineteen-sixty-one, was that a good year for this?"

"A legend. I don't think I'd ever open it," said Nick.

"The oldest vineyards in France, the favourite wine of the Russian tsars," said Charles, almost reverently. "Even then it was the most expensive wine in the world."

By degrees, as each mythic wine had been followed by another, even more iconic, Charles was eating and drinking his way towards some comprehension of the Olympian ambition that Frank was displaying, but for what? Charles sensed – in fact, he was certain – that there was an underlying purpose to this gathering, but what it was, he had not yet worked out. Galia's status as a cultural icon ensured that they never lacked for invites, but Frank could have called on a Hollywood A-lister if he had only been looking to decorate his table – you can find them on every street corner in Saint-Tropez. Charles and Galia had known Frank and Claudia for years, but they were not close friends; on the French Riviera there is a big difference between the well-heeled and the fabulously wealthy. Frank wanted something – what did he want?

With the pouring of the Hermitage – if not well before – Papoche also, no doubt, like Charles, understood that this luncheon was 'about' something. By itself, there was nothing unusual about the super-rich flaunting their trophy wines. What was different here was the meticulous matching of the wines with the food, as if they were being driven in tandem somewhere, but where?

Manipulation or no manipulation, Frank's magic was working its spell. Papoche was mesmerised by the wine; he spoke out loud but it seemed more as if he were talking to himself, so wrapped up was he in his enjoyment.

"It is an unbelievable wine, Frank. This deep purple colour is

Villa Eilenroc

like a jewel. On the nose it is so rich; you get the aromas of smoked meat, pepper, soy sauce," he breathed in again, "new saddle leather, and so much fruit – blackberry, plum, blackcurrants. It is like an old master painting in Florence that has just been cleaned. You admire the perfect proportion exactly balanced with such humanity and concentration. It is immortal." Papoche stopped, as if he were embarrassed at this display of sensitivity. "Did you lay it down a long time ago?"

"No, I bought them only a few years ago, at an auction in London."

"I know it's not very polite to talk about money but ... " Galia let the question hang in the air.

"No secret. The case cost me a hundred and twenty-three thousand, seven hundred and fifty."

"Pounds or dollars?" asked Nick.

"Pounds."

"How many bottles in a case?" asked Galia.

"Twelve, darling, you know that," said Charles.

"I'm almost afraid to ask how much money I've just drunk?" asked the Baroness.

Frank was laughing. "One thousand, seven hundred and nineteen pounds a glass."

"Fuck," from Casimir.

"That's ... nearly three hundred pounds a mouthful," said Charles.

"This is the only time I've ever felt guilty about drinking the boss's booze," said Marcus, drinking another mouthful of the Hermitage. Bill had brought three glasses down to the kitchen, and he was also taking sips, as he scuttled back and forth.

"It's not a perk, Marcus, it's a duty we have, to make sure that it's not corked."

"Duty calls," said Imogen, imbibing.

Her question answered, the Baroness seemed uncertain whether to praise the wine, or devalue the excessive cost. "Definitely what they mean by conspicuous consumption."

"Some people drink the cost, Baroness, I drink the contents. That's the difference."

"Frank's on his hobby horse," said Claudia. "Don't get him started, Sophie, or we'll still be here tomorrow."

"Shall we talk about *haute couture*, ladies?" asked Galia, mischievously. "A serious discussion about something really important, like, 'What's the most expensive frock you've never worn in your wardrobe?'"

Ray was with the women on this one. "Always the one you buy when you're in love, and in a hurry."

Jade preferred the men's talk. "You make yourselves easy targets."

Papoche was attracted to her intelligence (the beauty was a given), as much as he was annoyed every time she said something.

"You think that we have no taste, *mademoiselle*?" He didn't call her Jade; that would have been a word too personal, one that took him into her territory, as if she were Morgan le Fay.

"I didn't say that."

It made no difference how carefully he phrased his words; this was a woman who knew both how to massage a man's ego, and needle him at the same time.

When a man is in super-rich company, the money rubs off. Charles had rarely been this close to a billion dollars' worth of table talk.

"You're right, Frank. It was different before the Internet; and the Chinese and the Russians piling in. People want a wine cellar immediately, and they can't wait."

Papoche allied himself with Frank and Charles, and fired a warning shot across the table at his son-in-law. "Because they value money more than family, that is why they do not lay down wine for their children."

"Like gentlemen, you mean," said Nick. Four words, and you can say so much.

Romanée-Conti

THE CHEESE WAS served, and with it the Romanée-Conti. Ray gossiped with the women, and flirted with Casimir. Claudia, Galia and the Baroness talked about this and that – how annoying it is to buy couture, and then see it on the red carpet in Cannes. Claudia said that she had told Stefano she would never buy anything again if she saw her dress on an actress: "It's taking them three thousand hours to make, Domenico himself is doing some of the stitching, and if I see it for a minute on anybody else, I told him forget it!" How St Barts was getting too Russian; and the best rehab.

Cassandra was still as quiet as a mouse, and picked at the cheese, which she said was "delicious."

This was Charles's cue. "Do you live on the Côte d'Azur?"

"No, in the summer we have a house in San Remo. Well, it's actually my father's house."

Galia was very alive to the nuances of real estate. "It's so different on the Italian side, don't you think?"

"Well, her father is Italian, darling, so that makes sense."

When a man calls his wife "darling" at lunch, it is rarely a term of affection; after so many years, one reads the signals. Galia shut up.

Cassandra did not seem so much offended by Galia's attempt at social downgrading as bored. "Yes, I suppose it is.

We live in Turin the rest of the time, because of the business."

Charles wanted something – information – and extreme courtesy was his favoured method. "Frank said that you make chocolates?"

"I don't make them! Although, when I was little, I learned how to make all of them."

"Sounds like a childhood dream, to grow up with chocolate."

"Yes, until you grow up with it."

It was at this moment that Charles worked out what the luncheon was about.

Nick was also longing to find out the reason why these particular guests had been invited – what was the connection between them, if any? – but had to make do with vague questions addressed to Charles, Ray and the Baroness about how they looked after their investments. Charles was his own money manager; Ray was always meaning to sit down and try to understand them, but didn't; the Baroness managed not to give anything away.

Jade was telling Papoche how the Syrah grapes for the 1961 Hermitage had been partly picked by her grandfather, who owned a small part of the steep granite hillside, making up the *appellation*.

"His hands are always rough to the touch because they don't use machines. They have to carry the topsoil back up the slope after each vintage, and the paths are so narrow you can only do it with a sledge."

Casimir couldn't leave well alone. "I bet he always has dirt under his fingernails."

The Baroness had decided that Ray was welcome to this young man (she knew the meaning of the boy's place at table). "So much nicer than a pianist's fingers. You can always trust a man who works with his hands."

"A pianist does work with his hands, Baroness."

Frank intervened. "It's six hectares he has, if I remember. It's been a while since I visited, you were just a little girl, so that would be worth what now … " Frank put his Turing brain to work, "probably more than fifteen million."

Nick was enjoying the cheese. "She really is amazing, your catering countess, Frank," said Nick, "She makes everything into a work of art."

"Yes, she is, isn't she? So good, I almost married her."

Claudia was horrified. "Oh Frank, no! Not that story! Charles and Galia have heard it a thousand times."

"Nobody else has."

"We don't mind hearing it again," said Charles. "It's a very good story."

"And Claudia will never invite us again, Charles," was Galia's comment.

Claudia knew that Frank would tell his tale, and angled for a compromise: "Okay, so tell it if you must, for a laugh, but please, don't make it seem as if I was just a scheming little minx."

"I married you because I loved you, Claudia, still do."

"Oh Frank, now, I've gone bright red! Oh, this is terrible. Tell it!"

"Okay, here goes. When I was courting Claudia, she was always inviting me to supper at the apartment she shared with a girlfriend in Geneva. I hardly ever saw the friend who had a very busy social life, by the sound of it, out every night. Of course, I was delighted because it meant we had the apartment to ourselves. Every night I was there, the food was unbelievable. Night after night, Claudia served these amazing dinners, better than any restaurant I had ever been in – candles, wine, soft music, a beautiful woman who could cook – my God, I was in heaven! This went on for weeks, by which time, I knew that I wanted to marry her. Then, I thought that I should start to take her out, to show her that I wanted to give her a life outside of the apartment, give her a break from the kitchen. First night, we went to a restaurant, and that was where I found out the truth. I had the ring in my pocket, ready to get down on one knee and propose."

"What happened?" Ray loved a good story.

"I can remember exactly what we were eating: an *hors d'oeuvres* of quails' eggs in mayonnaise. I wanted to make a good impression, show her how much I cared about her. I mean, that ring was burning a hole in my pocket! To show her how much I appreciated her cooking, more than restaurant food, I asked Claudia how she made her mayonnaise."

Claudia was in an anguish of embarrassment: "I can't bear it! You make such a meal of it! I didn't know how to make mayonnaise! I told him it came out of a bottle."

"I didn't know how to make mayonnaise either, but I knew that you had to have eggs. And somewhere I had read about Escoffier codifying sauces. And I asked her if mayonnaise was one of those sauces."

"And I didn't know who Escoffier was!"

"But what about the ring?" Ray was rapt.

"I kept it in my pocket. I didn't say anything, just carried on eating and drinking and flirting. I soon worked out that it was the missing flatmate who had been doing the cooking. So, I started arriving early for dinner at the apartment to try to catch them out, but that didn't work, they were too clever. Then, I insisted that her flatmate should join us for dinner, and that's how I dug out the truth. First evening, I casually mentioned Escoffier, and Imogen went on about him for hours. I got to know her quite well, after that."

Ray's mouth was wide open. "The same Imogen doing the

cooking today, your catering countess, wearing that camping equipment?" Frank nodded. "Oh my."

The story had stopped being funny.

"But you married Claudia?" asked Cassandra.

"Claudia had other talents to appeal to a man."

"I think, given the choice between a man who could cook and a big cock, I'd choose the cook every time. This cheese is impossible to resist," said Jade, who had an appetite to rival the men.

"It's so much harder to find a good cook than a big cock," said Ray.

Perhaps the Baroness saw something of her younger self in Jade, because she clapped.

"How liberated you are! I think it's wonderful."

"Thank you, Baroness. Only if I were a man, and I had talked about the choice between a woman with big tits, and one who could cook, nobody would have turned a hair." Not even pausing for breath, Jade addressed Casimir. "Can you cook?"

"You are a bad girl!" said Ray, longing to hear what Casimir would say.

Casimir scored his first point of the day. "Come round and you'll see."

Papoche continued to be intrigued by the menu: "Interesting, Frank, you want to pair this Romanée-Conti with cheese and with chocolate? No Sauternes?"

Frank played the first move of his endgame (first game of the first round). "Yes, it's a bit unexpected, I agree, but I'm hoping you'll approve. People often let their tastes stagnate, don't you think? Takes the adventure out of life."

Papoche nodded, but said nothing.

"What do we think of this Romanée-Conti?" asked Frank. "Baroness?"

"I don't know how to describe it, not like Jade, or Nick, or Papoche. It tastes very nice."

"Can you describe what you're wearing?"

The Baroness caught the meaning, smiled, nodded her head, and gave it a go. She copied the actions she had seen everybody else make, not quite in the same way – more hesitant. "I'll just say the words that come into my head, not wine words." She paused, collecting her visual sense, her sense of smell, her taste buds; finding, perhaps unexpectedly, in her imagination and memory, more than she had thought possible, or even wanted to find. In a glass of wine, she was drawing on all of the colourful lives that she had led; now, at this luncheon, she was older, she had more to regret.

"Colour, a dark red, like the liquid dye that runs down the narrow streets of the *medina* in Fez, pouring out of the tanneries, and he lifted me up in his arms. Smell has … spices … not the dried variety – the cooked spices of the street food in Bangkok. Damp earth … not the wet tarmac, fake grass and gas fumes in Palm Beach; no, the leaves fading and decomposing in the woods surrounding the *schloss* in Mecklenburg. Riding leather, just after you take it off a sweating horse … and that gamey smell they have in the butcher's in Mount Street. It's not very fruity, I mean it's not like smelling a bouquet of flowers. The taste is very concentrated, and it's difficult to identify one dominant flavour, like trying to work out the fruit inside a jar of homemade jam, when the label has been lost. It's like it waits for you to uncover what's been hiding in the ground, like walking into somebody you used to love very much. It's a wine for grown-ups."

Now, it was Jade's turn to clap. "Bravo! Bullseye!"

"I agree," said Frank. "Enjoyment and appreciation go so easy together."

Papoche did not call her by her title. *"Très bien fait*, Sophie."

The Baroness deflected the intimacy. "It's just a glass of wine."

Jade was quicker than anybody else. "You two know each other?"

The Baroness batted away the question. "For a long time."

Papoche was more exact. "Thirty-two years."

"Where did you meet?" asked Cassandra.

"I really don't remember," replied the Baroness, rather too quickly.

Charles had a question: "Who made up the rule that says you have to have white wine with dessert?"

"Good question, Charles, don't know. Anybody?" asked Frank.

Jade was helping herself to slices of cheese, but still had a mind to joke. "The *Bordelais*."

"Clever girl," said Papoche, laughing for the first time.

"I don't get it?" Ray asked Casimir.

"The *Bordelais* live in Bordeaux, and they make a sweet white wine called Sauternes."

"Do you have a sweet tooth?" asked Ray.

Casimir gave Ray his very best smile. "I'm as sweet as anybody wants me to be."

The cooking finished, Marcus and Imogen had been tidying up the kitchen, and listening to the play on the terrace. "So, you could have been a billionaire's wife, Mo. Are you all right? You seem a little out of sorts."

"Me? I'm fine. As always."

There was a goodness of heart about Marcus, although he showed it in a roundabout way. "Do you know why I'm fucking Massimo?"

"Because he has the most gorgeous ass on any man I've ever seen?"

"And that's all anybody ever sees. I hate those Bikkembergs he wears. Look at me: I'm the original weed. I was teased at school. No chest, no biceps, tongue-tied, no sweet talk. I'm nothing outside of a kitchen. What chance did I have with a man like Massimo? I take off my clothes, and my skin looks as if it's been roasted alive. He got the job on the new *Claudia* because he's training to be a captain. You wouldn't think so to look at him, would you? For months, I couldn't find the courage to talk to him, just handed him the plates through the serving hatch, like a dumb fuck."

"Dutch courage?"

"No, I probably would never have asked him. Just carried on telling him excruciating details about every dish he was holding in his hand, just to keep him there a few seconds longer."

"So, what happened?"

"A few weeks ago, that's all it was, he was holding the Beef Stroganoff – we had that Russian, Andrei, here again – and I was telling him that it's a fake dish, how they made it up for a competition; and he just asked me, right off: 'Are you ever going to ask me out?' Said I was the first man, or woman, not to zero in on his ass."

Frank could be heard saying, "And now for the final *dégustation*."

"That's my cue to join them," said Imogen.

"Now, this should prove interesting."

Haute chocolaterie

IMOGEN SAT DOWN, and Frank immediately stood up. "I've asked Imogen to join us for the chocolates because she didn't have to cook them! Well, I think it's now my turn to propose a toast. The food has been magnificent, Mo, and we owe you a vote of thanks: Ladies and gentlemen, please raise your glasses to the catering countess."

There was a chorus of approval, and Imogen felt a little silly.

"Imogen, that was simply divine," said Galia. "One of your best."

"Thank you, Galia. I'm happy that you liked the grapes."

"I still can't turn over an omelette, even after living so long in France. Isn't that terrible?" Galia made it sound as if it were not really so terrible.

Bill and his staff laid out the chocolates, arranged on individual plates, not circular in shape but square. Six chocolates were placed on each plate, wrapped in black matt paper, each one bearing the words *"Les voiles,"* printed in red script.

"I thought that we might finish lunch a little differently," said Frank. "Instead of a winding down, end on a high note. We're eating the chocolates from left to right. And there's tea for anybody who wants it. Bill has the list; you just have to ask."

Papoche looked at the unfamiliar brand. "That's a chocolate name I don't know, Frank."

"For sure, because I had them made especially for lunch, hence the name."

"My, but I sure don't have room for chocolate!" exclaimed Ray, unwrapping the first one, and popping it into his mouth.

"Can we just save them for later?" asked the Baroness.

"If you like but you have no idea what you're missing, Baroness. Like I said, I had them made especially, and flown in from Brussels. And you'll miss the game."

"Game?" asked Jade.

"Guess where the chocolate comes from, and there's a prize at the end."

"Cash?" asked Casimir.

"Food vouchers?" joked Nick.

"No, really, what's the prize, Frank?" asked Charles.

"It's a surprise."

"More chocolate!" joked Claudia.

"But I don't know anything about chocolate," objected Ray, "so, I'm bound to lose."

"The runners-up all get a consolation prize. Anybody care to hazard a guess where this one is from?"

"I have no idea where to begin," said Galia.

"Well, this one is definitely a dark chocolate," joked Ray. "Does that get me a prize?"

The table erupted into laughter, and the game began.

"Anybody?" asked Frank.

Papoche knew his chocolate. "If I am not mistaken, I think this little one is the rarest of the rare; from a tiny estate called Hacienda Chuao, on the coast of Venezuela. In the chocolate business, it is what we call a *Grand Cru*, made out of a single type of Criollo bean."

Charles was enjoying the game (he could smell the money). "Well, you'd expect a man who owns a chocolate company to know his chocolate!"

Frank was concentrating. "And the taste?"

"Very distinctive. That is why I recognise it. When you bite into it, the first impression is very bitter, then a delicate fruity taste, balanced with acidity. Notes of caramel and fresh hazelnuts, with a hint of honey."

"Epic," was Casimir's word.

Jade was impressed. "Wow, all that from a bite of chocolate."

"All that, *mademoiselle*, from a mouthful of wine."

"*Touché.*"

Imogen joined in the game. "The taste lingers in the mouth, it's quite yummy."

Claudia was laughing. "Yummy? Oh Mo, that's such an English way to describe chocolate!"

The Baroness had decided not to take the chocolates home. "I think that yummy is a good way to describe it."

Frank was also laughing: "Right, so we're all agreed, this is yummy. Papoche, care to give us a crash course in chocolate, before we taste the next one?"

"My pleasure. I will sing for my supper. People think that the cocoa content is what matters in chocolate – seventy-eight per cent, eight-five, ninety – but fine chocolate is not about the numbers, it is about the type of bean, where it comes from, how it is grown, how it is harvested, how it is roasted. The finest chocolate comes from plantations covering a clearly defined area. We call it *Grand Cru de Propriété*."

"Just like wine," said Casimir.

"I didn't even know that cocoa trees could be different," said Charles.

"Chocolate for connoisseurs is about the estate, the *finca*, the *hacienda*, the *fazenda*, all the words we use to describe a wine *domaine*. Below the *grand cru*, you have the farmers' cooperatives covering a wider area, and there we talk about the chocolate region."

"Like a Burgundy?" asked Jade.

"*Exactement.*"

"Fascinating," said Ray, opening up the second wrapper. "This one I know! It's a white chocolate! I claim my prize!"

"But it doesn't taste like milk chocolate," said Imogen. "It's very strong."

"Nick, you're a chocolate man, how about this second one?"

"I was waiting for that, Frank. Imogen's got it right; that's the whole point about this one, I think, it's a trick chocolate. And Ray is right because it looks like a white chocolate but it's not, and when you taste it, it's very dark."

"Ooh, that's intense," said Casimir.

"It's very strong," said Galia.

"Well, whatever it is, I like the pairing with the Romanée-Conti. Sauternes would have been much too sweet. You agree?" Jade was finding common ground with Papoche.

"Yes, one hundred per cent. Now, I am waiting for Nick to say exactly what it is."

Nick accepted the challenge, and played a bold hand. "I'm pretty sure it's Finca la Joya, from Mexico. It's a dark chocolate Criollo, but it's a white-coloured bean, and so they call it Criollo Porcelana. That's what makes people think it's a milk chocolate."

Frank was looking pleased. "On the nail, Nick. Tasting notes?"

"Very yellow fruit flavours. Like everybody says, it's a powerful taste, and, once you've tried it a couple of times, for me, it's unmistakeable."

Frank had also been doing his homework. "Did you know that they even pollinate the trees by hand? To keep the beans that pure."

"Unbelievable, Frank. I would never have thought there was so much to know about chocolate," said Charles. Tomorrow, he would buy more shares.

"Chocolate number three. Any takers?"

Everybody, even Galia, had entered into the spirit of the game, and tasted the third chocolate.

Jade spoke first. "It's delicious, but I can't say anything more than that. Papoche?"

The first time she had addressed him by his familiar name …

"I am not sure. Extraordinary." He might have meant that the chocolate was extraordinary, or how extraordinary that he did not know what it was.

Nobody had a clue.

"I think that it's from Cuba." Cassandra had said (and eaten) little or nothing, and now, without warning, she seemed to have woken up, talking like a woman who has come out of a coma, knowing another language. "From the village of Baracoa, it's at the other end of the island, driving from Havana. My father says that the chocolate from Chuao is the rarest, but I think that this more deserves that title. The bean is called Original Trinitario, and they've protected it, with little or no investment, simply out of love for what they do."

Imogen was astonished – and then not – to see that Frank did not seem at all surprised. The power game had taken a new twist.

"You are absolutely right, Cassie. And the taste?"

She could have been describing a perfume, no less passionately than the way in which Jade had described the Montrachet; it was as if she had scented a pheromone. "A very strong chocolatey taste, aromatic and fragrant, and tasting of dried fruit, some dry wood." She bit into the last piece of the chocolate; and then, with satisfaction, "Dry hazelnuts and hints of tobacco."

"My," was Ray's reaction.

Charles spoke for everybody. "Well, this is a lunch full of surprises."

Papoche and Nick were more amazed than anybody else at the table. Papoche was so surprised that he said nothing, looked at his daughter, had too many questions to ask in one sentence, and asked none of them.

"You never eat chocolate?" said Nick, half question, half accusation.

"You've never seen me eat chocolate." Cassandra smiled, demurely, but the unpalatable truth of what she said had demonstrated to her husband, perhaps for the first time, that not only was she her father's daughter, she was her own woman. This was the first time that anybody at luncheon had heard Cassandra gainsay her husband. It had been like watching a once loyal votary declare that she worshipped both the old gods and the new.

Imogen was watching closely. She was not surprised to learn that Cassandra had a secret passion, and neither were any of the women at the luncheon who had ever been on a diet; it was a shared women's understanding, the very reason why Nick – so masculine and seemingly so uncomplicated – looked like a man who has just found out that his wife loves somebody else. Imogen felt sorry for him. Was it possible that he had never understood until now that his wife was stronger than he was? Yes, men were like that, so obsessed about the bullshit externals, and rarely able to look on the inside; to know the woman they had married. Imogen looked at Frank; was he surprised? This was his game; was Cassandra part of the game plan? But Frank gave nothing away.

The Baroness deftly moved people's thoughts away from the subject of Cassandra's unwrapping. "Are you going to tell us, Frank, who makes these chocolates?"

"Of course, Baroness. These first three chocolates are made by Pierre Marcolini. He has a shop in the Place du Grand Sablon, in Brussels."

"I've been," said Casimir. "It's like a temple to chocolate, and he's the high priest."

Ray was ahead of everybody, popping the chocolates. "I love soft centres. Isn't this what they call a praline?" He gave the word a Texas twang, making it sound like Dolly Parton singing *Jolene, Jolene* ...

Frank nodded. "It is."

"It's very sweet," said Galia.

"Which provides the clue."

Casimir spoke. "Just an educated guess, is it made by Neuhaus?"

"It is. Well done, Cass. They call it a *Manon sucre vanille*."

Jade, unusually for her, smacked the ball into the net. "How did you know that?"

"Because Jean Neuhaus invented the praline. You didn't know?"

"Right." Now that they had all but stopped throwing poisoned arrows across the table, Jade and Casimir were finding in each other that solidarity of the young and beautiful.

Imogen looked longingly at the praline. "I think I'll pass on this one. Looks very sinful."

Claudia laughed. "When Mo and I were at convent school together, we lived in fear of Sister Ursula. She said that men and chocolates were the work of the devil; except for Adam ... and After Eights."

"I think this one is more interesting than the Neuhaus," said Nick, speaking like someone who has lost the trail of a conversation and is trying to get back in.

"Definitely," agreed the Baroness, taking pity on him, "but I don't recognise the taste."

"Lemony," said Galia.

Charles had more than an inkling of where his profit was

going to come from, and which way the wind was blowing. "I agree, Nick. Nice and simple, very modern. Sort of a new taste."

Frank explained. "Very perspicacious of you, Charles. The fruit is called a *yuzu*, or Japanese citron; like a cross between a lemon and a grapefruit. It's made by Laurent Gerbaud – a very adventurous *chocolatier*. He sources the chocolate from Ecuador and Madagascar."

Jade never lacked for an opinion. "Makes the Neuhaus praline seem a little old-fashioned."

Papoche defended his way of doing things, his tradition. "There is nothing wrong with old-fashioned, Miss Jade. You could call it a classic."

"I didn't say there was."

"Your family has been making wine in the same way for centuries."

"I'll give you that point."

Frank unwrapped the last chocolate, and wrapped up the luncheon. "Number six. Papoche, what do you think?"

The slightest hint of a smile played around the old man's dimples, the surviving dimples that had made him a lady-killer in his youth. The Baroness caught the wry smile, and kept her own melancholy smile in check. She watched Papoche bite into the *ganache*, and kept the chocolate memories to herself. He spoke cautiously. He was not so naïve not to understand that he was being set up; he also understood that this luncheon was only a skirmish, setting the boundaries of a future, much bigger conflict.

"The chocolate is very good. Acidity well balanced with fruity end notes. A little lacking in character. Not a *grand cru* ... a little *vin de table*."

"It's wicked good," joked Casimir, looking at Imogen.

At last, Frank laid all of his cards on the table: "The chocolate comes from Sur Del Lago, in Venezuela; and Ghana. And it's sugar-free. Made by Pierre Marcolini. Like you say, he's the high priest of fine chocolate, and he makes sugar-free chocolates. Perfect for you, Mo – guilt-free pleasure."

Imogen confessed. "My fridge is full of them."

Ray was curious. "But it tastes so sweet."

Sensing at last the point of the elaborately arranged luncheon, Charles asked Nick the big question of the day: "You're in the chocolate business, aren't you? How does he do it? Seems to me like you can't tell the difference."

Papoche answered, a little too vehemently. "He cheats." The accusation of cheating encompassed the *chocolatier* and his son-in-law.

Nick looked his father-in-law straight in the eye. "It depends what you mean by cheating. He replaces the sugar with Maltitol, a mix of maize and wheat, both naturally occurring."

Papoche threw down his gauntlet. "We will never make such chocolates."

"You think there's a market for them, Nick?" asked Charles.

"Absolutely. They're less fattening. Women don't eat old-fashioned chocolates, but these they will eat."

"Pleasure without the guilt. What a lovely idea," said the Baroness.

Imogen was looking at Frank, and thinking, "The man's a genius. He's been manipulating us all through luncheon, waiting for this one moment." Looking around the table, she sensed that not everybody understood how they had been played. How could they, if they didn't know that this had been a luncheon as tightly structured as a Chopin sonata?

Her eyes went round the table. She decided that Papoche had worked out where the luncheon was going quite early on, perhaps as early as the reading of the menu, certainly with the

Chablis. Jade? Had she been in on the whole heist? If Frank really was fucking her, as Marcus thought, perhaps she had been primed to play a part; if she had been an innocent, then she was a remarkable woman. Charles, he was like a reptile, getting fat in the sun. Nick? He had known what the luncheon was about, but had he understood that it was anything more than a business meeting masquerading as a pleasant afternoon on the terrace, with good food and fine wine? He was clever but was he agile enough to divine Frank's byzantine machinations? Galia, well, she was a piece of antique silver, to decorate the table. Cassandra, yes, she was difficult to divine, the joker in the pack: she knew her chocolate – Frank might not have known – but for all that, she had declared herself unknowable.

Imogen liked Ray, for his refusal to be anything other than himself; it would take him a few days, perhaps, but he would work out what that praline had been about. It was difficult to like Casimir; he was gorgeously handsome and extremely clever, and she had nothing against a man on the make, but his ambition was so blatant. The Baroness shared her dislike of him; that made it okay, because she thought that the Baroness had more class than all of them put together. Most of all, Imogen was proud of herself, that Frank had entrusted her with the planning and execution of the luncheon.

She said her goodbyes, as the guests were leaving, and went back to the kitchen, to say thank you to Marcus, who had a date with Massimo.

"It went very well, Mo. You should be really pleased. As for me, it was a pleasure, as always." He kissed her fondly, and whispered: "Don't look round but Mr Right is here. Don't do anything I wouldn't do. I'm off, *ciao bella*."

Imogen turned round, to watch Marcus go; and saw Nick coming towards her. "It was wonderful, and I didn't want to go without saying thank you, properly." He kissed her, only on one cheek. "Let's do lunch. I'll cook."

And then, just as suddenly as he had appeared, he was gone, leaving her with the fragrant trace of his Green Irish Tweed, and a joke.

Imogen stood for a moment, alone in the kitchen. She was trying not to think about what she was thinking, concentrating on something else to distract herself: "I hate that silly chandelier," she said out loud, "it's like cooking in a ballroom." But the thoughts kept on coming, followed by the tears. No, it was not the releasing of tension after the stress of cooking; it was the release of a balloon full of sexual frustration. She sobbed.

Claudia came in. "What's the matter, Mo? Why are you crying? The luncheon was a big success, everybody raved about the food. Frank's over the moon, we both are!"

Imogen wailed. "Oh Clod, forgive me!"

"About Chanel? Forget it. I told Karl it was PMT. There's nothing to forgive, you're my best friend. But I still don't understand?"

It all came rushing out. "I know it went well, and Marcus is so nice, and you should try and persuade Frank to back him in his own restaurant."

"And take Massimo with him?"

"You know?"

"I'm thick, not blind, Mo. And I don't like giving things up that easily. That's it?"

There was more. "Look at me, Clod, I'm the fat friend who cooks, and is always happy."

"You're crying."

Imogen was in despair. "Oh Clod, don't you understand! Just once, I don't want to cook for money. I want to cook for love! I want a man to come home to me, and eat my food with love. And it's never going to happen!"

Claudia started crying. She threw her arms around her friend. "Mo, I love you, we both love you! Okay, so you're fat, fatty, but you're really beautiful on the inside. There'll be somebody for you, somewhere, who sees that. There must be."

As Frank and Claudia's guests were leaving, the winning captain, of the first day's racing at Les voiles, *was sounding pretty pleased with himself: "It was a very difficult start, very tight on the start line, but we managed to get some clean air. Got up to first mark and slipped away with the wind, fantastic ... perfect conditions for us, and a wonderful sail. After the leeward mark, we hung up to windward until we had about twenty degrees, then off the mark we had to come inside. Then we picked up a whole new breeze coming down towards the finish. The whole crew performed superbly."*

"I know now that what you said in *Tender is the Night* is true. Only the invented part of our life — the unreal part — has had any scheme, any beauty."

Gerald Murphy to F. Scott Fitzgerald

Thinspiration

Thinspiration

CASSANDRA WAS ALWAYS thinking about fitting her body into something, anything. If she walked past a park railing, she thought about squeezing herself through the wrought iron bars. She was reading a book about Marie Antoinette – her history as a clothes horse – and she loved to read about those bone-crunching corsets: *grand corps* in stiff whalebone, cinched and laced up so tight that you couldn't breathe. Cassandra even imagined encasing her neck in those hoops that Masai women wore.

It was not difficult for Cassandra to be thin. Thinspiration was a state of mind. It wasn't about painful, stomach-wrenching denial, if you thought it right. Cassandra was thin, firstly, because she wanted to get back at her father; secondly, because that was what was expected of a rich and beautiful woman; and thirdly, because she didn't want to lose her husband.

Thinness went back to chocolate; not because she associated chocolate with getting fat, or being fat – strange as that might seem; no, she associated chocolate with unhappiness, or a lost happiness – not the same thing.

They had once been a happy family. Cassandra's first clearly formed memory was the all-enveloping smell of cocoa in the factory, as she walked around as a toddler; her father would lift her up, and pretend to drop her in a vat; her mother would beg him, with her alluring voice, not to play such silly games; and Papoche would joke about his little girl becoming a "chocolate doll." Only a few years later, every day after school, Cassandra preferred to go to the factory and 'play' – sitting in the line of women in their white hats and uniforms, making chocolates by hand: *ganaches*, truffles, pralines ...

She had a taste for chocolate, not eating it, but an ability to know one type of chocolate from another. She could close her eyes, and the women would 'test' her. Lucky for her: if her father had wanted a son to carry on the business, he never said so; the women on the line were always telling her that she would one day be a "chocolate queen."

She was popular at school – of course she was, her father made chocolate. She was quite clever, but this was not encouraged, not by the teachers, or her parents.

If there was anything wrong with her parents' marriage, Cassandra, for many years, knew nothing about it – Italians cloister their unhappiness behind the green shutters. Infidelity, however, sooner or later, is always overheard. For children, the effect is deep and lasting, the more so for the childish lack of understanding about sexual betrayal.

Papoche was rarely home for dinner – away 'on business.' He had married Cassandra's mother for her home cooking and the chocolate business she brought to the altar. He went off the cooking, six or so years after the wedding; and the business had become his, with the wedding ring. He also went off her body. Still, for quite a while, Papoche kept a lid on his disgust and revulsion, lying next to his wife's enormous thighs. One line, however, is all it takes to wound for ever; first the nitpicking, then the accusations, the heated recriminations, and, finally, the *coup de grâce*:

"You know what you remind me of? *Prosciutto crudo!*"

You can destroy a marriage with that; and ferment a phobia in your children.

Her mother had spent the rest of her life – four and a half years – crying; and then she killed herself, expertly, with a stiletto blade in a hot bath. From her mother, Cassandra learned one deadly lesson: you lose your looks, you lose your man.

She had grown distant from her father; the more so as he made more and more money, and tried to marry her off to eligible Italian men from the upper classes, with titles to match the *palazzi* and *castelli* they lived in – *marchese di* something or other – and first names like Tazio, Anselmo, Oberto, and Michelangelo (Michelangelo by name, Michelangelo by nature). She drank espresso, and ate ice cream with each of them. They posed naturally – pouting was their default expression – lounging in a *caffè* in Turin or Rome, a look modelled on the dark, *craquelure* canvases of their ancestors. They all had floppy raven hair as teenagers, exquisite features, translucent skin, wore Tod's shoes, pressed jeans, immaculate linen shirts; and had summer houses in Lake Como or Portofino that had been in the family for generations; and where the plumbing worked on and off. How could they not be beautiful, those delicate boys, with all that late-Renaissance, Mannerist blood.

They wanted her dowry, to pay for the repairs to the frescoes in the *piano nobile*. She would have happily paid for the repairs, if any one of them had been able to give her an orgasm, but they were too beautiful to be good in bed; and she was too naïve to criticise their foreshortened foreplay, and forty-second fucks. They smelled lovely – Acqua di Parma – and they had pretty, rosebud lips no plastic surgeon could ever reproduce, but it was a sterile loveliness, ideal for the artist's studio, hopeless for the marriage bed. There was nothing wrong, as such, with their Renaissance-sized cocks – they were nice to look at and easy to handle. But straight or gay, they loved themselves too much.

Deep down, of course, her father despised them, for their soft hands, although he liked the mothers, with their blonde highlights, and open-necked blouses. Cassandra wondered if he really loved her, if he was prepared to see her married off to a man – any highborn man – she didn't love. Her marriage was to be the summation of his career, from nobody to somebody; age-old mercantile snobbism, the same reason, she supposed, why he had taken an aristocrat as his mistress.

So, partly to spite her father, she had married the gardener. Her father had first sung Nick's praises as a 'green-fingered genius;' and then, when the gardener borrowed the money from a pawnbroker (against his watch), to put an engagement ring on the finger of the boss's daughter, Papoche referred to his son-in-law either as a "peasant," or a "foreigner." An English aristocrat would have pleased her father; a middle-class Englishman with a middling, unfinished education (Hull, not Oxbridge), enraged Papoche. He threatened to cut her off from the money, and she threatened to get pregnant, unmarried.

It wasn't only spite and defiance; it was the mown grass that had clung to Nick's dripping chest, glued with sweat and bergamot suntan oil, that made him glisten and ripple like a god in the Uffizi; he had smelled anything but lovely – salty and ripe. The tan had long since faded but not the memory, which was still as potent as the first time she had seen him from her bedroom window, at their holiday villa in San Remo.

She had come back from Turin the day before, after yet another matchmaking week. She had had another row with her father who had told her that he would make the choice of husband for her if she didn't make up her mind soon. She had the feeling that this time he really meant it. She understood that she was running out of options: marriage, a nunnery, or become a woman making it on her own, like Chanel.

The noise of the lawnmower was driving her mad – she was reading *Eugénie Grandet* – and she angrily flung open the shutters, and began to curse at the young idiot, in loud Italian. He didn't hear her at first, which infuriated her even more, although she had soon noticed that he didn't look like a lout – they didn't wear tennis shorts – anyhow, it was too late to backtrack, and she kept hollering until finally he noticed; and switched off the engine. She was still shouting at him, above the abrupt silence, just to make her point; and then she fell in love with him when she heard him speak – it still brought tears to her eyes: "*Scusi*, but I don't speak Italian."

The cadence and beauty of his voice pushed her back a step from the window, the book in her hand, Balzac half in her mind. Unable to collect her thoughts, she had to say something that would say nothing about how she was feeling. "I was trying to read;" lame but true. Now, at least, he knew that she spoke English (two summers in London, and a summer in Cambridge).

She had expected him to respond to her beauty – as men always did. This one, however, said nothing, sort of smiled, and went off to rake the gravel in the driveway. How dare he!

She went back to her book, reading on the white wrought iron bed. She managed just a few paragraphs, then she stood up, and went back to the window. The gardener was nowhere to be seen. It was a big garden, and she guessed that he had to clear the swimming pool. She put down her book, looked at herself in the mirror, and rather liked what she saw – a tight-fitting Sonia Rykiel pink, round-necked soft merino wool jumper, with three-quarter length sleeves and yellow striped detailing, short in the body so that it showed her toned midriff; and with matching striped pink and yellow knitted shorts that showed off her tanned legs. She took off her bra, and put the sweater back on – the woollen fabric tickled her nipples; brushed her hair, put on a pair of old espadrilles, last season's because she didn't want to look like a little rich girl, and went down to the kitchen, where Beatrice was preparing lunch for one – Papoche was only at the villa at weekends.

Usually, when she sat in the kitchen, she chatted with Beatrice about the many failings of the latest blue-blooded beau who had bored her in the *Duomo*. Beatrice knew all there was to know about the family; she had been housekeeper to Cassandra's mother (it was she who had found her, dead in the bath). On this day, Cassandra was tongue-tied. She wanted to ask Beatrice if she knew anything about the new English-speaking gardener, but that would have been too obvious.

"Is lunch nearly ready?"

"Lunch is always at one; it's only twenty to."

"I could make some lemonade, then, couldn't I, and read my book outside?"

"You could, if you hurry, but where's the book?"

"I'll make the lemonade first."

In silence – unlike her – she pulverised the lemons, crushed the ice, added the sugar and a few mint leaves, then a touch of syrup – Beatrice's recipe. She picked out a silver tray, and the best crystal pitcher from the antique dresser, a white linen napkin, and two of the best tumblers. Beatrice watched her, and kept her thoughts to herself. It was nearly one o'clock.

Cassandra avoided looking Beatrice in the eye as she carried the tray out to the terrace, with its uninterrupted view of the Ligurian Sea – the view had cost her father six million euro. She bypassed the large wooden table and twelve chairs used for big gatherings; and walked down the long gravelled central pathway, with its alternating yellow and red tea roses, planted sentry-like, that ran the length of the garden. By the fountain, she took a side path, heading for the cluster of spreading palm trees, right by the perimeter wall, close to the main road, and within smelling distance of the sea. She placed the tray on the small, circular wrought iron table, with the four chairs, painted dark green, arranged beneath the palms, and situated close to where the gardener had left the lawnmower.

She sat down, out of the sun, and waited. There was no sea breeze, not at midday, and the palms were petrified in the heat. From here you had the best view of the house, with its luminous white walls, floral stucco plasterwork, and pale green shutters. Really, it was much too big for the two of them, she had told her father when he announced, only a few years ago, that he had bought it: eight bedrooms, and he never invited anybody to stay; his women never slept here. He was waiting for her to fill it with his grandchildren; some hope ...

She abruptly remembered that she had forgotten her book – she was meant to be reading. She stood up, and immediately sat down again – she would admire the garden, instead; reading in the garden would make her look too bookish. She poured a little of the lemonade. He was a good worker, she noticed; already, the garden looked much better than it had before, for any of the previous summers they had been there. Only, there was no gardening sound anywhere, and she was annoyed to think that he might have left for the day. Was he living in the rooms above the old carriage building, she wondered. Then, she heard the familiar sound of the door to the orangery closing, and the glass panes shifting in the frames. Moments later, he appeared, loping towards her. She wondered if he had been watching her from somewhere. She tried not to look at him, or any part of his body, but she had forgotten her book so she could hardly not notice him.

He was dressed in a pair of white tennis shorts, soiled with grass stains, and a very old pair of tennis shoes, with no socks. She noticed that he wore his hair very long – Renaissance style, she thought – and the waves were so pronounced that it looked as if they had been styled in a hairdresser's. He should have been pretty, with hair like that, but somehow it made him very masculine. He came straight towards her, which unnerved her a little.

"That's nice of you," he said, breezily. "Is that a peace offering after shouting at me?"

"No, it's not for you. Just in case my father arrives."

"He said that he wouldn't be here until Friday. He's never here during the week. It's Tuesday."

"You know more about my father's movements than I do."

"Maybe, but I'll drink the lemonade anyhow, seeing as how it's here, and you're obviously offering."

He helped himself, and gulped it down. She absolutely and positively disliked him; even a Michelangelo was better than a rude gardener. Uninvited, he even sat down, instead of standing at a respectful distance!

"It's a lovely old-fashioned garden. Full of *Bourbon* roses, did you know that?"

"You know a lot about roses?"

"Yeah, especially the really old ones. I'm big on *Empress Josephine*."

"So was Napoleon."

He grinned. "I wish it were mine. You can do so much when it's sub-tropical. It's a lovely house too, very grand for a holiday place. When was it built, *Belle Époque*?"

He was very familiar, she decided, for a gardener. She tried to ignore the fact that he worked for them.

"In Italy, we call it *Stile Liberty*, after the shop, did you know that? Strictly speaking, though, this was built before, in 1874. It was one of the first villas to be built after they completed the railway. It was owned by a Russian Grand Duke."

"I saw the Russian church the day before yesterday, on my day off. Strange, must be like being in Moscow in the blinding sun."

"And you probably walked along the Corso Imperatrice. They named it after a Russian Empress. She paid for the palm trees. There were lots of Russians here in those days. Tchaikovsky wrote some music here, a symphony or something, and the last tsar stayed here as well."

"Shouldn't have gone back, should he? This is a lovely place for exile."

"People come here because it's so beautiful."

"Yes, but I don't suppose it makes them happy, just because they've left the Russian winter behind them. I bet that's why Tchaikovsky liked it so much, sunlight only makes you more aware of the shadows."

He spoke to her as if he were sitting there in a crisp linen suit, sporting a Panama. He had the ease and assurance of a buttoned-up character straight out of E.M. Forster, perspiring in Tuscany, except that the top button of his shorts was undone, and the trail of dark pubic hair that ran down from his belly button, travelled more than a little way below the danger zone. No matter that she might have only looked for a fraction of a millisecond, there was no mistaking the outline of his curled up cock and balls, or the fact that he was wearing white underpants – Jockey, she could see.

"You like Tchaikovsky?"

"Yeah, why not? My parents forced me to play the piano, and then I got good at it. He wrote a lot of stuff for gifted amateurs like me."

"So, you garden and you play the piano."

"Yeah, I'm good with my fingers."

He could talk, she would give him that, but, except for his locks, there was nothing Renaissance about him she decided, nothing refined; his body was lean and crude. He leaned back in the chair, slouched quite low and relaxed. Seated, the tops of his tanned, hairy legs were very white. She didn't know where to rest her eyes – anywhere on his body, and she worried that she might somehow give herself away. She settled on his eyes – "*Che figata*! They're blue!" – only to be completely unsettled when he squarely met her gaze. The lemonade had been a very bad idea, she was thinking; she should have discussed it with Beatrice first, a plan of campaign.

Feeling undefended – she should have kept her bra on – she made to pour herself more lemonade. Instantly, panther-like, he stood up, very gentlemanly, before her hand had barely touched the pitcher; close to, his thigh muscle was so developed, it looked as if he were a sprinter crouched in the starting blocks. Beneath his outstretched left arm she caught the tangle of hair in his armpit; beads of sweat were forming and dripping in a steady stream down past his nipple. He missed nothing:

"Sorry, I ran out of deodorant. I'm not much good at living on my own."

He let the sweat keep dripping – it dropped on to the table. He poured the lemonade, and sat down again.

"You're a long way from England."

"It's a summer job. I answered the ad. Your dad thinks English gardeners are the best, which is true, if you ask me. I failed my exams so I might be staying longer than I planned. Might get to see the flower festival. Burning the candle at both ends. Still, it was fun, and nobody got pregnant."

She had never met a man so openly sexual. What was

strangest of all, was that she didn't get the idea that he was undressing her, even if her tits were on show. Italians could be so ridiculously voyeuristic, and then muffed it in bed. This man, whose name she didn't know, was talking to her as if they were old friends. He liked women; yes, that was it.

"Do we feed you?"

He laughed really loudly, showing all his teeth, very white, although one of the front ones was pushed back – that was very English. "You mean is feeding the servant a part of the slave wages your father is paying me, or you're offering me lunch in the big house?"

There was no hiding from him; he was so quick to see right through her; and yet he could then instantly make it all right, with the mollifying phrase that followed: "It's nice of you to ask. Beatrice feeds me. She's a great cook, but if I eat too much of that pasta I'm going to get a fat gut, like a rich man." He ran his index finger affectionately down his pubic trail; and Cassandra followed the movement of his finger in her mind, imagining what his total nakedness looked like when he pulled off his shorts. She crossed her legs. He looked at her again in that very direct way he had.

"You don't look as if you touch the stuff. You need feeding up, my mum would say."

Cassandra decided that honesty was her only defence. "I just thought that you might be hungry, after all that hard work."

"I'm starving, it must be lunchtime. Don't worry, you don't have to entertain me. I'll eat in the kitchen, as I usually do."

Cassandra decided that he had given her the brush-off. Yes, probably he had a girlfriend back in England – more than one. She set her mouth, stood up, and picked up the tray.

"No, don't! I'll do it. Put it down. Wait two secs and I'll walk back with you."

Unusual for her, she did as she was told; and watched him as he walked off a little way to where the hosepipe was lying beneath the rhododendrons – browned and past their best. He turned it on, and then hosed himself down, from head to toe. He shook his head like a horse at a stream, and rubbed his hands all over his body, rinsing off the grass and dirt. She watched him; she tried not to, but she did. He spoke to her, dripping in water, glistening like marble.

"I'm Nick, by the way. You must be Cassandra."

"Obviously."

"That's a name full of …"

"Full of what?"

"Classical meaning."

"I know what my name means."

He was rubbing the inside of the front of his underpants.

"I'll call you Cassie, not so dangerous."

"Nobody calls me Cassie."

"Good, so I will."

He turned off the hosepipe, and retrieved his T-shirt that had been hanging over the arm of the statue of Spring – Papoche had bought all four seasons for the garden. He struggled to put it on as it clung to his torso. He walked back towards her, and saw that she was watching him very closely. "It'll dry in five minutes."

The T-shirt was white, with words printed in black over his chest that she couldn't read. He picked up the tray, looked down at his chest, and then at her, reciting his T-shirt. "I'm a rugger bugger." He turned round to show her the words on the back.

"Bugger me …" and then turned back round again, rather elegantly she thought. "Bugger me, get it? I play rugby, you see. Pretty good at it, too. Winger. My mum gets tired of dusting the trophies."

She said nothing; the English were funny that way. They walked back to the house side by side.

"What are we having for lunch?" he asked, boldly.

"I don't know what you're having," she replied, trying, and failing to put him in his place.

She was undone by Beatrice who had laid two places at the kitchen table, expressly against the wishes of Papoche who had said, more than once, that his daughter was always to eat in the dining-room, not in the kitchen like a servant. Beatrice said a cheerful, *"Buongiorno*, Nick," but apart from that, she said nothing, not about the fact that lunch had been ready for some time, or the table for two; and Cassandra said nothing. She sensed that Nick was laughing inside, at the situation, and at her. She was furious with Beatrice, doubly so when she saw that Beatrice adored him; that was painfully plain to see. She fussed around him, almost clucking, pushed food on to his plate, chatted with him in voluble Italian, even though she knew that he understood hardly a word, and then switched to French, which he spoke, and not so badly.

"You speak French but not Italian, and then you get a job in Italy?"

"My parents have a house in Brittany, and, anyway, I like this garden. It's been neglected but it could be really something. I've counted more than a hundred different plant species. By the time I've finished, your father will be able to open it to the public."

It annoyed her that he knew more about the garden than she did. "Your father's a gardener?"

"Sort of, they run a nursery in Yorkshire."

She misunderstood. "Teachers?"

He laughed, and she wondered why the English never had their teeth straightened. "No! A plants nursery, they grow plants to sell to people to grow in their gardens."

She hardly touched her food. He had an appetite big enough for the both of them. He was appreciative of the food – said so many times to Beatrice, using the few words of Italian he had picked up; and talkative: he talked about what he had done to the garden so far, and what he was planning to do.

"I've never had the chance to work in a garden all on my own, not a serious one like this. I just wish I knew more about what it looked like when it was first laid out. It looks to me as if they've mucked it about a bit since. I'm sure the roses are not all original. There are some that don't make sense. I think there must have been a pattern, only I haven't worked out what it was."

Cassandra was mystified.

"All I know, is the name of the family that used to own it. Russian right?"

"Yes, like I said, it belonged to a Grand Duke. That was enough for my father."

"If I had a drawing or something, I could work from that."

"Look in the library."

"With my Italian?"

"If it means so much to you, I'll help you."

"Thanks, I mean it, only you're probably busy?"

"*Magari*! Oh yes, I'm busy, looking for a husband."

She surprised herself, with the sarcasm aimed not at him but at herself; and it surprised her that he didn't seem at all surprised by anything she said. He didn't try to bat away the husband-hunting, or try to stand up for her father, his employer; he just let her say it. She understood that he didn't seem very interested in her, he was just being polite, in exchange for lunch. She was miffed that he didn't flirt with her; and yet she would have given him the brush-off if he had. He asked her very little about what she was doing with her life, nothing about how she spent her days; she wondered how much he already knew about her –

perhaps her father had told him to keep his hands off. She didn't know what to think about him. She was attracted to him, he was not attracted to her; she had told him she was looking for a husband, only he was not husband material. She wasn't sure that she wanted to get to know him better.

"What's *magari* mean?"

"I wish, let's hope, maybe."

"I'll remember."

Beatrice had made profiteroles; Cassandra never ate profiteroles.

"*Il nostro cioccolato*," Beatrice explained.

Nick nodded, his smile a little smeared with dark chocolate.

"Your father's chocolate?"

"Yes, your Italian's getting better."

"I'm teaching myself. Do you know anything about cocoa beans?"

"My father makes chocolate."

"Did you know that he's trying to grow cocoa beans in the orangery?"

She hadn't been to the orangery for a long time. "You mean cacao beans, not cocoa beans. They're called cacao beans when they come out of the pod, but cocoa beans after fermenting and roasting."

"I stand corrected. Anyway, they're tricky buggers to grow. I'll show you, if you like."

"All right."

"But not today because I'm going to work on the roses this afternoon. I'm quite good with roses. We sell a lot of them at home, so I thought I'd get them in order first. I'm leaving the sub-tropicals to last, after I've read up on them."

How organised he was. She was certain that her father had little or no idea of the gardening talent he had imported. This annoying Englishman was only here on a summer job, and yet he had taken it upon himself to restore the entire garden. He was so horribly confident in his own ability; no doubt, with that much confidence, he had said nothing to her father about his grand plans. For as long as he was working in the garden, it was Nick's domain.

It was not until after lunch, when he had profusely thanked Beatrice for lunch, and reminded Cassandra about her promise to help him research the history of the garden, that, upstairs in her room, and unable to concentrate on her book, she thought about the paradox of what she had learned about him so far: he could set himself a task, plan it all out in his mind, recruit people to help him find out the information that he wanted, be endowed with all of the talents that he needed to make that task a reality; and yet he had failed his exams. Somewhere, he had a weakness; that clarifying thought made her feel better, and she went back to her book.

Up in her room, she had also resolved that if they were destined to meet – of course, they would keep meeting, how could they not – it was going to be managed, and on her terms. From Beatrice she could expect no impartial advice.

After lunch, when Nick had left, leaving the two women alone together, Beatrice had tried her hardest not to sing his praises too much.

"A man like that doesn't appear by accident. All I'm going to say is that he's a nice, hard-working boy and handsome too."

"Yes, and we'd have lovely looking children, why don't you say that as well? He's a gardener."

"He's a student."

"He failed his exams."

"Failure is good for a young man."

"You think that I should marry the first handsome man who walks into the garden?"

"No, you could be a *marchesa* instead."

A Hothouse Atmosphere

For certain, Cassandra was on her own in the management of this seduction. Nick had volunteered his working hours – every day, Sundays off – and told her about his living arrangements: as she expected, he was lodged in the carriage house. He took breakfast, lunch, and dinner in the villa. That left her with something of a problem: she could hardly take her meals in the grand dining-room on her own, not now that she had sat with him in the kitchen. No, from now on she would have breakfast on the balcony of her room – sitting above him, and monitoring his movements; she would make sure that she was not at home for lunch. Dinner was more tricky because she could not be seen to eat out on her own in a restaurant – not in Italy; her father would get to hear of it, somehow or other, and that would only cause more drama. She thought about inviting some of her friends from Turin to join her, but most of them already had their summer plans fixed, and, anyway, Nick's virile presence would probably start a vicious competition amongst her girlfriends for his favours. How would he measure up to, and perform, she asked herself, in the presence of a Tazio, Oberto or Walfredo?

She managed to stick to this determined resolution until lunch time the following day, Wednesday. She didn't see him at breakfast, and she happily went shopping on the Corso

Matteotti, where she bought three outfits in Versace: a silk chiffon blouse in swirls of tangerine, yellow and dusky pink, worn over white tight cotton trousers; a green floral silk wraparound dress with a plunging neckline – she thought that it would look good drinking lemonade; and a very revealing long evening dress, in lime green swirling silk, slit at the thighs, and with even more *décolletée* than the afternoon dress. As she tried them on, she realised, both annoyed and pleased, that she was asking herself if Nick would like them; the first time that she had ever bought clothes with a man in mind. She bought shoes to match, telling herself that, no doubt, she was wasting her time, and her father's money, on a rugby-playing gardener with no fashion sense.

She got back to the house at a quarter to one, and went straight to the kitchen to show Beatrice what she had bought. Beatrice had made lemonade:

"You can show me after lunch; why don't you take this out to Nick? You should see what he's done with those roses. He'll be dying of thirst, poor boy. Then I can carry on with the cooking. No need to hurry."

It was pointless to refuse, and she did as she was told. She thought about changing her outfit, perhaps give the new afternoon dress its first outing, but she decided that what she was wearing was okay for a 'waitress' – pale-blue T-shirt dress, with a rope, tasselled belt, and a pair of 'old' espadrilles.

She dithered about the straw hat that she had worn on her shopping trip – it was very Marie Antoinette at the Trianon, but was it too much? She stood in front of the mirror in the back hallway, putting it on and taking it off.

"Too much," said Beatrice, from the kitchen.

The moment she stepped out on to the terrace, hatless, she could hear that there was somebody in the swimming pool; it could only be Nick. The pool was hidden behind the rhododendrons, and she walked towards the splashing. Nick was swimming naked, making a fast crawl away from the shallow end closest to the house, so that she had a clear view of his tanned back, and white ass, rolling a little from side to side. She put the tray down on the table beneath the sun umbrella, beside his shorts, with the underpants tucked inside. She sat down on one of the white-painted iron chairs, and watched him make a very professional turn underneath the water at the far end, his bare ass rising up momentarily, showing the dark hairs between his buttocks, and matted at the tops of his legs; and then, cleaving very fast through the water, coming straight towards her. Was there anything he didn't do well, she asked herself.

When he touched the blue mosaics at the shallow end, he paused momentarily, before lifting himself out of the water, and landing, cat-like, on the edge of the pool. He was bent over, panting hard, his hands on his knees; he stood up, hands on hips, looking away from her, towards the sea.

"Enjoy your swim?"

He turned, surprised, saw her looking at him, and then, instantly turning round on his heels, dived back into the pool. He swam a few lazy strokes, obviously to compose himself, and then swam back slowly to where he had been. This time, he stayed in the water, his elbows resting on the edge of the pool, looking at her, she thought, a little hesitantly.

"A bit late for that, really," she said. She had no intention of sparing him any embarrassment.

"I didn't see you."

"No, but I saw you. Beatrice made lemonade for you, and asked me to bring it."

"I think we've got things the wrong way round here."

"Oh?"

"I'm in the swimming pool, and you're bringing the tray."
"Right."
"I thought I'd have a swim before lunch. You don't mind?"
"Why should I mind?"
"It's your pool, and I work here."
"Did my father say that you couldn't use the pool?"
"No, he didn't say anything."
"So, then you haven't done anything wrong. You want some lemonade?"
"Love some, only my shorts are on the table."
"Didn't you bring any swimming trunks?"
"Yes."
"But you're not wearing them?"
"No, you know I'm not. You're enjoying this, aren't you?"
"Yes, very much. You want me to bring you the lemonade?"
"No, I'll get it myself, thanks."

He got out of the pool, walked towards the table, looking straight at her, picked up his shorts and underpants, put them on, in no particular hurry; and then drank the lemonade.

She stood up, and started back to the house, saying only, "Lunch is ready."

She wasn't hungry, but she sat with him while he ate two platefuls of *carbonara*, salad, cheese, and ice cream.

He wasn't talkative today, and she sensed that he felt he had overstepped the mark, either swimming without permission, or standing in front of her naked. She was happy for him to feel uncomfortable. Beatrice did the talking for him, saying that he had done wonders with the roses, and asking him what was next. Given that he understood little or nothing, Cassandra, by default, was his translator.

"Beatrice says that the roses look much better. What's next in your restoration plans?"

"I've had an idea about how to look after the chocolate trees. Well, it's not really my idea but I want to give it a try."

"Oh?"

"Do you want to have a look?"

"I told you I would."

"What did he say?" asked Beatrice.

"He asked me to marry him."

"*Santa Maria!* What did you say?"

"That I've had a better offer."

"Oh, Cassandra Lascari, they gave you the right name when you were born."

"Did you finish your book on the balcony?" he asked, excessively politely, she thought. She understood that he was worried he had upset her; was he worried about his job, or he liked her?"

"I went shopping."

"Buy anything nice?"

"A few things, nothing special."

"Anywhere I know?"

She didn't understand what he was trying to say; he seemed to have lost his sure footing. She liked him better for it.

"Just some shop."

"Does it have a name?"

"Versace. Does that mean anything to you?

"Do you think that if he had just slept with the kid, that he wouldn't have shot him?"

"I wouldn't have thought that a sporting hero like you would be up on gay relationships."

"I went to an all-boys' public school; and with hair like this I had my fair share of Versace romance."

She looked at him in astonishment, or rather, she tried not to look as astonished as she felt inside; she was only glad that

Beatrice didn't understand a word. She had never met a man so honest about something so ... well, not talked about. She wondered if he ever lied; and then hoped that she would never find out if he did.

He stood up. "Do you want to see the orangery?" He seemed very sad, as if he were offering her a parting gift.

"If you like."

"*Grazie per il pranzo, Beatrice, è stato meraviglioso come sempre.*"

He had been practising. Cassandra stood up and followed him. Beatrice seemed even more sad than he was. "Why can't you just be nice to him?"

The orangery was more humid than Cassandra had remembered. It was not unpleasant, not suffocating; unfamiliar, like being in a new world, yet with familiar scents and smells that were more concentrated in such an enclosed space. Her nostrils and lungs needed time to become used to this glassed-in, alien world. She could smell the damp soil, the fetid aromas of sweating leaves, and hothouse plants breathing in and out. There was a soft hissing sound of water being sprayed all around.

"Welcome to Venezuela," said Nick.

"Where they grow chocolate trees."

"*Theobroma cacao*, yes, only the rainforest there is natural. Here, we're growing Criollo and the hybrid Trinitario, trying to trick them into thinking this is a rainforest."

She liked the way he proudly said "we."

"They look quite healthy, like the ones I saw in Venezuela."

"You've been? Wow!"

"Business trip, my father called it. I was twelve years old."

"Do any business?"

"I kissed my first boy."

"Sounds like a business trip. Does it feel more humid in here, to you? More tropical?"

"I haven't been in here in a long time."

"Well, it's different. I called a friend of mine at Kew, and asked him how they look after their chocolate tree. He said they try to recreate a semi-shaded rainforest canopy region – something about mother trees protecting them – using spritzers to mist the air."

"Dry air kills them; and too much light; and cold. You see, I did learn something."

"Right, and that's what I've done, increased the humidity. I drilled little holes all along the hosepipes, instead of just having a single nozzle spray, so it feels like it's always raining."

"I should have brought an umbrella. Do you think they'll ripen?"

"I think a few might. I'd like to have a go at the whole chocolate-making process – fermenting, roasting, grinding, making the paste ..."

"I'm not sure that we have a machete for cutting the pods. And you really need a *torréfacteur*."

Nick looked at her, not understanding. "Like a baker, only specialising in cocoa. My father is ... was one of the best."

"*Magari!* We can make a chocolate bar, I'll call it Cassie Number Five."

He was going to say something else, quite happy to talk with her on 'his' territory, but he suddenly stopped, aware of the phrase too far. That lost look appeared again on his face; he had been talking about chocolate, and somehow it had got mixed up with feelings he was not so willing to express. She looked at him, at his 'lostness,' as she already called it, and she felt an involuntary shiver go through her body. She had known him all of twenty-four hours, and yet, in the artificial heat and tropical dampness, she reached an understanding of him, sensing, with a horrible sadness, that here, in the hothouse, he was showing at his best – blooming, perhaps more brightly and more completely than he ever would again, living his life at this moment to the maximum of intensity. It was not only his youth and freshness and vigour, it was a self-sufficiency; he needed nothing more in his life than to grow these chocolate trees to fruition – no parents, no friends, no women.

She had been looking at him in the wrong way, looking for something that he was not: he was not a Roman god, not a Renaissance golden boy, he was a green-fingered artist. Inside the orangery, and outside in the garden, like an artist in his *atelier*, and painting *en plein air*, he was completely at one with his chosen environment. She looked at the sensual way that he touched the cacao pods – tenderly, lovingly – and asked herself if he would ever touch her in the same caressing way? He didn't know it – for certain he hadn't planned it – but he had touched her conscience: should she really be even thinking of taking him out of the garden? She wondered what would happen to him if he were taken out of this natural environment, and placed in her world. Would he thrive? Or would he wither?

Her reading of nineteenth-century novels – that library mark of a lonely childhood – told her that an orangery was a place for divining the essence of romance: the plucking of an exquisite flower, the exotic bloom held up to the nose, the delirious scent, the quivering, erect stamens … Well, in San Remo – "Town of Flowers" – let it be a chocolate tree, she thought, just as delicate and vulnerable.

Nick was asking her a question. "Have you ever been to the Gardens of Queen Elena?"

"I don't think so. Where are they?"

"Here, in San Remo, at the top of the old town."

"Right. No. I don't know the town very well."

"Just the clothes shops." The frosty look on her face stopped the smile on his. "I thought I might have a look, later on. Eat afterwards, if Beatrice doesn't mind. Do you want to come?"

He was asking her to go with him somewhere. Did a garden count as a date? She had no time to think about how best to answer, in the most strategically effective non-committal way, that is; it wasn't as if he were asking her out to dinner – she had been prepared for that one. He had wrong-footed her; she had been thinking that he was drawing away from her, and now, this. Yes or no?

"Yes, I'll come."

The Gardens of Queen Elena

THE HISTORY OF San Remo starts with a villa – Villa Matuzia – and ends with lots of them: Villa Ormond, Villa Nobel, Villa Angerer, Mirasole, Rondinella, ad infinitum. Between 1874 and 1906 they built a hundred and ninety of them.

Caio Matuzio, a rich Roman, built his villa in the third century and, because he got there first, Caio got to name the whole town after himself – Matuzia.

Why then, is it now called San Remo, and not Matuzia? Poor Caio Matuzio; now all he has named after him is a road.

Saint Romulus of Genoa was one of the first Bishops of Genoa. We don't know his exact dates, but given that his coffin sits on top of Saint Syrus of Genoa, in the basilica of San Siro, and we know that Syrus died in 381, we can dare say that Romulus lived around the late fourth century. Why, we don't know, but he seems to have left Genoa in a hurry, and took up residence in a cave, close to the Villa Matuzia. We also don't know what Romulus did that was so saintly, but, whatever it was, the reputation for saintliness stuck.

When the Matuzians were being attacked, as they frequently were (this being prime real estate), they invoked the name of Saint Romulus. Eternally grateful, they adopted the new name of Civitas Sancti Romuli. They only came up with the more catchy name of San Remo in the 15th century.

Now we come to the intermingling of lovely smells and romance –

floriculture – that is the true history of San Remo. First, the smells. The humanist scholar Leonardo Giustiniani (1388-1446) described this area as a "land of lemons, limes, and oranges." The architect Leone Battista Alberti (1404-72) described it as "a pleasant and fruitful place, full of citrons, palms, and blossoms that send forth wafts of perfume."

By 1663, those wafts of perfume had become so strong that the geographer Galeazzo Gualdo Priorato could smell them, "as far as six miles off the shore."

We don't know if he was attracted by the smell, but Tobias Smollett stayed a few days in San Remo in 1765; and in Travels through France and Italy *(1766) he developed the nice idea of San Remo being a scented place for lovers. "The hills are covered with oranges, lemons, pomegranates and olives ... The women of St Remo are much more handsome and better tempered than those of Provence." This last phrase might well be a dig at Saint-Tropez, but one cannot be sure.*

The English, however, cautious travellers, waited another hundred years before they discovered San Remo; 1855, to be precise, when Giovanni Ruffini published Doctor Antonio – A Tale of Italy. *This is a gripping novel about swooning: the fluttering, weak heart of the beautiful, aristocratic Lucy Davenne, and the doctor, Antonio – handsome, Italian, charming – who examines her. The hot palpitations beat faster in the fragrant town of San Remo, set against the backdrop of the struggle for unification. All in all, a rich tapestry of Ligurian life and English society. A must read.*

The English always like to travel in books first, and then see what it's like.

And where the English step, the Russians are sure to follow (look at Tuscany ...). The Russian aristocrat, Baron Andrei d'Uxkull, stayed at the villa of Countess Roverizio in the winter of 1858-1859. He might not, in actual fact, have been the first Russian in San Remo, but he signed his name in the guest book. And that is how history is made.

All it needed was for the Tsarina Maria Alexandrovna to choose San

Remo as her winter residence, and the rest of St Petersburg followed. Soon, the Russian colony had a consulate, a baker's, a chemist's, and its own newsletter. In 1901, San Remo had 21,410 tourists and a local population of 22,440, which makes for a nice social mix – one servant for every visitor.

They opened the casino in 1906; and the Russian Orthodox church six years later – Russians like to gamble first, and light a candle afterwards.

One story about the casino is surely enough: King Farouk of Egypt claimed that he could win a poker game by laying down three kings; when the other players protested, he said, "I am the fourth."

Italo Calvino spent his childhood in San Remo, in the 1930s, and, from the sounds of it, this was exactly the sort of place guaranteed to nurture a future writer: "I grew up in a town that was quite different from the rest of Italy, in the days when I was a kid in San Remo, at that time it was still inhabited by old English, Russian grand dukes, eccentric and cosmopolitan people."

San Remo breathed its glamorous last in 1954, when Ava Gardner was in town to film The Barefoot Contessa. *She was not with her husband, Frank Sinatra, but with her new lover, Luis Miguel Dominguin, the bullfighter. Their fights were legendary.*

Nick Austin and Cassandra Lascari, however, were pretty much entirely ignorant of all this glorious, romantic, and rather fanciful history, when they went for a walk in the Gardens of Queen Elena.

Cassandra was admiring herself in the mirror when she heard Nick's voice in the garden.

"Cassie, are you ready?"

She stepped out on to the balcony and looked down at him. She laughed; she couldn't help herself.

"What's so funny? Because we're both wearing white trousers? You look amazing, by the way."

She was going to say that he also looked amazing, but that was not right for a man.

"You didn't iron those trousers yourself did you? Let me guess, Beatrice?"

"Right, but I could have ironed them, I do know how, only she wouldn't let me."

"Why am I not surprised. I'll be right down."

Nick was waiting for her in the front hallway, which gave her an opportunity to make a grand entrance, coming slowly down the marble staircase, flooded with early-evening sunlight filtered through the stained glass windows, patterned with pineapples, palm fronds and hummingbirds; her heels clacked on the marble.

"That's quite an outfit. I'm guessing Versace."

"You're not guessing."

"Well, I like it, and that's what matters, right? Bag's nice, too."

She was pleased that he looked at what she was wearing; and not at all pleased that he thought she had bought it just to please him.

"The bag's a Baguette, by Fendi."

"Good enough to eat, then."

He was in a very good mood, and he looked good: a yellow Fred Perry polo shirt, white jeans, tan leather belt, and weathered tan moccasins, worn without socks, she was glad to see. He was wearing a nice watch – Rolex Oyster. He saw her giving him the once-over.

"The watch was a present from my parents, for getting into uni. So, not ashamed to be seen walking with the gardener?"

"I thought that you were going to walk behind me?"

"Nice view from behind."

Beatrice, unable to resist seeing them off, came into the hallway.

Cassandra had been expecting her. "Whatever you say, don't say that we make a lovely couple."

Not even Cassandra's sharpness could dent Beatrice's matchmaking happiness. "You make a lovely couple. When you get back, all you have to do is heat up the food, in the microwave. He'll be hungry. I promise to stay out of your way, all night."

"We're going." Cassandra was already out the front door.

Nick made a hurried wave to Beatrice, and followed. "What did she say?"

"That I have bad taste in men. Do you know the way, or I'm the tour guide?"

"Oh, I'm sure you'll make a good tour guide."

He annoyed the hell out of her, but she liked walking with him, and she liked being seen with him. He was good-looking, attentive and, mostly, charming. They did make a nice-looking couple, she knew; she could tell that, as well, from the admiring glances they were getting. From his first question, she also understood that this was a walk with a purpose.

"What's wrong with all the men your father wants you to marry?"

She tried to put him in his place. "Beatrice talks too much. Let's get one thing straight. I agreed to come for a walk with you, not to talk about my private life."

He immediately dropped back two paces, and walked behind her, like a bodyguard. When she turned round, he grinned at her.

"I know my place."

She stopped; they were standing next to the Saracen Tower, in the Piazza Eroi Sanremesi, busy with tourists, probably heading for the same place they were headed. She shook her head in mock exasperation; he was impossible.

"They have soft hands. Happy now?"

She wasn't sure if she had said the right thing, or the wrong thing because he kept grinning at her, the smile getting bigger and bigger.

"What?"

He walked towards her, and she thought that he was going to kiss her, but, instead, he stopped one step away from her and opened out his hands: they were rough, blistered and red with rose scratches – a gardener's hands.

She was determined not to lose control of this trip. She carried on walking, and now he walked beside her: "Do you know anything, Mr Austin, about where we're going?"

"Do you? It's the medieval part of town called *La Pigna*, which means pine cone, and they called it that because the streets and buildings are wrapped around the hill in the shape of a pine cone. See, I'm not just a pretty face."

"So I see. And now you can see it for yourself because we're here." They were standing in the Piazza Cassini. Cassandra looked lost. "Beatrice said that we have to look for an archway."

"Over there, follow the tourists with the American flag."

They walked beneath a gothic stone arch, and immediately left behind them the history-light modern world, stepping into a thousand-year-old medieval world. They call them *caruggi* in Ligurian Italian – dark and narrow, steep alleyways and cobblestone streets, winding and ascending; shadowed in *chiaroscuro* by a maze of terraced houses seemingly piled, precariously, one on top of another; and painted in late Gothic and *Quattrocento* colours to lighten the sense of dark claustrophobia: Naples yellow, earth, ochre, lime white, burnt umber, orpiment, vermilion, smalt, and carmine lake. Even with unpainted plasterwork, the twisted and exposed wooden beams, and hunchback doors gave these habitations a singular history that told of a time when people hurriedly shut their doors, crossed themselves, and hoped that the raiding Saracens would lose their way in the labyrinth. There were no hard edges here; everything was worn smooth by a millennium of people going up and going down. Look at the work of almost any late Gothic artist – Duccio di Buoninsegna, Giotto di Bondone, Simone Martini – and there you will see the likeness of *La Pigna*.

Unlike anywhere else in Italy – except for the *sui generis* Porto Antico of old Genoa – this is not a place where people sit outside, lovingly scold their children, and complain. Here, they complain high up, above the ranks of vaulted archways that buttress their leaning buildings, safe from the threat of earthquakes.

There was a hushed silence, as if the Catholic Church was celebrating communion for the whole reclusive populace. There were some signs of Italian life: Piaggio and Vespa scooters; a caged canary; a large family's washing, drying on a balcony – his and her underwear, the children's T-shirts, assorted towels – but this was otherwise a sepulchral place.

"Are you really going to be able to walk in those shoes on these cobbles?"

"I'm fine, thank you."

"I hope they have a hospital halfway up here, some of these tourists are going to need one. I bet they only get as far as the first photo opportunity, and then turn back."

She was not going to tell him that her new shoes were killing her; she would not give him that satisfaction.

"Why don't you take your shoes off?"

"Why don't you just shut up."

He did as he was told. Adding to her fury, she could see that he was right about the tourists turning back. The Piazza dell'Oratorio dei Dolori was the turning point, where they "oohed and aahed," took a few snapshots and turned back.

"The Square of Pain and Sadness, I take it? It's like a film set for *Romeo and Juliet*," said Nick. "Not very square for a square is it?"

Cassandra sat down on the edge of the water fountain, and watched him as he circled around the very small piazza."You could fit it into a doll's house. What does this say? Must be a church or something. I can only read the numerals, 1642."

She stood up and walked, now in even more pain, to where he was standing in front of a sign. "Hold on. I don't know all the words. 'It is forbidden to urinate or leave dirt under this archway ... with a penalty of four lire. Informers need not be afraid of ... revenge from the guilty people because the name of the informer will be kept secret.'"

"Right. Meaning, don't shit on your own doorstep. Good advice. Listen, do you want to stop? Take your shoes off? Don't get mad at me. That looks like a restaurant to me. Must be okay, looks popular. Are you hungry?"

"No, but I take it that you are?"

"Ravenous."

They sat down, outside, at one of the white plastic tables and chairs, beneath a bright red awning blind, the last free table. Nick looked at the name of the restaurant: *"Urbicia Vivas"* which is Latin for ... "City, or Town Lives."

"You studied Latin?"

"Oh yes, I had a very old-fashioned education. And plant names are always in Latin."

The waiter brought the menus, and, in response to Cassandra's questioning, made some recommendations.

"What's he say? Something about Ligurian food, which is local?"

"You don't really need a translator, do you? Yes, he says they specialise in Ligurian dishes. The goat is good, and the risotto with mushrooms and wild berries."

"What are you going to eat?"

"I'm not. Just a green salad, and San Pellegrino."

"Don't you ever eat?"

"I'm sure you'll eat enough for both of us. Does it matter?"

"You asked him what was good, right? And yet you're not going to eat, so that means you must ..." Nick stopped, and then waded in further. "I like women with a bit of meat on them, that's all."

"*Meno male*! And before you ask, it means 'Thank God.' I guess that means we're completely incompatible."

"I guess it does. I'll have the linguini to start, and the goat. And some wine – half a carafe of red. *Per favore*."

It was dusk. The last rays of the sun grazed the upper storey of the few buildings that lined the small square, but down on the ground, blanketing the grey cobblestones and the patchwork ornamental brick path that bisected the square, all was in shadow.

Nick took in everything around him. "Isn't it beautiful the way those plants on that roof garden get reflected on the pink wall opposite? Plants everywhere, if you look." He smelled the cut red roses in the centre of the table. "The smell of San Remo. Plastic furniture, but damask tablecloths, they do everything with taste in Italy, don't they?"

"Did you plan this?"

"No. It just looked nice. Why?"

"I wondered if this was something you planned with Beatrice?"

"You have a suspicious mind."

"I'm Italian."

"Beautiful too."

The waiter brought the wine and the water, and a basket of bread that Nick immediately grabbed.

"We're incompatible, remember?"

"Right. Bread's delicious."

Cassandra could see very clearly that this simple walk had morphed into a first dinner date. She looked at the Englishman she hardly knew, sitting opposite her, demolishing the bread; and looked about her at the other people sitting around them – Italians and tourists; and she thought that he couldn't have chosen a more relaxed, casual, romantic and atmospheric place, by accident or design (she would find out …).

Nick seemed happy just to sit there, and say nothing for the moment. She had the feeling that he was trying to take the measure of her in some way; and, in exactly the same way, during this silent interlude, she tried to compare him with all of the Italian men who had taken her out to dinner. They were beautiful to look at – well, Nick was nice looking also; and they dressed with very good taste – well, there was nothing wrong with Fred Perry, was there? They drove beautiful cars – did he have a car? They had perfect manners – mmm … there were a few rough edges about Nick that she would have to smooth out. They were blue-blooded and titled – did she want to be the *Marchesa di* something or other? Mrs Nick Austin? That was a difficult one. They were Italian, and so she understood them – could she ever understand an Englishman? Did it matter? The Italian men wanted her dowry – what did Nick think about the money? Was he a fortune hunter? Did he look at her and see a big fat bank account? Marrying a chocolate billionaire's daughter, that was a very good match, for a gardener. What else? Italian men never, ever upset her – he took delight in making fun of her, and making her lip tremble. But then, admitting it to herself, openly, for the first time, she understood, that was exactly the reason why she liked him. To him, she was a woman, not a chocolate doll; a little too thin, perhaps, for him, but she didn't think that really mattered.

"Try the linguini, it's wonderful."

The fork was right in front of her mouth, and she obediently accepted. She never ate pasta.

"It's very good. They have a good chef. You were right, that's why it's so popular."

"Wasted on you, though. I'm going to fatten you up. A couple of sizes bigger, and you'll be perfect."

"I'm happy the way I am."

"How can you be happy, not eating?" Nick was soaking up the linguini juice with the bread. "What were you thinking?"

"You really want to know?"

"Why not? Anyways, sooner or later, you'll tell me what you think about me."

"I'm comparing you with the Italian men who take me out to dinner."

"That's what I thought."

"You want to know how you compare?"

"No, you just told me."

"I didn't say anything."

"No, but you're still sitting here."

It was an arrogant thing to say, but he softened it, a little, with a slight smile.

"Do women always fall down in front of you? Like ..." She couldn't think of a good simile.

"Like ripe peaches falling from a tree? Pretty much. It's not very difficult to pick low-hanging fruit."

Cassandra was not going to take this conversation any further. She had heard enough. Perhaps there was not so much difference, after all, between a self-regarding Italian, and an overly self-confident Englishman. Like every woman, Cassandra had no desire to be one more peach in a big bowl of fruit. Was she repeating the mistake that her mother had made? Her mother had married the low-born Paolo Lascari against the protests of her parents who had said that he was marrying her for the chocolate. Her mother had trusted her instincts – putting her trust in love, charm and handsomeness; and there hadn't been a fairytale ending. How could you know if you were making the right decision about a man, or the worst decision of your life? What did you put your trust in?

The last of the sunlight seeped out of the piazza, and with it went the warm glow inside Cassandra's heart.

Nick didn't notice the chill. He was wolfing down the food, and knocking back the wine.

"This is a real find, this place."

"Yes, it's lovely."

"Think you can make it as far as the garden?"

"Yes, I'd like to see it. We've come this far."

"Okay, let me finish the wine, pay the bill, and we'll be off."

"You have enough money?"

"You think that I want your money?"

"I didn't mean it like that."

"Yes, you did, but it's okay."

She had brought up the subject of money, and she knew that she shouldn't have done; it wouldn't tell her anything.

He paid the bill, and then stood behind her chair, like a perfect gentleman, when she got up from the table. If she had upset him, he didn't show it. She took her shoes off, and as she did so, told herself that she didn't care what she looked like.

"Here, let me take them," he said, chivalrously.

It was now quite dark overhead, and the streetlamps had been switched on. They were large, old-fashioned, turn-of-the-century, with wrought iron frames; they gave the *caruggi* a bronzed and burnished warm glow, highlighting the exposed timbers and the vaulted roofs.

It didn't take them very long to reach the Gardens of Queen Elena, laid out at the very summit of *La Pigna*. With their ornamental flowerbeds and fringed palms, set against the night sky, and illuminated by sunken floodlights, and the glowing halo of San Remo below them, they had a shimmering, mysterious and other-worldly presence, like a tabletop painted in lacquered *palekh*. Nick and Cassandra were the only two people there.

"Wow! Some garden! I guess we just follow the path towards the church. So, who was Queen Elena?" asked Nick.

"No idea."

"Me too. Well, doesn't matter. She employed a good gardener. Flowerbeds are not my thing, but they're really well done."

"Do you ever walk around a garden, and not look at it like a gardener?"

"Point taken."

They walked along a broad avenue laid out with black and white sea pebbles. On all sides, they were surrounded by palm groves and giant ficus trees. The panoramic glow of San Remo peeped everywhere through the plantings.

Cassandra thought that it really was a very beautiful garden; it was having the effect on her that Queen Elena must have planned – an uplifting of the spirit. Nick was almost ecstatic.

"My God, it's like walking around a perfume shop. I can smell orange blossoms, can you? And pine cones, and roses. Romantic, huh? Have you ever been to the Alhambra in Granada? That's my favourite garden of all, but this comes very close."

"No, I've never been. You'd be very happy working here, wouldn't you?"

"Yes, but I'm very happy where I am."

They were standing in front of the Santuario della Madonna della Costa, a white, cream and pink rococo confection of pilasters, pediments, plump putti, Corinthian columns and lavish stucco plasterwork. Above the main door, the word 'Sanctuarium' was carved, set within a Little Bo Peep heart of palest sea blue.

"It looks like one of your father's chocolate boxes."

"You don't like our chocolates?"

"The chocolates are very nice. Lovely place for Goldilocks to seek sanctuary."

That was it. Cassandra walked beside the man she no longer liked. She had listened to her heart, and it had deceived her. She had run after this man, when she should have played it at a walking pace. Now, all she wanted to do was to run away from him.

They stood by the stone balustrade of the belvedere, the look-out point that offered an uninterrupted view over the Gulf of San Remo – magical, twinkling, exactly the right place for a first kiss, one to talk about in years to come. They were both silent; the only sound a fountain playing in the rockery behind them. Cassandra had no heart for the view; she could feel herself retreating from it. Nick breathed in as much as he could of the scented and fragrant air.

"*Riviera dei Fiori*. This part, I confess, I did plan."

She knew that he was about to kiss her. She had never felt so unsure of herself. If she kissed him back, that would be it – no going back. She was trying to find some courage from somewhere. She willed herself to look out at the magnificent view, hoping that the beauty of it all would find its way into her heart. She wanted to cry out, and break the spell of Queen Elena. She tried to stop breathing, in the hope that this would stop the notes of citrus fruits and floral blossom that were interfering with her ability to reason. She felt as if she had lost her mind; and mindless, she had only her unreliable senses left. Yes, he had planned this very well. He had known that here in the Gardens of Queen Elena, with their perfumes, and scents, and fragrances and vistas – all that was most beautiful about the world, he would be at his strongest, and she at her weakest.

"Before I kiss you, can I ask you a question?"

"What?"

"Why did your mother kill herself?"

She was almost glad that he had broken the spell for her. He had dared – presumed – to try to find his way into the deepest recesses of her being, and nobody was allowed there. Now, with her millions of euro adding to her coldness, she would make him pay.

"You have no right to ask me that question, Mr Austin. You are the gardener. You work for us, remember? What gives you the right to think that you can kiss me as and when you please? You think that I want to kiss you? You are arrogant and over-confident, with nothing to be over-confident about, as I can see. I am not a quick holiday fuck to add to your collection of sporting trophies."

She was hurting him. She could see that he bruised very easily; and she kept on hurting him, because she could. He looked at her in such pain that she thought he was going to cry. She could see the glistening in his eyes, and yet she carried on. She pushed the knife in as far as it would go.

"You like Tchaikovsky so much? Well, I don't want a relationship with a man who really wants a Versace romance! I want a real man!"

She looked at him in hot silence, for as long as she could; then she walked off, leaving him standing there, still holding her shoes.

The *Belle Époque* Railway Station Scene

WHEN CASSANDRA WOKE up the next morning, even as she was opening her eyes, she regretted every single hurtful word. How could she have been so stupid?

"Nick Austin. Nick Austin. Mrs Nick Austin."

She sat up. She liked him more than any other man she had ever met; so, then, everything would be okay. It was a mess now, but she would definitely make it right. He wanted her, and she was beautiful and rich; so, it was obvious, for good reason, he would get over it. It was a pity that she couldn't unsay what she had said, but she would make sure that she said the right things from now on, to make him forget about last night.

She sat in bed thinking about how she could make it up to him. She could help him in the garden – no, she didn't want gardener's hands. Why not say that he could take a day off, and go out with him somewhere that he would enjoy? Somewhere equally romantic like last night. There was no shortage of gardens to visit. Somewhere outside of town ... Villa Hanbury, with its tropical English garden, he would love that, or the Jardin Exotique in Monaco. If they went to Monaco they could have lunch on the terrace of the Hermitage; that would be a good introduction to the new life that he would soon be leading. Then it came to her – help him research the garden! Find out what it looked like in the beginning; that would make him understand how well she understood him. They would sit in the library, looking through old, musty books, and she would find a picture of the original garden; and then Nick would replant it, rose by rose, exactly as it had first been.

She jumped out of bed, happy that she had it all planned and sorted. She took a quick shower, and put on the floral green Versace dress; he would not be able to resist her in it.

She came down to breakfast, quite happy, thinking that Monaco was a good idea. She would buy him some clothes, and then they could go for dinner in the Louis Quinze; that would be the right place to show off the evening dress she still had to wear. That was the good thing about having lots of money – it could always get you out of trouble.

Beatrice was sitting at the kitchen table, immobile. She had been crying.

"He's gone. He left you this."

Cassandra picked up the sealed envelope, with her full name on it; she tore it open. He had nice handwriting.

"Cassie, I asked you that question because I didn't want you to make the mistake that your mother made. I'm sorry. I have to leave. Nick."

She felt sick to the pit of her stomach. "Where is he?"

"At the train station. He's flying from Nice. And if you don't bring him back, I'm going to leave as well."

"Why did you tell him?"

"Because he asked me, and I didn't want him to ask you. He worked the rest out for himself."

"Did you recommend that we go to that restaurant last night?"

"What restaurant?"

"It doesn't matter. You shouldn't have interfered."

Beatrice was sobbing. "I interfered because I love you as my own daughter, and because he loves you, only you're as blind as your father when it comes to love."

Cassandra sat down. "How can I be sure that he loves me?"

"Because."

There was silence for what seemed to both of them a long time, but it was not more than a few minutes.

"What do I do now?"

"Do what every woman does."

There was another silence. Shock, or setback, has a very focussing effect on some people (you either focus or collapse). Cassandra drank the remains of a still-warm *Americano* – Nick must have left it – and focussed. As a child she had not known what questions to ask her mother; as a woman, it had been too late, but this morning, post-tantrum, she knew what the answers to those questions would have been. She knew that she was about to follow in her mother's footsteps. It was a waste of time to ask what life would be like with a man tomorrow, to try to calculate how much happiness he might give you, and how much pain. "Seize the day," that's what her mother would have said, "before the train takes him away from you. Love is painful. You want epiphany, then you must learn to bear the stigmata."

Cassandra stood up.

"I'm going."

"You know where it is? You've never been on a train."

"I know what a railway station looks like."

Cassandra went back upstairs to get her bag – no time to worry about whether it coordinated – and three minutes later she was on her way to where she knew the station must be; the track ran along the coastline.

She was quite certain that he would be waiting for her – he didn't really want to leave. As she walked she thought about their first meeting, when they had sat in the garden drinking lemonade; when was that? The day before yesterday! There was a nice symmetry about the way she had talked about the opening of the railway station in San Remo; and here she was, on her way there, to tell him how much she loved him, to stop him from taking the train that was taking him out of her life. He would be sitting, forlorn and morose, on a bench underneath the clock, wearing the clothes that he had been wearing the night before. Probably he didn't have nice luggage, just one of those Adidas sports bags. She would walk on to the platform just a few moments before the train was due to arrive, and the pressure of the timetable would ensure that her emotions were heightened to their utmost by the need to say quickly what needed to be said.

She had seen pictures, so she knew that it was a very beautiful *Belle Époque* railway station, encircled by palm trees; you couldn't hope to find a more atmospheric and romantic rendezvous. Fifteen minutes, and she was there. Strange, but it was very quiet – no cars or taxis, no people coming and going; and no ticket office in the station building, just a small tobacconist's kiosk. She walked on to the platform: there was the clock, and the bench where Nick should have been sitting, only he wasn't. There were no trains in sight, not even rail tracks, but there were plenty of cyclists. Panic was setting in. She walked further down the platform that was no longer a platform, and stopped by a rank of parked bicycles.

Two well-upholstered, elderly English women were in fits of giggles, gaily trying to remember how to ride a bike – the gaiety of women who have paid off the mortgage and downsized.

"Felicity! Stop! The palm trees! You need stabilisers!"

"Laura, we need L plates! I wish I'd asked them for an automatic!"

There was no money left in Cassandra's small voice: "Excuse me, where are the trains to Nice?"

The tone was pitiable, and both Felicity and Laura instantly stopped larking about, and looked at Cassandra in the same way they would look at a dog that had been run over in Chiswick High Road.

Felicity spoke first. "Oh, you are behind the times. There aren't any trains from here. This was the station but it's not one any more, now it's a cycle path. The new station's underground."

"And a horrible soulless place it is too," added Laura.

"It's quite a walk, especially in those shoes. I'd take a taxi if I were you, if you can find one. Or there must be a bus."

"I don't think she does buses," said Laura.

Cassandra whispered, "Thank you."

The two women wobbled off, leaving Cassandra standing there, wishing that she had kissed him when she had the chance.

"That was always my favourite film," remarked Felicity.

"What was?"

"*Brief Encounter.*"

Unstabilised, Felicity and Laura could be heard rather over-dramatising the final parting torment: "'And then he walked away! Away!'"

"'Out of my life, for ever!'"

Would Nick have made the same mistake? No, probably he would have arrived by train. But surely, he couldn't be that far away. She walked back out into the street, to find a taxi. There were plenty of cars rushing past, but no taxis – no reason for them to sit at a railway station that was closed. She thought about calling Beatrice to ask her how to get to the new station, but pride stopped her. What would Nick have done? How would he have found his way to the horrible new station? How did people without money travel? By bus, and she was standing by a bus stop.

Cassandra wanted to ask the people waiting in a sheep huddle, if there was a bus that went to the new station, but poor people always looked so hostile. She willed herself to remain calm; she would find him in time. She would marry him.

She had only a few moments to wait before a bus arrived. She watched everybody else get on, and then followed. When she asked the bus driver a question he looked at her as if she were stupid.

"Do you go to the new train station?"

"It says station on the front of the bus."

Cassandra upset him even more because she had no small change. He waved at her impatiently to sit down; her first time on a bus, and she got a free ride.

San Remo looked different on a bus, less Italian Riviera and more a warm place where people tried to survive from loan day to pay day. Cassandra knew nothing about survival, but she could see that her numbed state was the same as all the other passengers. Her experience of the 'real world' – a world without lots of money – lasted no more than fifteen minutes, but its unpleasant memories stayed with her a long time after. She had never looked at people's faces before, and tried to imagine what they were thinking. Now, she looked at all of the bus faces, and she saw in each one of them something that she knew she never really wanted to understand – not her leisurely enjoyment of life, no, the chipped fingernails of a desperate scrabble for a foothold.

When the bus pulled up in front of the concrete and glass train station, Cassandra was already standing by the pneumatic door, impatient for it to open. As she ran towards the entrance, built into the hillside like a bunker, she could see herself in the wrap-around reflective glass panes. Is there anything more unsettling for the psyche than running towards yourself?

Laura was right, it was a soulless place. The old *Belle Époque* station had celebrated the journey; the new station just wanted to hurry you through as quickly as possible, and rush you off to your destination. Cassandra's heels clicked and slipped on the smooth marble of the ticket hall. She ran along the moving walkway that delivered her to the platform. It looks unfinished – that's the idea – a long tunnel with bare concrete shoulders and steel girders; the lighting doesn't illuminate, it creates an atmosphere of Stygian gloom. There is nowhere to sit down – "Be off with you!" it says. You would never want to hang around here, holding a bunch of flowers, waiting with excited anticipation for the train to pull in. This is a setting for Dante, the tracks on that side leading to Hell, on this side to Purgatory.

Nick was not on the platform; like everybody else he had probably just wanted to get the hell out of there. Cassandra looked at the read-out of trains – Nice due in six minutes. She could wait, or she could take a taxi; the train would be faster.

She waited. She took no notice of other people waiting. She was asking herself time and time again if she would catch up with him; no, *where* she would catch up with him. Perhaps he would change his mind, and wait for her? But how far away would that be? Perhaps he was testing her, to see how much she loved him. But did he know that she loved him? What if he were not at the airport – was he expecting her to fly to England? She didn't know where he lived. Her father would know, but she couldn't ask him. How would she find out? She didn't even have his mobile number. Perhaps he was on Facebook? That would look silly, asking him to make her his friend; she wanted to be his wife. What did it really mean when he wrote that he had to leave? What if it wasn't an invitation to come and find him? What if …

There was a monstrous cacophony of heavy engineering groans and screeches as the train emerged out of the tunnel, and pulled into the platform. Instinctively, she got into the first-class carriage. She took a window seat, not because she wanted to look at the view – she had seen it many times through a tinted car window – but because she thought she might see him standing at a station. Madness, she knew, but she couldn't stop now.

The inspector was soon standing in front of her. "Ticket, please."

"I don't have one. How much? Here. Is there a stop at the airport?"

"No, get out at Nice and take a bus." He gave her the same look as the bus driver. "Perhaps you'd better take a taxi."

The train moved forwards, and she went backwards, rewinding frame to frame, to the moment when she had first seen him in the garden. Was it really possible to fall in love with a man at first sight, before you had even spoken with him, or heard his voice? Yes; it had happened to her. Why had she not told him? Why had she played such a silly game? Because that's what we do when we think we have so much time left. What time was his flight? Was he the type of man who liked to cut it fine, reaching the gate just as it closed, or the type who liked to have breakfast and shop the duty free? She knew so little about him. How could she be so sure that he was the one? She was sure. Did it matter that she didn't know what aftershave he liked? Or his favourite colour? What would he say when he found out that she couldn't cook? Would she make him happy in bed? Would he make her happy? Only now, it didn't seem so important to have an orgasm. She just wanted to sleep with him. She thought about his nakedness when he had stepped out of the pool; yes, that had been the right thing for him to do – shock her. Was he cut or uncut? She tried to zero in on his cock, but she had only glanced at it – not really fact-checking – so she wasn't sure. The money was still the biggest problem. Funny that, people who travelled by bus, like today, probably thought that she could have any man she wanted; yes, but not for keeps. He had told her that he wasn't after her money when he paid last night; she hoped that she was reading him right, like Balzac. He was so confident in his ability to succeed, so that must mean her money was not a blandishment, it was more a turn-off, right. What was he thinking about her at this moment? Was she in his mind?

With the rush and jumble of all these thoughts, the stations passed by very quickly. She almost missed Nice Ville. When she got into a taxi she hoped that this would be the last stage of her journey. She had made up her mind – she would follow him until she found him. She realised that she hadn't cried, because she didn't think that she had lost him.

She knew the airport well – the private jet terminal, that is; still, she wasn't such a spoiled little rich girl that she didn't know where to go for the flights where you have to stand in a line, and check in. She scanned the Departures board; there were so many flights to London. Which one? He would take one of those discount airlines. What were they called? Look for people who looked as if they liked discounts. She looked, and headed for an easyJet check-in desk.

"Can you tell me if a Mr Nick Austin is flying with you today? Or he's already flown?"

"I'm sorry, but I can't give out that information. If he's flown, you've missed him; if he's flying with us, he'll be here."

How would she know where he lived? She would have to call her father, ask him for the address, get Nick's home number, and phone his parents; and what would she say? "Hello, my name's Cassandra. I want to marry Nick but I don't where he is. Actually, I don't know anything about him. I've known him for two days." Or look for a plants nursery; how many could there be in England? She couldn't wait here for ever; that was it, call her father. No, better to call Beatrice; she would know what to say, not to make him suspicious. She was walking through the terminal, talking to herself, panicking.

Then she saw him watching her. He was sitting on a bar stool, drinking beer. He didn't look unhappy, or sad, or regretful; he was laughing – laughing at her.

She was suddenly so angry at him that she wanted to walk straight past him; only, she couldn't. There was no time to decide what look she should be giving him. She had no idea what she looked like – like a woman who has chased all day after a man.

He was all smiles. "Are you looking for me?"

Was he happy to see her, or playing with her?

"I thought you were flying to London?"

"Right country, wrong city. Manchester. Yorkshire, remember? It's closer. I'll show you one day."

"I read your note."

"Obviously. What is it, exactly, Cassandra, that you want from me?"

"I walked. I got the wrong station."

He smiled.

"Then I took a bus – I've never been on a bus. Then I took a train. Then a taxi."

"Taxis cost money. *Magari*. If I ever have as much money as you, Cassie, I hope that I never forget to say sorry."

Then she started to cry.

Versace Romance

STUPID BITCH. Jesus fuck! Why didn't she just ... Fuck her, and fuck the money! Cunt! He wouldn't kiss her now if she were the last bitch in the world. Show her your feminine side – it was in *Maxim* magazine every fuckin' month. Try to think about more than getting your leg over, was the advice. Okay, right, that's what he did, he held back. Thought about her feelings. Okay, so her mother topped herself, that must have left a scar. He wanted to show her that he understood. He was being sensitive. Fucking waste of time that was. Should've just fucked her when he had the chance. He'd spent a week's money on dinner last night. Her father's such a fucking mean cunt.

It was frigging hot lugging his sports bag. Thank God the station wasn't far away. He'd taken the bus here when he first arrived, but Beatrice had told him the train to Nice was quicker.

He'd miss the garden; it was so fucking beautiful, he would have done it for nothing. He'd made a great job with those roses. At least he hadn't fucked that up. It had been worth it just for that. They really were magnificent; two were old favourites: *Empress Josephine* – he should have been her gardener – and *Souvenir de la Malmaison*; that was a textbook colour combination, white and pink. They were easy to spot, but what about the roses he still hadn't identified? Whoever had laid out the garden at the very beginning, he must have been working to a pattern. Would have been nice to have cracked it before the bitch sent him packing. Keep thinking about the roses 'n' perhaps he wouldn't get so steamed up. He should've jacked off before he left. Fucking heat and her parading her tits every opportunity she got, he'd been tugging it three times a day.

This was Corso Imperatrice, not far to go. Place must have been like an outpost of St Petersburg, or an upmarket Russian village. Little Russian Italy. *Blinis Quattro Formaggio*. You tell me, what's wrong with a man liking Tchaikovsky and playing the piano? Typical – they want sensitivity until you give it to them.

Russian gardens! That was the pattern – everything as Russian as possible! Now it all made sense: that first gardener, he'd been a rosarian. What were the roses with Russian names? *Anna Pavlova, Tchaikovski,* and another one he couldn't remember – *Princesse* something or other. Even if he didn't work out exactly what was missing from the original layout, he could plant a modern *Swan Lake* in the gaps.

He almost turned back, scenting the urge to go back to the roses. On the platform that somehow wasn't a platform – where the fuck was the railway track? Two Muscle Marys on bicycles were making jokes about riding side-saddle. He could tell they were queens because they looked at him that way they did.

"Where's the fucking train station gone?"

"Haven't a fucking clue, handsome."

"Somebody didn't get lucky last night," said the other one.

Nick was not in the mood for flirting. "You should be so lucky."

"You'll sell it before I do, handsome. Take the bus marked *Stazione. Ciao bella.*"

Jesus fuck. Why was he always the straight man in a gay world? Versace romance, is that what he'd called it? Yeah, then she'd thrown it back in his face. He should have kept his mouth shut, but you only let it slip if you know you've grown out of it, that phase.

At fourteen, he'd warded them off, scared shitless – his voice hadn't dropped 'til he was fifteen; red-faced, mortifying, having to sing soprano in a red cassock and a white frilly collar at the front of the choir, desperate to be a tenor. Still, he'd felt rather virtuous when Jed the housemaster had said that there was "too much homosexuality in 'A' Dorm." All around him the lights-out activity was pretty feverish.

His nicknames had changed with his voice – from "Squeak" to "Lashes," only that was nothing to do with being a longed-for tenor. "Lashes" because in art class they'd been looking at ideals of Renaissance beauty, and Mr Hindley had pointed out the long lashes of the Florentines; his classmate, Alessandro D'Achille, whose father was Italian, had joked about them being "just like Nick's lashes, sir!"

Even with that pretty obvious giveaway, still nobody guessed, not even Jed.

"Stazione ferroviaria?"

"Sì."

San Remo looked like a shabby shit hole from the back of a bus.

Nick didn't like D'Achille; he was a bully, and liked to throw his weight around, usually on top of Nick, who at that time had no muscles to speak of. In the fifth form, Jed put the two of them together in the small study. He'd said to Nick, "You'll be good for each other," meaning that Nick might become more sporty, and D'Achille more studious. Some hope; it was like Beauty and the Beast. D'Achille was not that handsome – broken nose, aggressive chin – but he had a body hacked out of marble. He'd come back every afternoon, muddy, sweaty, hot, horny; he'd fling his filthy shirt and shorts into a pile on the floor, and stand there in his jockstrap, leaning over Nick doing his homework, blowing into his ear and saying, "Suck me off, Lashes."

"Don't be disgusting."

Nick might have held out if it hadn't been for the lager. There was a school pub, to teach them to drink responsibly. He'd gone there to celebrate getting an 'A' in French a year early. D'Achille had slapped him on the back, and coaxed him into drinking as much as he could until they'd used up all their chits. Nick hadn't been able to walk back to the dorm unaided – couldn't stand up. He woke up in the Sick Room, with Alessandro lying beside him.

It had been quite intense, after that; fifteen, sixteen, seventeen, did it really go on that long? Amazing they'd never been caught, never been found out. "Lashes" had been more beautiful than Cassie, and the general object of unconcealed lust and leers, but who would have thought it of D'Achille, the mythical school sports hero, always in the First teams for rugby, hockey and cricket, even fives for fuck's sake. Every morning before Assembly, the lists for Away games would go up in the corridor, and it always seemed to Nick that D'Achille, A. (Capt.) was at the top of every team.

Nick, as dear old Jed had hoped, had indeed become sporty – cross-country running was best for making love in the woods. And Alessandro had studiously made love to Nick in the Old Library, late at night, with the leather-bound volumes of the *Pall Mall Gazette* for elevation.

It had ended when Nick started fucking the fat girl in the local fish and chip shop. Alessandro had been ... well, heartbroken. Nick had felt a pang, and moved on. He'd been in love, and then he wasn't.

He couldn't explain it even to himself, the new attraction. Some men like to dress up in women's clothes – skimpy knickers, suspender belt, stockings, and stiletto shoes (if they can find them in the right size), maybe even a wig if they're going the whole hog. Dressed in women's underwear, and with a dab of lipstick, they'll fuck with other men, but, and here's the funny thing, they won't kiss you; they're really straight, you see, and kissing is not for fantasy, it's for real relationships.

The thing is, if it gets you hard, then that's what you like, simple as that; no point in analysing it. Some men have a thing about big tits, no harm in that. The Victorians had a thing about feet. Now everything has to be shaven.

Fetish used to lie at the back of the cupboard, now it sits on the desktop. Go to Google, type in "porn," click on any site, and see how many different categories there are. Some men have a thing about fat women, men like Nick. You lie on top of a thin woman, it's like aching on a pebble beach; you lie on top of a fat woman, she gives in like a sand dune.

The new train station was like Colditz – you couldn't wait to escape.

It didn't matter, he wasn't in any hurry, he just wanted to make her sweat a bit, running after him, as he knew she would.

He'd played it by the book – nice 'n' slow, nothing crude. She'd got the message. Served her right if she got an eyeful by the swimming pool – now she'd know what she was missing. Just because a guy can tell a nice dress doesn't make him a bum bandit.

He'd miss it around here. Look at those villas, swimming pools, fast cars, yachts, marinas ... This was the life. What was not to like? Couldn't get anywhere in Ripon, could he? Snooty fuckers. County cunts. He never wanted to see another fucking clematis for as long as he lived. And he'd fucking blown it, dickhead.

She wasn't really his type – no fat on her – but she looked well fit. And she wanted it, badly. He could have fucked her when she surprised him in the swimming pool. Like she didn't stare at his cock with her tongue hanging out. She couldn't keep her eyes off him the moment she first saw him. Like he hadn't noticed everything. Lemonade! That was a good one. He'd watched her from the greenhouse. Fuck her! He was Jack the Lad and he didn't give a fuck. But the thing was he'd really fucked it up at uni. His parents went apeshit. Re-apply? Couldn't face that. Boy, he'd lucked out, as always. How was he to know that mean-fisted Italian git had a wad of dough and a daughter up for it. Fuck, she'd even told him she was looking for a husband!

She'd bought those clothes in Versace, wanting to please him, attract him; he'd been pleased. That see-through stuff. He'd seen through every move she made. She annoyed the shit out of him, but there was something about her. Money? No, for certain, it wasn't just the money, although there must be fucking millions.

He had a walk around Nice. Why not, she'd follow him, he knew that. All right, so she'd hurt him with that gay Tchaikovsky shit. Well, today was payback. They looked good together, and he couldn't be a gardener all his life, could he? "Do you have any trailing fuchsias?" He never wanted to hear that question ever again.

He hadn't bought a ticket. What was the point? He just had to sit tight at the bar, and she'd come running. And here she was, running scared, wearing Versace. Versace romance. Yeah.

"You can never be too rich or too thin."

Duchess of Windsor

Lose Weight through Sex

A Totally Fat Wardrobe

"*B*ONJOUR. How about lunch?"
"You mean with me?"
"Yes, why not? You do eat lunch, don't you? Or you just cook them? You know who this is, right?"
"*Ouais, je sais.*"
"Thought so. Tomorrow okay?"
"Yes ... no ... Yes."
"I'll take that as a yes. I'll pick you up. About one. The restaurant's a surprise."
"You don't know where I live."
"Yes, I do. *À demain.* See you."

Nick hung up, and Imogen stood there, in the *salon* at home, clutching her mobile like a rosary. She found herself unable to move. That lunch for Frank and Claudia had been two weeks ago. She hadn't given him two thoughts. There had been plenty of other things to think about since then. As so often, one lunch had brought in others. The Baroness had sent her a note:

Thank you for a wonderful lunch! Would you like to do the same for me? After I'm back from Palm Beach. For four. The menu can be all of your choosing but I would like to have chocolate somewhere. Something substantial and not too elaborate! Sophie

The note was written in ink on crested ivory-coloured paper. Jade had sent Imogen a one-word text: "Fab!" Everybody else had sent their rave reviews to Claudia. And there had been a christening party for twelve in Mougins. So, no, there had been no reason to think about Mr Nick Austin, with his wet nipple, and his Creed aftershave, and his bitch of a wife, or the coconut smell of his hair, and his care for roses, and the way that he hid the fact that he thought he didn't belong where he was.

She hadn't waited more than three or four days for him to call her ... because he had said that they'd have lunch, so it was reasonable to expect him to call, wasn't it? Who was she kidding! A man like him didn't go for fat girls like her. Two weeks! And why now? What did he want?

She was standing in the *salon*, looking out at the bay towards Juan-les-Pins. It was a Mistral day, and the rich early autumn leaves and baked pine cones were eddying and scudding about the terrace. Hers was an elegant villa, even if the décor was a bit of a mish-mash, what with the inherited Georgian walnut writing desk where she kept her MacBook, in front of the quill-pen ink stand; some Irish hunting pictures, and some really not bad portraits of O'Rorkes in taffeta gowns and powdered periwigs. These lived with a lot of white modern furniture – leather sofas, bookshelves bearing cookery books, a printer, and a Bang and Olufsen sound system, and a 1960s Arkana tulip table and chairs, the table laid with more cookery books and untried recipes; Persian silk rugs luxuriated all over the stone floor.

What to wear? Bet you anything Nick Austin wouldn't be thinking about what to wear; he'd look good in, and out of, anything. She went into the bedroom, threw open all the wardrobe doors, and took a step back. Nothing. Nothing to wear for a man who was everything in one piece. Knickers ...

Right on cue, Sister Ursula appeared. "Clean, in case there's an accident on the way."

"Yes, Sister Ursula."

Why was she thinking about knickers? Was it a date?

Did she have any sexy ones? Yes, somewhere, she'd had them made for a rainy day. She remembered, Rigby & Peller, a few years ago when she'd been in London. She'd undergone yet another one of those unsatisfactory mercy fucks – why were men always so merciful to her? Depressed, she'd cried her heart out to Claudia who had told her to, "Go and buy something sexy; something you'd hide from Sister Ursula."

She rooted around in the *armoire*. Found them. They were all still in the original boxes; she unwrapped and inspected them: Rigby and Peller Alondra black g-string (she also had them in red); and there were the Aubade Love Circus knickers, again in black and red; that was funny ... St Tropez briefs!

"Here goes," she muttered, and unwrapped her wraparound cheesecloth skirt – she had a wardrobe full of them, all of them brightly coloured, and all bought in Mumbai when she had gone on an Indian cooking course. She pulled off her Spanx undies, the Super High Power celeb ones (the ones Claudia said reminded her of playing lacrosse), and, trying not to look at herself in the mirror, she climbed into the red Love Circus knickers. Next, she threw off her oversized dark blue painter's calico shirt – like the skirt, and a lot else in her wardrobe it covered up a multitude of sins – and manhandled herself into the matching bra; it gave her so much cleavage she could have balanced a tray of canapés. What about the Aubade Amour Clandestin in black? Or the Aubade Lady Erotic in red; a plunge bra for lunch?

She remembered the fitting, around the corner from Harrods. She had been so embarrassed at the beginning, standing in a mirrored fitting room, with her tits on show while the talk turned to breasts. No, not a talk, a communion, the soothing tones of the solid saleswoman who had made breasts her vocation: "Madam, there's really no need to be shy, there's nothing we haven't seen before, from the Quantocks to Mont Blanc. Now, let's see how we can get you fitted. Back straight. The shape and size of a woman's breasts change a number of times in her life. This is mainly due to fluctuations in weight, sport, pregnancy, contraception, medication and diet." That word "diet" Imogen had felt was aimed at her; it wasn't. "That is why at Rigby & Peller we recommend that our customers are fitted every six months."

"That must work out rather expensive."

"We are talking assets, madam. Eighty per cent of the ladies who walk through our doors for the first time are wearing the wrong size bra. The biggest mistake women make is wearing a bra too small in the cup and too big in the back. When a woman's bust gets bigger she thinks she's getting wider in the back. She's not. It's her cup size that's increasing. We find over and over again that having been fitted in the right size, our customers can't believe the difference, and leave us feeling like a new woman!"

It was the best confession Imogen had ever attended. She had never before worn anything so close to her skin that felt so perfect in size, and made her almost unashamed of her mountainous appendages. Why, then, had she never worn these wonderful confections? Because she was a Catholic? No, she had looked at herself in the mirror at home, and decided that these were bras and knickers designed for a man to look at.

The ghost of Sister Ursula again appeared behind her.

"Would you take a look at yourself, Imogen O'Rorke? That is an abomination in the sight of God. What do you call those?"

"Dumplings, Sister."

"And these?"

"Muffin tops, Sister."

"And these lower down?"

"Ham hocks, Sister."

"Take them off at once."

Imogen did as she was told, but, when Sister Ursula had disappeared, she defiantly put back on the Alondra bra and knickers, in black.

"Now what?" she said out loud.

Call Clod for advice. Tell her everything. No. Why not? Because. Calm down. It wasn't a date. What was it then, a business lunch? What business? The only thing she had to wear to lunch was her underwear! Stop panicking. Concentrate. Start from the top – hair, nails, pussy, feet. She peeked inside the knickers; thank God, "Trimmed and ready for grazing," as Claudia would have said. Nails and feet had been done the day before yesterday, as always, after the *marché aux fleurs* in Nice – the whole of her life revolved around market days. Now, call Jean-Pierre; she could tell her hairdresser things she wouldn't tell her confessor:

"*J'ai une urgence.*"

"*Encore une?*"

"*Je déjeune avec un homme.*"

"*C'est toujours un homme, Madame Imogène.*"

"*J'ai besoin d'aide aujourd'hui.*"

"*D'accord. Donne-moi ... deux heures.*"

The dapper Jean-Pierre Caminade advertises himself as the "Coiffeur de Stars," offering, "Styling the Stars;" this being Antibes, it's actually true: Juliette Binoche, Audrey Tautou, Uma Thurman, and Imogen O'Rorke have all taken comfort in his hands. When a woman puts herself into his care the hair is only part of the story.

"*Il est bel?*"

"Divine."

"Married?"

"Of course."

"Satisfying?"

"We'll see."

"What are you wearing?"

"My underwear." Imogen opened her royal purple peignoir. "Do you like it? I don't have anything else to wear."

"For breakfast it is very chic. For lunch, perhaps a little something on top?"

"There isn't anything, I looked."

"Perhaps if we have a look together?"

"My wardrobe has always been the same, you know that."

"*Bien sûr.* And half of it you never wear."

"*Exactement.* The Princess Grace half."

"*Madame Imogène*, every woman has a thin wardrobe and a fat wardrobe."

"Some of us have a totally fat wardrobe." Jean-Pierre finished with the hairdryer, and then inspected the wardrobe. He pulled clothes off the rails and threw them on the bed as he was speaking.

"You want to take him away from his wife?"

"I want to murder his wife."

"*Ça veut dire* 'dressed to kill?'"

"*C'est ça* but it's not in my wardrobe."

Across the hallway, the door to her grandmother's old room was open.

"It looks like a museum in there."

"It is."

"What you have in those Vuitton suitcases?"

"They're called steamer trunks. Full of my grandmother's clothes from before the war. Vionnet, Chanel, Schiaparelli, Lanvin, Molyneux. She wore them all; actually she knew them all."

Jean-Pierre knew his couturiers. "Molyneux would look good on you. Very chic."

"They're too small. I keep them to remind me. I should really give them to a museum. I'm never going to wear them."

"*Eh bien*, his wife is very beautiful?"

"His wife is perfect. And I know what you're thinking."

"I am thinking what a man wants, and it is not perfect."

"He wants this?"

"He invited you to lunch."

"He probably just wants me to cook for him, *comme toujours*. A business lunch."

"Where is he taking you?"

"He said it's a surprise."

"So, then, it's not a business lunch."

This thought hadn't occurred to Imogen, and she instantly became more interested in what to wear.

"I could wear a long cashmere cardigan?"

"Why you want to cover all up?"

"That's what I've always done."

"We have to uncover you. How about this?" 'This' was a black quilted pea coat. "Why you never wear these Nicole Farhi clothes?"

"I don't know. They were one of my binge buys, straight into the dieting part of my wardrobe. What about underneath?"

"Chanel jewellery. Do the buttons up. And these black trousers. Very Marlene Dietrich."

"They're from London. Kilgour. They made my father's suits. I used to go with him for the fittings. Mr Smith made these."

"Aah, that is why they fit. *Ça c'est l'Angleterre à son* best."

"I was saving them for a special occasion."

"Yes, for tomorrow. And flat ballet shoes."

"I have lots of them."

"*Eh bien. C'est tout.* And eat! Don't say you're on a diet. For every man, it's a turn off."

A kiss, and Jean-Pierre was gone. Alone, Imogen looked at herself in the mirror, coiffured and dolled up in her finery. She still recognised herself – there had been no ugly duckling/swan transformation; everything fitted, there was just too much of it. There was no way that a man as perfect as Nick Austin could really be interested in something this big. And yet ...

She had to do something to calm down. Think about lunch for the Baroness. What could she make with chocolate? *Chili con carne*? No, too middle class – 1970s. The lunch must be something to do with Frank's deal – had to be.

She opened some old cookery books – Larousse, Escoffier, Carême – looking for inspiration. Thinking about food was a defence against rising panic. Be creative! She was trying to psych herself up for lunch with Mr Nick Austin, except that she only felt secure in a kitchen. She would be on show in a dining-room, and for every positive thought that she forced herself to clarify, a negative one came flying by. She remembered something she had overheard at a working cocktail party – a gallery opening in St Paul de Vence.

"Imogen doesn't do sex! Like, come on, that's too gross! Ugh! Like people doing it in wheelchairs."

She had been brought up to expect a life of ease and pleasure, and it had turned out to be a hard slog. She was starting to feel sorry for herself. She put on some sad music – always a bad sign: Fannie Brice mourning *My Man*, in 1921. Her grandmother had been sad to it.

She was no good at pleasure, and that was surely what Mr Nick Austin was looking for. Pleasure; she always paid for it. Years ago, on a stolen weekend to Paris, she had gone with Claudia to an all-night party thrown by a friend with a brandy fortune. She had got very drunk, on brandy and coke, and stayed up all night. Penitent, in the morning (without Claudia, of course), she had gone to church, the biggest one she could find – Notre Dame. Sitting at the front, to demonstrate her guilt, she had yawned repeatedly throughout the sermon; incensed, the archbishop had leaned over the pulpit, and addressed her very loudly. *"Courage, mademoiselle, j'ai presque fini."*

A Fuck Me Lunch

IMOGEN SCRUBBED EVERY crevice and crevasse, wallowing in the scented bath water. All around the white hip bath there were scented altar candles; crystal bottles iridescent with perfumed salts; and bowls of handmade soaps fashioned into fruits and vegetables. What was all this luxury for? What was the point of it? Every lotion and potion that she lavished on her body had never been fully appreciated by any man.

She dried herself, taking care not to stand up straight, full frontal, facing the mirror. She put on the new underwear, and then, realising that she still had hours to kill, decided not to finish dressing until later. She had had an idea about the menu for the Baroness. As always, when she was having a sliding-down day, she took comfort in food – cooking not eating; she was too keyed up to munch. She would cook *Bouef en Daube à la Niçoise*, with the famous bay leaf. That bay leaf had given her the one and only exam success at school. She had been dreading the exam – English literature was not her best academic subject. In truth, she didn't have any best academic subject – "Thick as a plank," said Sister Ava.

But when Imogen turned over the exam paper the text was about a woman cooking a *Boeuf en daube*. Imogen could tell that the woman had never been in a kitchen in her life because there was a line about the bay leaf being "done to a turn."

Imogen started off her answer quite sure of herself: "Virginia Woolf knows nothing about cooking. If she had read Elizabeth David (but she couldn't have because she killed herself before Mrs David started writing about Mediterranean food) she would know that you take the bay leaf out of the dish before serving. Mrs Ramsey doesn't even really do the cooking, the real cook is Marthe. But I think Virginia Woolf is right about the connection between food and love. If you want to get a man you have to give him the best pieces of meat . . ." Her pen flowed, and she passed with distinction.

It was a fluke; and that was why she didn't think she would ever be a celebrity chef or a television personality. Imogen was unsure about how to express herself except in her food; she could cook as well as anybody on TV, but she couldn't write the books, or put the cooking into words. And how would she market herself? *How to Eat on Five Million a Year*; *Cooking for the Rich*; *The Fat Woman Cooks*.

Somewhere, Escoffier had a recipe for a *daube*; of course he did, he had been born around here. Dressed in her underwear and wrapped in her peignoir, Imogen pulled out all his tomes, and went to work. Time passed as she lost herself in a culinary history, drafting a menu, going back, ending up with Carême, just like Escoffier, who had done to Carême what she liked to do with Escoffier – strip out the inessentials and the double-cream showmanship.

Turning the pages of *Le guide culinaire* brought an idea to mind: if the lunch the Baroness was giving was somehow a continuation of the lunch for Frank and Claudia, how about an all-Escoffier menu? Nothing too fancy – an *hors d'oeuvre*, a soup, the *daube* and dessert. After a few crossings out, she had it:

Jeremy Noble

Éclairs à la Karoly
Consommé George Sand
Bouef en Daube à la Niçoise
Bombe Nero

She had never made the éclairs, and they were going to be fiddly to make, so she would have to practise.

The throbbing sound of an approaching engine on the water disturbed her reverie; probably visitors mistaking her jetty for the one belonging to her much richer, Russian neighbour. She stepped outside to redirect them. What looked like a Sunseeker powerboat was aiming straight for the jetty – hers – throwing up plumes of spray, even as it slowed down and banked sharply like a skier braking in powder snow. This was a rare sight – the O'Rorkes hadn't had a boat in a long while; and the jetty needed new boards. Imogen took some steps down the path, and, shielding her eyes against the sun, tried to make out who it was – perhaps she could wave them on next door. Well, she was right, it was a Sunseeker, only it wasn't strangers, it was Nick Austin! He waved gaily at her, and shouted, "Can you grab the line?"

Imogen tightened her peignoir around her, which movement only accentuated the large body underneath, and walked down towards the jetty. "I'm not dressed! I forgot the time! I thought you'd come by car!"

Nick was concentrating on lining up the boat. "It's much quicker to get here by boat. Traffic's so bloody terrible."

Nick cut the engine, and immediately leaped to the side of the boat, to unwind the line. "You know how to tie it up?"

"I know my knots, thank you."

"One, two, three; catch!"

Imogen expertly caught the thrown line, but the athletic

movement caused the peignoir to come undone, revealing the black lacy ensemble.

"Nice underwear! You want to skip lunch?"

"I thought you were a gentleman," remarked Imogen, tying a good bowline to the post.

"Whatever gave you that idea? Can you tie up the stern too?" Nick threw the line. "Your jetty needs repairing."

Imogen tied the second knot. "I don't get many visitors arriving by boat."

"No, well, you couldn't fit Frank's boat in here."

"Actually, the last person to use the jetty was Picasso."

Nick jumped off the boat on to the broken boards. "A carpenter would have been more useful." He kissed Imogen on both cheeks. "You smell nice. I thought I'd surprise you."

"You did," said Imogen, leading him up the garden path back towards the villa.

"I meant surprise you in a nice way. You're not angry?" He sounded contrite.

Imogen melted like chocolate. "No. It wouldn't have mattered if I'd remembered to put some clothes on. I was planning a menu."

"Somebody I know?"

"The Baroness. You remember?"

"At the lunch? Yes. Interesting. What's the lunch for, did she say?"

"No, but she wants chocolate on the menu."

"Does she? Your garden's in a bit of a mess."

"It's better for wildlife if you let it grow wild. And full-time gardeners are expensive."

"You live in Cap d'Antibes! Are you going to be long?"

"Are we in a hurry?"

"No, nothing to do with lunch. Do you have any secateurs?"

"What?"

"Pruning shears?"

"Wouldn't nail scissors be better?"

"I don't want to cut my nails. I want to tidy up your roses."

"I thought you wanted to have lunch?"

"I do want to have lunch, but I can't leave your roses looking like that."

"You said the same thing to Frank."

"I did? Oh yes, I remember. *Bourbons*, they'd been over-watered. You must have been listening."

"I was just passing by when you said it."

"No, you were hovering."

"I'll find those scissors."

Nick had stopped by an overgrown rose bush. "This is a *Grace de Monaco*, did you know that?"

"Yes."

"You do? I'm impressed."

"Don't be, I read the label when I bought it. Give me two minutes."

Imogen returned with the secateurs; she almost dropped them, seeing that Nick was now wearing only his white underpants – Zimmerli, she noticed. He had carefully draped his clothes over a sun chair, and slipped off his moccasins.

"You don't need to undress on my account. I'm not wearing this to lunch."

"Pity. I don't like to garden in duck whites."

"Probably best, given our clothes history."

"I remember. You massaged my nipple."

"I think I'd better go and put some clothes on."

"Don't you want to keep me company?"

"Comme vous voulez."

Imogen watched as Nick got to work pruning. He had a

gorgeous body. Cassandra was a lucky woman. There was no point in not admiring it, seeing as how he had put it on show. *Déshabillée*, she had lost her fear of what he wanted.

"What's your favourite rose?"

Nick replied without hesitation. "Two. *Lady Mary Fitzwilliam*. It's the palest pale pink, like a woman's skin. Large double bloom, shapely and voluptuous. It's not the oldest rose – 1882 – but it's very rare, rediscovered in the nineteen seventies. I like the old ones best. Smells like heaven. It's a rose for rosomaniacs, like me. And I like *Madame Alfred Carrière*, it's the whitest of white, has the most lovely smell. So, what's your favourite dish? Apart from me. Chocolate for a chocoholic?"

An image of Nick wrapped in puff pastry, and decorated with white roses and dark chocolate, appeared in Imogen's private picture gallery, to add to all the other erotic images of him, hanging there, in her head – it was those éclairs.

"I don't know. Whatever I'm cooking at the moment. You should've been a gardener."

"Don't remind me." Nick's tone was almost sharp, at the very least it was regretful.

"I'm sorry."

"No, don't be. You're right, that's all."

"Frank says you run the company very well."

"Yes, I do. And it's made me a lot of money, which is what I wanted. But you know what they say about getting what you want."

"I'll go and get dressed."

Imogen walked off before Nick had a chance to keep her there. When she re-appeared, dressed to kill, Nick had finished the pruning; and put on his trousers and shoes. He looked hot. It was one of those days where the Riviera sun plays hide and seek with the clouds, but was still warm enough for a labouring man to work up a sweat. He also had a way of looking at her very directly.

"I see what you mean about dressing for lunch. I'd better scrub up a little."

"A shower or a lick and a promise?"

He laughed, revealing perfectly straight teeth. "Not a phrase you expect to hear in Cap d'Antibes! A promise."

"Guest bathroom immediately on the right. If you open the cabinet, I think my father's Green Irish Tweed is still there."

"You remember?"

"Yes."

There was no point in denying it. She was no longer nervous about what she knew she wanted – his body. But what about him? What did he want with her? Standing in the shorn garden, waiting for Nick to freshen up, Imogen was confused. Was he really flirting with her? Was he really planning to cheat on his wife, with a woman twice her size? What sort of a man was he that took off his clothes before lunch? Well, what sort of a woman was she not to get dressed? They had both unclothed their intentions. He had noticed her watching him at the lunch in St-Trop; she had remembered his aftershave. He was gorgeous. She was fat. He was married. She didn't care.

"What are you daydreaming about?" he asked, coming towards her, flicking his hair dry. "No, it's okay, I know what you're thinking. Where are we going for lunch?"

Imogen was disappointed. "You think I only think about food?"

Nick grinned. "You really think that was what I thought you were thinking about?" He stopped to admire his handiwork, and plucked a single rose. He smelled it, and then, walking up to her, he deftly placed it in her buttonhole. *Voilà*. Pink suits you."

"You don't think it's too much?"

"I like too much." He leaned even closer into her, and

breathed in the rose scent; his hair brushed against her *décolletage*.
"Heady, isn't it?"

His words were breathed into her breasts. Imogen swooned and shuddered. Nick stepped back.

"You're cold?"

"No, no."

"Sorry, I didn't tidy up. You don't mind?"

"I have a part-time gardener, believe it or not."

"Not a good one. Let's go." And he marched off down to the boat, with Imogen following obediently.

"She's very beautiful. Your boat. Very sleek."

"It's only money."

Nick helped her in, which was not as difficult as she had feared; and then he let loose both the lines, athletically leaping on to the deck as the boat slipped away from the jetty. He fired the engine; and Imogen felt a deep throbbing feeling beneath her legs.

"Am I going to get wet?"

"Not unless you want to. Hold on tight."

The boat growled and Imogen was forcibly thrown back into the passenger seat. Nick laughed as he opened up the throttle, and raised his voice above the roar. "She's called a San Remo. She's a fast little thing. Thirty knots."

"I believe you. Where are we going?"

"I told you it's a surprise. Relax! You're not being hijacked."

Nick steered the boat into open water, making a direct course for the headland beyond St Jean Cap Ferrat. Imogen knew exactly where they were; this was not a journey into the unknown, and yet that is what it felt like. What was it that she was so frightened of? She stared straight ahead, not daring to steal even a glance at Nick, in case he caught her looking at him, and dared her to say what she was thinking. Yes, there was something of the pirate about him; not an uncultivated wildness, but a cavalier attitude, as if he couldn't care less about the riches he had at his fingers. What was he? Level-headed? A risk-taker? A hedonist? He had not been born to riches. Most of the new-rich people Imogen knew – she cooked for a lot of them – spent their time planning the accumulation of even more. Nick had the Midas touch, and yet it seemed to touch him not at all. As she saw it, he could as easily set himself the goal of buying a boat as big as Frank's, as he might throw it all up without a backwards glance. You would not think so to look at him, but Nick Austin, she decided, was an outsider; he could have belonged, he just didn't want to. That was the attraction for her quite apart from the fact that he was scalding hot and yummy like a buttered crumpet. Of course, being fat made her an outsider also.

Imogen wondered if his wife was aware of the dangers. A mistress was not what Cassandra should be worried about – if such a woman ever appeared on the scene; no, the roses were the danger.

Out at sea, with the occasional sun illuminating and refracting everything around them – windscreen, sea spray, leather upholstery, screaming seagulls – she realised with a piercing clarity that she did not know this man, but that, perhaps, she did understand him; it came to her like a Renaissance annunciation – a shaft of light, a beating of wings, Mary shrinking from the awful truth – foretelling what would be Nick's story, their shared story: she already felt it; theirs would not be a happy ending.

Imogen thought that they might be headed for Monaco – she hoped not – too fancy. But as they rounded St Jean Cap Ferrat, Nick headed inland towards Èze.

"You want me to swim to the shore?"

"Why do you say that?"

"Well, how are we going to get from the boat to dry land?"

Villa Eilenroc

"Watch," said Nick, slowing down as he aimed for a jetty built beside a rocky promontory jutting out just before Cap Estel. "Belongs to people I know. They're away. They won't mind."

Five minutes later, they were standing on the jetty, with the boat tied up.

"Right, let's go and get the car."

"You think of everything, don't you?" This was more a statement than a question, as Imogen trotted behind him, over the artfully placed paving stones leading up to a white villa glimpsed behind thick foliage.

"Pretty much."

"I thought we might be hitchhiking."

"I'd pick you up."

"You say the nicest things."

"Here it is."

Nick waved his hand with a beam of affection at a white open-top sports car sitting in the gravelled forecourt of his friends' villa, where uncommon trees stood tall like guardsmen, and offered protection from UV rays and uninvited eyes.

"It's very pretty." Imogen meant the villa.

"Pretty? It's the most beautiful thing ever made on four wheels! A Dino 246 GTS. The paintwork's original – Bianca, it's called. She was the first thing I bought when I made some money." Nick opened the passenger door with a bow. "Might be a bit of a squeeze, and she'll blow your hair away, but she's worth it."

He meant that she was too big for his prized toy, but Imogen wasn't offended; he said it in such a matter-of-fact way that it didn't seem unkind. The effect of being with him was that she was starting to forget about being fat.

"How did you get the boat here, and drive the car?"

"The man who looks after the car brought it here from San

Remo. He's sitting in a café somewhere, waiting for me to tell him when he can take it back. Why?"

"Just asking. You think like Frank and Claudia."

"Is that a good thing or a bad thing?"

"It's just a rich thing."

Getting in to the car was rather like falling into bed; it was so low down. He was right, she barely fitted in. Nick settled down in front of the steering wheel, gunned the engine, and edged out into the Lower Corniche. Imogen was surprised that he drove so slowly, several cars overtook them, and two teenagers in a beat-up Peugeot whooped at them as they passed by.

"She needs warming up," said Nick, by way of explanation. "Like all the best females. Ready?"

"Ready for what?"

Nick let the car answer, as he pressed the pedal, and the car shot away, twitching as it made a sharp turn straight across the coast road, in front of oncoming traffic, and starting the rapid ascent into the hills.

A few metres above sea level the gorse and pine landscape was here and there blackened and parched from the fires that had raged in August. Trumpeting its arrival at every twist and turn, the distinctive Ferrari engine sound whined behind Imogen's head, rending the midday stillness.

"Sex on wheels!" exclaimed Nick as he pushed the car faster and faster around the hairpin bends; de-accelerating and double de-clutching into the turns, and immediately rocketing out with the blistering pace of a sprinter.

She was shit-scared but Imogen showed no outward fear; he was waiting for her to cry out, to urge him to slow down, but she wouldn't. She was sitting so low down that her sight line made it seem as if they were going off the road at every sign warning of *"virages dangereux"* – the awkward angle of a snooker player potting the white. She bit her lip when the Dino caught up with the old Peugeot, and the punk driver did his best to stay ahead. There was little or no straight road, and no way to get past safely.

Nick was enjoying himself; he laughed, and shouted, *"Neuf à la banque!"* He dropped down into second, swung out into the middle of the road, judged that he had the distance to get past and get back in, before hitting the oncoming bus coming round the next corner, and roared past the angry Peugeot.

"Le jeu est fait! Still hungry?"

"You only live once."

Five minutes later, and Nick slowed down as they drove into Èze-Village, and stopped in the car park just outside the walls of the medieval village.

Nick opened the door for Imogen, and helped her out – not so easy.

"Hold on a mo, have to get a ticket." He bounded off to the ticket machine, and was back in less than a minute. "I know it's very touristy but it's not inside."

"Let me guess, La Chèvre d'Or?"

"I was trying to think of somewhere you might not have been, but that seemed impossible, what with your line of work. Happy here?"

"Very."

They were walking along a narrow winding alleyway.

"Why are you smiling?" he asked.

"Rien."

"No, tell me."

"I thought that you might bring me here. Because of the view."

She thought that he might be offended that she had spoiled his surprise, but not at all; he shrugged his shoulders good-naturedly.

"I guess I'm very predictable."

"No, I wouldn't say that."

Their joint arrival perplexed the *maitre d'*; he clearly wasn't certain about which one of them to greet first: Nick, who was obviously a regular, or Imogen, who was in the business of food; so he went for a diplomatic dual approach. *"Mais non!* My two favourite customers together! *Monsieur Austin et Madame Imogène."* He put his left hand on Nick's shoulder, his right on Imogen's, and still somehow managed to kiss her cheeks, saying, "I will go straight into the kitchen and tell Fabrice that you are here."

More attention was the last thing that Imogen wanted. *"Mais non*, Jean-Pascal, let us give him a surprise later."

"Comme vous voulez."

Jean-Pascal led them through the dining-room. This was the moment when Imogen understood what she had let herself in for. It would have been different if she had been wearing the usual patterned carpet – then she would have felt as if she were here for a business lunch. Everybody would have thought, "Ah, *c'est Imogène la Grande"*, but dressed as if she were Claudia she felt more undressed than when she had been wearing her underwear in the garden. Nick knew three tables in the room, and she knew two; they made the obligatory air-kissing and handshaking tour of the room. *Bien sûr*, nobody said a word about the two of them being together – *'Perhaps he just wants her to cook something for him'* – but she looked so different, it was that noticeable how nobody said how good she looked. It took them fifteen minutes of chit-chat, promises to call, have lunch, *'Share price is doing nicely,'* *'We have a silver jubilee lunch coming up …'* before they made it out on to the terrace. Imogen felt like a tart who has walked into a convent.

"I'm not his mistress. Why do I feel like a kept woman?"

"Everything all right?" asked Nick, holding the seat for her. He had exquisite manners, she would give him that.

"I feel like the other woman."

"Isn't that what all women want?"

"Only the idea of it." She sat down and stood straight up again. "I think I'd better go and rescue my hair."

"Think you can brave the room without me?"

Nick didn't mean it unkindly, but his perception was disconcerting.

"You see too much."

"Yes, it's why we're having lunch. Drink?"

"Yes, you choose."

She braved the room rather well she thought, but in the ladies' powder room, viciously brushing her hair, she gave herself up to self-flagellation. She didn't need the ghost of Sister Ursula to castigate her, she could do that unaided.

"What is the matter with you? This is what you've always wanted, right? So why are you hesitating? With him I don't feel fat; away from him I'm a heifer ... You look amazingly different, but I don't feel different inside! This is your world, you know your way around. Think of it as a business lunch. Bullshit, I know what he wants! Sitting outside on the terrace of one of the world's most famous restaurants is a rich and handsome man who wants a piece of your big ass; and you have to think twice about it? Because he has a beautiful wife who's half my size ..." She was giving up something of herself – independence, self-worth, call it what you will. Look, she had already let him choose her drink for her, and what was she going to get in return? Wasn't this what she had always wanted – a grand passion? So why was she frigging about, hesitating? They were two consenting adults. He couldn't have made it plainer what he was after. Go for it. Be damned.

Nick was staring out at the panoramic view, taking in a good part of what made the Côte d'Azur the playground of people's dreams: majestic yachts, reclusive villas, turquoise swimming pools, things manmade and natural living together in an equilibrium of warm, rich beauty; paradise if you ignored the traffic and the over-building.

"It's an amazing view, isn't it? No matter how many times you see it."

"Yes, it's lovely," said Imogen, taking her seat, and not really taking in the landscape.

"Lovely? You know how much effort it takes to get to the Cote d'Azur? To play in the sunshine?"

"No, not really, I've always lived here."

"Bellini okay?"

"Perfect."

"See? I'm a good judge of character. What are we eating? You like the food here?"

"Yes, it's inventive."

"You always work in restaurants?"

"*Comment?*" French was her default language for mystification.

"I mean, do you ever relax in a restaurant?"

"Well, do you ever relax in a garden?"

"*Touché*. I'll say this for you, you give as good as you get."

She was irked, and she didn't quite understand why.

"Do you come here a lot?"

"I've never brought a mistress here, no." Imogen widened her eyes. "But then I've never had a mistress."

"You could get away with it. You have expert social skills."

"Didn't use to. My wife rubbed off all of my rough edges."

"I can't imagine that you ever had any."

"Cassie saw me as a rough diamond in need of polishing."

"She did a good job."

"You know what you're having?"

"Yes, *Capunatina* and then *sole de Méditerranée*. You?"

Nick answered, at the same time as he told the waiter. *"Le loup de mer et le caviar d'Aquitaine et après Veau de Corréze."*

The *sommelier* followed hot on the heels of the waiter. "Aah! Philippe, *que recommandez-vous comme vin aujourd'hui?* You like red or white?"

"I'm happy to let you choose."

"I feel like I'm being tested. You made mincemeat of me last time."

"I did?"

"Yes, when you told me I know nothing about food."

"You don't."

"And you trust me with the wine?"

"No, I trust Philippe."

"La belle dame sans merci hath thee in thrall." Imogen must have looked surprised at this. "Don't look surprised. I had an education. Who wrote that?"

"No idea."

"Keats. Champagne okay?"

"Lovely."

Without waiting for the *sommelier*'s recommendation, Nick made his own decision about the wine, with the terse brusqueness of the newly rich man who hasn't yet become used to the calming feel of money in his pocket. Imogen didn't like him quite as much at these moments.

"We'll have the 1990 *Legras St Vincent*."

Imogen thought that it was a very good choice, but didn't say so – he was daring her to disapprove.

Philippe nodded his approval, and glided off.

"You speak nice French."

"Nice of you to say so."

"Compared to Jade, I think I'm a pussy cat."
"True. She really scratched and clawed at Frank's poor Casimir."
"Your father-in-law didn't escape either."
"He can fight his own battles."
"You don't like him, do you?"
"He doesn't like me."
"What's not to like?"
"I don't have blue blood."
"Does it matter?"
"It matters to him."
"You've made a success of your life."
"In what way?"
"Money?"
"*Je m'en fou*. I think that's the most meaningless measure of a man's worth. Do you know who's coming to lunch with the Baroness?"
"No idea. You want me to ask?"
"Be helpful, yes."
Instant deflation. Imogen forced a weak smile, and looked away from him, out at the aquamarine, placid sea far below. He was going to use her.
"Aah! You wonder how I love to go on about not giving a fuck about money, and yet I still want to take control of the company, is that it?"
Imogen barely turned her head towards him. She sucked the slightly chilled pine air drifting down off the hills, into her lungs, but with it came the scent of the lovely rose at her breast, now hurtful like smelling salts.
Nick was watching her. "I've upset you, and I don't know why."
Imogen swallowed, almost looked at him, and said it. "You

want me to spy on my clients? Is that why we're having lunch?"

"For fuck's sake you asked me!"

The *amuse-bouche* arrived. Sensing the *malaise* at the table, Jean-Pascal decided against explaining what was lying on the almost empty plates.

Nick tasted the champagne. *"Très bien fait."*

Dismissed, the *sommelier* disappeared. Imogen let the bubbles settle in her glass, without touching it. She admired the presentation of the food in front of her, but didn't eat.

The terrace was busy – it always was; Les Remparts is one of those restaurants people have to say they've been to.

Nick never let an atmosphere get in the way of his food; and he only started talking after he had popped away the chef's tricks, and savoured the champagne.

"So, you think this was all a devilish plan? You think I'm playing you along just to beat my father-in-law? Don't you have any self-worth?"

Imogen wished that she had the guts to stand up and throw the champagne in his face. She should have known. She breathed in deeply, and the Monégasque rose scent stung her nostrils.

"You can say it, I've heard it before. What you really mean is that I'm fat, and I should just be glad that any man takes any notice of me, no matter what he wants, is that it?"

Nick didn't answer. He folded his arms and pursed his lips, mimicking Imogen's strop.

Imogen glared at him. *"Et quoi?"* Always in French for annoyance.

Nick picked up his fork, leaned over to Imogen's plate, speared a morsel of food, and put it up to her lips.

"Who's your favourite artist?" He knew that she was too well-bred to refuse – that would have attracted attention. She ate. "Delicious, isn't it? Who's your favourite artist? On canvas not in the kitchen. Let me guess … Botticelli?"

"No. Andrea del Sarto. He's a nuns' favourite." Her anger had almost run its course. "Who's yours?"

"Rubens." Nick let the word gain some weight before he continued. "Rubenesque women. Now, do you think we could enjoy the lunch? How do you like the food?"

She didn't get it, not immediately; then she did, and suddenly felt better – stupid but better.

"Fabrice? I think he's very talented. I don't like lots of surprises in food, and he knows when to stop.".

"I just realised ... you're a Catholic?"

"You've never had lunch with a Catholic?"

Nick laughed. "It explains a lot."

"I wish I could explain it. 'Never let a man lead you to the foot of the stairs.'"

"*Et pourquoi pas?*"

"That was one of the nuns' warnings. I can remember them all. 'Never ride a bike for too long.' 'Never sit in a very hot bath.' 'Never wear a dress more than five fingers open from the collarbone.'"

"That's a lot of nevers."

"Claudia never took any notice. I've never forgotten."

The *hors d'oeuvres* arrived. Jean-Pascal was relieved that his unlikely couple seemed to be friends again.

"For *Madame Imogène, Capunatina d'Aubergines*, and for *Monsieur* Austin, *le loup de mer avec l'Araignée de mer et le caviar d'Aquitaine*. Enjoy."

Nick had found his manners. "Jean-Pascal, looks amazing."

Imogen drank the champagne.

Nick raised his eyebrows. "Verdict?"

"Very not bad." She saw that Nick had been expecting more. "You don't like being ordinary, do you?"

"No, I got lazy. That's what money does to you – dulls the senses and shines the silver. People think that making money is about being clever. It isn't, it's only about cunning. A panther kills with cunning but you wouldn't take it to the theatre."

"My grandmother had a friend who walked her black panther in its jewelled collar every day along the Promenade des Anglais."

Imogen stopped talking; she realised that Nick was trying to tell her more about himself than she had been asking.

"You're right, I don't know anything about food. Money lets you get away with bullshit."

"I didn't mean …"

Nick cut her off. "I know what you meant, and it was good for me to hear."

"You explained the wine very well, at Frank's lunch."

"Half-remembered phrases from wine magazines."

"You could learn? Add to the roses."

"You read me very well."

An old-fashioned ringtone broke in on whatever Nick was planning on next revealing about himself. "It's Frank. You mind if I take it?"

"Be my guest."

Nick stood up and left the terrace, going through the restaurant and out into the street.

With nothing to do except look at the view, Imogen looked out at it, towards Èze, Beaulieu and the Cap; that finger of St-Jean-Cap-Ferrat, her birthplace, indexed for her, not the people who lived there now, but the ghosts of Marie-Hélène and her friends. From this distance – too far away to see the hot overcrowding – it was possible to believe that the rigidity of dressing for dinner, and the elegance of a White Lady cocktail at six on the terrace, had somehow survived. Somerset Maugham was still opening the doors of the Villa Mauresque to the Windsors and Churchills; and hiding his homosexuality. Resistant to the last, soldiering on while fading into sepia, living on their memories and not much else, the flappers, dewdroppers and Ethels had been carried comatose out of their empty villas; the Vuillard had been sold off at auction by the heirs, who had waited so impatiently in the northern rain for the old bird to lose her plumage; the rings had been reset; and the clothes given to the V&A. For Imogen, the view was not beautiful, it was haunted. She called Claudia. Claudia got in first.

"I hear the Baroness wants you to make a lunch."

"News travels fast."

"Frank was wondering if you knew what it was about?"

"You mean a death, a marriage or a christening?"

"You know what I mean. Is it anything to do with the deal?"

"How would I know? People don't usually include me in their business."

"Well, for friendship's sake and the new house on St Bart's, could you please keep your ear to the ground because that Papoche is a wily old fox."

"No, I won't. I'm a cook not a spy. You're the second person to ask me that today. And what new house? You've got a house there already."

"It's a secret."

"You don't know how to keep a secret."

"What's wrong with you? It's only me who can be horrible to you, not the other way around. Where are you?"

"I'm having lunch."

"Where?"

"Chèvre d'Or."

"Strange place for you to hang out. What's it for, a business lunch?"

"No, I wouldn't call it that."

"What other type of lunch is there?"

"Actually, Clod, I think I'd call it a 'fuck me' lunch."

The Plot Thickens

"SHE'S HIDING SOMETHING," said Claudia, annoyed, coming into the stateroom of the *Claudia*. They were headed for Portofino – a business lunch. Claudia didn't like mystery, not unless she was the one being mysterious.

Frank put down his weekend FT; he read the sections most readers avoided. Knowing how to make it was more important to him than how to spend it (for that he had Claudia). "Who is hiding what ... from whom?"

"Mo is hiding something from me. I think it's a fancy man."

"'Fancy man.' What sort of a phrase is that?"

"From school, the nuns."

"Those nuns had strange ideas about men."

"They had strange ideas about lots of things. You know, she didn't even sound like her."

"You mean frustrated and lonely. Why does she always go for the men she can't have?"

"Because she's thin on the inside."

"Did she say anything about the lunch?"

"Only that she doesn't know anything."

"Didn't think so. She's just serving at the edges. Nick's the one sitting at the table. I just got off the phone with him. Sounded much too happy for a man who isn't certain of winning. What's his marriage like?"

"You saw them together at the luncheon, you work it out."

"Yes, she gave him a surprise. I'm worried she might get a taste for it."

"Sugar-free?"

"Think not."

"Are you going to win?"

Frank shook his head in mock annoyance. "What is it that you want to buy?"

Claudia tried to play her usual arsenal. "It was in your newspaper, the pink one."

"The pink one? Why do you still do this to me? Don't give me an answer. A long time ago, remember, I found out that it was Mo doing the cooking, and I still married you. Where, how much and why?"

"St Bart's, don't know, and he's in jail."

Frank stopped preaching. "Who is?"

"I wasn't really looking, you know me, I can't read for longer than a cappuccino, but the man whose house you said you liked has gone to jail for doing something he shouldn't have done – I mean who cares if nobody get's hurt – and I was just thinking that he's going to need money for the lawyers."

"You were just thinking? Right. Did the nuns teach you all that?"

"All what?" Claudia was already tearing out the old kitchen.

"Ambulance chasing."

"If we offered him half of what it's worth that might reduce his sentence."

"Your thinking is skewed but immaculate."

"Of course it is, I was brought up by nuns." Claudia knew that she had won. Back to the deal that would pay for it. "I asked Mo to listen out at the lunch."

"Good, but without Cassie's support Nick doesn't stand a

chance. Have to play another game. You'd better tell Marcus to have a few more Russian dishes ready. That's why we're going to Portofino, just so you know. Have to find out if anybody knows anything, before calling in Andrei."

"Oh, Frank, no! Not more Russians! I thought the luncheon gave you enough to win?"

"That was before I saw Cassie humiliate her husband. We might need those Russians."

"So, I can make an offer on the house?"

"No."

This word came as a shock to Claudia; she hadn't heard it in a long time.

"Did you say no?"

"Because we can't afford it."

"But we can afford anything?"

"Not at the moment. Goldmine deal went wrong."

"How wrong?" asked Claudia, a little nervously. It was not like Frank to make mistakes.

"Bought at ten, now at two fifty, and I wasn't shorting the stock. Not enough to sink us but it made a big hole below the waterline. Which is why we're also going to Porto Montenegro."

"It's full of Russians!"

"Exactly. From Portofino we'll take the chopper to Tivat and meet the boat there."

"Frank, we have to think of something. Aren't there any Americans with money, or English? And what about Chinese?"

"I don't know any Chinese money. These Russians have money to invest, and they're getting quite good at it. So, you'd better start being nice to them. And whatever you do, don't mention the word chocolate."

Left Bank v Right Bank

FRANK SCHULTE NEEDED this chocolate deal. It couldn't have come along at a better time. And it was all thanks to Claudia's new friendship with Cassandra Austin.

They had both been on the organising committee for a charity ball in Monaco. Frank had bought an entire table of ten (for a hundred thousand euro), and Claudia had mentioned in passing that it might be good for them to sit with Nick and Cassie – "It's probably nothing, but Cassie said something about having to referee between her father and her husband. They're in chocolate."

Frank knew nothing about the business of chocolate, not at the start of the evening, but by the time they got to the auction he had made up his mind to take a punt. Over the next three months he had bought discrete parcels of shares, so as not to move the price too much. Then he called Nick.

"This is Frank. How about lunch?"

"Er, okay, what did you have in mind?"

"Hermitage in Monte Carlo. My office is around the corner. Can you do one o'clock the day after tomorrow?"

"Two secs ... okay, yes, can do."

"*Bon. À bientôt.*"

Nick had not been certain how to react to this approach – friend or foe – but he knew that he had no choice, so, yes, he had agreed.

Instinctively, Nick distrusted Frank. In Nick's Yorkshire eyes, people who grew or made things were moral businessmen, and people like Frank, who moved things around the board, were immoral, living off other people's misery. They restructured, rationalised, downsized, hived-off, turned around, sold-off, and sold-out, without a thought for the humanity buried inside a cash-flow.

Nick was uneasy before the meeting. He had little or no experience of high finance and corporate chicanery; the chocolate business had sufficient capital, and Nick tried to have as little contact as possible with the company's bankers because he knew that they were always reporting back to Papoche. Lacking the contacts, it was not so easy finding out about Frank who maintained a super-rich low profile. By the time he again shook hands with the man, two days after the surprise phone call, Nick knew only that Frank ran a hedge fund out of Monaco, that it had earned its investors consistently high returns; and one other piece of information, given by the CEO of a supermarket group that sold Nick's chocolates, and had 'enjoyed' Frank's attention: "Be careful, he takes no prisoners." In this game, Frank was a cardinal, Nick a postulant.

The first time he drove up to the front of the Hermitage in a Ferrari, Nick had been with Cassie. He had been trembling with excitement: everybody looking at them as they stepped out of the car; people taking photos – Nick had felt like the bee's knees. He took the key out of the ignition, and gave it to the doorman, asking him if he could look after it. Cassie was suddenly furious. "Don't ever do that, ever again," she hissed.

"Do what?"

"Show me up like that. You leave the keys in the car, and then you just walk away. I belong here. If you want to belong, that's what you do."

At the time, Nick had wondered if it worked the same way with a Ford Fiesta. How he'd changed: he had been in Monaco so many times since then that now he didn't see the people staring at him – they didn't belong. Inside the hotel, he took no notice of the marbled luxury; it was just a setting through which he strolled: young, confident and totally at ease; outwardly, at least.

Frank was waiting for him on the terrace, sitting at a good table with a direct view of the port, and chatting with the *sommelier*. It was a glorious Côte d'Azur afternoon, when the sun is shining so brightly that everybody looks as if they have money. As Nick approached, Frank didn't stand up, just waved a casual hand, and immediately included Nick in the discussion. "We have a young and thrusting Right Banker here, Nick. Thinks we Left Bankers are behind the times. Tried to pass me off with a Saint-Émilion. What do you think, find a better restaurant?"

The *sommelier* had obviously heard this line before, for he barely imitated a smile.

Nick understood that the *sommelier*'s opinion was not what mattered, it was what Nick thought about Saint-Émilion.

"Anybody who can grow grapes in that soil gets my vote." Nick was rather pleased with himself; he had played what he thought was a clever answer.

Frank shot back. "Of course you do, you were a gardener."

Was there mockery in Frank's reply? Or was Nick being over sensitive? And why should he be surprised at such a remark, anyway? That was being completely illogical: he had tried to find out about Frank, so why not the other way round? No, Nick was unsettled because Frank's easy way of saying important things offhand suggested to Nick that Frank knew all there was to know; and Nick knew very little.

Frank didn't look at the menu (he hadn't been given one, meaning that he came here a lot); and when the menu was placed in front of Nick, with casual authority he said, "I recommend the gazpacho and the steak tartare."

"Sounds good to me."

"You don't mind if I choose the wine?"

"No, of course not."

Nick could hear himself giving ground over the tablecloth; he was aware of Frank making all the running. He was even more annoyed with himself for both admiring and liking this player.

The first time they met, Frank had been at his most charitable. Now, with money on the menu, Nick had been expecting a more cold-hearted villain, but lunchtime Frank was no different from his charity ball self; dressed down in lilac polo shirt, khaki chinos and Tod's, he was exactly the same as he had been in black tie – affable, charming and disarming. He wore his clothes as easily as he lived comfortably with his wealth. He said very little about himself, because, as Nick well understood, he didn't feel the need to either impress, or stake out a position. He said only that Claudia was well, and he was taking delivery of a new boat.

Glibly, Nick said, "Hard work has its rewards," and then, too late, thought that might have sounded a bit too facile. Somehow, he couldn't quite find his stride.

"Sort of. The guy who ordered it ran out of money, so the shipyard was looking for a deal." Frank made it sound as if saving ten or twenty mill' was nothing out of the ordinary; like getting two for one in a supermarket.

Nick tried not to let his wordless smile express too much admiration, mixed in equal parts with a slightly queasy Yorkshire disapproval.

They drank Haut-Brion, the iconic 1989, but the white, not

the red, because, said Frank, "The red takes too long to open up, and no lunch is important enough to hurry a great wine."

Nick admitted that he had never tried an Haut-Brion white, which caused Frank to smile. "And it's owned by Americans. Clarence Dillon bought it in 1935. He was going to buy Margaux, but it was raining and Haut-Brion was closer to his hotel."

Nick understood this to mean that not all Americans in Europe were philistines.

Frank savoured his wine. "So, you're a *garagiste*?"

Nick shook his head. "I think that Bordeaux needed shaking up. They make wine with love."

"Wines that belong in the Folies Bergère?"

"Yes, where they make love with wine."

Frank enjoyed this quip very much, and laughed. Nick, emboldened, continued: "Mind you, I don't think you could call La Mondotte a garage wine anymore, not at that price."

Frank waved his hand at nothing, expressing disdain. "Agh! They're just picking the grapes one by one simply for the sake of it."

"Perhaps you're right. Still, I like green fingers. Like you say, I'm a gardener. I'm just not so keen on wines made by insurance companies. Who cares if a guy doesn't have a fairytale château to put on the label? I'd rather give him my business than drink a status wine like Pétrus with Russian oligarchs and members of the Chinese Communist Party who don't even know the difference between a Merlot grape and a Cabernet Sauvignon."

Frank shook his head, and smiled benignly. "They give themselves away too early. There's nothing to surprise you later on. This Haut-Brion, keeps talking to you, for hours and hours, lets you find out what it's really about."

And so it went on, as they took up entrenched positions on either side of the Garonne and Dordogne.

Villa Eilenroc

Nick wondered if they would actually ever talk about business. At last, over exotic fruit salad, unable to hold out any longer, he asked Frank why he had bought the shares.

Frank's smile was as well-balanced and restrained as the wine. "You made a good case for them. And now, I suppose, you want to know what I'm going to do with them?"

"Would be nice to know, yes." Nick was well aware that he was being much too eager; it was a reply without finesse, as if he had crashed the gears in his car. Part of him, however, inside, defiantly said, "Unctuous bastard." Was there anything that could break his seemingly impregnable poise?

Frank poured them both the last of the Haut-Brion. "Why don't you tell me again what you want to do with the company, and we'll see if we have the same ideas." He listened without interrupting while Nick laid out his well-rehearsed, sugar-free plans. When he had finished, Frank's summary of the situation was pithy and brutal. "So, you have to ease the old man out."

"Yes, but I don't really want to lose my wife at the same time."

"Then we'll have to think of something." Frank signed the bill and stood up. "Let's stay in touch."

Afterwards, driving the Dino back to Turin, Nick felt as if he had been interviewed, but he had no idea how the interview had gone. He had learned nothing about what Frank was up to, and yet he had the feeling that he, Nick, had given away much too much about himself. But what had he said? All they had talked about was fucking wine; and what did that tell you? He thought about it, driving too fast, and going back over the conversation several times. It came to him in the outside lane. Furiously, he railed at himself, over the roar of the engine: "You fucking amateur, Nick Austin! Drink the wine, and find the man!"

Montecatini Terme

*B*Y THE TIME *you read this, it will be too late: the Russians will have invaded Montecatini Terme, and checked into the Grand Hotel and La Pace Spa, en masse. Blame Svetlana Medvedeva, little Dima's wife, who likes to do good works in couture; she arrived with an entourage almost big enough to fill the hotel; it was out of season, but they opened up, of course they did. And where Sveta goes ...*

The Russians have been here before, a long time ago: in 1908, the Russian ambassador to Italy, Count Nikolay Muravyev, complained about the noise of – no, not other Russians – the cicadas whose chirruping upset his siesta. The quick-thinking general manager sent up to his room two guitarists whose playing put him to sleep; that is what you call five-star service. You might be wondering why the Italians were that eager to keep the Count so sweet? Because the Russians were supplying Italy with kerosene – the oil business has been fuelling hotel politics for a long time ...

A grand hotel is not a grand hotel simply because of the luminaries who have stayed there. True, La Pace has welcomed Giuseppe Verdi, Paul Cézanne, Clark Gable, Grace Kelly, Audrey Hepburn, and Arnold Schwarzenegger, which sounds like a catalogue of culture and glamour giving way to a precipitous decline. No, a grand hotel makes its reputation nowadays by the stories it can upload to the website: there was the Polish count who played a game of tennis in the restaurant; and the English aristo who played nursery games at dinner, flicking cherry stones at the other guests (nobody would have said anything in London).

It is touching the way in which the Italians bravely welcome the marauders: Massimo Giovannetti, who works in the town hall at Montecatini Terme, is absolutely convinced that the effects of Medvedeva's visit "will be seen in the coming months when Russian tourists who love classic spas will visit us in ever greater numbers." I like that phrase about their coming for the "classic spas."

Giuseppe Bellandi, the mayor of Montecatini Terme, has gone even further: he announced that from now on all the signs in the town will be written in Cyrillic as well as in English and Italian. That is very helpful: "Russians this way, Italians over there."

Nick Austin was not aware of the Hotel La Pace's new status, when he booked it for the start of his adulterous affair. He had been there several times with Cassie, during his 'apprenticeship,' as he had called it, otherwise known as an engagement. Cassie had never actually said that she thought of him as a rough diamond, but he knew that there was an underlying purpose to their many weekends spent making love in old European hotels, with four-poster beds and intermittent Wi-Fi – the Negresco in Nice, the Gritti Palace in Venice, Le Richemond in Geneva … It wasn't that he didn't already know how to tip the soup bowl away from him, only that in Cassie's rarefied world people ate oranges with a knife and fork, and couldn't live without grape scissors. He hadn't minded; he had found it easy to put away the gardening tools, and re-pot his life as a businessman and man about town. He had soaked up every experience she had given him, and made it his own – the perfect chameleon.

The big wedding was held at the Cathedral of San Siro, and

the reception at the house in San Remo. Nick's parents were over-awed by the guests' glitter, appalled at the ocean of money, and worried about what effect a life of lived dreams would have on him. Nick told them he would always be the same old Nick – a gardener at heart.

The dowry was even bigger than Nick had calculated: ten million euro deposited into his bank account ("For looking after my daughter, not to spend on yourself," admonished Papoche); two per cent of the ordinary (non-voting) shares of the company; and a specially created ceremonial role of Executive Assistant to the Chairman (Papoche). Faced with the choice of either bringing in an outsider to take over when he retired (many years away, in his eyes), or letting Nick into the business, Papoche had reluctantly decided in favour of family, not thinking that Nick might have had more than ceremony in mind.

Instinctively, Nick had applied gardening techniques to the old-fashioned chocolate empire: weeding out the parts that showed no growth, and bringing on the ones he sensed showed the greatest promise. At first, to keep Cassie happy, and with grandchildren to think about (they arrived two and three years after the wedding), Papoche had agreed to the changes Nick wanted to make, believing that he could always manoeuvre him back into line whenever he chose. That was a miscalculation. Nick soon acquired a taste for chocolate, and had no intention of stepping aside. Nick's success did not cause Papoche to like his son-in-law, rather the opposite; the old man had stopped being entrepreneurial years ago, and yet Nick's ambition was an achievement too far.

Nick's radical idea to introduce sugar-free chocolate into the product range was a line in the sand, not only between him and his father-in-law, but also between him and Cassie. Papoche was dead set against the idea – so much to be expected – but so was

Cassie. Nick had thought (no, assumed) that she would back him in everything when it came to the business, but Cassie said no, she would support him in whatever changes he wanted to make to the management, advertising, packaging, whatever, but not to the chocolates themselves. In the early years of their marriage, Nick would have been able to fuck her into agreeing with him; after the children were born, it was not so easy. Seven years in, measured by most yardsticks, their marriage was a success – moneywise, carewise, sexwise – but the sparkle had dissipated, like the lone glass of prosecco left on a tray at an art opening. Cassie loved her husband as much as she had ever loved him, but love was not the same as chocolate.

Fat Girl Rodeo

THE RUGGER BUGGERS played "Fat Girl Rodeo" at uni. You downed as many pints as you could, and then you jumped on the back of a fat girl, whooping "Yee hah!" until she bucked you off. It was just a laugh, really. And deep down they loved it. They really did. Seriously, they fucking loved it. You got extra banter shag points for "pulling a pig" – fucking the biggest and skankiest minger you could get your drunken hands on. Honestly, they should've been grateful. Herds of total mingers wouldn't have had a shag otherwise, so, you know what, they could think themselves lucky. It was good for them, like hot sperm gargle. Anyway, if they said yes, they were all slags.

Sitting in the Liberty Bar of the Grand Hotel La Pace, waiting for Imogen to come down, to join him for dinner, it was hard to imagine, and painful to remember, that "Fat Girl Rodeo" had once been Nick's favourite game. Was that how he used to be? Thinking about it now, he felt doubly ashamed: that wasn't the way to treat a woman, and he secretly liked fat girls. It was like being gay, and going out with your mates, queer bashing for a lark. Was he still, perhaps, in some way, that same rodeo man? In what ways had he changed? He had a lot of money, a wife and two children; did that make him any different?

He ordered a dry martini, and asked the barman to put a bottle of Ruinart on ice. So far, the subterfuge had all gone to plan: he'd got her here, she loved the hotel, said the suite was *très jolie*; and his wife was none the wiser. He'd had to make the arrangements himself – couldn't risk asking his secretary to organise his affair. He'd booked a private Cessna at Nice airport, to pick her up and deliver her to Pisa, where he'd picked her up in the Dino, having driven down after work, from the factory in Turin.

He turned around on the bar stool, to take in the vast *Salone degli Archi*, with its overstuffed sofas, palatial chandeliers, Persian carpets, and monastic echo. "My God," he thought to himself, "I've come so far: from easyJet to Netjets." This was the grandest of grand hotels: there was nothing intimate about this hospitality space; the enormous room could pack in a couple of hundred moneyed people – "Well, if you're gonna cheat, cheat in style."

He was alone at the bar; the season was almost ended, and the general manager had told him that there were not so many guests. "From Moscow, from Nizhny Novgorod, from Ekaterinburg, from Khanty Mansiysk." He pronounced the Slavic names without a slip, and with an uneasy smile. Nick had taken this to mean that there were not so many Russian guests as he might have feared.

A pianist was mechanically playing Scott Joplin, seated at a grand piano situated way down at the other end of the room. He was so far away that the sound lost its crisp syncopation, drifting across the ornate distance.

Imogen had said that she wouldn't be long getting settled in, but Nick told her not to hurry. "We're in Tuscany."

"And you live in Italy!"

She looked nervous as hell. In truth, he wasn't much better. He was happy to have a drink, and try to get his head around what he was doing.

He had been faithful to Cassie, up to now. He hadn't ever

been tempted by the high-class tarts who lounged in the bars of five-star hotels, pretending badly that they were meeting somebody. Sometimes, they did it so well they really could have been the real thing. Real thing? Everybody was on the make, so why not be a whore? He had no intention of fucking them, not because he thought that the sex would be mechanical, or he'd feel guilty afterwards. No, he'd avoided them because he was never going to pay for pussy. Why, then, did he now want to fuck a woman three times the size of his wife? Good question. Unless you were into big women, nobody would understand the attraction; that's just how it was.

He was taking something of a risk, make that a big risk. If he got caught, Cassie would never support him, whatever he wanted to do with the business. Then there was Frank; what was the fancy term for being stuck between a rock and a hard place? Scylla and Charybdis? He'd be up shit creek without a paddle.

After the lunch at the Hermitage, there had been the lunch in Saint-Tropez. That had been some lunch; the effect on Nick had been cumulative. As course followed course, and one great wine followed another, he had felt like a fag in the presence of a prefect; it had been a lesson in the uses of sophistication. Yes, Cassie had taught him only about the externals of being rich; Frank was initiating him into a secret society. Three days after the lunch, Nick had worked out, from digging around in the share register, that adding up the shares sitting around the table in St-Trop, came to eighteen and a half per cent – that was what the lunch had been about – but even with Cassie's shares, that still didn't give him control; and he couldn't be sure that Cassie would play ball. She'd told him she would never agree to a sugar-free product line. Fuck her.

He ordered another drink. And what were those new Russian

shareholders doing? Who were they? Frank, he suspected, knew more than he was letting on. Was he working in concert with them? If not, why had they bought when they did? It couldn't be coincidence. They had bought a big slice, with a web of dummy companies; and Nick doubted that he could find out who were the real people behind them, not without outside help. Well, they would show their hand soon enough. All in all, what with Cassie, Frank and the Russians, that made the prospect of fucking Imogen O'Rorke even more of a gamble, and even more of a turn-on.

He'd booked the second biggest suite in the hotel. He couldn't remember if he'd been in that room with Cassie or not; not that it mattered: to fuck or not to fuck, there didn't seem much point in having delicate moral scruples, not now – you can't have half an affair. He wasn't going to play that inter-connecting room bullshit game. If you want something that bad, play for high stakes.

Imogen was up for it. He hadn't asked her outright; he'd learned a few manners since uni, more subtle than, "Fancy a shag?" How did he know he was going to have an affair with her? Because she'd been giving off more "fuck-me" vibes than a fracking drill.

What was it about her? That was easy to explain: she was twin-engined – she was big, and she had class. Of course, Cassie had class, but Imogen had a different type of class, less uptight. Cassie never let up, not if she thought he was letting her down: the time he wore a dark blue suit to a festival party in Cannes, with a "Strictly Black" dress code; the party in Menton where Kate Moss was expected, and Nick asked his hostess, "Is Kate here?" And he wasn't allowed to look at other women, not even out of the corner of his eye, or she'd explode, there and then; she'd screamed at him once in the middle of a wedding reception, and thrown part of the cake at him. She was a jealous bitch – something to do with her mother, he guessed. Imogen, however, reminded him of the girls who went to hunt balls in Yorkshire, the "taffeta tarts" he and the boys had called them. You could give them one behind the marquee, or, if it was really muddy, with their legs jammed against the roof, clutching their tiaras, in the back of a Land Rover. Cassie was good in bed – thank God she liked big cock – but there wasn't an ounce of spare flesh on her, and she wasn't very adventurous. The best fucks were always the well-bred ones who'd been brought up on a farm or in a convent; pussy and pearls – a posh fuck is the best fuck.

His whole life at the moment seemed to hinge on a succession of lunches – Monte Carlo, St-Trop, Èze. That made sense: lunches were for manoeuvring, dinners were for doing the dirty deed. After Èze, he'd given it two weeks (to whet her appetite), and then he'd called her. He'd asked her point blank: "What are you doing next weekend?"

His day-dreaming was interrupted by a loud male voice booming next to him: "Do you know how to make a Moscow Mule?" The Russian accent was thicker than the traffic fumes on Kutuzov Prospect.

"*Si signor*." The barman set to work.

Nick turned his head slightly to see who it was. The man had the build of a weightlifter – medium height, cropped blond hair, bull neck, barrel chest. He was dressed in a very expensive pale grey silk suit, with an open-neck purple silk shirt; and he wore sharp alligator shoes that looked as if they might bite. He was clothed in gorgeous peacock fabrics, but there was menace in his demeanour, as if he might flex his muscles at any moment, burst the buttons on his shirt, squat down, and perform a clean and jerk, with whatever came to hand. Nick was fascinated by

Villa Eilenroc

his watch: it was full of diamonds that rolled around inside the case whenever he moved his arm.

Nick thought that he should be polite, and some aimless chatter would stop him from going upstairs, to try to get a fuck before dinner. "What's in a Moscow Mule? Snow and vodka?"

The man smiled. "You English are so funny. Vodka, ginger beer and lime." The man had the look of a brute but he was friendly. He put out his hand as if he had known Nick for years: "Tikhon. My friends call me Tisha."

"Nick, short for Nicholas." Nick was already more than a little drunk – too much Dutch courage before adultery. "And what do your enemies call you?"

Tikhon thought this was very funny: "I don't have any enemies!" Funny to him because he was the one still alive.

"Lucky you."

"No, they were unlucky." There was no darkness whatsoever in Tikhon's tone, but Nick's mind threw up images of silenced men hidden away in concrete suits.

"Where are you from?"

"Khanty Mansiysk. It's an oil town."

"I don't know any Russians."

"So, it is your lucky day, Nick."

Tikhon downed his drink in one gulp. "Listen, I go fuck upstairs, then I come back in twenty minutes." Tikhon put out his hand to be shaken, Russian style, ignored the barman – because he couldn't give a fuck about the bill – and strode off.

Shaken, Nick's hand still hovered in the air. Nick said only, "I'll be here." Without thinking it through, he had a sudden thought: "Why don't you join us for dinner? I have a friend, she'll be here soon."

Tikhon was already out the door, but he turned round, and

continued walking, backwards. "Nice idea! You like Château Le Pin?"

Nick was caught off guard by this – unusual choice for a bruiser – but he raised his voice to match. "Yes, of course, who doesn't?"

"I tell them in the restaurant. *Ciao*."

Nick had another drink, and then another. How many was that? Four or five? Fucking would have been a better idea than an aperitif.

"Penny for your thoughts." Imogen was standing behind him. She put her hands on his shoulders, the first time she had openly touched him like a mistress-to-be.

Nick leaned backwards into her touch, but his mind was not on dalliance. "Honestly, you couldn't make it up. Everything they say about them is true. Of course, he knows absolutely fucking nothing about wine."

"What's true?" Imogen had already decided, days before, that she would not attempt to scale a barstool, and suffer the humiliation of Nick having to crane her on to it. So she carelessly placed her clutch bag where her ass should have been, and pressed her ass against the mahogany counter, allowing her to admire, with a feigned appreciation, the vista of bourgeois furniture facing her.

"Russians. Look, over there. The older guy with the very young girl who isn't his daughter. They're looking at the jewellery."

"You mean my next-door neighbour?" If Imogen was surprised, she didn't let on.

"Neighbour where? The room next door?"

"No, in Cap d'Antibes. He lives next door. Not all the time. He's got houses everywhere, so he says. Aren't you going to offer me a drink? I'll have a Peach Bellini." Imogen kept talking because, standing, as she was, very close to Nick, was wrecking her equipoise. It was that so familiar aftershave, and the tamed waves in his hair; she wondered what it would feel like, later on, to run her fingers over the curling ups and downs, with his head on a pillow. "His name's Tikhon."

"Yeah, he told me. We said hello."

"It means fate apparently. I know him quite well. His guests keep arriving at my jetty. I told you. He comes over to apologise. Sweet of him, isn't it? He's loud, but I really quite like him. I think he's more clever than he looks. Horrible shiny suit."

"Good, because we're having dinner with them."

"*Comment?*" French for what the fuck are you doing. "You're not serious? You invite me away for a weekend, and then you invite people we don't know for dinner?"

"You just said you do know him. I promise I'll make it up to you afterwards."

"You're unbelievable. And you're drunk."

"You'd better believe it."

"You're up to something."

"Isn't that what you wanted?"

"You know what I mean! Oh, this is hopeless. What am I going to talk to her about? Have you seen the size of her?"

"Yes, scrawny. He must be buying her some baubles. You look nice."

Imogen didn't think that "nice" was a good enough word to describe what she was wearing, but she kept quiet. It had taken her a long time to make up her mind: a dark brown ruched silk cocktail dress, cut on the bias, with a long-sleeved lace bustier over her breasts.

Nick caught the disappointment. "Actually, what I meant was you look fab. Who's it by?"

"Giambattista Valli."

"Never heard of him, but it's still nice. They're coming over. Be nice, please, for me."

"I know how to behave, thank you."

Tikhon was striding towards them, with a girl by his side. He commanded attention no matter what size room he was in; from ten metres away his voice had an operatic reach. "My wife, she gets a dozen of roses. This one, she gets a dozen of rubies!"

Without breaking his parade ground stride, Tikhon marched up to Imogen, and put his arms around her, exclaiming, as he pressed himself enthusiastically against her breasts, in the most atrocious French accent: *"Mon Dew!* The world is a *petite* place! *Mon voizin!* This is Katya." He released Imogen, with a smacking kiss on both cheeks, and presented Katya, like a sergeant major showcasing the regimental mascot. "She dances a little and spends a lot of money."

Off-stage, the multi-talented Katya was much less dramatic in person than the roles that, no doubt, gave her character when in costume. She was a bob-haired brunette; gaunt, no tits, as thin as a lure coursing whippet, and with chalk-coloured skin that seemed to have been applied to her bones by a *patissier* working with filo pastry. She was wearing a severe black suede dress, of a schoolgirl cut, and tottering on very high black suede stiletto heels with tell-tale red soles – Christian Louboutin. She was weighed down by her latest present from the beneficent and besotted Tikhon: a necklace of cabochon rubies, bought a few minutes earlier, that flashed and sparkled with such explosive intensity, she looked as if she were dancing *The Firebird*.

Nick held out his hand to her. "Hello, I'm Nick, and this is Imogen."

Of course, Imogen instantly disliked any woman this size, and she had an urge to say, *"Écoutez moi bien, mademoiselle.* We're not married. We're just about to start an affair, and you're interrupting." Well-bred to the last, however, she didn't. The anger came out, she hoped, warm and deadly: *"Quelle surprise! We come all the way to Montecatini Terme, and here you are, mes voisins* – my neighbours." The translation was for Katya's benefit.

Katya, however, to Imogen's fury, had manners as vampy as her shoes, and an education to match. *"Vous êtes voisins? C'est drôle."*

"Mais oui. Vous parlez français?"

"Bien sûr, je suis une ballerine. Avec le Bolchoï de Moscou."

Imogen was now as angry as Katya's rubies. She raged silently at Nick, who was gripping the bar stool with both hands, whether from fear or alcohol she didn't much care. "How could you!" she screamed at him silently. "On our first night! I'm going to feel like a Jumbo parked next to a Gulfstream! And you've been drinking too much! You'll be no use to me later!"

Tikhon, catching her anguish, winked at Imogen, and in a low, conspiratorial tone said something in Russian that sounded something like: *"Ya lublyu potnikh zhenzhin."*

Imogen, understanding nothing, politely said, "Thank you."

Katya helpfully translated. "He said, 'I love women who sweat.' I think he means big."

Tikhon chided his most treasured possession, knowing that the goodwill of the rubies would last a little while longer. "Look at this one, she's only good for *Swan Lake.* Let's eat. I'm hungry." With that, he gallantly escorted Imogen into the restaurant, saying, "She is young. She will learn. 'Everything has beauty but not everyone sees it.' Old Russian proverb."

Imogen could have hugged him for that.

Nick followed, walking very carefully, with Katya by his side.

"Can you lift your legs above your head? I saw it done once. She was wearing rubies just like yours."

"Not real ones."

The restaurant was expecting a very generous evening; they could not do enough for Tikhon and his guests, fawning as if they could already feel the tips bulging in their pockets.

Tikhon was in charge of the proceedings. He told the *maitre d'* that he didn't like sitting in a corner, and commandeered the table in the centre of the room. He ordered for everybody, telling them what they would like. As far as Imogen could tell, they were not the only Russians in the room – she thought she heard the language at two other tables – but they were certainly the loudest. A table of stately Italians watched them as if this were an *opera bouffe*. Strangely, this didn't bother Imogen, she who was normally so socially correct. She liked the bold way Tikhon wore his money like armour, not for protection, but to charge into the furious *mêlée* of pleasure. And he was nobody's fool, she was pleased to see: when the first decanter of Le Pin arrived, Tikhon summarily told the *sommelier* to bring him the bottle; Imogen cringed, thinking that he wanted to trumpet something about the vintage, but when the bottle appeared, Tikhon didn't brandish the label for approval and attention. There was still a little wine left in the bottle; Tikhon poured it into a glass, drank from it, and said nothing; the *sommelier* looked a little discombobulated; and Imogen couldn't think what Tikhon was doing; and then he drank the mouthful of wine sitting in the glass, poured from the decanter. He made very little show of savouring the wine, merely nodded, satisfied, and said, "Okay, it's the same." When, after they had quickly got through the first bottle, and another decanter was immediately brought to the table – Tikhon had given orders for the wine to be free-flowing – the *sommelier*, without needing to be asked, brought the bottle for inspection, and Tikhon, having made his point, merely fanned his fingers. Nobody cheated Tikhon (and lived to tell the tale). He reminded Imogen of a medieval tsar, taking his very public pleasures with calculated care – terrible to behold.

Imogen looked at the four of them sitting there, and thought that they were a very mismatched quartet: she and Tikhon looked as if they belonged together; and Nick and Katya made a lovely couple. Nick was very quiet, playing page to Tikhon's knight.

Tikhon dominated the table and the conversation. "I bought a vine yard this afternoon," he announced, trashing the word "vineyard" so that it sounded as if he had picked up a bunch of grapes in a backyard.

"Pétrus? It's much more famous than Le Pin," said Nick, with a top note of sarcasm.

Imogen wished that Nick would tone it down. She was starting to understand why Cassie had embarked on a programme of cultivation; Nick was undeniably gorgeous, but he had a crude side that appeared when it shouldn't. Women only wanted a cock in the bedroom, not at the dinner table.

"Agh!" exclaimed Tikhon, dismissively. *"Nouveaux riches!"* This phrase he knew how to pronounce correctly. "What do they know about wine? I've been rich for ten years. What do these people know about anything who made their money yesterday?"

Imogen laughed. The evening was turning out to be more fun than she had expected; and there was sex for afterwards.

"Where is the vineyard?" she asked.

"Sauternes. You know where it is?"

"Is it in Bordeaux?" asked Imogen, innocently, not because she wanted to play with him, or catch him out, but because she was interested to hear what he would say.

Nick guffawed with laughter. "You know exactly where it is, and what it is! She's playing with you, Tikhon. Cooking is her job, you didn't know?"

"You can cook?" Tikhon sounded as if he were interviewing a prospective bride.

"She makes her living cooking! You've never tasted food like it. It's an education."

"You want to cook for me? Next week in Montenegro. I need to make them sweet, and make them sweat, get my money back."

Imogen smiled. "Well, you could do that with Sauternes."

Nick was instantly sober. "Deal gone wrong?"

Tikhon shook his head. "Another time, Nick. Never in front of women."

Chastened, Nick switched tack. "Why Sauternes? You didn't want a famous Pomerol like Le Pin?"

Tikhon was happy to talk with his mouth full. "You know the Russian saying 'A fool and his money are easily parted'? Perhaps it's an English saying? Who cares. What sort of a bargain is there in Pomerol? Russians have a sweet tooth. You know that the tsars drank Sauternes? That's a history worth selling. And I have a few wine shops."

"Hundreds of shops," said Katya.

Tikhon liked to spend his money, not to talk about how it was made. "Now, let's have Sauternes! Mine."

Nick couldn't imagine what the bill would be like. "On top of all that Pomerol?"

Tikhon, disdainful of economy, asked, "What is money? 'The one who dies with most toys, still dies.'"

And so they drank Tikhon's Sauternes.

When, at last, they parted for the evening – the last ones to leave the restaurant – Tikhon repeated his offer of work, to Imogen. "I have a boat in Montenegro. Come and do the cooking. We can talk over the fence in Cap d'Antibes."

Villa Eilenroc

She was lying below him, wanton. The dough of her skin settled down around her, spreading over the Persian carpet. Instead of trying to scoop it up, and hide it away, as she had always done, ashamed, now she let it ooze and seep. The rage of his cock gave her confidence.

Nick dropped to his knees. He scooped her left breast out of her bra; it blancmanged down the front of her stomach, like molten lava from a volcano. She put her hands up to staunch the flow; he wouldn't let her. He held her hands tight in his, and watched the lazy movement of the breast as it drooped and settled, like pizza dough finding its shape on a baker's shovel. He let the other breast alone, as if he wanted to see her lying there, slatternly. Before she could stop him, he had pulled her knickers off. Imogen clamped her hands between her legs, locked like a chastity belt. Nick prised them apart. He looked her straight in the eye, and said, tightly, "Nice vajazzle. Swarovski?"

If that was meant to put her at ease, it didn't work. Imogen immediately glued her hands together again, shielding herself. Nick shook his head, and let out an annoyed sigh. He lay down on his stomach, trying to find a comfortable position for his swollen cock, pressed stiff against the carpet. From her pillowed vantage point, Imogen looked over her freed breast, and watched him, looking up at her from between her legs. Nick raised himself up slightly, as if he were about to say something, which unexpectedly caused her to giggle, and mumble how, "A gentleman always raises his weight off his elbows."

Nick grinned. "They gave you an interesting sex education in that convent."

She relaxed the grip of her hands. His mouth was that close, she could feel his breath warming and teasing her pussy; that lovely, soft, caressing, catch-all word men use as shorthand for what surely deserves and demands a more detailed and intimate look: the raised mons (with a Hollywood, not Brazilian wax); the long, untanned lips of *labia majora*; the darker flower petals of *labia minora*, surrounded by Hart's Line. Hot breath – as if he wanted to inflate her insides like a hot air balloon. She tensed all of the muscles in her buttocks and thighs, squeezing, and closing off, but only for a few, delicious, milliseconds, the vestibule – "vestibule"! What an amazing word to describe the antechamber of all pleasure – "Come on in, right this way, sir." Inside, thousands of nerve endings shivered and tremored. The anatomy of desire.

God knows if she said anything that made any sense. "Nuns! Hah! You have no idea what they taught us. You were going to say something?"

"Yes." Nick paused, as if he were about to deliver a lecture, which, in effect, was what he did, in a low, enticing timbre; Miles Davis in the background.

"So, Imogen O'Rorke, here we are. Consenting adults? This is what I've always wanted, if I'd ever been brave enough. What? You think you can't have this?"

She confessed. "Women like me aren't built for love."

"You'll never believe it, but I like this size."

"You'll still hurt me."

"Yes. And I'm not going to leave my wife. And I'm not going to marry you. And it's no use praying. It won't last a lifetime – who knows, it won't even last a year."

She was thinking that he was anything but merciful. "That's what I meant. That's what frightens me – I get what I want and then I lose it."

"Everything gets lost. And when it ends you'll be miserable. I'll probably be miserable too. But we'll have fun while it lasts. Now, you want me to make love to you or not?"

There was a pause. Nick retreated, and his tongue grazed and probed the fleshy inside of her lips.

Imogen heard herself say, more pleading than agreeing, "Yes, I want to."

"Right, so, will you please move your hands away and open your legs wide."

Lucca

"YOU DON'T HAVE much money, do you?" asked Nick. He had to shout above the whine of the Dino engine, screaming right behind their heads.

"I have inherited poverty!" shouted Imogen. She had given up trying to hold on to her hair, and now it was streaming wildly off her scalp, Medusa-like.

Nick laughed. "As opposed to inherited wealth? I like that."

"You think that because I cook for rich people, and live in Cap d'Antibes, I must have money?"

"Now I've seen your garden, no."

"Is that how you tell if somebody has money? Because of their garden?"

"Yeah, I think it's a good way. A garden's about who you are."

"Most of the people I know are fucking their gardeners."

"And now you're fucking me, just like your friends."

"How many of my friends are you fucking?"

"I didn't mean it that way. What position did you like the best?"

"All of them. Mmm ... what did you call it? Reverse cowgirl."

Nick gave a whoop of pleasure. "Yee hah! You made me a very happy cowboy!"

"Where are we going?"

"I told you, it's a surprise. You want to stop for lunch or sex?"

Villa Eilenroc

"That's more direct than saying we've run out of petrol."

"It's not very far. You're not hungry?"

"After that breakfast, no."

"Scrambled eggs and cunnilingus. I couldn't eat another thing."

"Like I said, the nuns warned us about men like you."

"You have been warned."

They raced through the Tuscan countryside. Imogen marvelled at the way Nick threw the car around the roads. He seemed to have no interest in slowing down to look at anything picturesque; strange for a man who so liked gardens, which needed time to love; even his love of beauty was single-minded. She guessed that he was in a hurry to get somewhere; he wanted to show her something. She saw the sign for Lucca, and guessed where they were going.

Reaching the walled town, they drove through the archway of Porta San Pietro, and into mediaeval, renaissance, and tourist Italy.

"They don't like you driving into the town, but I suppose it's okay in a Ferrari."

"Spoken like an arrogant, rich prick. I bet you think they won't give you a ticket either."

Nick parked the car in a tiny, deserted square. He got out and came around to open Imogen's door.

"Puccini was born here," he said, and immediately went off to buy a parking ticket.

Imogen wondered what Puccini had to do with anything – they're being here. Some sort of operatic drama? Whatever. And then, as soon as she stepped out of the car, the elation of the drive disappeared. They would be walled in all day, and, although she had never been here before, she sensed that they had come to a place with a beauty that she would find as much claustrophobic and oppressive, as uplifting and romantic. Nick had brought her here for a reason; perhaps he thought that it would be a lovely day out – of course, much of it would be enjoyable and fun – but that was not the thought nagging uppermost in Imogen's mind. There was nothing in any way remarkable about this particular Italian square, nothing of any historical or architectural note, and perhaps that was exactly why, here, at the very start of their first public excursion as lovers, remembering what he had said the night before, head between her legs, she was struck by a horrible foreknowledge of what was in store for them. The whole arc and history of their adulterous relationship came to her with a terrible, stinging and prophetic pain; and she spoke the words, Cassandra-like, before she could think about the consequences.

"You're going to break my heart, aren't you?"

"Isn't that what you want?" Nick seemed unruffled by the question. He put the parking ticket on the dashboard. "Come on then. Bit late to have second thoughts."

Imogen walked in step with him. She wondered if he would hold her hand; if he did, she decided that it would mean he wasn't ashamed of how fat she was; if he didn't, it meant that she was just a fuck toy. He held her hand.

"I've never been here," she replied, by way of an answer to what he thought she wanted from their relationship, which seemed, to her, like a pretty good way of not answering. She was thinking about Puccini and grand passion going wrong. "I'll follow you, seeing how you know your way around so well."

"Okay, but today is all for you. We'll go wherever you want to go. But the last hour there's somewhere I'd like to see ... to show you."

"Is this where you bring all your mistresses?"

"I told you, I've never had a mistress."

"I thought there would be more tourists?"

"It's lunchtime, the season's over, and it's not half-term."

Imogen didn't want to be reminded of Nick's children. They were standing in front of a church. "How about a moment of reflection before the shops open?"

"You're the boss."

On the steps of the Chiesa dei santi Paolino e Donato, Imogen read an inscription on a municipal notice board. "In 1877, Puccini's first work was played here: Motetto for Baritone with four-part chorus and orchestra."

Nick was already at the church door. "He was a serial adulterer, did you know that?"

"So, we've come to the right place, you and I."

"I'm not into confession. But I'll buy you as many candles as you wish."

She wished that he could be serious sometimes, without the envelope of flippancy. "It's a church, not a bathroom."

Imogen followed Nick into the chilled interior. She devoutly crossed herself, and noticed that Nick didn't. He caught her looking at him.

"What?"

"Don't you believe in anything?"

"Oh yes. Me."

They were the only people there. They walked together down the nave. Imogen thought about a marriage ceremony, with Puccini's music. The lunchtime sunshine hit the luscious colours of the vaulted ceiling above the altar, and the over-decorated walls rising above the apse; writhing and ascending figures in exultant and soaring states of undress. On Imogen, the passionate vision had exactly that effect: filled her soul with joy. On Nick, there was no effect other than the factual.

"Low church nave, high baroque altar. Like a theatre."

Imogen tried not to make any sound with her shoes.

Nick was still thinking about Puccini. Perhaps the church was having some effect. "He also liked fast cars and yachts. Puccini, I mean, not Christ."

"Bit like you, then." Imogen didn't like talking in church.

Nick wouldn't let go of Puccini. "That's why he wrote adulterous music."

Imogen wondered if she could make him into a Catholic.

"You think that sex is the answer to everything."

"No, I think that sex is the key to everything."

They were before the altar. Imogen craned her neck backwards, her eyes rising up to the ecstatic epiphany of the barrel-vaulted roof.

"Make a nice chocolate box," said Nick. There was a pause.

"When was the last time you had an orgasm?"

"You want me to confess? Here?"

"Isn't it good for the soul?"

"Before last night, never."

There was a pause while he took this in. "There you are, then."

Outside in the street, the shops were re-opening.

"You don't mind if we have a look in some food shops?" asked Imogen.

"That's the same voice Cassie uses when she wants to buy clothes."

"Food is cheaper."

"I don't care about the money. This day is all for you."

Phrases like that can make a woman fall in love with a man, even if she has doubts about him.

In La Grotta di Calderia, Pizzicheria dal 1865, Nick paid for *Savini Tartufi, Pomodori secchi Italiani, Fungo Porcino, Lardo di Colonata,* and *Pecorino di Lucca.*

At the Apicoltura Guidotti open-air stall on Via S. Antonio, Nick paid for *Miele Italiano di Acacia e fichi.*

In Panificio Chifenti dal 1923, Nick paid for *Torta d'Erbi coi Becchi*. They ate it outside in the street, washed down with a can of Coke.

"I feel like a poor student again," said Nick.

"You wouldn't know how to live without money, not now."

"You think I'm too used to it?"

"It happens. Could you ever give up that Ferrari?"

"It would be very difficult to say goodbye to her."

"Me, you could say goodbye to."

Nick gave her a thin smile. Then, flicking a different switch, he suddenly started laughing.

"Now, what? Why are you laughing?"

"I'm just thinking that every shop we've been into has looked like a Disneyworld fantasy. Like this next one you won't be able to resist, La Bottega di Prospero."

Inside, Imogen went into raptures; she sniffed and smelled the bags of herbs and spices, like the nose in a perfume business. Finally, after much anguish, and because she felt guilty about Nick taking out his wallet so often, she chose only two: *Aglio Olio & Peperoncino* and *Gricliata Alle Rosa*.

"That's all? I can afford ten euro."

"So can I. It isn't about the money."

At Forno a Vapore on Via Santa Lucia, Nick paid for *Valdostana*.

"You know, you could almost believe this is how all Italians live," said Imogen.

"Instead of really going to supermarkets, you mean?"

They walked straight past Caniparoli Cioccolateria on Via S. Paolino. Nick said, "I don't want to think about chocolate today."

"And I don't want to think about your wife. Let's stop and have a drink. How about here?"

Nick read the ornate sign: "Ricci & Pieri, Antico Caffè di Simo. Sounds a lot nicer than Starbucks."

They ordered a glass of wine and tapas, which, for Imogen, proved to be a difficult choice: *Salsiccia, Pate di Fegato, Lardo, Panzanella* ...

"What is this?" she asked the barman.

"Fish."

"We'll have two of everything," said Nick, decisively.

An elegant old lady, dressed in a pale green silk cocktail dress, amber necklace, and bearing an immaculate coiffure of a colour that matched her necklace, walked in and stood at the bar, next to Nick and Imogen, nibbling their tapas, and enjoying the wine. She said nothing. A minute later, a tiny glass of espresso appeared on the counter. She sipped it very slowly, in complete silence. Imogen noticed that she was wearing navy deck shoes. When the old lady had finished, she laid out some money on the counter, and walked out, as peaceful and satisfied as if she had left the confessional.

"Some people have their lives organised so well," was Nick's comment. He was happy. "Puccini used to come in here for coffee. Played the piano over there."

"You have this day all organised, don't you?"

"I like to know where I'm going."

"You have the looks for an Italian tour guide."

"Ouch! And is all this food I know by now you're going to copy, for me, or for work?"

"I could cook it for you if you want, but I was thinking about cooking Italian for Tikhon."

"You think he was serious?"

"He sent me a text message this morning confirming. Said the menu was up to me. For up to eight people. It's on a yacht in Porto Montenegro. I've never been. It'll be fun."

"How does he have your number?"

"I gave him my card last night. You're jealous?"

"I just think it's interesting why he wants you to cook, that's all. Doesn't he have one?"

"You told him how good I am! I thought you'd be pleased."

"I wonder if Frank's involved."

"Why on earth would you think that? He didn't mention Frank."

"I don't know. Just a thought."

"You want me to tell you what happens, don't you?"

"I've learned my lesson. Not if you don't want to."

"I'll take that as a yes."

They walked down the Via Del Fosso, by the river, and into San Croce.

Nick was hungry. "Antico Osteria, *gia dal* 1650. How about lunch here?"

"No, too perfect."

"It's romantic."

"Yes, exactly, like we're in a film or something."

"You just spent hours going into shops straight out of a film set!"

"That was different. We'll find something."

Nick shook his head. "I'm starving."

Obediently, he followed Imogen while she looked for the perfect place to eat. A few minutes later, she stopped on Via Della Fratta, by a little trestle blackboard – like something out of a nursery school – that was propped outside what looked like a junk shop; this was La Bottega delle Cose Buone.

Imogen took one look and said, "Perfect."

Nick read the menu, written in chalk on the blackboard.

"Fifteen euro for a whole lunch? You want to eat here?"

"It says they serve *Vini I prodotti tipici lucchesi*." Imogen went inside.

Nick followed. "Glamorous place. Looks like they raided a junk shop."

"Yes, and there's also marble table tops and rattan chairs."

"If it makes you happy."

Nick was right, the restaurant looked as if the owners had furnished it in a charity shop. There was a delicatessen vitrine and an old-fashioned mahogany counter bar in the front section; and up a short flight of stairs, the restaurant area with six tables. Old black and white advertisements for Fry's Cocoa and Cadbury's Cocoa were hanging on the wall, together with a motley assortment of other framed odds and ends. Four voluble Italians were having a late lunch, chatting with a burly, bearded man in a chef's apron, whose confident manner suggested he could also be the owner.

Behind the bar stood a very attractive young Italian girl, polishing glasses. She was a long-haired brunette, pale-skinned, intelligent, virginal; T-shirt and jeans. Nice figure. She looked bored and tired.

"For two?" asked Nick.

The girl raised a glass in the direction of the restaurant.

"Menus are on the table."

They took a seat nearest to the bar, and looked at the short menu.

"How did you find this place?" asked Nick.

"I didn't. We walked past it."

"It wasn't planned?"

"No, I don't have a secretary."

"How?"

"Just a hunch: no tourists, no photos of dishes on a board outside, no pizza."

"And a bearded chef."

"Oh, yes, that was the deciding factor."

At that moment, a ginger-haired young man walked in; the look and demeanour of a backpacker who had stayed – tousled, studious, carefree, intense. Rolex watch. He sat down on a bar stool. He exchanged no greeting with the bar girl, and she said nothing to him. He ordered nothing. The bearded man, noting his entrance, leaned back in his chair. *"Buona sera, Ryan."*

"Buona sera, signor." Nice accent. Been here a while. Must be American with a name like that.

Studying the menu, Nick and Imogen heard everything that passed between the bar couple.

The girl polished the glasses, vigorously. "I told you, it isn't going to happen."

"I love you."

"I cannot leave my father. He needs me. He says he cannot keep it open without me."

"What about us?"

The bar girl left Ryan to his heart's unhappiness, and came to take their order. Imogen ordered for herself: *"Tortelli lucchesi al ragu, lo spezzatino di cinta con patate."*

"And for you *signor*?"

"Lardo della Garfagnana i trippa lucchese. And a bottle of the best wine you have. Tuscan. Your choice."

Nick was flirting. Imogen didn't mind, not that much, as long as he didn't think he could get away with it every time.

The bar girl gave the check to the bearded chef.

"Papa," was all she said.

The chef immediately stood up, excused himself, and went into the kitchen.

"You eat tripe?" asked Imogen.

"Sure do. Deep down, I'm still a flat cap Northerner."

"Flat cap?"

"Gardener class."

The wine arrived. Nick looked at the label – a Super Tuscan

2008, *Solaia, Marchesi Piero Antinori* – and had the grace to admit his surprise. "I'll admit I was wrong about here."

The owner's daughter smiled, and poured out the wine. "You haven't tasted the food yet."

"With wine like this, how could it not be good? And a glass for the man whose heart you've broken."

The girl gave Nick a look both pained and quizzical, but she poured out a small glass for Ryan, and surprised him with it at the bar, saying, "You make friends easily."

Ryan acknowledged the gesture, nodding politely at Nick.

"Thanks."

"You're welcome."

"I would never have thought it of you," said Imogen.

"Thought what?"

"That you have a heart."

Imogen was right about the food: served on chipped plates, and with mismatched cutlery, it was Michelin quality.

"You're amazing, you know that?" said Nick.

"I am? In what way? In or out of bed?" For Imogen, this afternoon, the convent seemed a very long time ago.

"On top of a restaurant table and underneath."

Ryan nursed his drink at the bar, running his forefinger around and around the rim of the glass.

"Are you going to sit here all night?" asked the owner's daughter.

"If I have to."

"I wish she'd put him out of his misery," said Nick.

"How's the tripe?"

"Delicious. Have you ever made it?"

"No. Perhaps I could make it for Tikhon."

"We could ask the chef for the recipe."

"I don't want this to be a working weekend."

Villa Eilenroc

Nick was laughing. "No, of course not! You just dragged me around a dozen food shops."

"You told me you didn't mind!"

"I don't. You want afters?"

"No. You sound very English when you say the word 'afters.'"

Nick left a big tip, and his compliments to the chef. On the way out, as they walked past Ryan, Nick gave him some advice.

"You have to be patient, but they always give in."

Outside in the street, they were both slightly drunk, after a bottle of wine between them.

"I would hold your hand," said Nick, "only I've got too many carrier bags."

"Is that the secret of your success? Knowing exactly what a woman is thinking?"

"Yeah. Good gardeners make good lovers."

They wandered into the Piazza Anfiteatro – a perfect circle, painted in shades of cream and beige; green shutters, wrought iron balconies – and meandered around the souvenir shops, buying nothing.

"Let's watch the people go by," said Nick.

They drank chilled white wine, sitting on tall bar stools in front of Pane e Vino. The sound of an anguished aria came floating out of a small shop specialising in Puccini – *"Folle di gelosia ... Vorrei non più soffrire ..."*

The square was full of budget families eating pizza. Nick had long forgotten what it was like to economise.

"They could almost put you off Italian food."

"Don't be such a snob."

"Don't you think that what they're doing is a sin against good cooking?"

"You're asking me? Yes, I do, but at least they're here, and not in Disneyworld."

Nick, she realised, was not listening. He seemed to have become lost in the music, transfixed – *"Te lo giuro, non tremo/ a vibrare il coltello/ e con gocce di sangue/ fabbricarti un gioiello!"*

She lacked his intensity, his capacity for drama, but she also knew that this was his weakness. Against a cold-hearted opponent, he would surely lose.

He snapped out of it. "The madness of jealousy. And this is the square of adultery."

"For a man who hasn't ever had a mistress you're an expert in the subject. Actually, I like Bellini better."

"I thought you said you wanted white wine? I'll ask them to change it."

"I meant Bellini the composer. I'm named after one of his heroines. An opera called *Il pirata*. My grandmother heard Callas sing it, and persuaded my parents to call me Imogen. She was big on tragic heroines."

"You don't strike me as being very tragic."

"Give it time."

Nick had had enough of looking at the hoi polloi. He stood up. "Now we're really going somewhere. It's only a few minutes away, I think."

Imogen pulled a face, although she was loving every minute.

"Yes, sir. It's like being on a route march."

A few minutes later, they were standing at the entrance to the Palazzo Pfanner. Nick bought tickets and two bottles of water; and then they stepped into the garden. They were the only people there.

They wandered down the central alleyway, flanked by white classical statues, of "Spring," "Summer," "Hermes …" They walked amongst lemon trees in terracotta pots; past red, pink, yellow, and white regimented standard roses; past potted red geraniums; and luxuriant potted palms with nodding fronds; and shy alpine plants peeping out from beneath mossy rocks. There were big, fat, pink rhododendrons massed against the south-facing wall; and there were soothing sounds: in the very centre of the main alleyway, the plash of water in a circular fountain; and the soft crunch of pebbled walks. They breathed in the heady scent of thirsty pine trees.

They sat down on wrought iron chairs, in the shade, in front of a copse of bamboo. Above them, they could see the joggers and the cyclists, sweating and peddling along the city wall, just outside the enclosed brickwork wall of the garden.

They said nothing for several minutes, maybe even five; they both drank from their water bottles. Nick spoke first.

"Italians, they've been good at design for ever, look at that bell tower: one row of columns at the bottom; two levels of two columns; and two levels of three columns."

"Do you think they felt safe inside this garden when the tocsin rang to warn that the enemy was outside the gate?"

Nick didn't answer at once; he seemed a little distant. "Tocsin, that's a nun's word. They didn't design this garden for safety, did they?"

Silence again. A pair of turtle doves flitted past, and came to rest in a magnolia tree; they immediately began to bill and coo. More minutes passed. The bell tolled six times, and yet, even as time moved forwards, still it seemed as if everything else in life had slowed down, almost to a standstill.

"I was wrong about you."

"Oh?"

"Why did you want to be rich?"

"Doesn't everybody?"

"Well, yes, I suppose they do, that's what they dream about, only not everybody makes it happen like you."

"What you really mean is why did I give up being a gardener?"

"Sort of, yes."

"I was seduced by the money. Now you'll say I don't have any willpower."

"No, I won't."

"That's what I like about you. You actually listen to me."

"Please don't say that your wife doesn't understand you."

"I thought you didn't want to talk about my wife?"

More minutes passed. Imogen tried not to speak; wherever Nick was, at that moment he wasn't with her – a man's moment, hidden from a woman. She relaxed, properly, at last; didn't feel obliged to make conversation. She knew that, however good it might be between them, it would never be this good ever again; that sated moment beyond sex. She waited for Nick to break the silence.

"There's only one pear tree."

She had the very odd thought that he was going to cry. She wasn't embarrassed or discomfited; she hoped that he would, and perhaps reveal whatever it was that lay deep inside. His tears would make her fall in love with him for ever. She wanted to make him understand that she understood, albeit dimly; she picked up his left hand, and kissed it, in a medieval gesture of courtly love.

He smiled, a little sadly. "What was that for?"

"For the rose life that you didn't have."

"Yes, I'm a rosarian. How did I ever forget?" There was a pause. Then he said, "You make me remember."

In the garden, she drew closer to the make of him. She had dragged him about the streets of Lucca, picking up food, for which he had absolutely no passion, and he had doggedly followed her, uncomplaining. She understood that this was the one place he had wanted to visit; and had kept it a secret.

"You had green fingers."

His tone wiped away the threat of tears. "Yes, and I washed them very thoroughly."

He stood up, said nothing, and she followed him, into the *palazzo*: up the grand staircase, where they both twisted their necks admiring the faded ceiling frescoes. They stepped back to enjoy the *trompe l'oeil* on the wall of the central *salon*. As they moved slowly through the small suite of parade rooms she watched him as he looked around at the decorative objects and pictures; she noticed the expert way his eye dismissed the second rate, and stopped only in front of the first class. He looked at the curtains, with their enormous pelmets, in embroidered, heavy fabrics, and, behind them, the off-white simple drapes, backlit by the early evening sun; unmanly, he looked closely at the turned mahogany poles that secured the curtains, and extended far out into the rooms.

"As my wife would say, 'Nice tie-backs.'"

As they walked back down the grand staircase, a man was sweeping the steps, just a little way below them. He was in his mid thirties, and well dressed for an odd-job man – blue polo shirt, beige chinos, and brown drivers. He stepped back to let them pass, and his name tag pinned to his breast announced that this was Dario Pfanner.

"Nice house you have, Mr Pfanner," said Nick. "Must cost a fortune to run."

Mr Pfanner extended his hand, and smiled in a welcoming way, as if Nick had dropped in for the afternoon, or to stay for the weekend.

"Dario. Yes, especially in these difficult times."

"Nick. Well, I guess this house has lived through many interesting times. The garden is very beautiful, only it would be nice to know what all the plants are in the garden. Very unusual to see bamboo in a Renaissance garden."

"It was replanted in the eighteenth century. Yes, a good idea, labels you mean?"

"Yeah."

"Hello, I'm Imogen."

"Your wife?"

"My mistress."

Mr Pfanner had impeccable breeding. "You've come to the right place for love."

Nick did all the talking, for them. "Yes, that was the plan."

"Three days in the Palazzo Pfanner, and the love is for ever."

"I wish that we had three days."

"Three days is all you need in Lucca." Mr Pfanner had a story to tell. "In 1689, Crown Prince Frederick of Denmark came to stay here. Three days. He slept in the state bedroom you saw. He met a young Italian noblewoman, Maddalena. They fell in love."

"Very quickly," remarked Nick.

"He went back to Denmark to become king; said that he would come back for her. Twenty years later he returned, as King Frederick IV. They told him that Maddalena was now a Mother Superior in a convent in Florence. Her family had shut her away when she refused to marry. They met again, we don't know what they said, but she gave him a silver crucifix; and he gave her his portrait in miniature. Then he left."

"Alone?" asked Imogen.

"Yes, alone."

They said goodbye to Mr Pfanner, and walked back in silence to the car. On the Via Fillungo, Nick at last spoke. "What are you thinking about?"

"Maddalena. You?"

"Frederick."

Figgy-Dowdy

"I CAN TRUST YOU not to talk, can't I?" asked Tikhon.

"You hardly know me," replied Imogen. They were having a talk 'over the fence' in Cap d'Antibes.

"You're an English lady."

"Irish."

"I don't understand the difference. And your friend Frank is coming."

"Frank and Claudia?"

"Yes. We are in the same boat, as you say. And no, I did not tell him I met you with Nick."

"Thank you."

"Now we can both keep a secret. And Katya is dancing *Giselle*, so we are only men on board. I want to eat English children's food."

This made Imogen laugh. "Comfort food we call it, for adults."

"Yes, roast beef and custard."

Imogen had understood that Tikhon was not expecting overcooked cabbage and a dry rice pudding; she had to give the menu some thought. She spent a lovely day reading through recipe books, and settled on a mix of the classics and the unfamiliar; showy, that was what Russians liked, but nothing fiddly or fancy, so:

Jeremy Noble

Miniature Cornish pasties
Shropshire Pea Soup served with Lady Arundel's Manchet
Scottish beef on the bone with Yorkshire pudding, horseradish sauce
and gravy; roast potatoes, buttered swede, runner beans
Figgy-Dowdy with custard
English cheeses

Probably nobody would get it, but she was really pleased with the idea for the pudding. Tikhon had asked her to e-mail the menu because, "I'll be where they make Russian gas," and she sent it with a request that she be allowed to buy some silverware. He replied immediately, and attached the contents of his stupendous wine cellar. "Figgy-Dowdy? You British! Buy everything you need. You choose the wine but my Sauternes for your English pudding. You know how it has to be. Tikhon."

It had been a long time since she had cooked these nursery dishes; she decided to practise on Nick when he came for dinner, a few days before she was going to fly with Tikhon to Montenegro – she could get quite used to all this private jetting about. She did tell Nick that the evening was a trial run for Tikhon's lunch, but she didn't tell him that Frank would be there. This lack of frankness caused her some standard Catholic soul searching; she wanted to be totally honest with him, even if this was a relationship with infidelity at its foundations, but she didn't want to be his spy.

Foodwise, that first evening at home as a mistress in Cap d'Antibes was a disaster: the soup boiled over because of a blowjob she gave Nick on the terrace; then, he went down on her – ecstasy, she had never known a man so enjoy eating out; he gave it all the attention of a gourmand unpeeling the petals of an artichoke, burrowing deep inside, slavering after the heart. The beef was over-cooked because, after the oral sex, they made love for a very long time in the bedroom. Even as Nick was inside her, she was thinking that she should turn off the oven; she didn't – the first time that she had ever put sex before food.

Nick didn't seem to mind the burnt offering of beef that she served him; he said that it was like the roasts his mother made. He ate everything she put in front of him – sex made him hungry – but she ate hardly anything.

"Off your food? Not like you. Or you just don't like your own cooking?"

"I'm not hungry."

"Not even comfort food?"

"Not even."

"What's for afters?" Imogen must have looked surprised. "Why are you looking at me like that?"

"Only because Tikhon calls it pudding, and you call it afters."

"And what do you call it?"

"Pudding."

"Yeah, well, like I told you the first time, I didn't always have money."

"It doesn't have anything to do with money."

Nick stood up and helped clear away the plates. "What does it have to do with? Aah! Upbringing. Class. Always saying and doing the right thing. So, now I'm being polished by both of you is that it? I do okay, I think."

"Well, you would have failed my grandmother's test. I didn't often bring boys home, almost never, but that didn't stop her from finding out if they were suitable. She sat where you're sitting now, and when they'd finished eating, she asked every one of them, 'Do you stack or are you gentry?'"

"I don't get it?"

"If you picked up the plates and stacked them one on top of

the other, you failed the test. The funny thing is, she had absolutely no background to speak of."

"Right. So I'm a social failure. New rich and vulgar like Tikhon, is that it?" Nick was trying to keep it light, but she had wounded him.

"Darling, I'm sorry. It came out the wrong way. I just meant that it was funny how Tikhon uses such old-fashioned words, and he's a new rich Russian."

"Seems to me you like lots of things about Tikhon."

She had hurt him. The whole evening was spoiled. She put the figgy-dowdy on the table, and started to cry.

Nick slapped his thighs with his hands in exasperation, and shook his head, but he was not that upset. "For God's sake! Enough! Pudding looks amazing. Happy now? So, what's this when it's at home?"

"Figgy-dowdy. It's like spotted dick but with rum."

"You've developed a taste for dick, Miss O'Rorke. What's in it?"

Imogen cheered up. "Sultanas, ginger, mixed spice, plain flour, shredded suet, caster sugar and rum. And the custard is homemade."

"Sounds horribly fattening."

"Are you trying to get back at me?"

"No. What is it with women and weight?"

"The two don't go together."

Nick couldn't stay the night, he had told Cassandra that he had a long meeting in Nice; that much was almost true. Waving him goodbye, Imogen experienced that fuck 'n' go mistress feeling.

After he had left she sat on the bidet, looking at herself, fold by fold, in the floor-to-ceiling gilt mirror that had come out of the bankrupt O'Rorke house back in Ireland. Well fucked, still she did not feel any better about her body. Nick had stopped her from covering up all the time during sex, with various strategic pieces of pretty fabric – "Drop the handkerchief pussy games" he had said – but she still found it unbelievable that a man whose treasure trail fell sheer down his flat stomach like the Lhotse Face on Everest, could have a sexual attraction for this amount of blubber. He did, she was sure of it, she had no doubt about it, for certain he wanted her only for her body; I mean, she had nothing else to offer, did she – he wasn't after her money – or was she such a good conversationalist? Just a good cook? She wanted to believe it, that he desired her, she really did, but a brace of shuddering orgasms in as many weeks was not going to change her fat loathing. Perhaps he really didn't like sex with Cassandra? It must be like fucking a stick insect. What was it then? Perhaps she, Imogen, was a slut? That was it; he liked fat sluts. A man wants his mistress to be a cheap whore. She was a slut because she hadn't tried to fight him off, a married man.

Facing the mirror full on, squeezing the dough around her thighs, and manhandling them; lifting up her tits and letting them droop like tubers, she sat up as straight as she could, and sucked everything in. When she breathed out, there was raw pork meat flopping all over the place.

In front of the mirror, stark naked, she played the fat girls' window shopping game: you stood in front of an outfit that had caught your eye, and then, ignoring the massively distorted reflection staring back at you, and with that lively creative imagination that fat women need to survive out on the street, you photoshop in your head, all of the gross bits you so hate, until you can fit inside the dress, modelled in a perfect size eight in front of you. In your mind's eye, at least, you look fabulous. Imogen imagined most of all what she would look like in Chanel.

The bidet was threatening to overflow. She stood up, and

looked down at the water: Nick's sperm was floating on the surface. She scooped up a handful of water, and carefully let it drain away through her fingertips, until only the sperm was left. How fertile he was. She wondered if they were still alive. She rubbed the sperm in the palm of her hand until it congealed into rubber-like globules. She wanted him again. She wanted him very much. She dried herself, flagellating her body with the fluffy towel. At least she didn't have to wait around until the next time, frustrated in her négligée and maribou; she had a lunch to worry about.

Moscow-on-Sea

WHEREVER THE RUSSIANS drop anchor becomes Moscow-on-Sea, so perhaps we are being just a little bit unfair to Porto Montenegro when we say that it is the only deep water port to be Russianised (overrun by Russians). We could say the same about Portofino, Monaco, Cannes, Antibes, Costa Smeralda, St Barts ... With so many places to park their boats, you might wonder why the Russians so love Porto Montenegro – because it's full of other Russians ...

It was Scott Fitzgerald who put 'Little Montenegro' on the map, when the country gave a medal to Jay Gatsby for heroism; that was its only claim to fame until rich Russians began to migrate there in the early twenty-first century.

Many people perhaps think that penis envy among Russian yacht owners began with Roman Abramovich when he unzipped the Eclipse from its slipway, and it became "the world's biggest superyacht." But they would be wrong because it was not Roman who started the superyacht size race, it was Tsar Nicholas II. His yacht, the Standart, was the biggest private yacht of its day (and that really upset the Kaiser), with a dining saloon that could seat seventy-two people. The Standart was named after the frigate of Peter the Great – the fastest ship then afloat – given to him by William III when Peter came to England in 1698. The history of Russian superyachts, then, is a long one. The Standart of Nicholas II measured 401 feet in length; Roman's Eclipse measures 536 feet.

During the Soviet period there was a ship of state called the Rossia, *used by Brezhnev and other gerontocrats; however, this was less of a yacht than a tub, and best not to go into too much detail. Talking about presidential yachts, the tandem of Dimon and Vlad – the couple who swapped jobs – recently spent some of the country's oil money on a second-hand yacht: the Turkish-built* Sirius *measures 177 feet, which is a very modest size for kleptocrats.*

People who gawp at the yachts riding at anchor in Porto Montenegro think that the marina is a playground for grown-ups with money; it's not, it's an open-air office. What poor men don't understand is that rich men do business anywhere they can show off their trophies – women, cars, paintings, trinkets, houses, and lunch in the sunshine on the saloon deck of a yacht measuring more than anybody else's in the harbour. A line of yachts is the ultimate parade of penis power. For a poor man, sporting nine or so inches is the most he can aspire to; a rich man sports in hundreds.

The lunch for Tikhon on board his yacht (238 feet, built by Lürssen, Germany) was an unusual occasion because Imogen was both cooking and serving; this was not because Tikhon didn't have crew on his yacht, only that they had been given the afternoon off. When Imogen asked why she would have to be running up and downstairs all afternoon, Tikhon explained why, in his usual graphic way: "I do not mind them seeing me fuck but I do not like them seeing me get fucked."

The setting was lovely – a natural bay framed with snow-capped mountains, and imported palm trees – but the lunch in Porto Montenegro was the worst lunch Imogen had ever catered. Pacing around on the saloon deck, around and around the teak table where his guests were seated, Tikhon was beside himself with anger.

"He told us it was a sure thing! The only thing I'm sure about is how much money I've lost!"

"How much are we down in total?" asked a man called Dabing; he was Chinese, with a South African accent. Imogen thought that he couldn't be older than fifty.

Frank knew exactly. "One point four billion, in less than a year."

A Russian called Oleg who looked like a retired boxer said, "I lost less money in the Credit Crisis."

Other than Tikhon and Frank, Imogen knew none of the guests; she was introduced to them only by their first names. There was an elderly man called Peter who must have been in his eighties, and whose accent she found impossible to place – East European mixed with North American; and a man probably no older than thirty-five called Andy, with an estuary English accent, who sounded desperate, as if he had put his career on the line with this deal turning sour – everybody else had lost their own money.

"So, what 'r' we finkin' then?" asked Andy, a good octave above his usual tone.

Oleg was in no doubt. "He's in trouble, you can smell it. Like shit."

"He cancelled his yacht," said Peter, as if the man in question had cancelled the newspapers.

"That means we're in trouble," said Dabing.

"He says he didn't like the design," said Frank, turning up his nose.

Tikhon had still not calmed down. "Bullshit! Didn't like the cost."

"It's only two hundred forty-one feet," said Oleg. "If you can't afford that, what can you afford?"

"And when are you going to get a bigger yacht, Tikhon?" asked Peter, only half teasing. "Looks a little small next to Frank's new monster."

"I'm not because I don't need to. I have a big cock," answered Tikhon, ending the subject.

Andy didn't take part in this conversation because he didn't have a yacht.

They were waiting for the last guest to arrive, the 'guest of honour,' as Tikhon referred to him, almost spitting with fury.

Imogen played her part, soothing tempers with the warm Cornish pasties; they had some effect – they were all eaten.

Tikhon uncorked the wine, frowning at the label – a 2004 *Cannubi Boschis Luciano Sandrone*. He had quizzed Imogen about it on the plane here. "Barolo? Don't the English drink claret with beef?"

"Not on a yacht. Too stuffy. And I didn't want to go overboard."

"You're worried I won't like your food and push you over the side?"

Imogen did her best to explain. She was very happy with the wine – she accepted a glass for herself, just to be sure – but this was not a lunch for vino snobbery; most of the guests were drinking Perrier. Only Andy was knocking it back.

The 'guest of honour' finally appeared, bounding up the gangplank. Imogen had no idea who he was; no introductions were made because, clearly, the guests all knew each other. She wondered what he would sound like.

"Sorry I'm late. I was in China."

Imogen decided that the mystery man was probably in his early forties. He had had work done on his face, and yet far from making him appear more youthful the result was owl-like and unflattering; the skin had been pulled back so tight that, around the eyes, the skin was whiter than the rest of his tanned face, making it look as if he had just wiped off a dollop of cold cream, or removed cucumber eye pads. His permanent half-smile had no wrinkles around the mouth; he looked like an overgrown schoolboy who has been found out doing something he shouldn't have, which was exactly the situation at this lunch. His crinkly dark hair was cut very short, and was thinning at the temples. He was dressed in a cream linen suit over a monogrammed pale blue open-necked shirt, which revealed that he had never been good at games. His suede loafers were a nondescript beige. Everything about him said, "Savile Row and St James's toff."

"Never trust a man who wears monogrammed shirts and suede shoes," was one of Imogen's father's many (failed) business maxims. This man failed the test on both counts. Unlike the other five guests, dressed in birds-of-paradise colours of turquoise, yellow, pink, orange, and scarlet, and with expansive gestures to match (except for Andy), there was a withdrawn, almost hesitant manner about this last guest.

"Have you been ganging up on me?" he asked affably, shaking hands with everybody, speaking with a cut-glass accent that Imogen recognised immediately – the well rounded vowels and lazy top-drawer delivery of an English gentleman with a very good pedigree. He was remarkably self-possessed, relaxed even; seemingly unconcerned that he had burned through more than a billion of other people's money.

"No," said Frank, "we've been calculating our losses."

"Just as well Tikhon doesn't have a sailing yacht, or I suppose you'd be stringing me up from the yard arm. Have I missed the Cornish pasties?" he asked Imogen, charmingly.

"I'll bring some more up," said Imogen, attentively, hoping that Tikhon wouldn't think that she was being disloyal, being nice to Enemy Number One. She knew what was happening: she was smitten; he was another Nick (although, of course, he probably didn't have Nick's taste in women …).

"Hanging's too good for you," said Tikhon, still angry. "You're lucky we're not in Moscow."

This was not a lunch for pleasantries. Peter launched his attack. "What was it you said? 'Our cash, your city connections, their gold.' Now where are we? We've lost our cash; you've lost your reputation; and they've still got the goldmine."

The mystery man put his hands up in mock surrender:

"Whoah! Gentlemen, please, this isn't a firing squad!" Despite the fact that he was on trial, he was leaning against the guard rail looking as if he owned Tikhon's yacht.

Imogen came back with more of the Cornish pasties. She made a point of offering them to Tikhon first, but he waved her away. The mystery man piled three on a plate, saying, "I'm ravenous. Very interesting menu, yours I take it? I'm Mat, by the way."

She had to reply; not to say anything would be rude, but she could feel Tikhon watching her. "Imogen. I didn't know you'd all been sent the menu."

"I only came for the food," said Mat, grinning, out of earshot of his accusers.

My God, she thought, nothing to look at, but he's to die for. You could eat him.

"So, what are you going to do?" asked Andy, aggressively. "Fucking mess you've made."

"Worried about your pension?" Mat's tone was icy.

Imogen liked him a little less.

Frank recognised a British class war when he saw one. "Guys, we're here to agree on a plan. Let's hear what he has to say, Andy."

"'Adversity teaches us life's most valuable lessons,'" said Dabing. "Chinese proverb. Let us see what we can learn today from all of our mistakes."

Imogen thought that he and Frank were probably allies. This was another one of those power struggles conducted over a tablecloth. Trust Frank to have a plan of campaign, even at somebody else's lunch.

Today, however, her loyalty was with Tikhon. She wanted to help him, not only because he was paying her for her services, but because she liked him, and he was her next-door neighbour. She guessed that he had not made his money in a boardroom; here, pacing around the deck, he was clearly frustrated at learning a new money game. He had purchased all the usual trappings of success – a villa in Cap d'Antibes; draped his ballerina in jewels; a Bentley in the driveway; and yet, his buying a second growth Sauternes vineyard rather than a trophy, first growth red, said to her that he had a deeper understanding than most New Rich Russians she had met, of the more rewarding ways his wealth could be enjoyed, beyond the surface level of one-upmanship. Tikhon was certainly clever, but, up against smooth operators like Frank, Dabing and Peter – even if they were his co-investors – and jousting with Mat, Imogen felt that he was at a disadvantage. Oleg, his fellow Russian, seemed more composed, as if he had less to learn. Andy didn't count; he was a hired hand.

At the time, in Montecatini Terme, Tikhon's offhand invitation to Imogen to cook for him had seemed to her a spur of the moment, unscripted decision; now, she saw how very far it was from that: Tikhon had asked her to cater this lunch, for carefully thought out reasons that had as much to do with her social background as her cooking skills. He understood that she had grown up knowing how to set the scene for whatever actions a host might like to put in play over a table. On Tikhon's yacht, she was a weapon in his armoury – a big cannon on deck.

This was an elegant game of do or die. Unusually, there were no advisers at this lunch, and no lawyers; they would be brought in after the rescue deal had been struck. In the time it took to clear his plate, a man could make a very expensive mistake committing himself to something he later regretted. Imogen was glad to see that Tikhon's anger had ebbed away; she hoped he understood that losing his temper had temporarily lost him the captaincy of his own yacht.

"Would you like me to serve the soup?"

Tikhon gave her a broad smile. "Yes, why don't we eat."

"Good idea. I want to try this English food with the funny names," said Oleg.

Imogen served the soup in an antique silver soup tureen, with a large silver ladle. "Trying to corner the market in silver are we, Tikhon?" remarked Peter. This caused a laugh – Peter owned a silver mine.

"You know how to live well, Tisha, for an old Soviet!" joked Oleg.

"Who was this Lady Arundel?" asked Dabing. "Manchet is a loaf of bread?"

Tikhon opened his arms wide to signify a complete lack of knowledge about Her Ladyship. He was, however, smiling, delighted that the lunch was making people think about something other than the money they had lost. Imogen came to his rescue.

"There was more than one Lady Arundel. The recipe is from the mid-seventeenth century, probably much earlier. It's a yeast bread from Sussex."

"Probably the Lady Arundel painted by Rubens, the one with the art collection," said Mat, easily. "And didn't she write a book of herbal remedies?"

Mat smiled broadly at Imogen. Out of loyalty to Tikhon, Imogen tried hard not to smile back. The unbelievable confidence of the man. He had the most to lose, and yet he was the only one enjoying the lunch. He possessed all of Nick's charm, and much more polish. She felt guilty at making such a comparison.

"I think we need more than herbal remedies to fix this mess," said Frank, deadpan.

Andy had failed to catch the new mood. "Pity you didn't use all that education to stop us from buying a pig in a poke." Mat kept his cool. He had taken a seat at the table, and was breaking the bread. "What was it you said, Dabing, when we were talking about this deal? 'If two men unite, their money will buy gold.' And that's what we did."

Andy pushed on, regardless. "Yes, we bought it, but now it's not there, and we want to know why."

"I've called an extraordinary general meeting. I'm going to take control of the board and make some changes."

"Have you actually seen this mine?" asked Peter.

"What's to see? Gold mines all look the same – they're just bigger or smaller."

Andy's blood was up. "This isn't a gold mine, it's a black hole!"

Time to serve the beef. Imogen wheeled a silver-domed trolley out of the lift, and parked it next to Tikhon. He loved the showmanship.

"First I lose money in gold, and now I lose a fortune in silver!"

He stood up to carve the meat, while Imogen busied herself hurrying between the kitchen and the saloon deck, laying out the vegetables. Everybody tucked in to the food, which put them all in a much better mood.

"Where did you find that cook?" asked Oleg.

"Next door."

"Next door where? You have a lot of houses."

"Cap d'Antibes. She has a small house next to mine. *Nyet*, I won't give you her number."

"I will," laughed Frank, "she's my wife's best friend."

"She obviously likes her food," joked Peter, as Imogen sashayed back to the kitchen. She heard him, but the thought of Nick appreciatively licking her tits allowed her to brush off the jibe.

"The marina here looks very good," said Dabing, looking around. "I should have put money into it."

"We did ask you," said Peter. "There's still a lot of residential going up."

"No, I only like to be in on something at the beginning."

"You still have your share, Mat?" asked Tikhon.

"Last time I looked, yes."

When Imogen served the pudding, Mat said, "Spotted Dick. It's like being at school."

"Sort of. It's Figgy-Dowdy," said Imogen.

"Aah yes, I'd forgotten the menu. It was a naval dish, wasn't it? How clever, for a yacht lunch."

Imogen had to give it to him, no matter how much money Mat might have lost his investors, he still had vintage patrician blood. She wondered if he was good in bed.

The pudding was a success, particularly the custard. Tikhon judged it the right time to broker a deal.

"Has anybody tried my Sauternes?" Tikhon was already filling the glasses.

"His new possession," remarked Oleg, enviously. He would buy a vineyard as soon as he could, to keep up.

"He's always trying to sell us something," joked Frank.

Tikhon made his move. "Is this plan of yours going to work, Mat? Let me get it clear. You want us to vote with you against the family that sold us half the mine?"

"Yes, if you all say yes, I think I can sort it out."
"Do we have a choice?" asked Oleg?
"That was a yes or a no?" asked Tikhon.
"That was a yes, *tovarish*."
"Frank?"
"Do we think the shares have further to fall?"
For the first time that afternoon, Mat spoke with conviction and enthusiasm. "Not if we show a united front. Or are you planning on shorting them?"
Frank smiled. "When you've lost this much money there is nothing else to do except grin and bear it. I'll only short them if I think you're going to fuck up a second time. In answer to Tikhon's question, yes, I'll give you my vote. Peter?"
"Profit is about confidence," said Peter.
"Oh yes, all we need is a little bit of confidence!" Andy was finding it hard to keep the hysteria out of his voice. In this company of hard-won fortunes, he still had a lot to learn.
Peter gave him a lesson. "I took the last train out of Germany in nineteen thirty-nine. I know about confidence. I give you my vote, Mat."
Tikhon looked at Dabing. Dabing pressed the tips of his fingers together. "A gem is not polished without rubbing, nor a man perfected without trials."
Tikhon raised his eyebrows. "Will somebody please translate?"
"That was Chinese for yes," said Frank.
"Andy?"
"Think of it as a deal pure and simple," said Peter, trying to soothe Andy's wounds, "not a test of wills."
Andy wanted to say no, but the decision had already been made for him back in London: he was to go with the majority.
"I'm against it, but we're still in."
Imogen served the cheese.

"You haven't told us, Tikhon, which way you're going to vote?" asked Peter.

"I'm going to vote yes," said Tikhon.

"Thank you," said Mat. He was home and dry.

"On one condition."

Mat was holding the Sauternes up to his lips, but he didn't drink. "Which is?"

Tikhon smiled sweetly. "You give us your stake in the marina here as a guarantee of success."

Lose Weight through Sex

*T*HE HISTORY OF *my Battles.*
Dieting is a religion: if you don't pray regularly, you won't go to heaven.

1 F Plan Diet – My first diet, at St Mary's.

2 Scarsdale Diet – My second diet, at the Sacred Heart.

3 Weight Watchers – My second and a half diet at Brillantmont.

4 South Beach Diet – Catholic battle between "good" and "evil" carbs and fats. Lost that battle.

5 Montignac (Businessman's) Diet – My fourth diet, in Geneva. Something about weight-losing carbs with a Glycemic Index less than 35. Hocus pocus. Yes, but it was working so why did I give up?

6 Soup Diet – Ugh, vast quantities of grey-green cabbagey slop. SO disgusting.

7 Mediterranean Diet – My 1st New Year's resolution diet, lasted January 1 to February 7. Not suitable for Cap d'Antibes.

8 Biggest Loser Diet – Short-lived (a diet for losers was what they really meant).

9 Flat Belly Diet – 2nd New Year's resolution diet, lasted January 1 to February 14.

10 Zone Diet – My 1st get-ready-for-the-beach diet. Lasted April 1 to May 6th. Impossible to stay in the zone.

11 Raw Food Diet – 3rd New Year's resolution diet. Raw foodism lasted January 1 to January 5.

12 Atkins Diet – My 2nd get-ready-for-the-beach diet. Had those lists of net carbs and foundation vegetables (lists now in kitchen drawer). Result: carbs make you happy, ergo no carbs make you unhappy, and it gave me bad breath, constipation, and I wanted to kill myself.

13 Blood Group Diet – Okay, that was a silly one.

14 Dukan Diet – Attack, Cruise, Consolation, Permanent Stabilisation. Too many rules just asking to be broken. I enjoyed the attacking, I cruised a bit too long, and then I consoled myself.

15 Slim-Fast – If something sounds too good to be true …

16 Anti-Inflammatory Diet – Did I start that one, or just bought the book?

17 Macrobiotic Diet – Dieting as a lifestyle (not the same thing as dieting as a way of life). Grains, fish, nothing processed. Would have been the perfect diet if only I could have eaten meat.

18 Lemonade (Master Cleanse) Diet – Worked for Beyoncé. Another Catholic purge diet – is Beyoncé a Catholic? My 4th New Year's resolution diet, lasted January 1 to January 19. Detox, starve, go mad …

19 Grapefruit Diet – Another Catholic purge diet. Half a grapefruit before every meal. I wonder if there's a Catholic flagellation diet.

20 Engine 2 Diet aka The Texas Firefighter's 28-Day Save-Your-Life Plan That Lowers Cholesterol and Burns Away the Pounds – My last get-ready-for-the-beach diet.

21 Therapeutic Lifestyle Changes (TLC) Diet – Sounded perfect for a New Year's resolution …

22 Mayo Clinic Diet – I have to confess: Catholic diets are not my thing. How can food be sinful?

23 Flexitarian Diet – What exactly is a casual vegetarian?

24 Jenny Craig – Frozen food, for me?

25 Paleo Diet – If the cavemen didn't eat it … Would have worked in the Bronze Age, only it's difficult to be a hunter-gatherer in Cap d'Antibes.

26 Volumetrics – This was my last New Year's resolution. Said I could quit "dieting" for good. I did.

27 ABSOLUTELY MY LAST DIET which I'm calling the "Sex Diet" – worrying about what he thinks when I take off my clothes. The best diet of all ...

"You've been fucked. I can tell," said Claudia, matter-of-factly. "And you've lost weight," she added, lazily, not getting up from her sun lounger, merely inclining her sun-glassed gaze in the direction of her best friend.

"Don't be silly, Clod, people like me don't lose weight, we just go on a different diet."

"Mo, a library of dieting books isn't the same as going on a diet, and sticking to it."

"Do you know that in my short life I've been on twenty-six diets? I counted them. That works out at about two diets a year."

"It doesn't show. And don't change the subject. You're lying. Who is he?"

"Who?"

"The guy who's making you lose weight. Nothing else has. He must be a great fuck."

"It isn't anybody."

"You're fibbing. I can always tell. Is he married? Don't you want to swim? There's plenty of water left even if you jump in."

"You can be so fucking horrible, do you know that?"

"You're used to it. I know I'm right. I know you, remember? Have you stepped on the scales recently?"

"No, because you know I don't like frightening myself."

"They have those extra big ones at the airport."

"I hate you, Clod."

They were sitting around the pool, on the *Claudia*. After the Tikhon lunch, Imogen had stepped off his boat, and straight on to the *Claudia*; the two boats were anchored only metres away, port to starboard.

Claudia had been topping up her tan, lying by the top deck swimming pool. Except for the exercise of her clitoris, this involved no effort on her part, but a lot of effort on the part of Massimo, lazily rubbing oil into her skin, as low down her back as he could, and then some way further inside her legs. Pleasured, and still trembling from the ripple of sex, Claudia waved him away when Imogen appeared. She noticed the tent pole in his shorts as he sauntered past her, smiling sweetly.

"How was the lunch?"

"Don't you have any shame? He has a boyfriend … Marcus, your cook."

Claudia sat up on her sun lounger. She was topless; defying gravity, her perfect breasts somehow kept their beautiful mango shape.

"Don't preach. I can't help it, he's a total hottie. Nice face, big cock, tight ass, equals perfect. *C'est un bon coup.*"

"I just hope Marcus doesn't hear you."

"Anyway, I've promised to pay for his ship's officer's course. Help yourself to a margarita."

Imogen eased herself down on to the sofa. "You're unbelievable. You have absolutely no guilt, do you?"

"No, because I'm not you, Mo."

"How do your tits keep their shape like that?"

"Not like Mount Vesuvius exploding, you mean?"

"One day, you'll be old, and ugly and fat."

This had no effect whatsoever on Claudia; she had heard the line a thousand times. But something else about the way Imogen was looking, caught Claudia's surgeon's eye. "When did you buy that? I've never seen you wear it. Blue looks good on you, much better than Highland plaid."

"It came out of the unworn part of my wardrobe. And the food went down very well, thank you. I gave them an old English menu. And why are you asking? You don't normally take any interest in my career."

"No reason. Who was there?"

"You saw who was there! You were leaning over the rail."

"Not for very long. And I didn't hear anything. What were they talking about?"

"Clod, what's up?"

"Nothing. Why should anything be up?"

"You seem a bit uptight."

Claudia pursed her lips. It was not like her to show any weakness. Still, she had had it drummed it into her that confession was good for the soul. "If you must know, Frank lost a ton of money in a gold mine."

"Yes, I worked that out at lunch."

"So, what did they talk about? What did they agree to do? I could wring that Mat's neck."

"I thought he was rather nice."

Claudia was very put out. "How could you be so disloyal! And since when did you start looking at men as sex objects?"

Imogen sighed. "If you're so worried, why don't you ask Frank? He's your husband."

"I don't get worried. Because, Mo, you're my best friend."

"Clod, I understand, I really do, but I can't, it wouldn't be right. I can't talk about what I hear when I'm working. I'd never work again if it ever got out."

Claudia pouted, and tried another stratagem. "Well, if you're going to be like that."

"Clod, that won't work, either. I'm sorry."

Claudia knew that nothing could move Imogen when she had that stubborn tone in her voice. "All right. So, are you going to tell me who's fucking you?"

"Can you ever talk about anything other than money and sex?"

"What else is there? And don't change the subject."

Frank appeared. "What subject's that then?" He kissed Imogen on her cheeks, and his wife on her breasts. "That was a very good lunch, Mo, Tikhon must be pleased, it went really well."

"Thanks."

Frank made himself comfortable on the sofa. "I didn't realise you two were neighbours. Quite a coincidence. Good for you, you're going to have a horde of Russian clients when the word gets around. I gave your number to Oleg, hope you don't mind? Might make Tikhon a little jealous. I think he has a thing for you."

"Don't be silly, Frank, we're just neighbours. I cooked lunch for him, that's all. It's my job."

"You've lost weight, suits you."

"You see!" exclaimed Claudia, triumphantly. "She won't admit it!"

"Admit to what?"

"She's got a boyfriend, and she won't tell me."

"Wise woman," said Frank, caustically, although he was also smiling. "I don't see the connection between having a boyfriend and losing weight. You still have to eat. Or am I missing something?"

Claudia was fully alert, sensing a trail that she could track for juicy clues. "So, you just happened to cook lunch for a man who's your next-door neighbour, who we've never heard of before, and you've lost weight, and Frank says he's a chubby chaser ..."

"Clod, you're being ridiculous," said Imogen.

"Rude too," said Frank; he didn't like jokes about Imogen's weight.

"And anyway," added Imogen, "Frank knows him."

"Don't think I won't get it out of you, Imogen O'Rorke. You know I will. You never could resist the confessional."

Frank looked at his watch. "Darling, are you going to get dressed? You haven't forgotten that Nick Austin's coming? He just texted me to say that he'll be here very soon. He's flying in, an hour for talking, and straight back to Turin. I've sent the car to pick him up at Tivat. Dressed would be nice."

Half-naked as she was, Claudia gave Frank a married woman's 'look' that said, "It wasn't me who lost all that money, and now you're asking me, who went to a convent and a finishing school, if I know how to behave in front of guests?"

Frank retreated. "Okay, okay, I don't suppose you have forgotten." The hole in his fortune was forcing him to make adjustments he didn't like. In every way he felt less powerful, less in control.

Frank's mobile rang. He didn't recognise the number, was going to ignore it, and then changed his mind – losing money was damned unsettling. "Hello?"

"Hello, is that Frank? It's Cassie, Nick's wife. I'm sorry, are you busy?"

"No, no, it's fine. Hold on a sec. I'm on my way to the study." Frank headed for the private deck. "When are we going to see you again in St-Trop?" He gave a little false laugh. "You certainly know your chocolate." He was keeping it very light; whatever it was, this was serious.

Whatever Cassandra wanted, however, she was poised enough not to rush. "I guess I must be my father's daughter, after all. And we'd love to see you again. You should both come to San Remo. You're in St-Trop?"

"No. On the *Claudia*. In Porto Montenegro. How's Nick? I didn't realise he knew so much about roses."

"Oh, he's fine. He's gone to a meeting somewhere in town. Well, he was a gardener before we married, so he knows his plants."

"That put Nick in his place," thought Frank, and wondered why Cassandra would want to say such a thing, and in such a way. "Really? I didn't know. Say hello when you see him. Sounds very quiet there, children okay?"

"They're at a birthday party, and the nanny has the day off."

Frank wondered if the two – Nick and the nanny – were connected. Cassandra knew that that was what he was thinking. She hesitated, not sure if she should still ask what it was that she really wanted. He sat down in his study. "So, what can I do for you? Charity gala? Claudia hasn't mentioned anything."

"No, it's nothing charitable." There was the briefest of pauses. The security of her pre-nup agreement gave Cassandra the confidence to press on. "I overheard you and Nick talking about a man who knows how to find out things, I don't suppose you remember?"

"I remember exactly."

"Oh, you do?"

Frank didn't need to ask anything else. This was looking all very interesting. He was suddenly in a very good mood. "He's a private detective, in Zurich. Name's Andrei. Finds things out, doesn't talk. Do you want his details? You have a pen and paper?"

"Hold on a sec." Cassandra made a pretence of looking (the pen and paper were on the table in front of her). "Got it."

"Right, here goes ..."

"Who was that?" asked Claudia, with not much interest, when

Frank returned. She was now wearing a wrap-around swathe of multi-coloured chiffon, secured at her breast with an outsize gold brooch sparkling with rubies; and gold, strappy sandals.

"Nothing. Just business. You look lovely. Nick will be here any minute."

"Imogen fancies him. And she fancies that two-faced Mat. Oh, and Russian Tikhon, of course."

Frank grinned, enjoying the joke. "Is this true, Mo? From zero to three lovers, isn't that a bit excessive? Tikhon maybe, who knows? Mat she only met this afternoon. And I'm not sure about Nick. She's only met him once. He's very happily married, everybody says that. Besides, he'd be a fool to play around, with anybody."

"Why's that?" asked Claudia.

"Because Cassie's the one with the real money, and I heard Papoche tied it up before the marriage. Mo, is this true?"

Imogen shook her head, too nervous to speak, and dreading Nick's arrival.

Claudia was adamant. "Of course it is! I got it all out of her while you were downstairs. She's become man mad. How else could she have lost weight? She's been on a diet since she was born, and look what good it's done her."

Frank's mood was rapidly improving. He would have to call Andrei later. "Man mad? I wonder where that idea came from. Couldn't have been your influence could it?"

Imogen cautiously led her words through the minefield. "I was only saying that there was something very attractive about a successful man. I didn't say that I was sleeping with them. I only met Mat this afternoon, and Tikhon's my neighbour."

"Well, that only leaves Nick." Frank was visited by the most ridiculous thought that he had ever had; he just as soon tossed it away.

As for Claudia, she was having almost as much fun baiting Imogen, as she had had being pleasured by Massimo. "Imogen O'Rorke, you can't hide anything from me, you know that, so tell us what's really going on? Say it isn't true, swear by all that's holy, on Sister Ursula's grave, that you're not being screwed by Nick Austin?" She was having such fun at her best friend's expense.

Imogen went for broke. "I admit it. I'm having an affair with him. He takes me away for dirty weekends, and he comes to the Cap in secret, and we fuck on the terrace in full view of the neighbours. Are you happy, now that you've got me to confess?"

Frank split his sides, laughing. Claudia was hurt at being taken for a fool.

Nick chose that moment to arrive, escorted by Massimo (without a hard-on). Imogen quickly downed a margarita.

"Have I interrupted something?" asked Nick, sensing an unusual atmosphere. He shook hands with Frank; kissed Claudia on both cheeks; and did the same to Imogen.

Frank was back to his usual control and wit. "You're very welcome, Nick. Absolutely not bad timing. Imogen's just been telling us a very funny story, and Claudia didn't get the joke. You remember Imogen from the lunch in St-Trop?" Frank was in a devilish mood. "She's visiting from the yacht next door. That one, do you see? It's actually bigger than mine. That's friendship for you. Isn't that right, Mo?"

"I'm afraid Frank's playing games, Nick. All I've been doing is catering a lunch for a neighbour."

"I wish I could have been invited. I still remember your wonderful food."

Nick had hardly sat down, next to Imogen, when a very loud voice could be heard bellowing and laughing half-way across the harbour. "Miss O'Rorke, your boat is leaving!"

Imogen jumped up. "I have to go!"

Claudia had not been expecting this. "Why? Just like that? I thought we were going to talk. Who is that man screaming the place down?"

"It's my lift."

"But we can drop you off. We're sailing overnight."

"Sorry, Clod, I promised him."

"Promised who!"

Imogen gave Claudia and Frank the very quickest of kisses, and then, trying not to look Nick in the eye, she let herself be kissed by him, hoping that the heat between them wouldn't publicly solder their skin together. In front of her closest, and most suspicious friends, she quickly drew away from him, not wanting to leave, and yet desperate to go. She pulled off the coldest voice she could muster out of her torment. "Nice to meet you again. I'm sorry I have to rush off. Please say hello to your wife."

Nick was silent. Imogen registered his pained confusion of bewilderment, surprise and hurt. Surely, with a face like that, he would give the game away?

Standing in front of the lift door, praying for the doors to open, at the moment when she should have most played it coolly safe, she knew that she was falling for him. "This is not meant to be happening, Imogen O'Rorke," she said to herself in a low breath. "It's just an affair with a married man who isn't going to leave his wife."

Burning, she could not wait for the lift, and she made for the stairs. She took a single step down, and only then did she dare to turn around, knowing that he was watching her. With an exaggerated wave of her hands, she shouted, "Love you!" When you want to cheat, honesty is the best policy.

Tikhon was waiting for her by the platform deck, his hand outstretched; a big, gentlemanly fairground bear. Imogen stepped on board. She kissed him on both cheeks, for a fraction too long, playing to the gallery.

"Oh my God, it's true," said Claudia, genuinely shocked. "She really is being fucked! I knew it. Frank, who is he again? The man who owns that boat? We have to invite him."

"His name's Tikhon. I told you, he's her next-door neighbour on the Cap."

"What's he like? Is he married?"

"Rich Russian. I don't know, I haven't asked. Like all of them. You know the type …" Frank hesitated. "No, come to think of it, no, he's not." The cogs of Frank's brain were spinning wildly, his mind was now on gold, not on chocolate. "He knows about things they don't. Yes … now, it makes sense. He said that he likes big women. We all thought that he was joking because he's going out with a ballerina."

"Frank, look at her! Imogen O'Rorke, you sneaky bitch!" exclaimed Claudia, but not so loudly that Imogen might hear her. "You made me think you were interested in one man, just to keep me off the scent of the real one. Frank, you saw how she's lost weight. She never has. It's a man. It's that man."

Nick said nothing.

"I paint a woman's big rounded buttocks so that I want to reach out and stroke the dimpled flesh."

Peter Paul Rubens

Rubenesque

Pierre Marcolini

"Volkov."

No hello, no courtesy. Cassandra was wrong-footed. "Cold bastard," she was thinking, and said, ultra politely, "Mr Volkov, good afternoon, my name is Cassandra Austin. Frank Schulte gave me your name."

"How can I help you?" Andrei Volkov didn't need to ask who this woman was, or where she came from; he had just got off the phone with Frank.

"Do you follow people, Mr Volkov?"

There was a short laugh. She hadn't meant it to be funny.

"Only when I'm working, and, mmm … when I'm in love."

He was playing with her.

"Mr Volkov, I think it would be best if I were to meet you in person. I would feel more comfortable about it."

"I'm in Zurich, Paradeplatz. Where are you?"

"I'm in Turin."

"And where will you be tomorrow?"

"Zurich."

"That is what I thought. You have a pen?"

"No, but I have a good memory."

"You know Café Sprüngli, of course."

"Why would I know that?"

"Your husband is in chocolate, Mrs Austin."

"You know my husband?"

"We're right next door. I can see you at twelve-fifteen. À demain, au revoir."

The only thing that Cassandra could think of when the line went dead was that Mr Volkov spoke French with a terrible accent.

The house in Turin where they lived during the week was unusually quiet: the children had gone to a birthday party; Beatrice would not be back from her day off until early evening; and Nick had told her he had a mountain of work to get through in the office, but would be certain to call if he was going to be late for supper. Cassandra had a few hours to herself.

She had ordered some of her favourite chocolate from Pierre Marcolini, to cheer herself up: a tablet of *Los Rios Équateur*; and a tub of something new that Pierre had sent with his compliments – *Chocolat Primitif*; a grinding of cocoa beans, cocoa butter and cane sugar; and then, without any more refining and shaping, just dropped in the box any old how – flakes, chunks, slivers, wedges ... She could hardly wait to pop the lid off.

The box of goodies was still lying on the kitchen table. It was a test of her willpower to see how long she could hold out; it had been nearly an hour since the box arrived.

Nobody knew, but Cassandra liked big, fat slabs of chocolate, not the fancy little morsels made by everybody, including her own family business. As a treat, this afternoon she would pour herself a glass of chilled Sauternes – Nick had bought cases of it a short while ago, saying that he had met the owner – some Russian – and it was bound to go up in price. She would leaf through the new French *Vogue*, and have a little *dégustation*, all by herself.

By way of experiment, she had also bought a tablet of the sugar-free chocolate they had tried at Frank and Claudia's lunch in St-Trop. That was something else she was going to do this afternoon (in addition to trying to make her mind up about her husband): try to make her mind up about this chocolate. Two big, and closely connected, decisions.

What time was it? The chocolates had arrived from Brussels an hour and a half ago. Okay, that was long enough – she had proved how much willpower she had. She unwrapped the Ecuadorean tablet first, broke off a big slice, and popped it into her mouth. My God! She shivered at the familiar intensity of flavours. She squeezed her legs together – it was better than sex.

Connoisseur that she was, Cassandra knew that Belgian chocolate was in no way as good as it was cracked up to be – too many manufacturers selling muck to people who had little or no idea about the mysteries and rewards of artisan chocolate. But Pierre Marcolini was one of the select few – a bean-to-bar *chocolatier*.

Carré[2] Chocolat Los Ríos Équateur Grand Cru de Propriété Hacienda Puerto Romero, to give it its full title, was a taste bomb in the mouth: *Nacional* cacao from Ecuador, hinting first at berry fruits; the tongue excavating deep down into rich seams of coffee and treacle; finishing with flowers that lightened up the almost suffocating darkness. She washed it down with the sweet wine – the ecstatic coupling of wine and chocolate was going to give her a sugar rush.

She leafed through the first pages of the magazine, then, only a few seconds later, decided that, this afternoon, she had no interest in Burberry, Gucci, Vuitton, and all the rest. She would think about her life. She snapped off another piece of chocolate.

There was nothing obviously wrong with her marriage, so why this sense of unease? Her husband worked hard, he loved his children, he was considerate, he didn't shout, he didn't drink to excess, he wasn't violent, they made love regularly; not as much as they had done before the children, but that was to be expected. You can't keep a marriage on the boil, day in day out, month after month, year after year. She had tried the usual spicing techniques – a red négligée, new perfume, higher heels, swallowing – and, to be fair to Nick, he had been complimentary, but no more so than if he had enjoyed a beef casserole. It seemed to her that her husband took more pleasure in smelling an old rose than breathing in the scent of *L'Air du Temps* on her breasts.

She took another piece of chocolate, and a sip of wine. Well, if she'd opened the tablet, she might as well open the tub ... It was packed like ice cream, and the word "primitive" was exactly right – in front of her was a mine of chocolate. How would she dig it out? With a spoon. She took one from the kitchen drawer, and dipped it into the tub, shovelling out nuggets that spilled and crowded on to the silverware; little flakes falling on to the table, and a cloud of chocolate powder rising into the air. This was probably what Heaven looked like. She ate a big mouthful. So different from the concentrated and balanced, sophisticated flavours of the *Grand Cru*; this was brutish, coarse and ravishing, sweet and fruity. She drank off half a glass of wine to wash it down.

She was still in love with Nick, more than she had been at the beginning, in San Remo, when, she now realised, she had been infatuated, not in love. In every way he was perfect: looks, charm, body, sexiness. When he took off his clothes, it still gave her the same visceral thrill she had experienced when she first saw him mowing the lawn, half-naked. And what a cocksman (a word she had learned from Claudia); she would never forget the first sight of that erection, when she released it from his jeans, in the hire car on the way back from Nice airport to San Remo, the afternoon she had chased after him; they had been in a frenzy on the back seat, barely parked off the main road, coupling in a copse of pine trees.

Villa Eilenroc

She spooned out another heap of primitive chocolate.

He could stay hard for as long as she wanted and needed. Before Nick, she had never made love in so many different ways, and in so many different places. If she wanted him to fuck her on the drunken way home from a party, he would stop the car by the side of the road; if she wanted it in the bath, he would oblige; in a hotel storeroom at a white wedding, he would take her, with her dress pulled up above her hips.

And outside of the bedroom, she had to admit, he had lost – no, she had rubbed off – all of those rough, gardener's edges that had so grated on her sense of ideal social behaviour. She had planned his education very carefully, taking him to grand hotels out of season, correcting any mistakes, making sure he was ready, before they went out into society. It had worked; Nick was a big success. None of her friends had any idea where he had come from; the standard response to that question was always: "His parents have a horticultural business."

She might as well finish off the tablet of chocolate. There was not much wine left in the bottle. Should she open another one? Nobody would notice; downstairs in the cellar there were thousands of them. No, better not.

And her body was as trim and firm as it had been before those awful, disgusting pregnancies. The work she had put in after the births: personal training, running, swimming, stretching, massages, spa treatments ... Nick hadn't noticed; absolutely no acknowledgement of how much effort she had put in; no, worse, he had told her she had put on weight, actually said that he liked her that way. She was furious; told him she didn't need his sympathy and pity. Then they had had an argument about her mother; Nick had said that he wouldn't leave her just because she had put on a few kilos, "Not like your father dumped your mother." She had shouted at him never to mention her mother ever again! Perhaps she had gone a little over the top, screeching like a wounded soprano. He had looked upset, went very quiet, and left the house. That had really spurred her on – more time at the gym, extra running, Turkish baths.

That woman who had cooked the lunch in St-Trop, Imogen, she was bigger than a house. Just being close to that size had made her feel quite sick. How could women let themselves go like that? You could never be a part of anything, never belong; and no men. Discipline, that was all you needed.

She had eaten the whole tablet of Ecuadorean chocolate. She was half-way through the tub; what did it matter, if her husband no longer wanted her.

Did he still love her? Had he ever loved her as much as she loved him? What if her father had been right all along, and the gardener was only after her money? Well, he wouldn't get anything like as much as he might have done if her father hadn't tied it up. No, she musn't think like that; he had loved her very much, she was sure of it, but what about now? What was this cooling down that she could sense in her bones, this dulling and ebbing away of lust and desire. How, when she was so desirable?

She put the top back on the tub – it would be nice to have it around; yes, but where would she put it? No, she'd have to finish it off, and put all the packaging away at the bottom of the bin. There were only a few spoonfuls left; and a chunk of the *Grand Cru*.

She opened the sugar-free chocolate – how did it compare? Perhaps she'd leave it lying on the table as a challenge to her husband; perhaps she just might scoff the lot. She sniffed: it had the aromas of chocolate, perhaps a bit sweeter, which seemed illogical. Still, sugar-free means guilt-free. She tried a piece. Yes, it was not bad; her father had been wrong about it being an abomination, but what did that matter? This was not about taste, it was about winning. Either she would get her husband back, or she would get her own back on him, with his beloved sugar-free chocolate. Let's see what he wanted more – his wife or his deal.

She polished off the wine. She finished the chocolate.

A Woman Scorned

At 12.15pm on the dot, Cassandra pressed the buzzer marked Volkov & Associates.

"This is Cassandra Aus ..."

The black painted metal and plate glass door clicked open; and she was inside an expensive building: a black and white marble floor giving way to a thick pile carpet in scarlet, which made her Louboutin heels wobble – red on red; Casa Blanca lilies, statuesque in a tall crystal vase; silk wallpaper in pale ivory; and a Dutch landscape.

The gated lift was very old – Thyssen 1936 – and manually operated: open out the heavy main door; slide back the clanging concertina of steel; step inside; lug and heave the door back into place; let the outer door maddeningly slowly click back into place; and press the polished brass button marked 3. To Cassandra, the slow journey upwards, with the creaking and straining pulleys above her head, visible through the metal grille cage, seemed to be conveying her to an appointment with a private eye in *film noir* – Sam Spade, Philip Marlowe – the scorned woman seeking redress, and finding romance. Of course, our Hollywood heroine is not as naïve and helpless as she seems, the scheming little minx.

The warning notice said that the lift could hold a maximum of two people, or 240 kgs (German engineering for American football players?); this meant that four of her could easily fit in, without any danger of the cables snapping. Fit in, that is, a few weeks ago because the chocolate diet was starting to have an effect on the scales; she was heading towards that 60 kilo barrier, beyond which she had never ventured, ever. Yes, but, as she reassured herself every day, assessing her lovely body in the mirror, those extra kilos didn't show, so no harm done, and nothing to hide.

A matronly woman, who would have needed the two-person lift all to herself, was waiting for her when Cassandra pushed open the resisting lift door. Like the lift, the secretary was from another era: silver beehive, pink twin-set, black pleated skirt, and black patent court shoes. A little forbidding although she smiled warmly at the new client; a smile that would not normally have been returned in anything like equal measure, but today Cassandra was not her usual imperious self.

"Hello. Those lilies smell so lovely. I'm sure you know who I am, but I'm Mrs Austin. Mr Volkov is expecting me."

"Yes, we know. Please come in. I must congratulate you. Not many people get the accent and stress for Mr Volkov's name so exactly right."

Cassandra smiled, and did not say that she had checked the pronunciation this morning; establishing authority, that was one of her father's tricks. She was pleased with herself, and feeling altogether better about this silly cloak and dagger nonsense.

"You would like a coffee? If you would care to take a seat, Mr Volkov will be right with you. Skimmed milk?"

"Please, yes, please."

What Cassandra had been expecting was Sam Spade's office – raffish and seedy – but this was much more Poirot: mahogany panelling; more Dutch pictures; a Chesterfield sofa with finely turned legs, upholstered not in the usual, tired gentleman's brown leather, but in cream and green Loomstate calico, with yellow silk cushions; and she recognised the coffee table – Isamu Noguchi. Mr Volkov had taste; she wondered if he had chosen the design, or an interior decorator. She could not have done better herself.

The matron sat behind a desk, with not one piece of paper lying around; what you might expect, thought Cassandra, from a business of secrecy. She might have been sitting in the outer office of a Swiss private banker – her banker. The coffee was fresh, and there were unread magazines and heavyweight coffee-table books, catering to every taste – yachting, fashion, business, antiques, design, country pursuits, planes, houses, art – all indicating an international clientele.

Cassandra sipped her coffee, and leafed through *Country Life*; not a magazine she ever read, but perhaps she might learn something about English women, and their husbands. *Country Life* was very worried about the collapse in the bee population – so British, trying to save their honey bees instead of their marriages. "Bit late to find out about a nation, Cassandra Austin, after you've been married to it for six years," she said to herself. Yes, that was silly, but then this was all very, very silly. Look, it was not as if her husband had installed a *maîtresse-en-titre*, and she had to corset and suffer her agony in public, maintaining her dignity with the flick of an outraged fan, her shame magnified a thousand-fold in a mocking hall of silvered mirrors. No, she just wanted everything to be back where it had been in San Remo. Perhaps she should have let Nick stay a gardener.

She was startled by a voice interrupting her admiration of an Elizabethan herb garden.

"Mrs Austin, I presume."

What is it about a sleuth that so fascinates us? Because he always gets the girl? Because he knows how to wear a suit without it wearing him? Because he possesses all those cynical macho qualities men like to affect? Perhaps, only people forget that Chandler named his classic private eye after Christopher Marlowe, poet and brawler; well, lots of men are brawlers, but very few of them are poets. The sleuth is a rare breed: the man women want; and men very rarely are.

At first glance, Cassandra would not have said that Andrei Volkov possessed a rare quality about him. Nice quality clothes, yes, but not the formal suit she had been expecting: grey cashmere sweater over a grey shirt; Armani jeans; tan Gucci horsebit loafers. When he shook her hand, she noticed the Patek Philippe Calatrava on his wrist; a watch worn by a man who uses his brain not his dick. So, very expensive casual clothes; what of the man inside them?

Cassandra had been expecting a cautious and reserved man, dry and anonymous; a man who blended into the background while he dug up the dirt on people's hidden lives. Wrong, the man standing in front of her was the very model of a Hero of Socialist Realism. Andrei Volkov could once have been a poster boy for the square-jawed men who always seemed to have their brawny arms upraised, pointing towards a glorious vision of the future that somehow never came. That is exactly the type of hero Andrei had been; and those same lost ideals were the reason why he was now shaking hands in Zurich, with an heiress to a chocolate fortune, and not pawning a living on a spook's salary in Moscow.

At thirty-seven, he still had the looks of a dreamboat icon: hair cut severely *en brosse*, of a colour that changed with the seasons; in summer bleached by the sun; in winter, turning darker; a broad chest and shoulders that said "special forces;" and he was tall, tall like the guards of the Presidential Regiment that you see standing ramrod to attention at the entrance to the St George's Hall in the Kremlin (exactly where Andrei himself had once stood). Yes, Andrei Volkov had got out of a suffocating system, and done well for himself.

He ushered Cassandra into his office.

"Do you choose your own furniture?" she asked as he gestured to a chair she recognised.

Andrei was surprised. He looked at Mrs Austin with more interest. "I've never been asked that question. But yes, and I am sure you know that this is a Wasily chair by Marcel Breuer, named after Vasily Kandinsky, Breuer's friend."

"And you bought the Kandinsky behind you to go with the chair."

This Cassandra Austin was nobody's fool, thought Andrei. Frank Schulte hadn't taken the correct measure of her.

"So, you want me to follow your husband."

"I didn't say that it was my husband."

"No, you didn't. Are we talking money, another woman or a man?"

"My husband is not like that."

"Mrs Austin, if you knew what your husband was really like you would not be here."

Andrei's smile was bright, but the tone of voice was dark.

Cassandra recoiled.

Andrei caught her turmoil and hurt. "It is not my job to be nice, Mrs Austin."

Cassandra softened. "Can I ask you a question first?"

"Fire away."

"Can you keep a secret?"

"It's my business."

"Good." Cassandra paused. It was a fine Kandinsky. This man had an eye for detail; and that was what she needed. She plunged in. "I don't know what it is, only that something's wrong, and I want to know."

Villa Eilenroc

"I understand. That's it?" Andrei waited just a few seconds, for any further questions. Cassandra nodded. "Some other things: I run the show, and you don't play assistant detective. I will give it one month. If I have no results at the end of the month, I will advise you to drop the tail. I charge five thousand euro a day plus expenses whether or not I myself am doing the work or one of my colleagues. If you want to call it off now, no offence taken."

Cassandra did not hesitate. "I agree, and now I have some other things. You will tell me exactly what you do every day. You will tell me exactly what my husband does, and who he meets. Oh, and you had better come up with results, Mr Volkov." Andrei was surprised, and pleased to see that Mrs Austin had some backbone in her. If her husband was playing around, he was a fool. "I have no proof, just feminine intuition. I get flowers on all the right occasions. He's a good father and loves his children."

"The perfect marriage."

"Yes."

"But even the best silk shirt, Mrs Austin, has small imperfections. So, I will start very soon, and send you a report in one month."

"Nothing else?"

"What else would you like?"

"I thought that you would ask me lots of questions about my marriage."

"Such as?"

"Well, our sex life ... my husband's sexual fantasies."

"What fantasies does he have?"

"I don't know. He hasn't told me, and I don't ask."

"Mrs Austin, no matter how tempted you might be, please, don't ask him any questions. I will give you all the answers."

Pros and Cons

Orgasms
He's married.
Great body
That thing he does down there
I can't text him
He fucks me like a whore – that's a pro?
He wants the lights on when we make love
He tells me non-stop that he loves my body
Big cock – no, that makes no difference, or does it?
I'm losing weight – what's that all about?

Pros – 4
Cons – 3
Undecided – 3

Cherchez la femme

COCKS CANNOT LIE; cunts can. When a man gets a hard-on he has nowhere to hide; when a woman is up for it she can keep it a secret. That is why the word "cunt" is a swear word, signifying the ability to cheat; nobody talks about "cock" to mean cheating. You might call a man a "dick" or a "prick," but you only mean that he is stupid. Why then, if it is so difficult for a man to cheat, do men apparently cheat so much? Because they're dickheads.

Andrei Volkov liked to narrow his investigations down to the essentials: you look for the weakness in a man, that was what Andrei had been taught. That faultline is where a man is vulnerable, and open to being used (if you think that he can be useful), or where he reveals himself (and gets found out). *Kompromat* is the Russian word, meaning compromising material; Andrei had seen how effective *kompromat* could be, most of all where a cock is involved.

Forget about the word "cocksure;" a man's cock is his biggest weakness. Why? Because he's in love with it. If you want to see how obsessed men are with their cocks, look at all the selfies on Tumblr, Kik and Instagram. Oh, how men love and adore their cocks! They always have: it was exactly the same in the days of oil on canvas – look at all those lovingly observed codpieces. To understand men, today, you just need an iPhone. That obsession is why his cock always gets a man into trouble; and cocks have been responsible for all sorts of troubles: a marriage is destroyed by a straying cock; a war is waged by fighting cocks; a financial crisis is caused by a big swinging dick.

If you can find out where a man likes to put his cock, you can find out almost everything there is to know about him. In any investigation, sexuality comes first: gay, and you are not going to be looking for a woman; straight, and *cherchez la femme* is the way to go. Before that, however, as Andrei well knew, you have to find out if your target is gay or straight; not always easy to identify. You do not need to be a private detective to know that a married man – a 'straight' man married to a woman, that is – might also be gay. The fact that Nick Austin was married meant zilch. Moreover, in Andrei's experience, the more successful the man, the more successfully he can lead a double life. Up to a point. A cheating man, or a man who has something to hide, is very often over-confident about not being caught. Deception is difficult to maintain over long periods (even for spies, for whom deception is a way of life); cheating is for sprinters.

You do not start to follow your target immediately. First, you try to find out as much about him as you can, sitting behind your desk. What do his parents do? What do people say about them? Where did he go to school? What did he get up to at school? Any known liaisons? Find out about previous partners. What do they have to say about him? Who are his friends? Academic record. Work history. Business dealings. Phone records. Criminal record. Internet surfing. Build up a profile, put together a file. Somewhere, there is a weakness. Where does all this information come from? People leave big footprints, especially when they don't know that they are being followed; you just have to know how to find them. Stealth and patience are what you need – exactly the same as tracking a wild animal.

Within four days of Cassandra Austin coming to his office, Andrei had found out that her husband had once had a gay side. Nick Austin had had a long relationship at his public school, with a sporting hero, but the trail went cold after that – only girls; must have been a phase. His parents ran a successful garden centre, in an affluent area of North Yorkshire in England. Having spent three years on a posting in London, Andrei knew that this profession placed them outside the British class system – an English gardener is classless. Nick had been thrown out of university; Andrei thought that was an interesting piece of information. This was a man who had gambled on himself – his ability to wing it – and lost; and then won back big time when he married a rich Italian. Quite a student hellraiser too, drinking and sleeping around, mainly with 'dogs;' now he had a very beautiful wife. Well, that was the British for you – champagne money and beer taste. This, then, was not a man who liked to play a waiting game; he liked to leapfrog – a man in a hurry; to go where, though? A man who liked to take risks, certainly. Perhaps gambling was the weakness? Nick was sociable, that fitted the pattern of behaviour and character that Andrei was forming about him in his mind. Mr Austin was nice if it got Mr Austin what he wanted. Nick had had lots of friends, but they had fallen by the wayside (or he had dropped them) after his marriage. So, Nick Austin was ruthless and charming; the classic social climber.

What was it that he had to hide? A gay lover? A mistress? Drugs? Money worries? Something kinky? Somewhere, Nick Austin was covering his tracks – if Cassandra Austin's instict was right.

Where to start? Look for the pattern that is out of the ordinary, or doesn't make sense for this profile and lifestyle – low-life acquaintances, bad neighbourhoods, brushes with the law; anything that suggests a life being lived outside the comfort zone. No man is an angel, but the Devil started off in Heaven.

Andrei enjoyed picking up the scent, and then following his nose during the chase. Only there was no scent; either his wife had got it all wrong or Nick Austin had gone to ground. Andrei had sent an assistant down to Turin to track Nick's every move, and then to San Remo. The report made for boring reading. Nick Austin led a regulated life, moving between family and work; he left the house at the same time every day; he had lunch delivered to his office; he rarely worked late. There were the occasional business meetings, mainly to do with chocolate. They had friends to dinner, or they went out to restaurants, leaving the children in the care of a housekeeper who was an old retainer. A glamorous couple, perfect in every way. That was it, of course, there was no such thing as perfection. Where was the flaw in the diamond?

Andrei looked through the file again, cross-checking Nick's comings and goings. He knew all about the day trip to Montenegro because he knew all about the chocolate deal, in the same way that he knew all about the gold mine without any gold; they were both Frank's deals, and Frank was one of his best clients. Andrei also knew who had been on Tikhon's yacht because it was his business to know; he knew the players who had been on board (he had a file on every one of them), and the keepers who had looked after them – the captain, the army of staff (who had not been on board, for secrecy's sake), and the fat woman who cooked the lunch. Besides, Tikhon was also a client. No, there was nothing strange or suspicious about that day.

Where were the gaps? A secretary with big tits? Massage parlours? Nick looked at straight porn; well, a few furtive wanks onscreen don't break a marriage. Still, it also doesn't make a man 'straight.' So, any pretty boys met 'by chance' in a café, or wined

Villa Eilenroc

and dined in a style they might not be used to? Any young and handsome colleagues seen meeting with Nick over a 'business lunch' or 'assisting' him at a conference or trade show? No, nothing. Even so, Andrei had not entirely ruled out the possibility that Nick had that very English tendency of marrying one sex and playing with another. He had all but ruled out another woman.

Hour by hour, there was a record of every step Nick had taken – every walk, drive, coffee, lunch, meeting, drink, jack-off; and nothing, absolutely fucking nothing.

Well, if there *was* somebody, he or she was hiding or buried in that file. Andrei's tail, the guy who had followed Nick, had confirmed that there was no lover or mistress waiting impatiently at a love nest somewhere, dressed in a jock strap or maribou, for Mr Austin to come calling; they had found no evidence of that sort of set-up; that would have been nice and easy – too easy.

A good detective – the spy also – is a codebreaker, decoding the cheating stratagems. There are two ways of cheating: you do everything you can to hide it, bury it out of sight; or you deliberately bring it out into the open, into your 'normal' life, in the hope of openly escaping detection. Both strategies are doomed to failure. Encryption, decryption; Andrei would have to go through the file, again and again; and then step away from it to think.

He looked through the headshots of everybody with whom Nick was associated. He was not looking for beauty, or rather, he didn't think that was what he was looking for; he was looking for whatever it was, not necessarily a person, that drove Nick Austin to risk everything he had; some inner compulsion, addiction or demon that he could not escape. Sooner or later, Andrei would find it; cheating is always a losing game.

Frank had asked Andrei to keep him informed. Poor Nick, did he have any idea that whatever it was he was up to, would be used against him; Frank would show him no mercy. Andrei knew from Frank that he and Nick had met on four occasions in the recent past: the charity ball where they had first met; a business lunch in Monte Carlo; a finding-out-about-people lunch in Saint-Tropez; and Montenegro. According to Frank, Nick had driven to Monte Carlo, and back to Turin the same day; and the talk had been all about wine and chocolate.

Andrei went back to the lunch in Saint-Tropez when Frank had entertained Nick, his wife and the hated father-in-law. Did Frank perhaps know about Nick's dalliance, if that is what it was (and was keeping it in reserve) or just have his suspicions? Or, and this was quite possible, had Frank put temptation in Nick's way? The lunch had been connected with the chocolate deal, so did that mean that one of the guests had been invited undercover? There had been one beautiful girl; no, it couldn't be Jade because Andrei knew that Frank was fucking her; and a beautiful young man, Casimir, who had the track record for that sort of thing – upmarket whoring – but he did not appear anywhere else in the file. What about a member of Frank's staff? Frank was quite capable of whoring out somebody who worked for him if that was what a deal needed. There was one obvious candidate, the trainee Massimo; only he was fucking Mrs Schulte, and being fucked by Frank's chef. Yes, Frank kept quite a menagerie. There was nobody else who might have appealed to Nick.

What was it, then, that had aroused Cassandra Austin's suspicions? Lipstick on the collar? No, she had said nothing like that. Andrei was certain that this suspicion was something fresh in her mind. Cassandra Austin was a determined woman, spoiled, yes, but nobody's fool; she was used to getting what she wanted, and keeping it. She would not allow her husband to stray for too long before she pulled him up, or threw him away.

Andrei looked through Nick's credit card statements, searching for payments away from Turin and San Remo. For a man who had started off as a gardener, Nick Austin certainly knew how to spend money: Hermès, Bottega Veneta, Ferrari, mooring fees and maintenance for a very expensive boat in San Remo; Netjets, Berry Bros, Huntsman ... Andrei had identified the journey to Monte Carlo, when Nick had met with Frank, from the petrol stations: Nick had filled up on the A6 in the morning; and again in the afternoon.

Andrei went back further: there was a bill for La Chèvre d'Or in Èze-Village. Had Nick gone there with Cassandra? Unlikely; 266 kilometres was a long way to go for lunch. The next item caught his eye. That didn't make sense – why had Nick put fuel in his boat the same day? Had he gone out in the boat as well? Andrei checked the calendar. What, on a weekday, Nick had driven from Turin all the way to Èze, and then on to San Remo? Very strange. Who had that lunch been with? He could ask Mrs Austin what it meant, but, if she had not been with her husband, she would not be able to resist confronting him. Andrei would have to do the digging himself.

His senses quickened. There was a substantial bill for a very grand hotel in Montecatini Terme. And the next day some purchases in Lucca; lots of food he noticed. He recognised the shops – La Bottega di Prospero, Forno a vapore ... Andrei could see the shops in his mind's eye; he knew Lucca quite well – he liked cooking Italian. That weekend had probably been with Cassandra, but best to double-check. Some money to the hotel staff, and he would have the answer.

Andrei closed the file, and locked it away. He left a note for Ingrid on her desk, asking her to find out with whom Nick had spent two nights at the Grand Hotel La Pace. He closed the office, switched on the alarm system, and went out into the early evening street. Rush hour in Zurich, and it looked like a Sunday anywhere else. He remembered commuting in Moscow, when the crowd at the doors to Barrikadnaya metro had been twenty deep. Not his favourite city, but you had to know your way around it. Good that he was from St Petersburg; that was where the power lay, in his business, anyway.

This evening he would cook, it would help him to think. He would make something fiddly, something that needed concentration. *Pelmeni*, a taste of Russia. Apart from business, food was the only connection he still had with the Motherland. When the Swiss had granted him asylum, he had vowed never to return, and he never had. It had not been a bad deal; he had given nothing away of any significance, nothing that could compromise any of his former colleagues, but, even so, on Russian soil, you could never be too sure. Mind you, even after he had "gone over to the other side," they were still his colleagues, only now they were strictly "commercial." How things had changed: they had used to believe in something – what was it they had believed in, he couldn't rightly remember – now, the only thing to believe in was your wallet. God, the money he was putting their way, in exchange for information, very valuable information. His office was like a cloud storage facility. Russians everywhere.

He headed for Jelmoli, where he bought more food than he needed for one man living alone. It had been a long time since he had lived with a woman – fucks don't count.

He bought cheese in Chäs Vreneli. He was thinking about cooking – did Cassandra cook? Lucca ... why all that food? Rich women don't cook, certainly not women like Cassandra Austin. Did Nick Austin cook? That was quite possible. No, buying that food probably meant nothing; it was the sort of thing an Englishman would do.

Andrei's penthouse apartment did not say, "Lived in by a Russian" – no icons, no *palekh,* no brightly painted spoons ... The day they had given him a Swiss passport, he had told himself that he would not surround himself with memories. Lucky, if you could call it luck, that his parents had died in the traditional Russian way – alcoholism and lung cancer. No siblings. Some aunts and uncles in Archangel, but he kept his distance.

The apartment was decorated in minimalist style; neat and tidy, not because he was particularly houseproud, only that he had a good cleaner. The place had cost him a fortune, but he was making a fortune. He didn't like cats, and he didn't want a dog; that left cooking.

It wasn't completely true that there was nothing Russian in the apartment. He had a nice collection of Soviet nonconformist art – Ilya Kabakov, Komar and Melamid, Viktor Pivovarov, Oleg Tselkov ...; and there were quite a few cookery books, all of them in some way connected with Russian cooking, including a first edition of Carême's *L'Art de la cuisine française au dix-neuvième siècle. Traité élémentaire et pratique.* Paris, 1833–1847. And the first edition of *A Gift to Young Housewives, or a means to reduce costs in the household,* by Yelena Molokhovets, first published in 1861. Interesting how much she had borrowed from Carême; that cross-pollination between French and Russian cuisine was what most interested Andrei.

The apartment had come with a very swish Bulthaup kitchen, and Andrei had bought every utensil a cook could ever need. He laid out his shopping on the central marble counter, and set to work – mincing the meat, chopping the onions, rolling the pastry. He smiled at himself. So much for cutting all ties with Russia; who was he kidding? He was making a classic Russian dish, and listening to Rachmaninov's *Prince Rostislav*! Pity he didn't have anybody to share the food with him. He had never made a conscious decision to live alone, and it had nothing to do with doing what he did; yes, he had lots of secrets, but they were money-making secrets, not deadly. Why then, was he alone? Too picky? What did he want in a woman? A housewife? A daily fuck? No, he wanted a soulmate. There was no shortage of candidates, but nobody who fitted the bill.

It was his looks, they were the problem; was it right for a man to say that? He didn't trust them, the looks; he never had. He had enjoyed them, but that was not the same thing. He had been what, fourteen or fifteen, when they first started to get him what he wanted – first kiss, first grope, first fuck. Later, the looks had got him into the Presidential Regiment – like a beauty parade it had been; looked up and down, pinched and poked, and put through your paces, like choosing a stallion at a gypsy fair. Mind you, he'd looked good in the uniform; they even taught him to ride, parading in front of gawping tourists. After that, the right college; and then the Service. It had all been so easy, such a smooth upwards trajectory. Of course, he had the brains to match the heroic features, but, like every man with a plenitude of talents, he valued them cheaply. Because he didn't trust them, those kiss-me looks, he didn't believe in them; same as he'd never really believed the bullshit they had fed him. He had never trusted what the looks gave him – success at work, success with women; how could you be sure that she wanted you for what was inside you, and not that killer smile? "It's those cheekbones," one of his first girlfriends had said, "they cast their own shadow." Oh yes, he understood Nick Austin; it was like looking in a mirror. So what was it that they both wanted, Mr Volkov and Mr Austin? Something they couldn't have? Or something they shouldn't have?

He was boiling the dumplings when he realised that there was something strange about that Netjets item in Nick's credit card statement. For a start, Nick Austin had a private jet, or, at least, his father-in-law had one; Nick and Cassandra had the use of it whenever they wished. Why would he charter a plane from Nice to Lucca, when he was in Turin?

Andrei abruptly left the dumplings on the boil, and sat down at his laptop to check out the geography of Tuscany on Google Maps. Of course, Lucca was the nearest airport to Montecatini Terme! Business meeting? No, couldn't be; the type of people with whom Nick did business didn't need to have planes chartered for them. So, who had been on that plane?

He strained the *pelmeni*, put them into an enormous bowl, and slathered sour cream over them. His doctor had told him to be careful about his cholesterol count – at his age! Low fat tomorrow. He poured himself a glass of Barolo.

He had no evidence yet, but Andrei was certain Nick Austin had not been with his wife that weekend; and probably he had not been with her in Èze either. It was cock. *Plus ça change*; find out where a man has been putting his cock, and you can find him out. And that's when a man turns out to be a cunt.

Rubenesque

"*Of, RELATING TO, or suggestive of the painter Rubens or his works; especially: plump or rounded usually in a pleasing or attractive way.*" *That is what the dictionary says. Strange, but Rubenesque is a relatively new word, apparently, only first coined in 1913. Were there any Rubenesque women in 1913? Surely, they were all in corsets?*

Poor Peter Paul Rubens (1577-1640), so multi-talented – spy, diplomat, knighted by two kings, painter of Counter–Reformation altarpieces, portraits of haughty aristocrats, mythological and allegorical scenes – only to be remembered for his fat – sorry – Rubenesque women.

But what did he expect! Look at the size of his women. Take his Venus at the Mirror; she is gi-normous! Look at that ass! Those thighs! Is that sexy? Is that pleasing to the eye? Well, why not? As she is beautiful to Rubens, so might she not be beautiful to us? Take a closer look at that lovely milkmaid face, those rosebud lips, the mass of golden tresses. Rubens can't get enough of her, that is why he paints her face twice. In profile, the face is imperious, a little bit serious; but when we look at her in the mirror, and she looks out at us, she is full-on beautiful. Flirtatious, confident, knowing, quizzical, she gives us the merest hint of what a strumpet she might be in the bedroom. Rubens is enamoured of her, every inch of her. He gives her skin a lacquered sheen, shimmering as if he has polished her with his hand. Those shoulders;

we just know that Rubens indulged in them, nuzzled his cheek against her neck; as we do, worshipping her with him. Here is an unapologetic sensuality bursting out of the corsets that imprisoned women in restrictive fabric. Unclothed, caressed only by sheer silk, Rubens has set Venus free; she is earthy, she is a goddess. This is an aesthetic that holds in perfect balance, the impulse to fuck, and the impulse to paint. What the word Rubenesque really means is nothing to do with size, it is about what it means to love women.

He couldn't get enough of her. When they made love, Imogen felt as if he were eating her up. Sex with Nick was like a blow-out Christmas dinner.

"Do you only want me for my body?" she asked, sated. She was lying naked on a four-poster bed in the presidential suite of the Grand-Hôtel du Cap-Ferrat.

Nick was wolfing down a full English breakfast, seated naked at a dining-table. "I love your body, every inch of it."

"Yes, I know, I have the stigmata to prove it, only I feel like I'm a part of room service. Just another something on the menu."

"You don't like being a sex symbol?"

"I don't want to be *just* a sex symbol."

"What else do you want to be? Are you sure you don't want something to eat? Don't you like the idea of breakfast in the middle of the afternoon?"

"I'm not hungry. I've gone off food. I want to be a mistress. I'll have some of the orange juice, no champagne. I'm sick of bubbly."

"You are a mistress."

"I'm not a stay-at-home maribou mistress, I'm a hole-in-the-corner mistress. How many hotel suites have we been in, in the past seven months?"

"You're counting the months?"

"We're on a time limit, remember? I feel like we're going through a list of 'Best places to fuck on the Riviera.'"

"Nice. I always get the penthouse suite."

"That's not what I mean. I don't want to sound ungrateful because I know how much this sex is costing you, but I've developed an intense dislike of anything that is 'tastefully decorated;' and I absolutely hate beige. And if I sit in another jacuzzi my skin will shrivel like a prune."

"Mo, you want something I can't give you. I told you that before we started on this thing. You know, you can always tell if it's a really good hotel if they can make scrambled eggs."

"So we're having a thing, is that it?"

"I thought you were enjoying this thing?"

"I am enjoying it."

"Doesn't sound like it."

"You're not listening to what I'm really saying."

"Aah."

"I won't deny that the sex is the best I've ever had."

"Thanks for the compliment."

"But you can't keep a relationship going on sex alone."

"Why not?"

"We never talk! All we do is take a hotel suite and fuck! And then say goodbye! I know this is meant to be everybody's dream, but now that I'm living it ..."

"I'll make sure the next room isn't in beige." Nick was smiling, as he put a glass of orange juice to Imogen's lips.

"Be serious."

Nick sat down on the bed, cross-legged. "Okay, I'm really listening."

Imogen got up from the bed, so as not to be too close to him. She knew that he would be at her body – the man was always hungry – and she would be helpless to resist. She seated herself at the dressing-table, and looked at him in the reflection of the mirror. She brushed her blonde hair for want of anything else to do.

"I'm not asking for love. I'm not asking you to leave your wife. I'm asking for ... I don't know ... going out to a restaurant, the theatre, a film."

"You know why we can't do that."

"Because you're afraid of getting caught."

"Seems like a pretty good reason."

"Oh, I know it is, Nick. But we had lunch in Èze at the beginning."

"Yes, and how many times did you say afterwards that it made you uncomfortable thinking about what people were thinking?"

"That was different then. Now I've been condemned to hell and damnation, I don't think I mind."

"I mind."

"Because you just want to have your cake and eat it."

"So that's what this is really all about."

"It's true. You've got a good thing going here. All pleasure, and no guilt."

"I feel guilty as hell."

"You don't show it. What's wrong with our having lunch in public, and if anybody asks we can say that I'm going to cook for you."

"It will get back to Cassie."

"What makes you think she doesn't know already?"

"I thought we had agreed we wouldn't talk about her? What makes you think she does know?"

"Women's intuition. You told me she's put on weight."

"I don't see the connection."

"Don't you? No, probably you don't."

"Je bande pour toi."

"Is that all you can think about? Your cock?"

"It's the only thing a man thinks about. You look very sexy from behind, you know that."

"With my ass spreading all over the chair?"

"Especially. Very erotic, that silk scarf."

"I didn't mean to sit on it. Well?"

"Well, what?"

"Lunch, dinner, a film, anything in public that's decent, only not breakfast in the afternoon."

"Tu me casses les couilles."

"Et t'es rien qu'un petit connard."

"I thought that's what you liked about me?"

"You want it both ways, don't you? You can't have a hard-on and then say I'm busting your balls."

"Okay! You win. I'll think of something. By the way, you've lost weight."

"You almost sound disappointed. Most men would be pleased."

"I'm not most men."

"And how am I now then?"

"Rubenesque."

Combattente

"You've put on weight."

"I haven't."

"It's not an accusation."

"I'm not guilty of anything."

"What's that supposed to mean?"

"I'm just saying that's all."

"There's nothing guilty about putting on weight. You look very Rubenesque. I keep telling you I like it."

"Stop telling me."

"Cassie, what is it with you? You're like a bear with a sore head, morning, noon and night. You're even short with the kids."

"How would you know? You're always in a meeting."

"You know why. I want this deal. If we're to survive, we need this deal. We need these sugar-free chocolates. I know your father's against it, and I know he thinks it's personal but it's not. The company needs this deal."

"I liked you better when you were a gardener."

"You didn't want me to be a gardener, remember? You said that you were going to dig the gardener out of me."

"What makes you think I'm going to support you in this deal? You want me to vote against my own father?"

"Better if you tried to persuade him that I'm doing the right thing. You think I want to fight all the time? It's a family business."

"Yes, Nick, it is."

"Oh, and what, suddenly I'm not a part of this family? The outsider? Daddy and daughter closing ranks? Thanks a million."

"What did you expect? You just ignore me. Papa was right, you married me for my money."

"I'm not going to have this argument. I married you because I love you. I still love you. I always will."

Beatrice came into the kitchen, timing her entrance to maximum effect. She would do anything she could not to see a repeat performance of the way in which Cassandra's parents had destroyed their marriage: *"Combattere di nuovo? Solo l'avvocato vince."*

Nick tried to make light of the ill-feeling. *"Il tempo di preoccuparsi è quando smettiamo di lottare, Beatrice."*

"Andare via e fare qualche soldi!"

Thank God for Beatrice, thought Nick, giving his wife as much of a kiss as she would allow. "Money, money, money!"

When he was gone, Beatrice busied herself in the kitchen. Cassandra sat at the kitchen table, silent. Many years ago, at this same table, Beatrice had seen exactly that same look on Cassandra's mother's face – pain, agony, hurt, anger, fear, shame; the malignant maelstrom of a marriage going wrong. This was a repeat performance: Cassandra's mother had also put on weight; and that had been the decisive blow, the death knell. Personally, Beatrice thought that Nick was right, Cassandra looked better with a bit more weight on her – quite a bit more – but there was something else: she had stopped taking care of herself; and that was where she was going wrong.

When Beatrice judged that enough time had passed, she asked the only question that mattered: *"Lo ami?"*

The answer was a long time in coming. Beatrice could wait. It was not that Cassie did not know the answer; it was the consequences.

"*Sì.*"

"*Così, Cassandra, allora devi combattere.*"

The voice was small. "I'm not sure I have the stomach for a fight, Beatrice."

Компромат

Sex and money; they are the twin pillars of *kompromat* because people – not just Russians – have such a liking for them; a liking often outside of the boundaries of the law, and what passes for public decency.

In his time, Andrei Volkov had instigated any number of compromising situations. He disliked 'set-ups,' the belaboured manufacturing of compromising material – call girls cavorting with a politician behind a two-way mirror. That was too 'clunky' for him; he much preferred naturally occurring *kompromat*. Experience had taught him that if you give your target enough rope, he will hang himself. So it was with Nick Austin.

Andrei had been right to have his suspicions about the connection between the lunch in Èze, the Netjets charter, the hotel in Montecatini Terme, and the shopping in Lucca. He had found out soon enough that Nick had used his boat the day he was in Èze; from the fuel consumption, out of San Remo, Andrei had pretty much worked out that Nick had piloted the boat close to Èze. Neither had it taken him very long to come up with a name of the somebody Nick had met, but that only caused Andrei yet more consternation; he had been so surprised that he had asked for the information to be double-checked. No doubt about it, was the answer: Imogen O'Rorke. Okay, no reason to be suspicious there: she cooked for Frank, she had cooked for Tikhon, now she was cooking for Nick; that was how she picked up her clients – word of mouth; yes, that was the obvious explanation. Say that was true, though, then where was the mistress or the boyfriend?

At that moment, Andrei might have been willing to give Nick the benefit of the doubt, and advise Cassandra Austin to drop the tail, except that when she came to his office for a report on her husband, Andrei knew just from looking at her, that Nick Austin was up to no good.

Andrei was shocked. He could barely recognise Cassandra as the sleek and well-groomed woman she had been such a short time ago: her hair looked a mess; she had chipped nail polish; and she had put on a lot of weight.

Neither was she the self-assured woman she had been. "I don't understand, Mr Volkov, why you want me to continue paying you when you have found out nothing?"

"It is the nothing that is bothering me, Mrs Austin, as it is you also, no?"

Cassandra thought about this for a moment. "Yes, I suppose that's it. I can't put my finger on anything. Nothing concrete."

"I am going to handle this on my own now, no assistants. If I do not find anything, I will not charge you for my time."

"You must be very confident of finding something."

"Please leave it with me."

That conversation had been only a few days ago. Now, Andrei was following Imogen O'Rorke. She was in Monaco, shopping.

Andrei followed Imogen from one expensive shop to another, as she spent money like water – Nick Austin's money, no doubt. Nick had withdrawn 20,000 euro a few weeks before, from an ATM inside the Grand-Hôtel du Cap-Ferrat, and Imogen was paying in cash. Well, it certainly wasn't workwear she was buying, not unless she was changing career: little bags of lingerie and frippery from Hermès, Valentino and Prada.

He watched her linger in front of Chanel. She seemed to be looking as much at her reflection as at the display models, like a doctor examining an X-ray, the thin model bones showing up against her outer, bigger shadow. He watched as she walked away a few paces, and then, abruptly, she returned, head held high. She stepped inside. He waited – nearly an hour. She emerged, dressed in a pale pink suit, over a cream shirt, and carrying several bags. She was smiling – she seemed pleased with herself.

From across the street, he watched as she bought a pair of shoes in Stephane Kélian (platform sandals in khaki and ebony woven leather, crossed straps).

She must have had some spare change, thought Andrei. Now he was almost smiling as he watched her walk into Chopard, with a wonderful, easy confidence. Was she buying something for herself, or for Nick, he wondered. No, it couldn't be for him, that would be too risky; he might wear it by mistake, in front of his wife. Something to go with whatever she had in those Chanel bags, then? What, they were going out somewhere in public?

Andrei was surprised, but he understood the motive: they were going to brazen it out, daring people to think that they were a couple. But, and this was what he could not get his head around, was it really possible? Could it be that this was the mistress, the woman for whom a rich man with everything, with so much to lose, would risk his all? What did this woman have that Cassandra Austin lacked? Size, for one thing; she was not as big as Andrei had thought she would be, from the photographs in the file, but she was still big. She reminded him of those women painted by Rubens – larger than life – but this woman was real. Tikhon had mentioned her when they had been talking about the gold deal.

"Fuckable, like a merchant's wife she is. That picture by Kustodiev, you know? Where she's drinking tea."

"Yes, I know it. With the samovar and the table full of food."

"Yeah, that one. And she can cook. What a wife she'd make."

He walked right behind her, knowing that he could get much closer to her on the pavement because she had no idea he was there, than if he were following somebody who suspected they were being followed. He sized her up, observing the straight-backed poise that struck him as being not very Monte Carlo, more English gentleman farmer's wife. She was different from the other women around her, not so much because of her size, although that was what everybody noticed first – people did a double-take, turned their heads to watch the rear view moving away – no, it seemed to him more like a deliberate unbelonging; and yet she *did* belong here. Not forgetting the stupendous tits, he wondered if that was what Nick found attractive about her, that she walked, lived, and no doubt fucked, with centuries of good breeding, as if, in her mind, the family silver was always shining on the dining-room table.

She swayed, that was what he noticed about her; not the chaotic swaying of a goods train, but the elegant controlled motion of the TGV Sud. It was an anti-aesthetic, completely out of sync with the stick-thin ideals of glossy magazine beauty. Andrei was starting to understand that a man had to look at Imogen for some time to appreciate her attractiveness; and he did find her attractive.

He watched as she sat down at a table right at the front of the Café de Paris. He took a table at the back, in a corner, and watched. She ordered juice and a salad. She was sitting in full view of the world going by, albeit hiding behind Persol sunglasses.

He was certain that she was waiting for somebody, was it

Nick Austin? If this was what she was doing, he had to admit that she was carrying it off with *savoir-faire*. It took some guts to sit in the Place du Casino, waiting for a rendezvous with a married man. With her sunglasses, her pink suit, her shopping bags, she could have been waiting for George Clooney. Perhaps Tikhon had been right: whatever it was, this woman had something.

As he watched Imogen sip her juice and pick at her salad, Andrei thought about what he knew of her, from the little that was in the file. She had breeding – Irish blue blood on one side, Czech money on the other; that explained the class. Cassandra Austin also had class, but her father had started out with nothing. For all his faults, however, Nick Austin didn't strike Andrei as a snob. Imogen would know how to behave in public, but that was hardly a reason for adultery. Money? Nick didn't need money, and, in any case, from what he remembered, Imogen had very little. Little, of course, is a relative word when you are living in Cap d'Antibes ... Imogen was making money from her cooking, but when you compared her finances with Cassandra's ...

It had to be sex, it couldn't be anything else. What it came down to, then, was this: Nick Austin wanted sex with Imogen O'Rorke more than he wanted sex with his wife. Andrei found that hard to believe.

He had been sitting, observing Imogen for some forty minutes, when he saw Nick's white Ferrari coming round the square. That was some car, thought Andrei, who was something of a petrolhead. Andrei watched as Nick stopped the Dino in front of the Hôtel de Paris, got out, left the keys in the ignition, and just walked away, heading towards Imogen. "These rich people," thought Andrei. "They're something else. Possessions mean everything, and absolutely nothing to them." Dressed down in chinos, a lilac polo shirt, and Tod's – clothes that he could himself afford, easily – Andrei nevertheless knew that he was envious of Nick's nonchalance. Rich as he was, he, Andrei, would still have wanted to ask the doorman to look after the car.

Andrei watched as Nick kissed Imogen on both cheeks, and took a seat next to her. Andrei couldn't hear what they were saying, but he could guess: she was telling him that he was late …

"Sorry, I couldn't get away from the office."

"I feel like I'm on show here."

"Adultery becomes you."

"That isn't funny."

"Are you sure you still want to go through with this?"

"Are you kidding?"

"I thought that you might be having second thoughts?"

"You think I'm going to waste this suit? You have no idea what it cost me." Nick smiled. "You know what I mean! These shoes? And wait until you see what I bought for this evening, boy would Claudia be amazed if she had seen me. I felt like I was in *Pretty Woman*. Second thoughts? Forget it, lead on MacDuff."

"No, let's have a drink first."

"You can really wait that long?"

"The wait is always worth it. I want to watch you being watched."

"You're a pervert, a voyeur, you know that?"

Nick just grinned. He ordered a *citron pressé*. For half an hour, Andrei watched them watch the people go by, just another well-heeled couple enjoying the sun and each other. Then they stood up.

Andrei's eyes followed them as Nick and Imogen walked the short distance to the Hôtel de Paris, and went inside. Andrei gave them ten minutes, and then he went inside the hotel. He looked around; they were not sitting anywhere. They had taken a room. He took a seat in the bar where he could watch them leave, whenever that would be, and waited.

He waited more than three hours. He was used to waiting. Years ago, he had done this exact same thing, as a rookie, sitting in the Hotel Astoria in St Petersburg, watching and waiting for foreigners.

Andrei liked sitting alone with his thoughts; thinking backwards, and thinking forwards. Pointless looking back – you couldn't change anything that way. What was he going to do with his life? He was well established, making good money; and dissatisfied. What did he want? He was thinking about writing a book, about foreign chefs in Imperial Russia. Alone in bed at night, he was reading up on Alexandre Dumas, who had been in Russia for two years, from 1858, and had written about the native food. He knew that there was plenty of material for such a book, in the archives, waiting to be used. He was not proud of his line of work; digging up people's secrets was not a noble profession. He smiled at himself, thinking that that was exactly what he would be doing in the archives …

When Nick and Imogen stepped out into the lobby, it was early evening, and Imogen was wearing the dress that she must have bought that afternoon in Chanel – a silver evening dress that emphasised all those delicious curves. Andrei had to admit that she looked a picture. The woman had class, and, yes, Tikhon had been right, she had sex appeal.

"How do you manage to walk in those things?" asked Nick.

"With great care. Do you like them? Stephane Kélian."

"Very nice. I like the earrings."

"Chopard, rose gold and amethyst. They weren't very expensive."

"You look good in my money."

"This evening, I actually believe you."

"Okay, here we go. Ready?"

"In for a penny, in for a pound."

They walked into the Louis XV restaurant. Andrei should have waited, but, quite out of character, and breaking all the rules, he walked into the restaurant, a little behind them. He was lucky, there was a table – it was midweek. He wanted to observe the lovers at close hand; he had to be sure. Sure of what? That they were having an affair? How much more evidence did he need? Besides, he had never eaten here.

In this place, where everybody was rich and glamorous, Nick and Imogen did not attract attention. Of course, Andrei understood that was why they had chosen this particular restaurant. They might have been able to sit there all evening, unnoticed, except that Alain Ducasse almost immediately came out from the kitchen to say hello. *"Eh bien!* The lady from the market at last comes to my restaurant!" He kissed Imogen affectionately.

If Imogen was in any way flustered, it did not show. "Alain, please, you should not be leaving your kitchen for me. I have been here many times, and you very well know it! May I introduce Nick Austin."

Nick stood up to shake hands. Everybody in the restaurant was watching. "The lady from the market? I don't understand?" he asked.

Alain was smiling broadly. "We have been meeting in Nice market for years. How many you think?" he asked Imogen.

"Too many to remember."

Alain was in an expansive mood. "If I do not arrive before her, *bien sûr,* the best is gone, into *Madame Imogène's* basket! *Eh bien*, this evening, there is food but there is no menu. You are in my hands, *non*? You like truffles?"

Imogen looked at Nick for his agreement. Nick was at his

most charming. "Love truffles. Your surprise is our pleasure, Monsieur Ducasse."

"Alain, please. I go. We will have a little drink later."

After Alain had left them, Nick sat down, and rolled his eyes. "Is there any restaurant we could ever go to, where we might eat in peace?"

"I didn't think."

"I couldn't have put it better. Well, at least we don't have to look at the menu."

"You're not annoyed? Really?"

"No, it's fine, really."

Like everybody else in the restaurant, Andrei had heard every word, and, knowing what he did, he might have applauded the sparkle and brilliance of the performance. No one would have guessed at their guilt; the adulterers had come across as polished and innocent. They would be difficult to catch, if they had not already been caught.

Andrei found himself ignoring his food, which was magnificent, and looking at Imogen. As course after course was wheeled in over the plush carpet, he was trying to see what it was that Nick saw in her. At a distance, he felt as if he were receiving only an approximation of her attractiveness. He could not hear what they were saying, and this allowed him to observe the body language. Yes, just occasionally, he could have guessed that they were lovers, but you needed to look very closely, to catch the flirtatious smile, the ironic glance. Once, Imogen looked directly at Andrei – for a split second – as she looked around the restaurant. He held her look, she barely noticed that he was there. Was she in love with Nick Austin? Maybe. Hard to tell.

They drank brandy with Alain Ducasse, who worked the room at the end of the evening. Andrei did not stay for this ceremony; he paid his bill, and then went to drink a tisane, in the Café de Paris, waiting for the lovers to leave. He was certain that they would not be staying the night.

When they emerged from the hotel, it was a little before midnight. As they came down the steps, and waited for Nick's car to arrive, they were on their best behaviour, not holding hands, or leaning into each other. Andrei admired their self-control. But, it deserted them when the Ferrari was brought to the steps. Imogen did not get into the car, but stood with Nick by the driver's door. They were talking – what a lovely evening it had been, not getting caught, next time ... Nick embraced her, and, just for a moment, Andrei imagined what Nick felt. Imogen kissed her lover full on the mouth, for no more than a moment, but there was such a hungry passion in the kiss that Andrei, gutted, felt the lack of it. Without doubt, it was the most beautiful thing that he had ever seen in his life: a man and a woman kissing by the side of a white Ferrari Dino, in front of the Hôtel de Paris, illuminated by the night-time glamour of Monte Carlo. That was *kompromat*.

A Balanced Diet

*I*T'S ALL ABOUT *control, that's all*
Lose it, keep it off
Turn off the hunger switch in your head
Failing to plan is planning to fail
Men hate it when "she's on a diet"
Chocolate misshapes have no calories
Anything you eat standing up has no calories
Anything you eat standing by the fridge door at 2am has no calories
Anything you eat while Beatrice is cooking has no calories
Anything you eat on the sofa in front of the TV has no calories
A balanced diet is a piece of chocolate in both hands

Nico pointed at Cassandra's cream linen sleeve. "Mummy, you have chocolate on your arm. Mummy ate chocolate before lunch!" His little sister joined in, and they both started chanting, "Naughty mummy! Naughty mummy! Naughty mummy!"

Cassandra screamed at them, her anger and shame uncontrollable. "Stop it! Don't be horrible! Stop it! Be quiet! Beatrice! Take them away! Get them away from me!"

The children were suddenly silent, rigid, fearful; this was not the mummy they knew. Cassandra looked at their stunned faces, and froze with them. The memory of what had happened to her in this very room, her mother incoherent with angry confusion, aiming for the easy target, jerked her out of her crucifixion.

Like so many years before – the short-sighted past rushing back into horrible clarity – Beatrice again came bustling to the rescue, running into the drawing-room, throwing her protective arms around the children, promising to take them out for the afternoon. Obedient, silent, the children allowed themselves to be shepherded away to safety. There were no words for Cassandra from Beatrice; the two women had hardly spoken for days. Cassandra could feel the reproach, the pity, the fear emanating from the woman who had brought her up.

Left alone, for a painful length of time, as she allowed the laceration of hurt to pierce her every pore, Cassandra moved not one inch, transfixed by the dregs of her outburst. It was almost impossible to look out of herself, to focus on the world around her unless it was about Nick and eating. She was fighting a losing battle; and now even the children knew. Oh God! She shouldn't have shouted at them.

She didn't need any proof from a private detective, to know. You don't need to find out anything, you just know. Before two people fight, they withdraw from each other, like duellists retreating to the line of fire. Words are exchanged, exploratory, like the surgeon knifing a cancerous growth, but words produce only a surface wound. To be effective, marital hurt has to act like poison, cell by cell. There was an increasing distance that was opening up between them, husband and wife; they were like paper boats thrown into a stream, drifting apart. The further the tide carries them away from each other, the more soggy and misdirected the navigation.

She heard Beatrice leave the house with the children. She waited for the silence to settle in the house, and then she headed for the kitchen. Her only solace was in eating. The viciousness with which she unwrapped the packaging of something she had previously denied herself, anything, she didn't care what it was – sausage, cream, pasta, pastry – the more she enjoyed the taste. She no longer cared if it were illicit, no longer cared about being caught, except by the children.

She would have to buy a new wardrobe, almost nothing fitted. Serve him right if he stopped loving her, this size. He hadn't loved her when she was thin, so what was the difference if she was getting …? The word wouldn't come, it was there, weighing on her mind, but it was not yet out of its box. She had given him his chance. Eating was her revenge.

Hours later, in the half light of dusk, Beatrice found her, curled up against the fridge door, surrounded by tubs of Häagen-Dazs. Beatrice said nothing, no reproach, no exclamation. She had found Cassandra's mother dead in the bath, the water dyed with blood. Cassie was alive, and she needed saving.

Beatrice took a spoon out of a kitchen drawer, and sat down next to her. Saying nothing, she began to dig with relish out of each tub of *gelato* – black cherry *amaretto*, *cappuccino*, dark chocolate chip, *limoncello*, sea salt caramel, *stracciatella*.

Häagen-Dazs call their range of *gelato*, "A Spoonful of Italy." They have a forty-second video to go with it: a couple arguing like cats and dogs, until she spots the tub of *gelato* he brought home, in his bag; there is a spoonful of peace, until they start bickering again. That is how the world sees an Italian relationship. What happens when you add an Englishman to the mix? You get English taps – they always seem to have been made in Birmingham in 1907 – where you can't mix the hot and the cold …

There was silence, broken only by the guttural sound of Beatrice indicating if she liked the taste of whatever tub she was excavating. Minutes passed, many minutes, then, Cassandra leaned against her, and started sobbing.

Pros and Cons (again)

*G*REAT SEX – *fucking amazing*
Hate that he always wants to do it in front of mirrors, with all the lights on
Size makes a difference?
I hate penthouse suites
It drives me insane when he repeats the same thing over and over like a parrot
I love his voice
He's paranoid about getting caught with me
He gave me 20,000 euro for spending money – is that a pro or a con?
I don't want to be responsible for breaking up his marriage
What am I? A mistress or just a quick fuck?
It's a fling – I've been flung as far as I wanted

Pros – 2
Cons – 5
Undecided – 3

Thigh Gap

CASSANDRA HATED GROUP therapy. For three weeks she had played along with the game, listening to the hard luck and sob stories: a man who said that he was a banker told them how he couldn't leave a party if there was still coke on the table; a porn addict went on and on about wanking; an alcoholic poured out his troubles ...

They had all been told to keep a journal of their addictions.

"Three burgers on the way there, and a six-pack of doughnuts in the supermarket as I walk around."

"Bingeing is sinful I know, but it makes me feel so good."

The remedy was always rhetorical. "Look for the similarities, not the differences. An addict always believes himself different. Listen to all your stories, you are all the same. All addictions are lying in the head. The gourmet eats for the taste, a compulsive over-eater eats to fill a void. But we deserve as human beings to be happy, wealthy and productive, to have everything that's positive. People get what they think about. Now, Cassandra, tell us your story. How are you going to fight your addiction?"

Cassandra had been hoping that this moment would not happen to her. She slowly stood up. She looked around at all the expectant faces, anticipating her distress, her fear, her terror, her collapse into confession; they were like the mob in the Roman

Coliseum, joyfully waiting for the wild animals to tear apart the Christians.

"I ... I've ..."

"Go on, Cassandra, we're all with you."

"I've always fought against being fat. For years I fought a very successful campaign. I've always beaten the calories, never put on even a pound. I starved myself. I'd never eaten a dessert in my whole life. And I hate Caesar salad. I was always the thinnest woman in the room. I used to have a thigh gap, do you know what that is? It's the gap between your legs to show that you are thin and desirable. I used to have the widest thigh gap. Nick, he's my husband, used to say that the gap between my legs was so wide, my clitoris made a shadow on the sheets. I don't have a thigh gap any more. If you wanted to see some light down there, you'd need a weightlifter. You see, my husband Nick is having an affair."

"How do you know that he's having an affair?"

"I just know that he is. I don't need to be thin anymore because there's no point."

"Well, that's an interesting way of looking at things, Cassandra. You know, we only change in life through tragedy. But we don't really change, we expand."

Cassandra had had enough. She had never ever, believed in prayer; how could she believe in self-help and life coaching? The floodgates opened, she couldn't stop herself.

"Bullshit!" she screamed. "Fuck it! I want to be fat!"

"When you don't cry it's because you no longer believe in happiness."

Coco (Gabrielle Bonheur) Chanel

Food for Thought

La Croisette

"I DON'T UNDERSTAND WHAT this is all about Mr Volkov?" asked Nick. "I know who you are but I don't think we've ever met before? You ask me to come to Cannes for a meeting, say that this has something to do with Frank Schulte, and now you say he won't be here. And why here? Your office is in Zurich. And yes, I do my homework. An explanation would be nice. I'm a busy man."

"I will not keep you any longer than you wish to sit here, Mr Austin. The sun is shining, we are living on the Côte d'Azur, we do not owe anybody any money. Should you wish to talk to Mr Schulte, you will find him and his boat in the harbour. How well would you say you know Miss Imogen O'Rorke?"

Nick first stiffened and then shifted in his café chair; the rigid metal resisted, creaked; and gave him away. He dunked his croissant in his cappuccino. "She's a brilliant cook. I would recommend her to anybody."

"Let me summarise for you the report I am about to send to my client, Mrs Cassandra Austin. You and Miss O'Rorke are having an affair. For her, it is of no consequence, she is single, and therefore a free agent. But for you, Mr Austin, that is not the case. You are a married man with a lot at stake, and I am not only talking about your marriage."

"Aah, so, now I get it. Are you trying to blackmail me, is that it? In return for your not sending that report, I give you a bucketful of money?"

Andrei had ordered the English breakfast. "Does this look like an English breakfast to you? Not like the breakfast I remember when I was living in England. No sausages."

Nick was nonplussed by the non-reply. It took him a while to figure out the meaning. He relaxed his guilt. "Fried eggs, bacon, tomatoes, mushrooms, baked beans, fried bread, yes, and sausages. Omelette is French."

Andrei smiled. "No Yorkshire black pudding?"

Nick shook his head. "No, that's Lancashire. How do I know you have anything on me ... on us?"

Andrei was enjoying his omelette; he kept Nick dangling for a few moments more. "Hôtel de Paris?" Andrei went back to his breakfast.

"*Va te faire foutre*. You've been following us? How lovely. Nice job you have. Hardly a grown-up profession, is it? Do you wear a mac?" Andrei let Nick have his say. Nick was cornered; and they both knew it.

"What do you want?" he finally asked, acknowledging his defeat.

"To save your marriage?"

"I very much doubt that. Why are you so interested in saving my marriage?"

"Your wife?"

"My wife knows nothing."

"You think she knows nothing."

"So then, you could just as easily wreck my marriage."

"That is your choice."

Nick was the type of man who thinks better when he is being baited. "You don't want money, apparently, so, what is it exactly that you want in return for being so magnanimous?"

"Let us wait and see."

"Nice. You mean you want to keep me in your back pocket, is that it? To use me whenever you feel like it?"

"One good turn deserves another, isn't that what you British say?" Andrei put down his knife and fork, and sipped his coffee. "And you end it today, over lunch. The food is very good at the Moulin. That should make it easier."

"Wow! You know everything, don't you?" Nick was as much impressed as he was disconcerted. He fell silent, thinking through his limited options. Then, "You don't give a man much time to think."

"How much time do you need in such a situation? Your mistress or your marriage?"

"Frank was right about you."

"He was?"

"You take no prisoners."

"No, Mr Austin, you locked yourself in."

Oh s'io potessi dissipare le nubi

Musikhalle, Hamburg, 15 May 1959

I GAVE THIS CHAPTER an Italian title not to confuse you, but to try and show you that dieting is all in the mind.

Go to You Tube, type in "Maria Callas – Oh! s'io potessi dissipare le nubi," and feel the pain of a woman going out of her mind. This is a concert performance, not a theatrical staging, but look at that acting: the tentative way she raises her left hand to her hair, and pushes it back behind her ear, already she has our attention; the way her hand grips the bar of the conductor's podium like a ballerina in class; the artless way she looks down while the music – nearly a minute and a half – underscores her torment. Every instrument has its part to play: the melancholy French horn, the unsettled violins, the cor anglais that haunts her with a bittersweet melody.

Suddenly, doom-laden strings rising, timpani tolling her fate, she lifts her head, not at us, but far off somewhere into the immeasurable distance, facing some remembered, heartfelt pain; and we are electrified. No matter that she has yet to sing a note, whatever she is feeling, we are going to feel with her. This is not a performance, this is a woman who has lived, as Callas understood only too well: "An opera begins long before the curtain goes up and ends long after it has come down. It starts in my imagination, it becomes my life, and it stays part of my life long after I've left the opera house."

We don't need to know the plot of this opera, the far-fetched twists and turns that have brought this woman to the abyss of madness; we don't need to know the misfortunes that have befallen her, the men who have failed her (men, of course ...), because Callas emotes it all here. This woman is never going to dispel those clouds.

Above all, there is that voice: the luscious bel canto tone and timbre. Thrilling tessitura. Spellbinding coloratura (even if she does avoid the top C at the end of the scene, which high note, however, she nails in Amsterdam two months later). The phrasing is heartbreaking – "L'abbracci e mi perdoni anzi ch'ei mora" – how she gives weight and feeling to that last dying word. And those pizzicato strings plucking away at her strength. When people talk about singing your heart out, this is it.

So, what does this have to do with Imogen O'Rorke? Because Callas is singing the role of Imogene, and our Imogen is named after Bellini's heroine in Il pirata. *Imogen's grandmother, Marie-Hélène, who took for herself the privilege of naming her first (and only) grandchild, liked to identify herself with tragic heroines; it was a choice between Imogen, Lucia and Tosca ...*

Oh, and something else: Callas used to be very fat, big as a house. You find that hard to believe, that this svelte and totally glamorous siren was once grossly overweight? Absolutely, no exaggeration. In her own words, talking about her childhood, "I was the ugly duckling, fat and clumsy and unpopular." Still not convinced? You want proof? How about the photo from the late 1940s, of Callas standing with the conductor Serafin, wrapped in a fur coat that makes her look like a brown bear – that fat unrecognisable face; or Callas rehearsing I vespri siciliani *at La Scala, Milan, in 1951 – dumpy and dowdy, look at those pasta hips; and, most affecting of all, in her dressing-room, again at La Scala, in 1952, looking in the mirror at herself, before a performance of* La Gioconda *– the archetypal operatic porker. It is a photo that mines the inner Callas, quite unlike the thousands of ice-cold and* haughty sculptured images that she later liked to present to the world, the ones we remember. It is not too fanciful, I think, to suggest that the reflection she sees in the mirror is not how she wants to see herself. No woman ever entirely likes what she sees in a mirror, but Callas, here, is the extreme archetype of self-loathing – what we now call negative body image. She seems to be asking, almost accusing, herself: "You're fat and ugly, how can you go out there and make them believe in your tragedy?" The answer, of course, is to be found in the very question. When one understands what Callas used to be, one begins to understand what she became.

But how did she do it? Go from ugly duckling to beautiful swan? Answer, she went on a crash diet. One moment she looked like a shotputter, the next she was posing in Dior.

There are all sorts of stories about how she did it, and why; some say that she swallowed a tapeworm! The truth is almost as unpleasant. In 1947, Callas weighed 108kg. We know that she was depressed, and believed that she was too fat ever to be loved (and there you have the reason why she sang tragic roles with so much emotion). Luchino Visconti told her to lose the pork, or she could forget about working with him. Never one to do things by halves, within two years Callas had lost 40kg (Visconti had only suggested 30kg). How did she do it? Willpower. However she did it, careerwise it worked – Visconti hired her; and then the real battle began – how to keep the weight from coming back.

Callas kept the pounds off by getting as close to food as she could, without actually eating it. This was a woman who loved her food, loved to cook, collected cookery books; and denied herself the pleasure, so as to gain a different goal. She collected recipes for dishes that she had barely touched; in restaurants and hotels around the world, she would ask for the recipe of a dish that had taken her fancy, but had left on her plate; her handbags were stuffed full of scraps of paper, scribbled with ingredients for veal l'oriental, pound cake, chocolate-filled beignets, *sauces to go with the underdone steaks she always ate before a performance; and, what she called "my cake," an over-rich confection groaning with sackfuls of sugar.*

The recipes were sent back to the Paris apartment, to be cooked up for her dinner parties. Her guests would eat their fill of her magnificent table, while Callas played at eating. That was how she maintained the legend. It has to be said, however, that the transformation from wallflower to sunflower had an unfortunate side effect: the voice was never as good as it had been when she was overweight. Yes, beauty has its price.

"*Bonjour*, it's me." It was Nick. "What are you doing?"

"Thinking about you."

"So am I. Imogen, how are you fixed for time on Thursday this week?"

"Where did you have in mind? No beige, remember?" Imogen giggled.

"I was thinking lunch."

"No pudding?"

"I thought you'd gone off eating?"

"Who's talking about eating?"

"Let's go somewhere different. I have a meeting in Cannes in the morning. I'll book a table at Le Moulin de Mougins. Should we say one o'clock? Can you make your own way there?"

"Oh, all right. And they have rooms. Sounds good to me."

"See you. I have to go. *Je suis pressé*. Bye."

He had never called her Imogen on the phone. That was it, she decided: his wife knew.

Culoni

CASSANDRA HAD A hot dog craving. Yesterday, she had gorged on Flame–Grilled Double Whoppers with Cheese; the day before that, a bucket of KFC. When the dieting dam bursts, only carbohydrate sandbags can do the job – pile them on, one on top of another, until you stop the rush.

There is so much junk food in Italy, and a lot of it is Italian. Fancy a quick slice of re–heated pizza when you're out shopping? Every Italian street corner can fulfil that desire. Cassandra favoured Spizzico.

Super–sizing Italians are a little bit ashamed of what they have done to their food habits. That is why they give their junk food – their *merendine* – American names: *Dixi*, *Yonkers*, *Wacko's + Sorpresa*, *Fonzies Gli Originali* … The old *Pranzo* way of life is being hurriedly replaced with *da portare via*.

Cassandra spent her days shopping, just as she used to do, but not in any of the shops where she had once been an ornament; now, she avoided the high–end designer boutiques. For her new wardrobe, to go with her new larger size, she favoured the high street chains and the malls.

She had been rejected, and so she would reject everything and everybody that had failed her; only her children and Beatrice were exempt. The pain of rejection was arthritic, an all-consuming, constant presence, at any moment ready to stab her with a searing reminder of Nick's betrayal.

She was no longer hot with anger, such an anger always comes off the boil; no, that gorgon fury had been replaced with something much more terrible – a cold-blooded, visceral determination to tear down the edifice of her old life. Even as she raked over in her mind the ashes of her ruined perfection she was stoking the fires of a conflagration that would terrify him. As yet, she had only lit the gunpowder trail; it was fizzing towards a barrel of dynamite that would explode every certainty that she and Nick had built together.

Like the starving maw of a coal-fired steam engine, the hurt he had caused her needed to be fed, stoked with bucketfuls of retribution. All of her energy was concentrated on a sweaty, muscular and grimy vengeance. Nothing in their 'old' life was safe from her thunderbolts – the house, their friends, the business, her wardrobe, her body – everything was flung into the roaring furnace.

She called in the decorator, and told him that she wanted a new look in the Turin house. "Get rid of all the antiques, the pictures, the Persian carpets. Make it minimalist and uncomfortable. Take your time, make as much mess as you like, and money is no object."

She stopped giving the dinner parties that doubled as networking occasions. Fridays and Saturdays had been reserved for friends, for keeping their place in society, and promoting the business; that all stopped. Cassandra told Nick that she couldn't entertain while the house was in an uproar. She refused to go with him to any business events, where she had been expected to adorn her husband's arm. Let him take his mistress if he needed an escort.

She let him fuck her, if he wanted; she even kissed him, but it was a harlot's kiss. After a few weeks of this false intimacy, Nick stopped trying.

She would scupper the sugar-free chocolate deal, by voting her shares against the proposal that she knew Nick was planning to present to the board. She told nobody of her plans; she knew enough about the business to plot her husband's defeat without anybody's advice. She ordered an up-to-date share register, went through it with a fine toothcomb, and then called Andrei Volkov.

"I have something else that I want you to do for me. I want you to find out who are the Russians sitting in my company. Can you do that?"

"I can try."

"Why don't we make that a try as hard as you can. Do you have any other news for me?"

"I soon will have."

She gave her entire wardrobe to the local church, where she had been christened, taken her first communion, and worshipped all her life. On a couple of occasions she saw her old clothes being worn by immigrant women who looked guilty at displaying their finery in front of the primped and gowned priest.

She stepped on the bathroom scales of a morning with grim satisfaction, coaxing and urging the needle to a bigger payload. Then she would have breakfast, the first of many times when she sat in the kitchen.

She had never before been food shopping. That had been Beatrice's daily task. Now, Cassandra became a housewife, accompanying Beatrice to the daily market, piling the basket high with fresh produce, in quantities that would have fed an army, methodically wheeling the trolley down every aisle in the hypermarket, picking items off the shelf with abandon, snacking as she went. Before, everything that she had put in her mouth had been religiously checked for the lowest fat, sugar and calorie content – a few less percentage points on a 'lite' yoghurt label, and a 'low fat' cottage cheese, had once been an occasion for apostolic fervour – now, like an apostate, released from the tyranny of numbers, she zeroed in on the foods that she had once shunned.

At first, Beatrice had been disconcerted and alarmed by this new regimen, most of all by the complete lack of planning. Cassandra would refuse to discuss in advance what they would be having for lunch or dinner, or what the children would have for their tea; meals were decided on the spur of the moment. "We'll decide when we get there," was Cassandra's standard response. And she cooked; the woman who, before, had no idea how to cook *tagliatelle* or layer *lasagna*, began to take lessons from Beatrice. As a result of this apprenticeship, eating became a hit and miss affair; they ate at all hours – lunch at eleven in the morning; dinner at four in the afternoon, or, if Cassandra had decided to try out a complicated recipe, nearer midnight. The children never went hungry; there was so much food in the house that Beatrice could always rustle up something, if Cassandra's painfully acquired cooking skills failed to keep up with the kids' hunger pangs.

What did Nick think of this new life – the chaos, the builder's mess, the disintegration, the complete and total abandonment of the ties that had kept everything together? He saw everything; he understood everything; and he said nothing.

The tight–laced hourglass that had been Cassandra's perfect life was unhooked from its eyelets, clasp by clasp, and Cassandra let the contents spill out wherever they would. Before, she had divided her days into small, rigorously controlled portions, disciplining the hours into responsible activities; now, each day sagged into a shapeless and formless blob. Cassandra, nevertheless, lived her days with an enormous appetite; she got out of bed, put on whatever clothes she found lying around, barely looked in the mirror, and headed for the kitchen. Buying food, cooking food, eating food, this was the trinity of her new life. Italians have a word for people who love their food in this shameless and abandoned way – *culoni*.

À la carte

NICK SMILED AND stood up to greet her when she approached the table. He kissed her on the lips.

"What's the matter?" she asked. "You just kissed me in public."

"And you look different."

The headwaiter ceremoniously presented them with what looked more like a graduation certificate than a menu, at the same time asking if they would like an aperitif.

"Bloody Mary. I'm sick of champagne."

"And for you, *monsieur*?"

"The same is fine. And give us time to read the menu, would you." The waiter nodded and withdrew. "What's eating you, my little piglet?"

"I'm sick of all this cloak and dagger life. And I'm sick of iconic restaurants."

Taking her hand, Nick's velvet voice purred. "Mo, please, don't. I've been very upfront since we started, and regardless of what I might feel for you, I am a very married man. I told you I couldn't afford for my wife or anyone, for that matter, to find me out."

"I know all that and I understand, but I don't like having to duck and dive from my friends. Claudia is my oldest and best girlfriend, and because I'm always putting your paranoia first,

I'm shunting her aside. Because I can't tell her why, she's feeling very hurt."

"Darling, I really value both your appreciation of my situation and your sense of discretion." Imogen was thinking that this all sounded rehearsed ... "We've been very careful, and ..."

"And what? We got away with it?"

"Not quite."

"She knows about us?"

"I think so."

"*Merde*. How did she find out?"

"She followed us, or rather, she got somebody to follow us ... everywhere."

"*Bordel de merde.*"

"*Exactement*. Deep shit. Only I think that I contained the situation. She doesn't actually know that it's you."

"Like that's a blessing in disguise is it? What difference does it make? You might as well try to contain a nuclear explosion in a dustbin. She wanted to find out, and now she has. And what's she going to do? Wifey loves her naughty cheating hubby and forgives him? Or you've wriggled out of it somehow?"

"Don't make me sound like a worm. And try not to make a scene."

Imogen downed her drink. She was thinking that he seemed unreasonably calm, for a man who had been caught out in adultery.

"It'll be okay. She loves me."

"Just like that?"

He gave her that handsome escape smile. "Why not? So, what are we eating?"

"I hate that word 'so,' you know that? It means that you've ignored everything I've been trying to say, like you always do. You never actually listen to me. I bet you never listen to her either. Poor cow."

"Can we please just order? I'm starving."

All of a sudden she realised what it was that had been forming a live mould around her consciousness these past months, when they had been tumbling into all those five-star beds; what it was that had been disturbing her hitherto stable sense of herself: she no longer liked this man, in fact, she actively disliked him. She disliked his arrogant certainty of himself. She disliked his cold, unheeding dismissal of uncertainty, his never allowing another human being to feel doubt. She disliked his inability, his unwillingness, his refusal – who cares what failing it was – to consider, no matter in what small degree, something or somebody else. She even disliked his handsomeness, seeing it now as a weapon he used to control anything and anybody, a shield he bore to keep people away. Such handsomeness, she understood, made him horribly untouchable; he was a man who could only live on the lacquered surface of life, a performance artist, existing in his own one-man museum, strutting through one gorgeous room after another, a Damien Hirst manufacturing his spin paintings – master of spin – and all the while mocking the scraping and bowing of his courtiers. That was why Nick so loved these fancy restaurants – they suited the set design of his theatrical life, all flats and trick perspectives.

She felt sorry for Cassandra, his wife; and she regretted cheating on her, for that was how she now saw their adulterous relationship – they were both guilty, she and Nick, of cheating. She hoped that somehow Cassandra would get her own back on him.

She wanted to strike some sort of blow. "What does it matter what you eat? You know nothing about food, absolutely nothing."

"Guilty as charged. Now, what are you having? Let's splurge."

"I'm not hungry."

"Jesus Christ! Are the two of you ganging up on me or what? You don't want to eat, and Cassie can't stop eating. She always seems to have her hand on the fridge door."

"I used to know how she feels." Imogen wanted to have her say, something like, "Nick, this has been a lot of fun but I don't want to continue. There is never a nice or gentle way to put it, to soften the blow."

He beat her to it. "If you're so unhappy perhaps we should take a rest?"

Imogen didn't hesitate. "Yes, let's do that. Only, I'm not so easily replaceable. How many fat women are there, orbiting around your planet?"

"My wife for one. And who says you're fat?"

It was all over, and they hadn't even ordered. Nick reached down to the floor next to his chair, and handed her a bag from Van Cleef & Arpels. "I got you this. I hope you like it."

Imogen thought that it had better not be too valuable or she would give it right back. She undid the ribbon from the box; inside was a filigree clip in the shape of a flower petal with leaves, fashioned out of amethysts, emeralds and diamonds. It must have cost him a fortune. She was remembering what she liked about him. "It's lovely. No, it's exquisite." She kissed him on the cheek. "Thanks."

"It's from their *Jardins* collection. It's called Rosing Park. I thought a gardening connection would make for a nice memory."

Imogen gave him half a smile. "I remember. Mr Darcy lived in Rosing Park. Did you know?" Nick shrugged, uncomprehending. "So, this is goodbye, right?"

Nick relaxed; she was making it easy for him – no tears, no hysterics. He was already regretting that his cock would no longer quiver in her mouth.

"You've lost weight. You're not as big as you were."

"You really know how to play a final scene for laughs, Nick."

"Piglet, I love first times, and I don't like last times. It would have been different ... if I weren't married."

Imogen heard the catch in his voice, and she was pulled up sharply by the martingale of his emotion. *"Alors,"* she thought. "He actually has blood in his veins!" She needed to have the last word.

"T'es un salaud."

"It's part of my charm."

Nick stood up. He bent over to kiss her on the mouth; the taste was dry. "Thanks for the lovely ride." He dropped a five hundred euro note on the table. "For lunch."

"We didn't eat."

"You need feeding up. I have to go."

She watched him thread his way out of the restaurant. He had kissed her twice in public; and he had binned her.

Size matters

"You've lost a lot of weight," said Claudia. "I don't understand why you look so unhappy?"

"It's over."

Claudia was sitting in the spa salon of the *Claudia*, her face wrapped in a green mud mask, being attended by Amina, the full-time beautician from Algeria, who was rubbing cream into her heels.

"Well, if I knew what was over, I might be more sympathetic."

"My relationship. It ended an hour ago."

"In which case, the first thing you need is a drink. We'd better drown your sorrows. And then we need to look after you. Press that button there, and Massimo will come running. We'll have champagne cocktails. You still haven't told me his name. Now that it's over, you can, come on, spill the beans."

"Clod, please, just drop it. Okay? And I'm sick of champagne."

"Top marks for discretion. I get that he's married, but it really doesn't matter anymore. You know I absolutely won't tell a soul."

"Please!"

"Okay! Okay! So, then, Dry Martinis. Anyway, you look much better. You must have gone down four sizes."

"For the moment only three, but soon I'll be stealing your clothes, or my old grandmother's."

Villa Eilenroc

Massimo came loping in like a faithful spaniel. He was dressed in full white uniform – peaked cap, jacket, trousers, brass buttons and epaulettes.

"Aah, there you are," said Claudia, from behind her mask, "I hope you've been studying hard. We'll have six Dry Martinis, three each, and ... what do you want to eat, Mo?"

"Nothing, I just had no lunch."

"My God! It must be serious. Just the Martinis then."

Massimo nodded, and went out. "Doesn't he look unbelievable in that dress uniform? And he's studying so hard for those officer exams, I almost have to drag him away from his books."

"I bet. Marcus must love you. What's the occasion? Am I missing something?"

"Not now you won't. We're having a party tomorrow evening. I would have invited you, but you've been completely incommunicado of late, so I thought there was no point."

"Clod, I am sorry. I don't know what came over me."

"I do. *Et bien*, Amina, what are we going to do to *Mademoiselle* Imogen, to make her the belle of the ball?" Without waiting for the docile beautician to reply, Claudia made up her own mind, reciting from a menu of treatments: "Osmo-Thermy rejuvenating body treatment, recreates the beneficial effects of sea salt on your skin. Lymphatic drainage procedure with honey. Anti-cellulite treatment with seaweed. And something new this season! An anti-stress body cocktail. You fancy a Mojito, a Tequila Sunrise or a Pina Colada?"

"You're pulling my leg, right?"

"You are so far behind the beauty times, Mo. First, Amina will give you a relaxing massage with chocolate candles."

"Ugh! Sounds revolting. I'll get all sticky."

Claudia peered towards Imogen, sitting on the white leather sofa. "The face needs work. Ultrasonic facial cleansing. Then, an alginate mask like this one, don't you think, Amina?" Amina duly nodded, as most people did in Claudia's frightening presence. "Dermabrasion with ANA and cranberry. And to finish, eye contour treatment."

Imogen knew better than to argue with Claudia where beauty was concerned. "You're sure you won't have missed any part of me, after it's all over?"

"Darling, you'll thank me. *C'est le must.* There are going to be so many rich, powerful and sexy men here tomorrow, and I'm going to make sure that you get at least one of them. Some of them you already know and like; we'll concentrate on them first. But I'm afraid that Russian who gave you a ride home, the one you've been fucking, he'll be here."

"Tikhon? I wasn't fucking him."

"Whatever. If that's his name, yes. And Mat will be here."

"I'm surprised he's still alive after all the money he lost you."

"Frank's hoping we might get some of it back at the party. Everybody who was in Montenegro will be here."

"Everybody?" asked Imogen, with misgiving.

Before Claudia had time to reply, Massimo came back with the drinks. Claudia took a big sip through her mask.

"I've had an idea. Why don't you, *mon cher*, carry on with my feet, and Amina can start on you, Mo. But take your jacket off, darling, there's a lamb, and put a towel over your trousers. Put my feet in your lap, and rub as hard as you can, won't you. Mo, sit in Frank's chair next to me. Take off your clothes in our bedroom; robes and towels are in the bathroom. And drink a Martini first."

Imogen thought that it was rather odd for Claudia to address her cabin boy as 'darling,' but she kept her counsel. She undressed, wrapped herself in an oversize towel, and then allowed herself to be placed in the second treatment chair, which worked much like a dentist's – seat pushed down, and a powerful floodlight first beamed into her face, and then over her whole body. Amina adjusted the lamp, for a more mellow mood, and set to work. There was a slight smell of chocolate in the air. Imogen exhaled; it was nice to let go. Her mind, however, was full of Nick.

"I thought I was going to cry."

Claudia didn't have to think about this for very long. "What you mean is that you didn't."

"How do you know that?"

"Call it an educated guess. I don't have a heart, remember?"

"Because it didn't mean anything?"

"Everything means something."

"Why then?"

"Big girls don't cry."

"Thanks."

"I didn't mean it like that."

There was silence for a while; Claudia was wiggling her toes in Massimo's lap. Imogen was almost relaxing.

"You know, Clod, I was sort of hoping today that he would tell me how good I looked, since I lost all that weight stressing out about him. All he said was, I looked different."

"Perhaps he liked you as you were?"

"Do you think that's possible?"

"No, not really, but he must have liked something about you at the beginning. Still, I really don't understand why you're even thinking about him. I thought you wanted it to end?"

"I did! Sort of. I was bored. I got tired of him treating me like a sex symbol. I mean, what about me?"

"You're kidding me, right?"

"I was tired of everything being so fucking perfect. Five star this, five star that."

"I can't believe you said that! All your life you dreamed about this! And then you just throw it away!"

"He dumped me, remember? Although, it's true, I would have got in first if he hadn't. Look, it wasn't what I wanted! I mean, the sex was great, and he made me feel good about me, how big I am ... was ... but there was something wrong, and not only because he was married."

"Why then?"

"There was no room for me and his ego."

"Well, it would have needed a very big room." Imogen made a flailing action at Claudia with her arm. "Just joking! All right, now what?"

"Work as hard as I can to forget about him."

"Wrong! You look for the next one."

"Just like that? I'm not you, Clod. I have to grieve, first. Besides, I have lunches to think about. I've sort of been ignoring the business while this was going on."

"Lunches you won't tell me about, even though it might get us out of trouble."

"I already explained. I can't gossip about my clients."

"I remember. Serve you right if we have to sell everything, and we come to live with you, like we used to in Geneva."

"Is it really that bad?"

"I don't know. Frank's working round the clock. All I ever hear about is gold and chocolate. A massive cash flow crisis. That's why we're here for the festival. The harbour's full of Russians. Apparently, they're the key to our everything."

"Oh Clod! I didn't realise it was so serious. Look, if I can, I will try to help, I promise."

"Good. I knew you would, in the end."

"You were always good at taking me on guilt trips."

"Perhaps we really should try to fix you up with a Russian. Did I say that we're having Russian food?"

Imogen thought that she caught the meaning. "Oh no!

Absolutely not! I am not setting foot inside a kitchen!"

"There's no need to over-react. Marcus has everything under control, doesn't he, Massimo?"

Massimo actually spoke. "Yes, *madame*."

"And Bill has waiters lined up to pour the drinks and circulate the trays of food. And we have ice sculptures for the caviar. That just leaves the biggest question of all: what are you going to wear? I suppose you could always go home, it's only around the corner."

"That won't do any good because nothing in my old wardrobe fits anymore, not even the hopeful end. I haven't quite got used to this new me. You remember those deportment lessons we used to have? Mademoiselle Beauclerc shouting, 'Girls, think of yourselves as weightless!' Well, it's like that, trying to walk downstairs without bannisters."

"I remember. You wobbled a lot. You need a new look."

"Thanks. I've tried. I bought an outfit to wear for our last evening, only at the time I didn't know it was the last time …"

"With his money, I hope?"

"I'm a fast learner. I could wear that I suppose, I've got it with me." Imogen knew that she had better let slip her little secret. "There's something I have to tell you, well, more confess really … I went into Chanel."

"When?" asked Claudia, aggrieved. "In your dreams, maybe."

Imogen gave a mock Gallic shrug, with an expression to match. "I bought a suit and a dress, in Monte Carlo, without telling you, I'm sorry."

Claudia removed the cucumber slices from her eyes, and turned her head. "That suit?" Imogen nodded. "Let me get this right: after what happened in Saint Trop, you simply walked into Chanel in Monte Carlo, without me, I might add, and you walked out again with a suit and a dress that fitted you?"

"No, I walked out wearing the suit. Fitted me like a dream, as you can see, now that you've taken the salad off your eyes. I wanted to have a Chanel day. I had to wear it again, just to pinch myself that it was really me. Only, the thing is, it seems I wore it just so he could break my heart." She paused. "I've decided, that's when women start to wear Chanel."

"*Comment?*"

"To show that you've been hurt."

Claudia thought about this for a moment. "Right." There was another pause. "Don't tell Karl."

"I don't know why you're so upset. You were the one who wanted me to wear Chanel. So I took a leaf out of your book. High heels, the works, and I felt – still feel – as if everybody's looking at me."

"They probably do."

"Right, the same way they looked at me when I was fat."

"Oh buck up, Mo, please. You just have to think differently, that's all."

"I'm starting to realise that looking different is not the same as thinking different, Clod. I feel a bit helpless, if you want to know the truth. No more need to hide, no more shame about the size of the shadow walking behind me, no more wardrobe panic ..."

Claudia's mind was alighting on other things. "Are you uncomfortable down there?"

"No, *madame*."

"I wonder, *peut-être*, if I'm not too hard on you?"

Pelmeni

THE OLD HARBOUR in Cannes at night, during the Film Festival, is the most glamorous and tawdry reflection of a rosy-fingered vision that we poor humans cannot resist. Children play at dressing up; and that is what the adults are doing on their floodlit yachts – most of them rented – riding serenely at anchor, while harbouring a hornet's nest of couture ambition.

On the *Claudia*, Claudia was amazed with the transformation.

"Mo, you look like Audrey Hepburn!"

"I wouldn't go that far. This is still plus size remember. There's still a way to go yet."

Imogen was looking at herself in Claudia's cheval mirror, and doing a double-take. She almost didn't recognise herself, wrapped in knee-length midnight blue velvet, cut on the bias, the amethyst brooch clipped to the clinging fabric, in the very centre of her cleavage.

"Another two sizes and you'll be wearing Marie-Hélène's old clothes."

"Pigs might fly."

"Well, now we can see they can."

"*Ta gueule!*"

"The brooch looks perfect. He gave it to you, didn't he?"

"I don't see how you can know things like that?"

"Because I always do, remember? Now, let's go upstairs and make our fortunes again."

The saloon deck of the *Claudia* was already glittering with guests. It was the usual Festival crowd, made up of a few members from each of the categories one needed to make this annual party look … well, how one imagines a yacht party should look: a director with a film in competition; a couple of producers who have actually made some films; a sprinkling of competing actors; a Hollywood A-lister whose film opened the week; a few members of the jury; some very beautiful young women and very handsome young men (all of them available for purchase, Casimir included); and, most important of all, people with money and power. On the *Claudia*, because Frank and Claudia had no interest in appearing in the pages of a magazine, or advertising their business, there were never any PR people or journalists or photographers; this made their parties something unusual in Cannes – exclusive. Imogen fitted in just fine – category of friend.

"Nice jewellery," said Nick, in a voice that was equal parts admiration, equal parts melancholic.

"A present from a secret admirer," replied Imogen, a little bit too loudly. She clutched her champagne flute. She understood, as Nick did, that they were both going to brave it out in public, no matter what was turmoiling inside. What else could they do, avoid each other? No, but what were they going to talk about?

"My admiration is not a secret," said Mat, all of a sudden appearing out of a throng of guests, and kissing her on the hand in a courtly fashion. "Could this lily-white hand really be the one that makes pastry lighter than air? You look good enough to eat. I take it that you're taken?"

This was full-on flirting, and Imogen was wickedly delighted to see that Nick looked so put out at having his thunder all too easily stolen. She made the introductions. "Nick, this is Mat, we met in Montenegro when I was cooking for Tikhon. Mat, this is Nick." She was going to explain who Nick was – Mat was too well known to need explaining – but Mat did it for her.

"Aah, yes, the chocolate man," he said, stressing the confectionery. Imogen inwardly smiled, catching the ever-so-slight putdown. Nick loathed him on sight, for that remark. Mat followed this up with a body blow. "Are you going to win this boardroom showdown?"

Nick was wrongfooted, and admitted as much. "Do you have an interest in it?"

"Oh, I'm rather fond of chocolate, aren't you?" he asked Imogen airily, smiling broadly and clearly enjoying himself.

"I used to be," she replied, looking at Nick.

Nick had to ask Mat the question. "You like it?"

Mat was on top form. "Oh, I only ever buy very large boxes of chocolates."

From this, Imogen understood that Mat was mixed up in the chocolate deal too; and that made sense, with Frank in the middle of both deals – gold and *ganaches*.

"Would you come to London to cook for me?" asked Mat, provocatively.

"Lunch or dinner?"

"How about every day? I think I need to snap you up before anybody else does. Tikhon has his eye on you, did you know that?"

"Well, it's easy for him because all he has to do is look over the fence."

"Yes, he told me. Is the house on the other side for sale?"

Imogen thought that Nick looked a little seasick. Could he really be jealous? Well, too late ...

Looking around at the ebb and flow of guests, Imogen

understood that this party was a continuation of the business lunch in Montenegro, wrapped up in pretty packaging: Peter was talking with Dabing and Andy; all three of them went over to talk to Frank. Tikhon, she could see, was talking with Oleg and a man she didn't know, but whose face she thought she recognised. Frank left his group, and went over to talk to them; and, almost immediately, Tikhon left them talking with Oleg, and came over with the unknown man, to say hello.

"There are no chocolate people here," Imogen was thinking, "and I bet that means Nick's in for a surprise." Should she express her fears to him? Did she owe him anything?

Tikhon was his usual larger-than-life expansive self, full of devilish *bonhomie*. He kissed her warmly on her cheeks, and on her shoulders, which she rather enjoyed. "You look splendid! And you taste very nice! Are these men bothering you? I will throw them overboard!" He greeted Nick warmly, Mat less so. "And let me introduce Andrei. He's another Russian! Tonight, we are taking over the world." He said something in Russian to Andrei, which must have explained who she was ...

Andrei bowed his head in an old-fashioned way, as if they were at a ball in St Petersburg. "Tikhon was right when he said that you come out of a famous Russian painting. But the painting does not do you justice."

Nick, Mat, Tikhon, Andrei ... Imogen's head was in a spin, trying to remember who knew what about whom, and how much she was meant to know about each one of them. Did she know anything about Andrei? She asked him outright. "Have we met before?"

"Yes, in the Russian Museum when I was hoping that you might step out of the picture."

He was full of compliments, but she was not sure that she liked him.

"I'll leave you to your admirers. I'd better circulate," said Nick, already moving off.

"He looks like a man who lost a pound and found sixpence," thought Imogen, watching him go. She was surprised that she felt no regret; why was that? It had only been how many hours ago; and that was when the heartache was at its most heartburning – or should have been ... Had she ever really cared for him that much? Was he something that she had just needed to get out of her system – the big fling?

His place was taken by Oleg, who kissed her hand – a gesture that did not suit him; and who instantly made it known that a party was a competitive event – he was not going to let himself be outdone or outbid by Tikhon. "Whatever Tikhon has offered you, I will double and treble it."

"But you don't know what he offered me!"

"The catering countess is wasted on a *moujik*." Oleg had done his homework on her. Imogen smiled, thinking that she had become a tradeable commodity.

Tikhon swore coarsely in Russian, but he was also smiling.

"*Moujik* you call me! I wouldn't let you pick my grapes!"

"You look as if you're surrounded by cavaliers," said Claudia, coming up behind her, and whispering in her ear, in a schoolgirl way. "Have you made your mind up? I wouldn't be able to choose. Could you imagine all of them at once?" Claudia was gone before Imogen could think of a riposte.

Massimo was hovering close by, agitated. Imogen sensed the urgency.

"*Qu'est-ce qui se passe?*"

"*Excusez-moi, Madame Imogène, mais pourriez-vous venir à la cuisine?*"

"*Pourquoi? Je ne cuisine pas ce soir.*"

"*Il y a eu un petit accident.*"

"I just knew it! *Bon. Allons-y!*"

"A problem?" asked Andrei, gallantly detaching himself from the musketeers who were already talking business.

"Something in the kitchen. I have to see."

"Can I help?"

"I don't think so. You shouldn't. You're a guest. Claudia would be furious."

"I don't think so. She doesn't like me. She would be happy for me to disappear. And do you know anything about Russian food?"

"Absolutely nothing."

"So, then. Let's go."

Imogen excused herself from her cavaliers. "Gentlemen, duty calls."

In the kitchen, Marcus was nursing his left hand, and cursing. "Fuck! Fuck! Fuck and double fuck!"

"What did you do?" asked Imogen, rushing to his aid.

"I burnt my stupid self, that's what! Now I can't hold a fucking thing! Fucking *blinis* stuck to the pan! I forgot the fucking oven glove!" Marcus just as suddenly went quiet, staring at Imogen as she held his hand under a cold tap. He lowered his voice, trying to get his head around what was different about her – at once shocked and approving. "What the fuck happened to you, sister? You could package and sell that diet."

"It wasn't a diet, and keep your voice down."

Marcus immediately sensed what had happened, in a way that a straight man never would. He whispered, aware that Andrei was watching them. "The broken heart diet, is that it? Let me guess, Mr Drop Dead Gorgeous Lick Chocolate Off My Cock found somebody bigger and better."

Imogen had not been willing to tell all to Claudia, out of

loyalty to Nick, but now, the rawness of her dismissal yesterday was already eliding into a nagging need for a little vengeance. She wanted to give her feelings a name; and if one person in the world was going to know, it might as well be a gay man who could sympathise. "He didn't break my heart; he changed my sense of self-worth."

"Right, so that's what they're calling it now. I see that this one followed you into the kitchen also."

"What are you trying to cook?" asked Andrei.

Marcus raised his voice. "Who's this?"

"This is Andrei, he's a guest, so try to be nice to him. This is Marcus, he's the chef, so please be nice to him too."

"Not in my kitchen," announced Marcus, truculently, then, "The menu's on the fridge door."

Andrei read the list: "*Pirozhki, pelmeni, Tsar's blini* ... nothing too difficult. Do you have an apron?"

Marcus flounced. "You're joking, right? You think I'm going to let a stranger loose in my kitchen? And who says you can cook?"

"Listen" said Andrei, taking charge, "you can take a risk of success down here, or you can be certain of failure upstairs, your choice."

Marcus had no choice, and he knew it. He looked at Imogen.

"What are you looking at me like that for?" she asked. "I've never cooked Russian!"

"If you stayed to help?"

"Marcus! For once in my life, I'm a guest!"

"This is an emergency, Mo. There's a lot riding on this, and you know it."

Imogen mellowed. "Yes, you're right. Give me an apron. Better give him one as well."

Bill came in, sensing that something had gone wrong. "You

plonker," was all he said to Marcus – Bill didn't do sympathy. "Right, salads and colds are on the tables, so it doesn't look too bad. What's going to be ready hot first?"

"Some of the pies," said Marcus, calming down.

"As soon as they are, give them to me, and I'll decide who eats them first."

"I'll make the *blini*," said Andrei. "What are you making them with? This mixture's too thick. We'll start again. I'll call out the ingredients, you deliver."

Bill raised his eyes at the sight of a guest in an apron, in the kitchen. Imogen smiled at him, and shook her head to signify, "Say nothing."

Bill looked at Marcus. "Twenty minutes, or you'll be opening that restaurant sooner than you planned." He went out.

"Cunt," said Marcus, after him.

"I could make the *pelmeni* if you show me how," said Imogen.

"*Pelmeni*," said Andrei, correcting her accent.

"Right, *pelmeni*."

"Filling's in the fridge, Mo," said Marcus "and pastry's under the tea towel. They're fucking fiddly bastards."

"I'll show you how," said Andrei, to Imogen, businesslike. "Stand next to me. Just roll out the pastry as thick as a euro coin. There isn't time for Tsar's *blini*. Marcus, bring me plain flour, semi-skimmed milk, eggs, white sugar, salt, olive oil. What are you filling them with?"

Marcus glared, and then thought better of it: one-handed, he brought the ingredients to Andrei who immediately started preparing the mixture. "I was going to pile them high, and let people put caviar on top. We have loads of the stuff."

"No, best we fill them here. Much more Russian, and easier for people to eat. And please make some water to boil. You have smoked salmon? Sour cream? Boiled eggs?"

"Yes, yes and yes."

"Cooked chicken, mushrooms and onions?"

"Yes. I get it: chop the salmon and chicken, fry the mushrooms and onions, right?"

"Exactly. Can you cut like that?"

"I'll manage. And there's always the mixer."

"And truffles if you have them."

"Those, we always have, don't we, Mo?"

"Sure do."

"You like them?" asked Andrei.

"Love them. And I love to cook with them."

"I'll have to remember."

Imogen knew, even if she couldn't see, that this had registered with Marcus. She kept her head down.

For five or so minutes, there was silence in the kitchen, as Marcus, Imogen and Andrei concentrated on the rescue operation. Andrei was beating the *blini* batter in a bowl; standing shoulder to shoulder with him, Imogen stole sidelong glances at his profile, as she cut out circles of pastry. He was much too perfectly handsome for her taste – you could make a cheese grater out of that square jaw. He caught her looking at him, and smiled.

"You cook for a living?"

"Yes, you? You look at home in a kitchen."

"I cook to relax, not to live."

"Oh, what do you live on?"

He laughed. "My wits."

"You have a British accent. Tikhon and Oleg speak English like Americans."

"I was in London for three years."

"Business?"

"Embassy."

Imogen had been taught that it was rude to pry, so she left it at that. "Show me how to make the first ones, and then I can manage."

She caught Marcus mouthing and apeing her genteel diction. He was feeling better ...

"Of course." Andrei leaned over to show her. She was watching his hands and the back of his neck – he must have had his hair cut just a few days ago; she caught the smell of an aftershave she didn't recognise. She tried to concentrate on what he was saying. "Take a pinch of the mixture in the fingers, like this. In the middle of the circle. Fold over. Squeeze the edges together all the way around, and pinch the edge down until it looks like a woman's twisted hair."

"Braid, you mean?" *Pelmeni*, braid – now they were even.

"Braid, yes. Now, you try."

Imogen had a go; she could feel Andrei watching her closely. She was feeling warm under his gaze.

"Good," was all he said. "When you have twenty, drop them into boiling water, with a drop of olive oil. When they rise, they're ready. Now, Marcus, watch." Marcus stopped his simultaneous chopping and frying, and obediently came over for his lesson. "Get the pan very hot. Put two tablespoons of the mixture into the corner of the pan. Tip from side to side until it covers the surface. It has to be as thin as possible. As soon as it starts to turn brown, flip it. Tip onto a plate. Spread a little butter on top of each one to stop them sticking together. That's it. You have a go. I'll fill them the Russian way."

"They're just pancakes," said Marcus, trying to regain his authority.

"Yes, but you only make them once a year, on a Tuesday. We make them a lot."

The kitchen was like an assembly line, with Imogen braiding and boiling, Andrei filling and rolling, and Marcus ostentatiously swirling the skillet, and flipping. When Bill returned, with Massimo in tow, the first batch of *pirozhki* was ready; a pile of *pelmeni* was steaming in a large ceramic bowl – Provençale red and yellow; and a plate of *blini* rested on another brightly coloured serving dish, like a pile of miniature birch logs.

"I bought a whole load of these ceramics," said Marcus. "I thought they'd make the table look Russian."

Bill also didn't do praise. "What's in the *blini*? So I know what to say."

Andrei seemed not at all put out, only proud of a good job done. "Here, caviar, chopped egg and sour cream; here, smoked salmon, lemon juice and sour cream; this, mushroom, truffles, onion and sour cream; and chicken, onion, sour cream."

Bill was impressed, but would never say. "You use a lot of sour cream in Russian cooking?"

Andrei acknowledged the hidden praise. "We'll keep going until you tell us to stop."

Bill went out, Massimo following, trays in hand.

"Poncey fucker. I'm going to open that restaurant sooner than he imagines," muttered Marcus, though not as violently as before. "Let's open the boss's champagne, and we'll carry on. And thanks," he said to Andrei.

"My pleasure. It's a nice party down here."

Imogen decided that he was right; and that she quite liked him. "Well, that's obviously why I wore my very best party dress, to go under my apron."

Marcus was singing off-key as he popped the cork. "That's why you'll always find me in the kitchen at parties!"

Caviare to the General

"*A FANABLA!* I'm not going! I don't care how important it is! No, I'm not going because it *is* important!"

"It's business! Your business, so you keep saying! We have to show a united front! Or you want to lose it all? You think it won't happen? I'm telling you, the vultures are circling, waiting to swoop and pick us clean."

"That's what you want, isn't it? So you can go back to being a gardener! Where you belong!"

"What's got into you? What have I done to you? You really hate me that much?"

"*Cazzo si!* I loathe and detest you."

"Show me something, anything, that I've done to hurt you?"

"I'm not going to Cannes to that stupid party, and that's it."

"That's not the real reason, is it? You won't go because you don't want to face them. Look at you." He had meant to hurt her – perhaps it might shock her out of whatever crisis it was she was going through – and he had; he saw the momentary look of painful truth on her face, instantly replaced by a look of proud and sullen defiance. She looked a mess: hair unwashed and unkempt; clothed – she no longer dressed – in a shapeless black top and leggings that suggested shabby mourning; and only emphasised the spreading tree trunks of her thighs. He loved her for that refusal to bend. She would shout and scream, but she would not cry. There had been no tears since Nice airport. But she was quite capable of throwing something at him – mostly wedding presents – and, if he was not to lose her, he had to reason with her. "Where's the woman I married?"

"She left with the man who married her for her money."

"You are impossible, you know that!" It was useless. There was no talking to her, not like this. Defeated, Nick abruptly made a strategic withdrawal. He left Cassie standing in the drawing-room, or what used to be a room with that name; now, it was a war-strewn shell, full of builders' equipment and detritus, step ladders and paint pots.

He drove from Turin to Cannes; he could do it in less than three and a half hours, and the drive would help him think his way out of this mess. He would stay in San Remo on the way back; the children were there with Beatrice who had said that the builders' dust was bad for them. Cassie had not objected – she wanted to be left alone, she said. Perhaps tomorrow he would do some gardening; he could plant something with the kids, something that would grow quickly, that would interest them in the garden – get them away from TV and computer screens.

His handling of the Dino was always a pointer to his state of mind: in anger, he would throw it brutally around corners, floor the pedals; happy, he would drive with skill, feeling at one with the gearbox and engine. This evening, the car gave him no pleasure – he should have taken the BMW – and he drove like a pensioner, ignoring the constant challenges from drivers who wanted to race.

It was not true what she said about the money; it was not true now, that is. Admit it, Nicholas Austin, the marriage had included a measure of financial calculation – he had been on his uppers – and now that he was rich, he was ashamed of that earlier interest in her dowry. Now that he had had time to get used to the money, he felt only the responsibility of it all, the need to look after it, grow it, keep it safe as an inheritance. Except for the Dino, nothing that the money had bought had given him any more pleasure than he could have had as a gardener – houses, boats, clothes, food, wine, they were only commodities. When he analysed it – the meaning of his life – as he had done many times since he had married into money, the only thing he valued was beauty – Cassie (as she had been before bloating ...), roses and the Dino. Okay, so he was a guy into beauty, but where did Imogen fit into that beautiful picture? Aah! That, he understood only too well: the attraction had all to do with cock; and a cock has a mind of its own. When a man comes only once, it's a matter of simple drainage – a release of pressure; when he comes two, three or four times in a fuck marathon, as Nick had done with Imogen, it leaves him balls-aching emptied – the tip of his cock all passion spent; and that's when you can finally stop thinking about pleasing your cock, put your head down, and, at last, concentrate on whatever work your cock has been putting off.

She'd lost weight – why the fuck did she do that? He'd liked her exactly as she was – big and classy. Sizewise, Cassie would soon be up to where Imogen had been, but there was nothing sexy about fat and slatternly.

He had ended it, the affair, against his will – a man could wish to be buried in that cunt of hers – but perhaps being found out had also done him a favour? Yeah, right, now he had nowhere to bury his cock. The question now was, could he keep his cock under control in the future? That was a lot to ask of a man.

He knew that Cassie knew that he had been up to something – deep down, in her marrow – and yet he also knew that she didn't, in fact, know anything about Imogen.

As long as that Andrei fucker kept his mouth shut, he might just be able to dig his way out of trouble.

He tried to think about the upcoming board meeting, when he would put the sugar-free deal to a vote. It was not looking good: without Cassie's shares, he was going to lose. With so little time left, there was no chance of sweet-talking her into changing her mind. Frank was his only hope; that was why he had agreed to go to the party. "You might find it interesting," was all Frank had said, but Nick had understood this to mean that he should definitely go.

The first person he saw when he stepped on board the *Claudia* was Imogen. She looked pretty fucking amazing – all curves and clinging velvet; and she was wearing the clip he had given her only yesterday. Without hesitating, he went up to her. "Nice jewellery." He sensed that there was a tremor in his voice – the sticky residue of his feelings for her.

"A present from a secret admirer," she said in a voice that he understood she hoped would carry.

He wanted to try to square things with her – he had literally walked out on her yesterday – but that toffee-nosed cunt, Mat, had butted in, claiming her for himself. He hated him on sight: the upper-class drawl he used to belittle the chocolate business, the social privilege he used as an entitlement to anything he wanted; money had coursed through his veins since birth, and, unlike Nick, this genetic wealth meant that he had no doubts about how to live with it. Disconcertingly, Nick had realised that Mat also had his finger in the chocolate deal – was he in league with Frank? Swallowing his pride, he would have liked to probe a little more, but Frank came over to say that he wanted to introduce some people.

The two men negotiated their way through the party, with Frank playing the role of host with an easy grace – handshakes, kisses, brief exchanges about films nobody had seen – and yet never losing sight of his targets. He allowed Nick to chat with Claudia who asked him why they never saw Cassie any more. Was she okay? He explained about redecorating the house. Frank propelled him onwards: he met an old guy who talked about buying the yacht that Mat had cancelled – the only thing to cheer him up; a Chinese businessman living in South Africa, who wanted to talk about gardens; and an English fund manager who talked about the price of houses. The word 'chocolate' was not mentioned. While he was making the rounds, he noticed with proprietorial jealousy that Imogen was surrounded by men – Mat, Tikhon, Andrei and a mean-looking Russian he recognised from newspaper articles. He would have liked to talk with Andrei on his own, but he disappeared with Imogen, which really riled him. Couldn't she have waited? Shown him in some way that they had meant something together?

He was out of sorts; and the arrival of the hot food completely chilled his mood. It reminded him of that day when he had first met Imogen, in Frank's kitchen; then, he had shown himself up as an ignorant food snob; this evening, having learned so much about food, eating it with Imogen, now he couldn't, had no desire to eat. He wondered if it was her food on the trays being passed around. *Blini* with anything you could imagine; and so much caviare that, for no good reason, it turned him against everything Russian, turned him against the whole party. He had an urge to scoop out the caviare from the iced swans, and scatter it across the room, over all the guests. All this exquisite food was wasted on them; raining caviare down on them seemed an appropriate action, for the puritan feeling he had that he no longer belonged here, in this milieu. Frank and Claudia's Festival gathering was all so fucking perfect; and there was nothing about his life that came close any more to perfection. This was such a beautifully choreographed scene, the pinnacle of what passed for glamour; yet all he could think about what was how he wanted to just sit out the dance.

He made his excuses and left – to Claudia, something about having to get back to the children; to Frank, needing to prepare for the showdown. Frank clapped him on the back and said, "Good luck."

He drove slowly along the coast road. He could have taken the *péage* but he had no desire to drive fast. Driving through Èze, he wished that he had taken the motorway. Abruptly, he turned off the road, and drove down to the beach. Hitting the sand, he stopped, turned off the engine, and switched off the lights.

He sat there in silence, looking out at the sea, and looking into himself. Running his fingers round and round the steering wheel he started to cry. There was nobody there to ask him what was he crying for so he told himself. He was crying for all the mistakes that he had made – that didn't seem like mistakes at the time: Versace romance, marriage, adultery, money, chocolate, things ... Most of all he was crying for his manicured hands. He wanted to feel again the sharp, intense pain prick of a rose thorn on his finger. He was crying because his hands had become soft, and his heart had become calloused. He had bought into the Ferrari lifestyle, and now he was paying the price.

Escoffier

"Imogène? This is Andrei ... Andrei Volkov. Frank gave me your number. Would you like to go truffle hunting?"

"Just like that? It's out of season."

"We already did dinner, remember, in the kitchen? It's out of season for big white Alba truffles, yes, but there are always *bianchetto*. And does it matter? The excitement of the hunt is always in the chase."

"If I didn't know you were Russian, I would think that you were English, with a remark like that."

"I will take that as a compliment. So, you will come?"

"Where?"

"Just outside of Alba. Next weekend, okay? I've emailed you the details. Come. It will be fun."

Imogen read her email. Mr Volkov clearly didn't like leaving anything to chance: how to get where they were staying – an *agriturismo* farmhouse – by three different routes; a detailed itinerary; and names, telephone numbers, addresses ...

She immediately called Claudia. "Clod, what do you wear for truffle hunting?"

"Sensible shoes, same as for beagling, why?"

"That Russian, Andrei, who helped us in the kitchen, just invited me."

"Oh."

"I thought you'd sound more enthusiastic. You told me to take up with somebody else right away, and he's amazingly handsome."

"Handsome isn't everything. I don't like him. I don't like what he does."

"They're not the same."

"He follows people, finds out things they really don't want other people to know." Imogen was wondering if Andrei had been following Claudia. "I thought you might take up with Mat?"

"Be serious, Clod! Men like that want a glamour puss."

"You looked pretty glam at the party."

"That isn't the type of relationship I want."

"You don't know anything about relationships, that's your trouble. Truffle hunting? Well, don't say I didn't warn you."

Imogen made up her mind to go. The worst that could happen was that she ate too many truffles. Sex, would there be sex? Like asking yourself would there be trifle ... She was missing it, like a car running out of petrol. "You slut, Imogen O'Rorke," said Sister Ursula, right on cue. Imogen snarled back at her accusing conscience. "Oh, go away! You're always trying to stop me from having a good time!" Sister Ursula retreated.

That was always the weekend away dilemma: pack a bag for sex, and look too eager; not be ready for it, and look unbecomingly unprepared.

She could always compromise by wearing 'country' on the outside, and a g-string beneath her Barbour. But nothing fitted! She was smaller now than even the optimistic 'thin' side of her old wardrobe. Could she really face shopping, starting from scratch? No, not yet; she would find a seamstress to take things in, while she got used to the new reduced size, low-fat Imogen. In the meantime, she had to make sure that she was ready with the lunch for the Baroness.

As always, Escoffier was long on poetry and short on detail: *"These are little Eclairs stuffed with a purée made from the entrails of woodcock with champagne. The purée is buttered and slightly seasoned. Cover the Eclairs with a brown chaud-froid sauce, mask them with game jelly, and serve them, iced, on ornamented dish-papers."* She had served woodcock at a corporate lunch a while ago, when they had still been in season; and saved the innards for use at this lunch. The sauce could be tricky; cooling it down without congealing, that took patience. What did he say in the original French? She skimmed through it, and burst out laughing: *"Fourrées purée de parties internes de bécasse à la fine champagne beurrée ... décors de truffes."* Truffles – it was fate, she decided.

Truffle hunting

Imogen took in the simple stone walls, green wooden shutters and timber beams. "When you said a farmhouse, you really meant it, didn't you?"

Andrei seemed genuinely confused. "What did you think I meant?"

"Some men say 'farmhouse' when they really mean *castello*."

"You're disappointed? It's eighteenth century."

"Quite the opposite. What's not to like? Vineyards, olive groves, forests and a view of the river. I love it."

"Good. If you're happy, I'm happy."

"You look very English in those clothes. Brogues, green cords, and that jacket looks very lived in."

"I have been hunting all my life. And you look very English too."

"Irish, please. Did you think I would wear high heels?"

"I think that you are a woman who knows exactly what to wear. I'll show you inside."

Imogen was still wondering if he were expecting to sleep with her. Well, it didn't look that way – they had separate rooms.

"I thought we could go into Alba, have a walk around, and then an early dinner? We have to be up early tomorrow."

"I'm in your hands." She wished she hadn't said that; not that it mattered because he gave no reaction. After Nick's predatory ways, she found this gentlemanly reserve both reassuring and disconcerting.

She couldn't help but make comparisons with Nick: Nick had let his money look after her; with Andrei, she felt so much more independent, as if she could think for herself. She had driven here, followed his instructions to the letter, and still arrived late. She could have texted to let him know, but she wanted to see if he would ask her where she was? He didn't, which made her smile at his misplaced confidence in her.

"How did you know I hadn't had an accident?"

"Then you would have texted me."

They smiled at each other.

He had a nice line in dry humour.

She had become so used to the Ferrari that when she sat in Andrei's hired Fiat Punto, she was very aware of how basic it was, and underpowered – they overtook nothing on the way to Alba.

Andrei missed nothing. "What were you expecting? A Ferrari? I don't like to attract attention."

"What is it about men and Ferraris?"

"I wouldn't know. I drive a Maserati."

She caught the smile on his face, but couldn't decide how much truth he was telling. She wanted to know more about him.

"Do you miss Russia?"

"I miss some things."

"Such as?"

Andrei did not hesitate – what a man misses in his life is always fresh in his mind. "White nights in St Petersburg ... the view of the Neva river from the windows of the covered bridge over the Winter canal ... the smell of candle wax in St Nicholas Cathedral ... jumping into the snow after a *banya* at the dacha ... and Temirkanov conducting Tchaikovsky's last symphony at the Philharmonia."

"You make me want to go. What don't you miss?"

"That would take a very long time to explain."

"We have all weekend."

"You can never find out anything important in a hurry," which Imogen took to mean, "I'll tell you when I'm ready."

They drove the rest of the way in silence, with Imogen thinking that she was attracted to that part of Andrei she did not know. There was a withdrawn quality about him that she wanted to uncover. She had the idea, however, that finding out about him would not be straightforward. Here was a man who made his living out of secrets; perhaps being secretive about himself might have become second nature. She wondered how much he knew about her? She could have asked him, but she preferred to let things unfold as they would.

"Alba is made out of truffles," she said, after they had been there all of twenty minutes, walking down via Vittorio Emanuele II. "Truffle purée, truffle mayonnaise, truffle pasta. Is there anything they don't make out of truffles?"

"Well, you have oil towns, steel towns and nickel towns, why not truffle towns? You want to look around?"

They did the tourist sights – Palazzo Comunale, the watchtowers, the Church of San Domenico – and Imogen wondered how Andrei knew his way around so well. He pointed out interesting pictures, frescoes, architectural elements, and dismissed what he thought was not worth seeing, with authoritative firmness. "No point in seeing the Duomo, unless you want to see what happens when people don't respect the past. But if you want to, we will."

"No, you lead, I'll follow. You make a good tour guide."

He would zero in on the tiniest detail, and illuminate it with a wider reference. He particularly wanted her to see the frescoes in San Domenico. Nobody else in the church gave them more than a cursory look; and Imogen might have done the same – they were cracked and incomplete – but Andrei gave them his full attention. "It is always interesting to imagine what has been lost, as much as to see what has survived." She liked the way he carefully measured his words, meshing them with his thoughts.

"Piecing together the missing pieces, you mean?" She paused. She wanted to draw him out, like winkling a snail out of a shell. "Like getting to know somebody."

He did not answer immediately, carried on looking at the frescoes, and then, in no hurry, and rather distantly, "We can only ever know the fragments, *Imogène*. He pronounced her name with a soft French accent, which she found dead sexy.

"Where would you like to eat?"

"Your choice."

"Truffle menu?"

"I can never tell when you're being serious. I take it that's why you're so good at your job."

"Did I tell you what I do?"

"No, you didn't, Claudia did. I don't mind as long as you don't follow me."

"I know exactly where we'll go."

"I'm happy to follow you," said Imogen, gaily.

It is easy to miss La Bottega del Vicoletto – the entrance looks as if it belongs to a private house. The place was winding down after lunch, but the welcome was far from tired: Bruno Boggione, seeing Andrei step through the door, hurriedly left off writing in chalk on the large school blackboard that functions as the menu, and moved expansively towards them: *"Signor Andrei! Sei tornato così presto!"*

There was an exchange of voluble Italian, Imogen was introduced to Bruno as *"una signora che sa tutto sul cibo,"* which she understood was meant kindly; and they sat down. Bruno said that they were in his hands; they were not to look at the menu.

"It's a husband-and-wife team," explained Andrei. "Ilvia, his wife, does the cooking."

"You come here a lot? You like truffles that much?"

"I've been coming here on and off for the past year. It's nice to get away from the office."

Imogen was oddly disappointed, and couldn't stop herself from showing it. "I somehow thought this weekend was a special treat."

"This one is. And wait until you see the food."

For the next hour, Bruno brought to the table a feast: venison *prosciutto*, Jerusalem artichoke flan, snails in tomato sauce, roast squab with truffles and *parmigiano;* and to finish, *torrone semifreddo* with chocolate sauce. To drink, there was *Dolcetto d'Alba,* from a nearby vineyard. All the while, they talked about food and cooking, particularly Russian cooking. For once, it was Imogen who listened about menus and recipes as Andrei talked with knowledge about the dietary restrictions imposed by the Russian Orthodox Church, about the arrival of French chefs in the nineteenth century, and what a difference they had made.

On the way back to the farmhouse, they swapped stories about literature and food. Imogen made Andrei laugh, with her story about Virginia Woolf's *bouef en daube*; and Andrei talked about Gogol's *coulibiac,* "which was one of the first Russian dishes to be exported."

They drank Barolo in the kitchen while Andrei made what he promised her would be "a very light dinner." No man had ever cooked for Imogen, and she kept asking him if he didn't want any help.

"No. This is how I planned it."

"You plan everything in such detail?"

"What is life without a plan?"

Seated at the kitchen table, itching to hold a saucepan, or stir something, she watched him put together three *antipasti*, with professional expertise: a warm salad of wild rabbit marinated in basalmic vinegar – "I shot the rabbit here last week;" a fritter of diced artichokes; and grilled porcini with *fonduta*. Unlike Imogen, he cooked without a mess, cleaning up as he went. Despite what he had said about going to bed early, they didn't get around to the pasta course – *agnolotti*, with slices of *bianchetto* – until nearly ten o'clock in the evening. All this time, and yet she had learned nothing about him other than the fragments she pieced together from what little he allowed her to know: he was from St Petersburg, he had served in the Presidential Regiment in the Kremlin, he had worked in the civil service, he had been in Geneva during *perestroika;* and that was when he had decided to stay in Switzerland.

She was more than a little drunk, yet she knew what she was doing; she could hear herself not asking him searching personal questions. Looking at him, cooking for her, at his ease, she asked herself, why didn't she ask him more about himself? Because she didn't want to know. They were playing an undeclared game of cat and mouse. When he had told her about shooting the rabbit, that had been enough for her. A hunter is a loner; a woman who falls for such a man must needs tread carefully. Unlike Nick, she understood that Andrei was not a man who needed a woman to run his life – he was self-sufficient. Nick used his handsomeness to get what he wanted; Andrei, unshaven, sleeves rolled up, talking about food in *Anna Karenina*, seemed to have discounted his looks.

Nevertheless, Imogen was thinking – hoping – that he might make a pass at her, but Andrei gave no indication that sex was on his mind. He was a difficult man to read; still, when she retired to bed, Imogen had made up her mind, much too quickly she knew: this was a man after her own heart. Perhaps it might happen tomorrow evening, if she stayed another night ...

The alarm clock on her mobile woke her at six. Her head was a little woolly. She wrapped her purple peignoir around her, and looked out the window. A mist was blanketing the countryside, and levitating above the Tanaro river. It was a *gouache* morning, all of Piedmont's pantone colours washed out in the shivering air.

A cheerful voice from below said, *"Buongiorno.* How did you sleep?" It was Andrei, looking up at her.

"Very well. I think I drank too much wine." Had she given him a good enough look at her breasts – juicy in transparent purple. "I'll be down soon."

When she came downstairs to the kitchen, dressed all in green and tweed, there was fresh coffee on the table, and a mushroom omelette.

"Never hunt on an empty stomach," said Andrei, "it makes you impatient, my father said."

Imogen, not hungry, dutifully ate the omelette. "That's the first thing you've said about your parents."

He surprised her with his response. "I don't keep everything a secret, you know. My father taught me to hunt, and my mother to cook. She said that if I knew how to feed myself, I wouldn't marry the wrong woman."

"Every woman except Claudia thinks that the way to a man's heart is through his stomach."

"Not this man."

It was almost like flirting, but it was interrupted by a gundog careering into the kitchen, followed by an old man telling the dog to behave. He was of medium height, with a weatherbeaten face, and patrician bone structure – the type of man who is handsome at any age. He was dressed like hunters everywhere – green Wellington boots, moleskin trousers, Barbour; only the Piedmontese cap gave any clue as to where he hunted.

The two men shook hands, exchanged a few quiet words, and Imogen was introduced. "This is Aldo, our *trifolau*, and this is Diana. As soon as you're ready, we can start."

"I'm ready."

They walked through the ranks of *Nebbiolo* vines, heading towards the forested plateau that skirted the river. They kept a few paces behind Aldo, who was beating the underbrush with his walking stick and encouraging Diana. *"Beica bene!"*

"You know anything about truffles?" asked Andrei.

"Uhm ... I use them in my cooking, of course, and I like to think I can tell the difference between a white Alba truffle and a *bianchetto*, but I know almost nothing about the hunting. Oh! They used to hunt them with pigs, but everybody knows that. I'd like to learn."

"Well, you know of course that you find them close to the roots of trees – oak, chestnut, limes, hazel, beech. When the dog smells something, you'll see Aldo dig with that tool hanging from his waist – they call it a *vanghetto*. He picks out the truffle very carefully ... if we're lucky."

They walked on without talking. Imogen was enjoying the silence, broken only by the occasional sharp whistle of birds. Diana began to paw at the base of a hazel tree. Aldo hurriedly ran over to stop her.

"You have to stop the dog from digging or the truffle can be damaged," explained Andrei. "Hazel trees usually give black truffles. We'll see."

Aldo took out a biscuit from his pocket and gave it to Diana, patting her with words of praise in a dialect of Italian, Imogen didn't recognise – Albanese.

"He rewards the dog, no matter what she finds."

Aldo put on his glasses to take a closer look. He rooted around with his hands, sniffed the earth, and began digging with the *vanghetto*. After a few moments, he brought out a very tiny black truffle. He handed it to Imogen, turning up his nose in disappointment. "*Scotsori*. You can always find black truffles." Imogen was surprised that he spoke English – Aldo was not a village hunter.

Andrei explained some more. "They call them *Scotsori* because of their thick skin."

Aldo carefully replaced the soil. "To keep other hunters off the scent?" asked Imogen.

"Not only. The spores that drop from the truffle he collected will help to grow more truffles next year." They walked on. "The truffles on this side of the river have a better perfume. The soil on the other bank is sandy; the truffles look nicer, but they have less aroma and flavour."

"You know more about them than I do!"

They continued with the hunt, Diana zig-zagging through the undergrowth. She began to scrabble beneath an oak tree. This time, both Andrei and Imogen stood close by as Aldo prised the earth away with his hands.

Imogen sniffed the air. "It's amazing how you can smell it even when it's still under the ground." Aldo pulled out his trophy, and held it up with a smile. "It's a *Bianchetto*, yes?"

"Yes, a white spring truffle," said Aldo. "It looks like the famous white Alba truffle, *Tuber magnatum*, but it is smaller and the flavour is completely different. Smell."

Imogen put her nose to the truffle. "It's very garlicky."

They met another *trifolau*. Imogen heard Aldo complain about the slim pickings. "Lousy day. Nothing whatsoever. We'll leave you here, see if we have better luck somewhere else."

"Aldo guards his territory very jealously," remarked Imogen, as they walked off.

"With good reason. There are stories of dogs being poisoned by rival hunters."

"A dangerous business."

"You have no idea how true that is. And a very profitable business too. All you're doing is pulling things out of the ground ... No expenses except you and your dog."

"Just exactly how many times have you been here in the past year."

"Quite a few."

"This isn't a casual weekend, is it? You don't have to answer if you don't want to. I'm happy to mind my own business."

"No, that's okay, there is a reason for my being here. I'm happy to tell you, as long as you do not tell them in Alba. I have a client with a big share of the truffle market. More and more they are finding Chinese truffles mixed in with Italian."

"Well, I can tell you as a cook that the Chinese truffles have no perfume and absolutely no taste."

"Yes, because they pull them out of the ground not with dogs, which can recognise ripeness, but with spades. But you think everybody who orders an Italian truffle in a restaurant can tell the difference? A real Italian truffle is worth its weight in gold, a Chinese one is only good for pig feed. That is why there is such a big black market."

"So, first the Chinese counterfeit Louis Vuitton, and now it's truffles. I don't see what you can do?"

"The truffle market is an insider's market. You find somebody who is on the inside, and you find out what he knows."

Villa Eilenroc

"Aldo?"

"Sixty years of truffle hunting is a lot of information."

"And information is your business."

"Yes. That is not a secret."

"You've been giving away a lot of secrets today."

"Too many. I think it's time to be going back, and have some lunch."

They parted from Aldo at the farmhouse. Andrei said that he would cook lunch. They both freshened up, and took their places in the old-fashioned, stone-flagged kitchen.

"I feel very strange not cooking."

"You don't like it?"

"I could get used to it. You already planned the menu, of course?"

"*Tagliatelle* with today's truffles, grilled rabbit liver, salad, and *Barbera d'Alba* to drink."

"And I don't have to do anything except watch!"

"And talk. I talked about my parents, you talk about yours."

"My grandmother was a much bigger influence."

"I'm listening."

So, while Andrei busied himself with the food, Imogen kept him amused with the many stories she had to tell about Marie-Hélène – love affairs, eccentricities, strange beliefs ... He listened without interruption, or impatience because, she understood, he was interested in what she had to say – that was what she liked about him.

"Are you like her?"

"No! Well, I don't think so. I don't look like her at all. I mean, I can't fit into her clothes."

"Is that important?"

"It used to be. Perhaps it still is? I suppose I do like to be different, to take risks. Starting the business was a big risk."

They were getting on so well; it all went wrong when Andrei

served the pasta, and began to slice the truffles, slice after big slice.

"In the Louis Quinze you're lucky to get four shavings!" exclaimed Imogen.

"Yes, I remember."

Without thinking – almost unheard of – Andrei had dropped his guard; and the fallout was nuclear. Imogen looked down at her plate; then she looked at Andrei, forking his pasta. She could feel her insides chilling and contracting. The words came off her tongue with resistance, like skinning a rabbit. "None of this is an accident, is it? You want to tell me what's really going on? Am I useful to you in some way?"

"I don't understand?" Andrei did understand – he was no longer eating.

"I knew I had seen you before. The truffles made me remember. You were sitting on your own in the Louis Quinze when I was there with Nick ... Nick Austin. I always notice people sitting by themselves. That was our last evening. In Mougins – our last lunch – Nick said that somebody had been following us, and it was you, wasn't it? Who else could it be? You've been following me all this time. Oh God! What an awful thought." Imogen kept going, hoping he would deny it, but he heard her out in silence. "I suppose you know why he ended it, don't you, so suddenly? Did you have a hand in that as well? I thought it was unlike him. Claudia was right, you are in everything, aren't you? Let me guess, there are Russians involved in his chocolate deal, aren't there? Russians you know? Tikhon? Oleg?"

As she spoke, her pain and fury rising above the stave, she was swiftly piecing together all the fragments of what she knew. "Claudia says that Frank gets all his information about people from you – information he uses for making money. That's what you do, isn't it, you run a mining operation – gold mines, chocolate mines, people mines, scrabbling around in the dirt for anything of value. That's all I am to you, isn't it, a mine of information? On the *Claudia*, you came down to the kitchen because you wanted to find out more about me."

"Not in the way that you think."

She was not listening. "Claudia was so right – truffle hunting. That's all you want, isn't it, to know what I'm thinking, to know what everybody's thinking?" Finally, at bay, having chased her thoughts into dense undergrowth, she stopped. Then, drooping, "I think I'd better go."

She stood up. She could be packed and out of there in five minutes.

"Please, don't follow me."

Le déjeuner

Éclairs à la Karoly
Consommé George Sand
Bouef en Daube à la Niçoise
Bombe Néro

THE BARONESS WAS not at all sure about this lunch. For thirty-two years she had put that man out of her mind, and now he was coming back, for lunch. What was she thinking? That they could re-heat what had long gone cold, after scalding them both? He had left his wife; she had not left her husband. *Noblesse oblige*? No, she and the Baron were childless, and she had not the cruelty to take Paolo away from his daughter. Cassandra had lost her mother, that had been enough trauma. Oh, what nobility in that self-sacrifice, Sophie! Yet sacrifice always drips blood – High Priestess and victim spattered both.

The housekeeper – what was her name? – had rung her the evening Cassandra's mother had slit her wrists, accusing her of murder: "May God forgive you, I never will. Are you sorry? Are you? Pray every morning that Cassandra never finds out who you are. I washed that woman's blood off my hands, but you will never clean your conscience."

The blood prophecy is at the heart of tragedy, and that was how it was with the Baroness. Life became haunted and sterile; a life so elegant – diplomatic drawing-rooms and freshwater pearls – and yet so blanched of life. The nagging anxiety of our everydays merely unsettles the human psyche, guilt lacerates it; her conscience meant that the Baroness was never allowed to forget her bloody sacrifice, thrown back against the barbed wire of memory.

The Baron had been what people unfailingly describe as 'a good man' – kind, urbane, sympathetic and endlessly forgiving. How the Baroness would have preferred a little less bloodless *politesse*, and more of what Paolo had given her – the hot-blooded cocksure volatility of all-consuming love. Marriage to the Baron had meant that she had lacked for nothing; now there was nothing to remember.

Paolo had become Papoche – as confident as ever, richer than the Baron, a father and grandfather. It had been a shock to see him again, after all those years, at the lunch in Saint-Tropez. It was not his being older that had been so discomfiting – year after ageing year we reluctantly come to terms with the face we own, and yet do not recognise in the mirror; and all the other unrecognisable faces – no, it was the almost instantaneous realisation of how little had changed between them. They had exchanged only a few cautious words, and yet the hairline crack that she had lived with in her porcelain life had suddenly fractured into so many shards. With age comes a lengthening memory, a distant galaxy of opposing forces – the life you led and the life you were too afraid to live; and that lost trajectory is always out there somewhere, wilfully colliding with the orbit of your pedestrian life, and one day smashing to smithereens the capsule you have been hiding in.

She had sat tensely through the lunch at Frank and Claudia's villa, at first unable to look at him for fear she would give herself away. Frank's wine had loosened her tongue, and she had lost her accumulated reserve. As described by her, the Romanée-Conti had been a libation in memory of something that had refused to die. Love is what remains of us after the face has faded and fallen; buried but still alive, scrabbling and clawing on the inside even as we screw down the lid.

She had thought they would be four for lunch – Paolo, Frank and Claudia – but Claudia had called her just now to ask if they could come with Cassandra. "Because Papoche says she needs to get out of the house, whatever that means." What did that mean? And what was she meant to say? "No! It's too dangerous! What if she finds us out? What then?" What was he thinking? Why run the risk of re-opening an old wound? Trained in restraint, that was not what she had said; instead, she had sounded quite delighted.

What was it that she was so afraid of? An old flame, or the fear that there was no candle burning on the other side?

She had called Imogen to say that they would now be six – she was inviting that American, Ray, to make up an equal number. Imogen had seemed almost as disconcerted as the Baroness: "Oh ... right ... I see. Shall I keep the same menu? I mean, she doesn't eat, does she?"

The Baroness had smiled at the thought of Imogen being so concerned about somebody not eating, but she kept her thoughts to herself. "Well, eating wouldn't do her any harm, would it?"

What to wear? There had been a time when she had thrown on her clothes, any old how, so eager to run to Paolo and adulterate her marriage; today, she hated everything in her wardrobe – too fussy, too old-fashioned, too old, too young, too 60s, too 70s, too 80s, too 90s ... too whatever! She couldn't wear black – too much the widow; it would remind both of them of the Baron, to whom she had been loyal, which is not the same as faithful. She couldn't wear white – too immaculate. She could play it safe and wear grey; and then he would think that she was set in her ways; or she could wear pastel, and have him think that she was ... what? What did pastel signify?

"Keep it simple, Sophie." She picked out a pair of grey Chanel trousers, and a Lanvin silk shirt in palest pink, and capped-toe ballet flats in pink and black. "Yes, nicely casual, and not too grand."

That left the table to check. "Much too grand ... too formal," she said, rather imperiously, to Georges, the butler who had been with them for more than thirty years. "I've had a change of heart ... I've changed my mind, I think that we should eat on the terrace. And the flowers are much too big. Will you please call the florist right away and say that I want something *très simple*."

"*Oui, madame.*"

"And champagne as an aperitif. And the wine the best you can find in the Baron's cellar; in a decanter, and the bottle not on show."

"*Oui, madame.*"

She was aware that she sounded much too much "the Baroness." That grandness was what had attracted Papoche, the ancestral certainty of her knowing exactly what to wear, and how to behave. The very idea of her owning a tiara had been something to laugh at. Oh! if only they had owned up to each other that opposites attract – he wanted her class, she wanted him to take her with brute force.

He had always known where she lived. When she and the Baron were not away on a posting, the villa in Menton had been home. It was a grand turn-of-the-century stucco affair – Meditteranean marble graced with velvet pelmets and mahogany turned legs – set back in the hills, with a view out to the sea. This was where he had left her, at the iron gates, that last day, having exhausted his peasant stock of exhortations, pleadings, threats and prophecies. "You can spend the rest of your life, Sophie, telling yourself that you made the right decision, but one day, I promise you, the day will come when you will most regret this day." Was this the day?

Dissatisfied with life – a dispiriting *mélange* of regret and remorse – annoyed at everything, and furious with herself at having opened the door to a room in her memory that she had long ago slammed shut and padlocked, the Baroness went down to the kitchen, looking for some below-stairs companionship, only to be met with the downcast face of Imogen, mechanically stirring, and staring at ingredients as if she somehow expected – wanted to – fall into the mixing bowl.

"You look sad, my dear," she said, sitting down at a kitchen stool. Imogen looked up, attempting a smile. The Baroness understood. "Men can be brutes, but unfortunately we can't live without them."

"I would ask how do you know that it's a man but I guess you do."

"What else could it be? We only keep making mistakes about men and money."

"I didn't think that I was making a mistake."

"*Mais non*, of course you didn't."

It was an impromptu kitchen cabinet – baroness and countess. At some time in her life, every woman has been the other woman, and she needs to explain herself, to another woman.

Imogen tried first. "He was married, but I don't think that was the problem. I changed, only he didn't. The one immediately after that was the problem – the rebound. I don't suppose I'm making any sense?"

"Oh, you are, perfectly. I find confusion very understandable. I used to take off my wedding ring, before …"

"Did it make any difference?"

"Oh yes, I was horribly conscious of the red mark I made trying to pull it off." The Baroness looked at her flawless diamond ring. "I shouldn't be talking like this."

"No? We were always taught that confession is good for the soul."

"Yes, so we were. It isn't true. Men are so very sensitive, and it's so very easy to hurt them."

"I always think of them as soft fruit – easily bruised."

The Baroness laughed. "Do you always think in food images?"

"Almost."

"And how do you see in food a relationship that you can't bear to live with … can't stomach; and all your friends say is so wonderful?"

Imogen was quick with an answer – it had been her parents' marriage. "Anything in aspic – cold, trembling and transparent."

"*Mais oui!* That's perfectly horrible. Are those the éclairs? They look very difficult to make."

"Not difficult, just fiddly. I thought they would make a good first impression."

"I'm impressed but what makes you think that I'm trying to make an impression?"

"*Boeuf en daube* in this heat? You asked for 'something substantial,' and women don't eat substantial food. I think that is trying to say something."

"*Comment?* A menu can tell you all that?"

"A menu is an emotional experience. People use my food for all sorts of things – romance, celebration, farewell, making money …"

"Not because they like your food?"

"I think they like it more because I try to give it exactly the emotional meaning they're looking for. A restaurant can't do that."

"You never worry that a dish might not turn out exactly as you planned it? Over-salted? Over-cooked? Inedible?"

"It keeps me awake at night."

The Baroness picked up the black truffle that Imogen had brought back with her from her hunting weekend – presented to her by Aldo. She smelt it, inhaling the pungent aroma. *"Parfums de truffes.* I can remember so many of the times when I ate a truffle dish."

Imogen was in an anti-truffle mood. "Yes, they linger in the memory."

The Baroness seemed intent on her truffle memories. "Are they really an aphrodisiac? We used to buy them in the market in San Remo. He didn't really need truffles, not for love, but he loved to show off. If only a relationship could always be like a truffle – simple and perfumed."

It was a subject that Imogen wanted to keep away from. "Do you think the wife always knows?"

"Oh, yes, no matter how far away you go to make love."

"Perhaps they only suspect? I think suspicion must be far worse. Imagination is such a terrible thing. There's nothing a human being can't imagine. I keep thinking about her thinking about us."

"Yes, you do. Did it end badly?"

"Actually, it just stopped in the middle."

"Aah. *C'est ça.* A bad ending lasts for a very long time."

Imogen fiddled with the éclairs. "Do you think Cassandra will be upset by all this?"

The Baroness steadied herself on the stool, and replied cautiously. "In what way do you think we're going to hurt her?"

"All this food. I feel sorry for her. She didn't eat a thing in Saint-Tropez. I don't think she can even stand the sight of it."

"Her father has a big appetite. He likes to eat things up. And you've lost a lot of weight."

"Yes, and it's still the most noticeable thing about me."

Both women were startled by the sound of a clanging bell echoing throughout the house. The Baroness stood up, instantly becoming once more the *grande dame*, not a woman unburdening.

"Guests. Georges will let you know when to start."

Imogen nodded, equally formal. The conversation had never happened.

Boeuf en daube

IMOGEN SLICED THE truffle, and arranged the paper-thin shavings over the éclairs. The aroma sent her straight back to Alba. She tried to set up road blocks in her mind, thinking about something else – anything – but the smell would not let her go. She thought about Andrei following her, and involuntarily glanced over her shoulder, seeing only an unfitted kitchen, hung with copper saucepans, yet she was still trying to imagine what he would have looked like behind her. How far away had he been? Right behind her? A long way away? "Don't be ridiculous!" she told herself. "You never saw him." Yes, but why then could she not banish the shadow of him from her consciousness?

Frank and Claudia were the first to arrive. Imogen smiled; Claudia's voice was unmistakable – she still sounded like the netball captain. There was a murmur of voices, and then silence; the Baroness had led them out on to the terrace. The bell rang twice more: for Ray, whose extravagant twang vibrated through the house like a guitar string under a plectrum; and then for Papoche and Cassandra.

Imogen would ordinarily have gone upstairs to present the first course, and to say hello to everybody, but silver-haired and gold-buttoned Georges was very old school. Placing the éclairs on an enormous silver tray, he put Imogen in her place: *"Madame* likes the kitchen people to stay in the kitchen," and out he swept, grander than grand.

Imogen shrugged it off – let him run the lunch his way. She chopped the ingredients for the *persillade* – to sprinkle over the *daube* – and set the water to boil for the *macaronade*.

Georges glided in again, to return the empty plates, saying nothing about either the guests or the food – everything had been eaten, Imogen noticed, surprised – and to take back the *consommé*.

So far so good. She was not going to think about anything at all other than the job in hand – not about truffles, men, heartache, weight loss … "Take the *daube* out, and let it rest. Drop the pasta into the boiling water …"

Imogen was trying her hardest to concentrate on what she was doing, but today, unlike any other kitchen day, there was something missing – something about cooking had changed. She had often been alone in a kitchen, and the almost scholarly pleasure she took in getting a dish exactly right had always been the reason why she loved what she did, but today it was a chore. What had happened? What had changed? An inkling of what it was flitted into her mind, and she just as quickly tried to cauterise it by concentrating more than was necessary on making this lunch for the Baroness, if not a triumph, then at least a *succès d'estime*.

It was no use: truth is no respecter of the mind's contortions, and the truth was that, try as she might, she was doubting her vocation. Until today, cooking had never seemed like a lonely profession; it was lonely, yes, like all art, but the resulting pleasure of public delight had always been equal to the investment of solitary effort; and that equation had always validated whatever sacrifices she had made. Like every artist – singer, poet, concert pianist, couturier, chef … she had learned to accept loneliness as the price of creativity. Mmm ... was that entirely true? Or was it more truthful to say that cooking had been a substitute for happiness? Before Nick, hadn't she always told herself that what she most wanted was to cook for a man with love, not at a price for anyone and everybody? Yes, but had she actually cooked for him with a mistress's love or, more like a housewife, to satisfy his appetite? And still peering over her shoulder was the shadow of Andrei, the way he had seemed to be moving towards replacing Nick, the way he had cooked for her – the reversal of roles – the shadow becoming human. All this chilled her confidence; truth to tell, she no longer trusted cooking to tell her the truth.

Kitchened, she was too much the professional not to care, to give each dish less than her best, but why did it seem so strained of the stock of enjoyment? She drained the pasta, heaped it into a fine silver tureen that Georges had ostentatiously put in front of her, and poured over a little of the gravy from the *daube*. She looked at the tureen with disappointment; silver really wasn't right for a terrace lunch; hadn't the Baroness wanted this to be a casual occasion? What was the emotion that the Baroness was trying to elicit from her cooking? Versailles or Petit Trianon? Next to the earthenware dish in which she had cooked the *daube*, silver was much too grand. No, it was all wrong! *Merde*! Why hadn't she thought about this before? *Gesamtkunstwerk*, that was her credo: the food to match whatever emotion was wanted at the table. She had thought that this lunch was about the chocolate deal – the Baroness had specifically asked for something chocolate – but she had been mistaken; that was not what this lunch was about; their conversation earlier had revealed a much more personal intent.

Fuck Georges! Regaining her sense of solidarity with the Baroness, Imogen knew that there was no way she could go along with the gleaming aristocratic stiffness. She would have to find a serving dish to go with the rustic earthenware – something Provençale. She threw open all of the cupboards in the kitchen, leaving all of the doors frenziedly swinging back and forth. Nothing. Then she noticed the fruit bowl on the armoire; perfect – Matisse blue and yellow. She emptied it of fruit, washed it, and piled the pasta into it, just as Georges returned. He glared at her. She faced him down. *"Il faut manger pour vivre, et non pas vivre pour manger."* Something in her tone must have caused Georges to bite his tongue, for he pursed his lips, and then placed both the *daube* and the pasta on his palace tray, and exited.

There was nothing else to do except wait for them to eat the *daube*. She had made the *bombe* at home, and brought it with her in a freezer box. All she had to do was pour over the rum, and set it alight before serving. To appease Georges, she did the washing up – there was no dishwasher – which didn't take very long. Now what? Why was she so impatient to go upstairs? Because she wanted their plaudits? The food was praiseworthy but hardly spectacular. Because she wanted to see Frank and Claudia? She had seen them recently. What then? Why this impatience? Because, exactly as Sister Ursula would have urged, she needed to face up to her transgressions – Cassandra; she was suffering from guilt.

She had been feeling it ever since the failed truffle weekend, which, as she understood, was a little late. She hadn't felt a twinge of it while she had been cavorting with Nick in various beds across the Riviera, so why now? Because for as long as she thought Cassandra didn't know, it didn't keep her awake at night. Cassandra might have suspected but that was different; and she would never suspect that it could possibly have ever been, never in a million years, absolutely not be Imogen

O'Rorke. And why now? She was an ex-mistress. They had got away with it. Right. Well, Sister Ursula, it wasn't that simple: you don't need to be caught to feel guilty about the crime; you can find yourself guilty.

It didn't help that she looked so good on guilt; she was starting to enjoy not being fat. She had bought some new clothes only yesterday; the little black dress she was wearing today looked pretty damned good, even under an apron. Dior in a kitchen – that was a new look. No longer was she going to let Cassandra or Ray praise her food and damn her dress sense.

And what does a wronged wife look like? Spectacular; if she had any sense, Cassie would be doing all she could to remind her husband of what he had been avoiding, and almost lost. That was all there was to it: as long as Cassandra didn't actually know, there was no harm done.

Food for Thought

IMOGEN DECIDED THAT she would make her presence known. She was sure that the Baroness would not mind; and she wanted to see how the food was doing.

Even before she stepped out into the sunshine, she immediately sensed that the lunch was not going as planned: Ray could be heard exclaiming, "Oh my" at something, with such a weight of disapproval – real Queen Mary of Texas.

The terrace scene was a terrible sight, for anybody, that is, who had known Cassandra as she had been in Saint-Tropez – so thin that she cast no shadow. Now, she was a presence that all but blotted out the composition. She was standing, leaning over the table and liberally helping herself to more of the *daube* and the pasta. "Waste not, want not," she announced, piling up her plate. Nobody else was eating.

Swallowing their éclairs and sipping their *consommé*, the luncheon guests had had several courses during which time they had managed to swallow and stifle their reactions to this new Cassandra – think how people react when a waiter drops a loaded tray in a restaurant. Imogen, however, had barely a few strides to digest the blow-out. The shock was such that those few short steps were enough to make her instantly decide that she no longer wanted to ask about the food. Yet all the other social niceties that she might have employed seemed equally incapable of deflecting the fact – so in-your-face and stomach churning – of Cassandra's transformation from a coat hanger to a packed wardrobe.

Transfixed, Imogen stopped just short of the table, out of air-kissing range; and whatever she might have found to say didn't need to be said ...

Cassandra held her plate up, like a priestess bearing an offering. "The food is divine! You have to give me the recipe!"

Stepping forward to face Nick's wife, Imogen's first thought was, "Look at her! What a sight! What is she wearing! She looks like a brown paper parcel wrapped up with string!" Here was the opportunity she had been waiting for, to get her own back on the woman who had once wounded her so deeply; she hadn't forgotten that remark about not having that Brunello Cucinelli outfit in her size – "an elephant never forgets," as Claudia would have said. She was no longer an elephant ... Now, it was Imogen in her Dior – she'd taken off the apron – who could stick the knife in. She searched for the perfect putdown – "You look as if you're eating for two," "Would you like a doggy bag" – and she couldn't say it.

Right on cue, Sister Ursula appeared, to put a restraining hand on her shoulder. "Would you hold on now, Miss Imogen O'Rorke. Aren't you forgetting something? You've been fucking this woman's husband. Have you not thought that you might be responsible for all this?"

"It's nothing to do with me!" she heard herself say, out loud, banishing Sister Ursula, and trying to focus on anything except Cassandra. My God! What had she so nearly confessed! She saved herself with, "It's all to do with Escoffier!"

"Him again? Well, you and he go back a long way, don't you Mo?" said Frank, grinning with devilment.

"Frank!" exclaimed Claudia, meaning to urge caution, but

there was no need. Neither Frank nor anybody seated around the table had any intention of making food the subject of conversation.

Except Cassandra who knew nothing about Escoffier. "But I thought you were doing the cooking?"

Imogen recovered herself. "I am. Escoffier gave me the recipes."

"That was real nice of him," said Ray. "Cooks don't usually like to give up their secrets. Nice dress."

Air-kissing her way around the table, Imogen noticed that the Baroness and Papoche were both silent. If she had been asked to describe them, she would have said that they looked traumatised, like people sitting in a theatre, when the roof collapses on them, and the play goes on.

She watched them watching Cassandra tucking into her seconds. It was painful to watch: Cassandra putting away a plateful; the Baroness running her pearls through her fingers, over and over; Papoche winding and winding his wedding ring around his finger.

Imogen was aware of Frank keeping the conversation going. He was talking with the Baroness.

"Interesting that you've had the shares since the day the company went public."

"Have I?"

"You didn't know?"

"The Baron made all our financial decisions."

"He bought quite a stake. He could have sold many times, and done very well, really well, but he kept them. I guess he must have had his reasons."

"Perhaps he just liked chocolate," said Ray. This was not what he was thinking, rather he was aware of an uncomfortable undercurrent.

"Do you know if he knew anything about the company?"

Frank was pushing, which was not like Frank, thought Imogen. Why? Because he needed this deal so badly or it was a Frank-like stratagem?

The Baroness let her pearls slip out of her fingers; they fell back in a tumult against her blouse, making the soft clicking sound of an abacus, and leaving her right hand raised in the air, holding on to nothing. "I really don't know. He never told me, and I never asked him. It was something we never talked about."

Frank seemed to be going for broke, driving the conversation off the road. He turned to Papoche. "Did you know that the Baron had such a big stake in your success?"

"*Securo*. He told me."

Imogen noticed how the Baroness immediately clutched her pearls again as if taking comfort from a rosary.

"I guess he must have just had a sweet tooth," remarked Ray, laconically. "It's nice to own things you can eat."

The lunch was a disaster. What with Cassandra pigging herself, and the Baroness looking as if she would shatter into little pieces of Sèvres, Imogen couldn't bear it. She made her excuses, "I'd better get back to the kitchen … the pudding."

The Baroness called after her. "You will join us, won't you?"

Re-kitchened, Imogen didn't need Sister Ursula to flagellate her; she could do that to herself. Questions and answers ping-ponged back and forth in turbulent thoughts. "Why did Frank have to be so cruel? He is cruel. Why didn't Claudia stop him? Because they need this deal. And Cassandra, how could she have let herself go like that? Oh, you're a fine one to talk aren't you, Imogen O'Rorke, the original fatty!" The inner voices screamed at her. "I'll tell you why! Because she loved her husband, and you took him away from her! But he went back! *Évidemment trop tard*."

Georges returned with the remains of the *daube* and the pasta.

He was unmoved by whatever he had seen. That was enough for Imogen. She had to go back up; it was cowardice to sit in the kitchen. She poured rum over the *bombe* and set it alight. "*Allons-y!*" she barked at him; and followed him back up to the terrace.

Bombe Néro

THE *BOMBE NÉRO* had an explosive effect, if not quite as Imogen had intended. She was standing behind Georges when he placed the flaming dessert in the middle of the table. She scanned the faces of the guests, hoping that she might be able to rescue the lunch with a pyrotechnic display. Indeed, there were some gushing "oohs!" and "aahs!" from Ray and Claudia; excited staccato clapping from Cassandra; a dignified, *"Très bien fait"* from Frank; and from the Baroness and Papoche – shell shock.

All that Papoche could muster was an almost inaudible, *"Che meraviglia! Della ottima famiglia!"* which struck Imogen as a very strange way to describe a pudding.

Georges cut open the *bombe*, and chocolate oozed out on to the white serving dish. Imogen saw the Baroness close her eyes, as if she were a *suttee* widow anticipating the funeral pyre. A look passed between her and Papoche that should have alerted Imogen to the danger, but she had spoken before she had time to consider what she was saying. "You asked for something chocolatey, and here it is!"

Georges served the chocolate dessert in thin slices, and withdrew, leaving Imogen as a spectator. A chair had been brought for her, and she sat down, between Ray and Claudia, opposite Cassandra. She watched closely as Cassandra – wife of the man she had been screwing – put away three helpings; heaped together spoonfuls and slathers of ice cream, sponge and chocolate. She noticed the chipped nail varnish, the slapdash make-up. She recognised the fat woman's determination not to acknowledge the fact of her fatness. But this was different: this wasn't shame; there was fat and there was fat. Fat Imogen had cared about being fat, and done everything she could to compensate; she might have laughed off being fat, but she had always suffered from the stigma of fatness. Fat Cassandra didn't care what people thought, and that was what was most upsetting to Imogen. In looking at Cassandra, her ex-lover's wife, no matter what size she was, she would have felt unnerved; in looking at a Cassandra who had gorged herself on Imogen's food, Imogen's adulterous guilt was writ large; horribly visible, it was sitting right in front of her.

She was looking at Cassandra, and her mind was again all a jumble. "I did this. This is all my fault." What could she say to this wreck of a woman? Ask her what had happened? "As if you don't know! You're the cause of it!" Thank God, Cassandra didn't know they had once been love rivals. "What does it matter that she doesn't know! Look at her! This is what happens when you break a woman's spirit." She couldn't not say anything, could she? Oh yes, she could come clean. "Cassandra, I'm sorry, more than I can say. I confess, I fucked your husband. And now look at us: I lost weight because of it, and you've become a porker, but it's over, it meant nothing, and I didn't love him. He's a self-centred bastard, and you're welcome to him." Would that make Cassandra feel better?

Imogen had never been thin and beautiful, whereas all her life Cassandra had been used to people admiring her; and now they were wanting to say anything except tell her how wonderful she was looking. Of course the woman was in despair, or was she? Why was she so calm? Where was the venom she had once used to spit, to deadly effect? There was so much about this fat woman that Imogen couldn't comprehend. Why would she show herself in public like this? Imogen remembered again what her grandmother Marie-Hélène had said to her as a fat child, *"Tu sais, Imogène, ma petite*, being fat is being rude. You're offending other people's vision."

Imogen was conscious of a disturbing something else: that she was looking at her previous self – she had once been Cassandra. She had once been fat, Cassandra had once been thin; and now the tables were turning. Give it time, and they would each be where the other had once been.

Imogen took no part in the conversation. She looked, and didn't like what she saw. Frank she understood: he was talking about nothing in particular with Papoche, and yet all the while he was trying to find out what support the old man thought he might have from his shareholders. Claudia was pumping Ray for information about what he was going to do with his chocolate shares, with all the subtlety of a frontloader.

"But if you bought them so long ago, you'll clean up."

"But who can say no to an old-fashioned box of chocolates!"

Imogen was sick of the sight and sound of chocolate. Not so Cassandra ...

"Do you know anything about chocolate?" she asked the Baroness.

"I like it, yes." This seemed unlikely, thought Imogen, seeing how the Baroness had not touched the pudding.

"It seems strange that your husband would have held on to the shares so jealously. Did he like chocolate?"

"I'm not sure that he did."

"What about you? Do you like Belgian chocolate?"

"We came to know it quite well. We were in Brussels for three years."

"How funny. My father and I used to go there a lot. He called it an education. When was that? Do you remember, Papa?"

Papoche seemed not to like the pudding, which he had barely tasted. "I remember."

"Beatrice always came with us. My father didn't like to leave me on my own for so long, which was really kind of him. So many boxes of chocolates we took back with us."

"Your father is a generous man."

"Is he? Everybody knows that when you eat so many chocolates you get sick of them. I'm sure that I could eat all of this dessert, and I would never ever want to eat chocolate ever again." Cassandra gave a laugh that Imogen found quite curdling. "And chocolate is so fattening! The man who invents a chocolate that doesn't make you feel guilty is going to be a very rich man!"

"And very popular with women!" joked Claudia.

"Just like my husband." Imogen had no way of knowing if that remark was made in support of, or against Nick; in support of his chocolate skills, or against his philandering. Everything that Cassandra said was uttered with such careless abandon that it could be interpreted however one wished. But there was certainly menace in the air.

The more Cassandra talked in this way with the Baroness – it seemed to Imogen more like a cross examination – the more Imogen was asking herself, "Why? What's the Baroness ever done to her?" She wanted to cry out, "Don't blame her! I'm the guilty one!"

Georges served coffee and *petits fours*; not made by Imogen, she noticed, which enraged her. What was the point of asking her to create a lunch, and then buy cakes in a *patisserie*? How long could this nightmare go on? It was one of those lunches that you just wanted to be over.

Papoche put an end to it. Abruptly, he stood up, smoothly said his goodbyes to Claudia, Frank, and Ray, complimented Imogen on the food, and abandoned the table.

Cassandra had also stood up (the chair seemed to visibly relax as she did so); and she too made the goodbye round of the table – air-kissing Claudia, Frank, Ray. To Imogen she was especially gushing. "I'm going to ask you for all the recipes!" Then she had a sudden thought. "I've just had a wonderful idea – why don't you teach me how to cook? Look at me. You can see I'm that tired of Italian food."

"I don't normally give lessons." Imogen should have been less tactful – Cassandra sensed a weakness; an Irish unwillingness to say no outright.

"But it'll be such fun! *Dai!* We'll have a ball!"

"What sort of food did you have in mind?"

"Do you know how to make comfort food?"

"I grew up with it. I found it very comforting."

"Nick says that's what he misses most."

"Right."

Ray was an expert on the subject of men. "That's the problem with men I find ... they always expect to be comforted."

This caused smiles all round – even Papoche managed the trace of one – but it was not enough to deflect Cassandra from her objective. She might have gained a lot of weight but she had not lost her sense of entitlement – getting her own way. "I'll come to you. You live in Antibes, don't you? And I'll pay, of course."

"I ... I really wasn't thinking about the money."

"*Che figata!* So it's decided then. I'll call you."

What could Imogen possibly say other than to meekly acquiesce? "I'll be looking forward to it."

What happened next was something at once so direct and yet so nuanced that Imogen, and perhaps all of the guests, could not quite gauge the meaning. Cassandra barely pecked the cheeks of the Baroness. "Thank you so much. Everything was perfect, as I knew it would be. And I so wanted to get to know you better."

The Baroness somehow maintained her composure: *"Vous êtes trop gentille."*

Cassandra, however, was not quite finished with the Baroness. "And I've worked it all out. I think I know why your husband didn't sell his shares." There was a distinct silence. The Baroness was evidently incapable of responding. Cassandra gaily continued: "Chocolate has such a strong reaction with people. You either love it or you hate it."

That left the goodbye between Papoche and his hostess. As the Baroness allowed her cheeks to be barely grazed by his lips, he murmured something so softly in Italian that nobody could distinctly make out what he was saying, save for, *"Grazie."*

It occurred to Imogen that the two of them had hardly exchanged two words over lunch. But who, then, had been the guest of honour? For whom had the Baroness wanted "something substantial," if not for him? Not for Frank or Ray. To feed Cassandra? No, that was too horrible.

Papoche seemed to think that the lunch had been for him; speaking more loudly, he switched to English. "Truffles, casserole, and chocolate, you must have known they were my favourites."

The Baroness demurred. "A lucky guess, on Imogen's part."

And with that lie, because people talking about food helped her to understand them, Imogen at last understood what the lunch had been all about.

"Nothing tastes as good as skinny feels."

Kate Moss

Villa Eilenroc

"Nothing tastes as good as skinny feels"

"How was the hunting?"
"I got caught."
"Well, I told you so."
"You're always telling me, but I've stopped listening. If I wanted real sympathy I could have gone to confession."

More silence. Imogen was waiting for Claudia to explain the real purpose of this unexpected visit. She had called this morning out of the blue, said she'd be in Cap d'Antibes in a couple of hours; didn't say why; said she'd be driving up from Saint Trop, which was unheard of. She had said something else very odd: "Let's have comfort food for lunch." So Imogen made shepherds pie, and plum crumble, with custard. Claudia had eaten enough for two, and finished off what was left on Imogen's plate. Imogen was going to mention Cassandra, but left that subject alone.

They had been sitting on the terrace for at least an hour, drinking fresh lemonade, and trying to move as little as possible. It was baking hot; even in the shade, sheltered beneath a large peppermint green umbrella that had once been a deep eucalyptus colour, a potter could have fired his clays without a kiln, it was that hot. Through the exhausted pine trees and parched shrubs, below them, on the sandy curvature of Plage de la Garoupe, where no sand could be seen, the herd of August holidaymakers acted out a ritual that had been invented less than a century before, on that very beach.

On the terrace, there was no wind; the world was becalmed. Only the bees had the energy and need to be busy, raiding the roses, strafing the lavender, landing like helicopters on the slender, elongated stalks, and setting them nodding at each other in a frenzy, momentarily enlivening the still life.

So far, the two women had talked about nothing, with Claudia skirting around whatever it was she wanted to talk about.

"You've had the jetty repaired."

"Lots of people have boats. You're always saying it's much easier to come by boat from Saint Trop."

"Frank keeps saying that it's such a very expensive way to travel." Claudia didn't elaborate, and Imogen knew that this was something serious. Claudia changed the subject. "The garden looks different."

"I bought some roses."

"You've never taken any interest in the garden before."

"There are lots of things I'm interested in that I wasn't before."

"Marie-Hélène would be pleased. She couldn't get you to even carry a watering can. Still, I bet you don't know what you bought. What's that white one over there called?"

"*Madame Alfred Carrière.*"

Claudia folded her arms – harbinger of a 'serious' talk.

"Mo, what is this about not wanting to cook any more?"

"You came all the way here just to ask me that?"

Claudia seemed to hesitate. "Can I say something?"

"Why are you asking me? You're going to say it anyway. And I know that tone, it's going to hurt. I've been hearing it since I started menstruating."

Claudia suddenly giggled. "You remember how you thought you were dying? Said you wanted me to have your tennis racket?"

"I remember you told everybody. Say it!"

"This losing weight thing, and not wanting to cook anymore,

and the gardening, and all the other different things ... *tu sais*, it all seems a bit obsessive to me. Every time I see you, you look different. You know what? I just don't recognise you."

"Good."

"Is it, Mo? I mean, you look great on the outside, only I don't recognise the Mo I used to know, on the inside."

"*Foutre dieu*! Clod, you've spent years criticising how I looked, there wasn't anything you didn't want me to change: 'Lose some weight, Mo, try this lipstick, Mo, fuck some more men, Mo, let's go to Chanel, Mo.' Year after year after year. Well, I finally took your advice, and now you're saying you don't like the result? You know what? This is all your fault!"

"No, it isn't. You know what I think?"

"No, but of course you're going to tell me."

"You never took my advice. You never really listened."

Imogen furiously rounded on her best friend. "That's why all those diets failed, is it? Because I didn't listen?"

"No, because you didn't want to."

"Didn't want to do what? Lose weight? I was obsessed about losing weight! So don't tell me I didn't listen! I did listen! I tied myself up in knots listening."

"Not really you didn't. You were actually happy as you were, you just didn't know it."

Imogen pushed back as cruelly as she could. "*T'es vraiment trop con*, Clod. For somebody as thick as you are, you can be much too deep."

By now, Claudia was also close to shouting. "*Ta geule*! Okay, so tell me this, then: what diet are you on? Eh! Why is this diet so much better than all the others?"

"I'm not on a diet. But I am losing weight."

"Why? Go on, tell me that then?"

"How do I know! If I knew that, I could bottle it and sell it."

"Where are you, Mo? What the fuck has happened to you? You got what you wanted, a grand passion, and it didn't work out. So? It happens to everybody, even to me." Claudia couldn't sustain her anger. "You see?"

"See what? What am I not seeing?"

"Why you're doing what you're doing. I've been reading about it."

"Where? *Vogue* or *Tatler*?"

"Don't make fun of me when I'm being serious. I'm your best friend. I'm only trying to help."

"Somehow, I know I'm going to regret hearing this. Go on, out with it! Like a good Catholic, I accept my fate."

"It was seeing Cassandra …"

"Could we not go there."

"What you've both been going through is all about a level of body privilege."

"The what?"

"It's a fight that women have. Thin privilege versus fat stigma."

"Can we take this line by line, Clod, so I don't get lost? And I'm an expert on this remember. I get the thing about fat stigma, that's easy. It's where you think you're the only fat woman in a room full of thin people, and you can't stop thinking about it, because you've got this hang-up about being fat, and you think they're all looking at you, thinking how fat you are."

"Exactly."

"But that doesn't mean you're not fat."

"You have to stop thinking about being fat."

"Do you ever stop thinking about being thin?"

"That's different."

"Why did I know you were going to say that? Aah! Now I get it, that's what they mean by thin privilege."

"That's just thin people looking at you thinking how privileged they are to be thin."

"They are."

"You have to think differently. What they say is, you musn't put tickets on yourself."

"For sale? Parking tickets? 'Park your fat ass here!'"

"You have to learn to love and accept those horrible wobbly bits."

"I can't imagine what you mean? Thutts? Cankles? Side boobs, by any chance?"

"That sounds like them, yes. The thing is, you're still a fat woman in a thin woman's body."

"I should start feeling some thin privilege, is that it?"

"No! You have to get way from thin shaming."

"Oh, don't worry, I will. I'm not going to feel ashamed of being thin, not one bit. There's got to be some good come out of all this purgatory." There was a pause, as Imogen digested what had been said. "And that's why you came all the way here, is it? To analyse me?"

"Partly. There's more. Actually, there is something else, besides that, but I really don't want to ask."

"*Mouais*! Because you're very good at telling people what to do, just not so good at asking. Go ahead! Go on, ask me, I mean, you're not going to upset me any more than you have done already."

Claudia's voice was calm. "I'm not trying to upset you."

They had argued themselves into a stalemate. There was a hurt and hesitation in Claudia's voice that Imogen found far more upsetting than any words. She gave some ground. "All right, clever clogs, tell me, why am I losing weight?"

"Because you don't know who you are anymore."

"Oh, please, be serious."

"I am being serious."

"You don't know the meaning of the word! The only two things you care about are cocks and money."

"That hurt."

"You don't hurt."

"Don't I, Mo? You think it doesn't hurt when you say I'm thick."

"You are thick."

"I'm not. I just act thick. It saves a lot of hurt."

At this, Imogen was instantly no longer angry. She got up out of her chair and went round the table to embrace Claudia, leaning her head on to Claudia's shoulder. "Oh, Clod, I'm so sorry. I didn't mean to hurt you."

Claudia was also in a forgiving mood. She squeezed Imogen's hand. "It's all right. That's what friends are for." She sighed, expelling all of her anger. "Forget everything I said. *Eh bien*, what are we going to do with this new you?"

"Clod, don't you have other things to think about? Like surviving?"

"Yes, but not right at this moment, maybe later. Right now, I think I need to do something frivolous, it helps me to think seriously."

"*Che c'è?* Is it that bad?"

"Mo, I just don't know. *Ça craint*. I'm afraid to ask. All Frank says is, if the chocolate deal comes off, we'll be okay. And that's why we need your help. Frank was hoping you might talk with Andrei? Find out what he knows."

"He was following me! Like a spy. I haven't spoken with him since that hunting trip, and I don't want to either. And why doesn't Frank just talk with Andrei himself?"

"That's the thing, he has, and Andrei said that he didn't know any more than Frank, which, of course, can't be true.

Apparently, he said something else very strange."

"Strange in what way?"

"About closing his business."

"Why would he want to do that? God knows, I don't like what he does, but he's very good at it, I'll give him that."

"Mo, he must know something. Frank doesn't know which way to move, and our lives depend on it."

"Talk about making me feel responsible for your fortune."

"So you'll talk with him then."

"I'm wasting my breath saying no." Claudia mouthed a sloppy kiss at her best friend."And what are you going to do?"

"There's really nothing I can do, except carry on as if nothing has changed, and act as if we still have all the money we used to."

"You're not exactly going to be out on the street."

"Now you're trying to make me feel better? *Très gentille.* Money isn't what it's about. Well, it is but not really; it's my world, and I want to stay in it. You just get used to things, that's all. That's what we cling to. Didn't you get used to the old fat you?"

"*Bien dans sa peau*? I wish."

"*C'est dans la tête.*"

"How easy that is for you to say. I didn't want her hanging around me anymore. My best friend said the old me had to go, said it didn't suit me or her, so now I'm trying very hard to get used to the new me, which I think I quite like, but apparently she doesn't." Imogen paused for breath. "*Basta*! Could we stop this? I really don't want to look backwards, that's like standing still, trapped in aspic. Anyway, what's this big idea of yours?"

"Where are Marie-Hélène's old things?"

"Same place they've always been. I haven't touched them since she died in there. Why?"

"I thought we'd play a grown-up version of dressing up, like we used to."

"With you the centre of attention, and me with the hats and gloves, you mean? No thanks. Besides, I'm not sure I want to look through all those old things any more."

"Why not? It used to be you couldn't get enough of them. Ever since I can remember you've been going on about them."

"It was different when she was alive. Now it's like waking the dead."

"No, it's like learning how to live with them."

Taking charge, as she had always done, Claudia abruptly stood up, and marched off in the direction of Marie-Hélène's old room. Doubtfully, Imogen followed.

Le Numéro Cinq

"READY?" asked Claudia, already holding the door handle. Imogen shrugged, which was signal enough for Claudia. She opened the door, and stepped inside, immediately releasing a preserved smell of faded lavender, mothballs, and stale perfume. The old-style wooden shutters and French windows giving on to the balcony terrace were closed, the room dark and sepulchral, but the sun insistently pushed its way through the slats, creating those pinpoint shafts of light, which remind some people of an Annunciation.

Claudia unceremoniously unlocked the French windows, and pulled them open, inwards; she unbolted the shutters, and pushed them outwards, revealing a view that is familiar to anybody who owns a first edition of *Tender is the Night*, with that Scribner's dust jacket (illustrated by a graphic designer lost to history) announcing a vision of prelapsarian Provence, stylised in block reds, yellows, blues and greens, which herald a bright outlook, and so beautifully cover up the disintegration roiling inside.

With a satisfied air, Claudia said, "There, that's better."

Imogen blinked as the sunlight elbowed its way into the room, finding its way on to every surface, reaching under every piece of furniture, setting alight every object that Marie-Hélène had ever handled. She sat down lightly on the unsteady Regency chair, looking at herself in the rococo dressing-table mirror – two aged pieces of furniture (Catholic exiles sent over from the bankrupt O'Rorke ancestral home in Ireland) as defiantly flamboyant as their late owner: the chair, painted in faux-bamboo, white on blue *chinoiserie*; the dressing-table, painted ivory, a riotous, controlled elegance of flaking curlicues and gilt voluptuousness. Behind her, Claudia was determinedly pulling out steamer trunks, suitcases, shoeboxes and hatboxes.

Like a house museum, nothing had been moved for decades; and quite unlike a house where people lived, there was no dust anywhere – Imogen's cleaner had instructions to keep the room spotless. The silver-backed brushes were in the same place they had been when Marie-Hélène had picked them up to brush her hair, tresses that had lost their lustre, fading to a brittle iron grey.

There was the silver-framed photograph of Marie-Hélène's husband, the grandfather Imogen had never met, at the wheel of a Lorraine-Dietrich, losing at Le Mans; he seemed as distant in time as the eighteenth-century O'Rorkes hanging in the drawing-room. Next to it, the memory of all memories: a sepia photograph in another silver frame, of an early morning beach party, with Marie-Hélène in a long black evening dress and wide-brimmed straw hat, sitting between Sara Murphy, wrapped in a blanket, and Picasso – bull cock prominently displayed, filling out his trunks; a lithe Cole Porter prancing in knitted swimming trunks, twirling Sara's pearls around his neck; and standing behind them, Scott and Gerald, the former looking much the worse for wear, in white tie and tails, and the latter morose, but gaily dressed in a striped sailor's top, crisp white shorts, and sporting a turban. Imogen could describe every detail of the party they had been to the night before at Villa Eilenroc, so many times had she heard about it, sitting in this very room.

For Imogen, her late grandmother's room was both a

confessional – Marie-Hélène had had a love of confessing to her past sins – and schoolroom where, as a fat girl, she had come to be instructed in the ways of the (thin) world. The room was alive with her grandmother's spirit, crowded with the memories and ghosts of all the people she had known; the spiteful and amusing things they had said; the parties she had gone to; the cold sherry and little biscuits called *sablés* they had eaten on the beach at noon.

Most affecting of all were the perfumes arranged in a regimented row on the dressing-table: *Chanel No.5*, *Le Numéro Cinq*, *Arpège*, *Joy* and *Shocking*; the five fragrant coordinates marking the beginning, middle and end of Marie-Hélène's blaze of glory. These were the originals, not the later, adulterated updates. Marie-Hélène had bought them by the case, in the same extravagant way that she had ordered 1928 Krug, and made them last to the very last flacons, as if she had timed her death to meet the moment when her perfumed world would come to an end.

One by one, Imogen took the stoppers off the bottles and breathed in the contents, watching in the mirror as Claudia began to open the lids of every trunk, suitcase and hatbox. She opened shoebox after shoebox, lifting out piles of fragile, brittle, yellowing papers. "Look at it all! Theatre programmes, train tickets, restaurant bills ..."

"Don't look so surprised. You've seen it all before. You know she didn't throw anything away. Up to 1939, that is; after that, she never kept anything."

"Look at all these magazines! *La Gazette du Bon Ton*." Claudia thumbed and flicked through the pages. "Designers you've never heard of – Étienne Drian ... Gustav Beer ... look at that! Kriegck ... Larsen ... Martial & Armand. Where are Dolce and Gabbana?"

"People get forgotten, they stop being famous."

"How could people forget Tom Ford?"

"The clothes? Easily. Perhaps not the perfumes. And my hairdresser says his film is fabulous."

Claudia was trying on gloves: white satin opera gloves; Brussels lace wrist gloves; deerskin gauntlet gloves (for that knight in shining armour); cocktail party gloves sewn by hand with Sea Island cotton; and handmade soft ivory chamois. Imogen could hear Marie-Hélène lecturing her on glove etiquette: *"Faites attention.* Gloves have nothing to do with cold hands. Gloves are for sitting in church and nightclubs, for shopping and dancing, and unpleasant outdoor activities like walking. Do not carry your gloves; either you wear them or you keep them in your handbag; and never put them in your pocket because they make a woman look fat. *Écoute, ma petite, il ya beaucoup de choses que l'on ne le fait pas quand on porte des gants*: one never, ever, eats, drinks, smokes, plays cards, or puts on lipstick in gloves; doing any of those things wearing gloves makes a woman look available. And if you are going to make love in gloves, they must be long white evening gloves; making love in day gloves is for women who have too much time on their hands, the ones who always choose the wrong man." Imogen could remember the lecture, word for word, and for what? Nowadays nobody wears gloves! Her grandmother had been preparing her for a life that was dying even as she tried to keep it alive.

"Have you ever seen so many handbags!" Claudia was in seventh heaven: there were stiff handbags for afternoon visits, cut out of animals that could no longer bite; hand-tooled leathers, stamped and stitched by Florentine craftsmen; beaded bags for Black Bottom jazz dances, sewn by seamstresses too tired to even tap their feet; and clutch bags held tight on cool summer evenings, forged of molten aluminium, steel mesh, and chrome, by furnacemen who never dreamed of the fancies their labours would produce.

Imogen wasn't paying attention to what Claudia was doing; she was trying to concentrate on remembering the momentous occasions these perfumes had evoked in her grandmother's memory when she had lifted off the stoppers, and held up to Imogen's nose the commingled and intoxicating scents – all the perfumes of Arabia concocted into an iris oriental, a floral fruit chypre, a floral-aldehydic, that had instantly ignited in Marie-Hélène a gorgeous reverie of fanciful reminiscences.

Imogen had always listened with respectful girlish rapture. But in truth she had learned nothing, thinking then that Marie-Hélène's life was as meaningful to her as a fairy story. Why was it so important now ? Because, before, fat as she had been, she had only listened at a distance, knowing then, deep down, subcutaneously, that the imperfectly remembered experiences were not yet meant for her. This afternoon, however, thinner as she was, she knew at last that she had come far enough as a woman to unlock the key to Marie-Hélène's vanished world, to walk around in it, and perhaps, finally, even though it was too late to say thank you for the life lessons, to understand what it was that her grandmother had been trying to tell her all along, that how you lived your life had to be about something more than how you wore your gloves, it was about who you held on to – who was holding on to you – when you were wearing them.

Claudia broke into her thoughts. "Have you finished day dreaming? I've been asking what you think of these?" Imogen turned round from the dressing-table. She recognised the shoes that Claudia had tried on – silver lamé with Louis heels.

"Her favourites. She danced the nights away in them."

Claudia sniffed the air. "Now that smells like something your grandmother would have worn."

"She did."

Claudia came to the dressing-table, attracted by the smell. "Why would anybody call a perfume *Le Numéro Cinq*? Remind me, who was Edward Molyneux when he was at home?"

"Molynooks, not Molyneux; remember, he was English not French. He made clothes for Marie-Hélène. They're here somewhere. Don't you remember what she said? They were friends."

"She was friends with everybody."

"True. Don't you remember her saying he was a hero or something? He had a shop in Cannes, lived in Monte Carlo.

"I remember ... and had two nightclubs."

"I always thought that sounded strange for a man who made dresses."

"That explains the friendship then. I mean, did she ever spend a night in?"

"The watercolour up there's by him. It's Marie-Hélène."

"A very young Marie-Hélène. Nice frock. *Très raffiné.*"

"He was talented."

"Not enough for anybody to remember him, though. But the pong's not bad. It grows on you. You could still wear it today. Pity about the name."

"I remember the story: according to Marie-Hélène, he had a bet with Chanel. They would both call their perfumes 'number five', and see who won."

"Obviously, he lost."

"Yes, but you just have a thing about losers. It doesn't mean he wasn't any good. Look, he dressed Greta Garbo and Marlene Dietrich."

"Never heard of them."

"Oh, please! Go back to your shoes. Or wrap that fox around your neck."

"No way! It's still got its head and tail, and those feet are really just creepy! Like it's going to grab you by the throat."

"Try the hats on then." Imogen wafted the flacon of *Arpège* under Claudia's nose. "How do you like this?"

"*Arpège*? I wear it."

"Yes, I know. Is it the same?"

"Same as what?"

"As it is now. This is vintage *Arpège*. They've played around with it."

"No point in asking me, I can't tell the difference. But the clothes I like."

"Old Lanvin or new Lanvin?"

"Search me. What can you smell in it?"

"Experience."

"That isn't a smell."

"No, but unless you're an expert it doesn't really matter what's in it, does it? It's what it means to you. And it can only mean something if it's as complicated as you are."

"You get all that just wearing a perfume?"

"I do now. You have to have lived to like these perfumes."

"If you ask me, she just wore them to keep reminding herself."

"That's what I mean by experience. How about this? Original *Joy*."

"How about this? You'd never get a suntan in it, would you?"

Claudia was holding up a beach ensemble – a black crepe beach coat with white terry lining over a white scoop-necked top, with matching black shorts.

"Suits you. Who's it made by?"

"Says Jean Patou, Paris."

"So? Look at the name on the bottle! He also made the perfume."

"Well, that's how you get remembered. She sure bought into the lifestyle."

"No, she was the lifestyle. Would you wear it?"

Claudia took a deep breath of *Joy*. "For having sex at a cocktail party? Yes."

"About which you have lots of experience. And I bet you'd wear this in bed."

Claudia breathed in a long sniff of *Shocking*. "Ugh! Talk about raunchy! You could only wear it in bed. Smells like you're just about to give him a blowjob."

"Claudia Schulte! You are such a slut!"

"Only when I'm lying down. And stop being such a Mother Superior. Anyway, you're a one to talk. At least Massimo isn't married."

"No, but you are, and he soon will be, if Marcus could ever find the courage to ask him."

Claudia looked very surprised. "How do you know that?"

Imogen had said too much, but it was too late; it had been said. "Just kitchen talk."

"Don't give me that."

Hiding her hurt, Claudia took another sniff of *Shocking*. "Anyway, as far as the Pope's concerned, it isn't legal."

"That's all right, then. You have such progressive views when you need them."

Claudia moved on. "Look, do you want a dress or don't you? They're all in this trunk."

She began to unwrap the tissue paper that protected the cache of evening gowns; and tossed them carelessly on to the bed: a cornucopia of frocks and frippery – velvet, organza, silk moiré, metallic thread, rhinestones, mother-of-pearl, wool, feather, linen, and fur – reading out the labels as she did so. "Patou ... Lanvin ... Vionnet ... sorry, Chanel ... Schiaparelli, and ... here's the Molyneux! You remember her telling us the story of every dress?"

"Like a catechism. Every film star she danced with, every

writer who used her as a character, every man who fancied her."

"So which one is it going to be?"

"Man?"

"Dress! You have no taste in men."

Imogen had made her mind up a long time ago. "The Molyneux. It's the one she's wearing in the watercolour."

"Now that's what I call a gown. Try it on then! You've been waiting a lifetime."

"No. There has to be an occasion."

As always, Claudia had been only momentarily downcast. The frock conversation had done her a power of good. "*Eh bien*. So, when are you going to wear it? More important, who's it for?"

"I don't know. I haven't got that far."

"I've got it!"

"Got what?"

"Where you're going to wear it! What do you do when you stand to lose everything?"

"Pray to the Virgin Mary for deliverance. You're a Catholic, Clod, you know that."

"We'll throw a party! A Marie-Hélène party. A nineteen-nineteen to nineteen thirty-nine party!"

"Where? Not here, it's too small. In Saint-Tropez?"

"No, Villa Eilenroc, Marie-Hélène's old stamping ground. And for the first time ever, you won't be asking me what you're going to wear."

Cooked English

NICK COOKED HIMSELF a slap-up English breakfast – two fried eggs, four rashers of smoked bacon, two Cumberland sausages, grilled mushrooms and tomatoes, baked beans, three slices of white toast, smothered with salted farmhouse butter, and thick-cut Seville marmalade; and thought about how it was all working out rather well, considering. Nothing like a good breakfast for seeing things in perspective. Thank God he'd never had to think about his weight; it was bad enough Cassie piling on the pounds. Mind you, that wasn't turning out to be such a bad thing after all; it was amazing how much she looked like Imogen – Imogen before she slimmed down, that is. The break-up had been nothing like as bad as he had feared, at least she hadn't cried; and Cassie was finally coming round. So she should be, seeing how since he'd stopped fucking about with Imogen he'd been trying really fucking hard. He hadn't done anything that might upset her, just let have her way. If she said something horrible, which was less and less, he hadn't responded, just looked hurt. Well, it was working, as he knew it would; women are not difficult to bring round – like feeding oats to a horse. She'd finally stopped storming about. Amazing, but she'd even become a half-way decent cook – limited repertoire, admittedly, but he'd been really encouraging, told her that would come. Redecorating the house in Turin must have had a cathartic effect. Still, typical woman, she gave off conflicting signals; one moment she was nice as pie, the next she looked as if she'd been sucking on lemons. Okay, so she seemed a little distant, and hardly said a word to him, but that would wear off. Just give it time.

He hadn't so much as mentioned the deal, not even alluded to it. He'd done the numbers, and whichever way he looked at them, it still came down to Cassie and the 'Russians,' as Frank kept calling them. With Cassie on his side – if she was on his side, no, she had to be – that just left the Russians, and fuck knows what they were after, or who the fuck they were. Were they even all Russians? That was just what Frank had said. Frank said he didn't know – Frank only ever said as much as he wanted – and Nick didn't know whether to believe him or not. For somebody who professed "in all honesty" to know nothing, he seemed to know a hell of a lot. What, did they think he was that stupid? Like he didn't know that they were all in it together – Tikhon, Oleg, that wanker Mat, the old guy – what was his name – Peter, the Chinaman from South Africa, and that yes-man from the City, with the paid-off mortgage. I mean, please! Of course, they hunted in a pack, why else were they always together? Yeah, right, like it was fucking yacht envy. Whatever they were up to, that Andrei Volkov certainly knew. Nick hadn't forgotten that little talk they'd had in Cannes. No doubt, he'd come out of the woodwork soon enough. And? Nothing Nick could do. All he could do was play it cool; keep his head down, and hope for the best.

They were in San Remo for the summer. The children were at the beach most days with Beatrice, which meant the two of them pretty much had the house to themselves whenever Nick could get away from the office. The old man came for the weekends, which was not as bad as it might have been; they had an unspoken rule not to bring work home, so it was civil. It could have been worse.

Cassandra came into the kitchen, wearing his old school dressing-gown – it reminded him of Matron.

"Where's mine?"

"All you have to do is sit down and eat it."

"You made me breakfast?"

"Yeah, why not?"

"Where's yours?"

"I thought I'd work myself up an appetite in the garden first."

"Whatever makes you happy."

He was thinking that things must be better because not so long ago she would have said that was where he belonged.

He tidied up and watched as Cassandra ate his breakfast – anything for a quiet life. My God! She was eating the baked beans! She'd always said she couldn't stand baked beans; said they were common. But not much surprised him anymore about her eating habits. He had got used to her eating whatever was put in front of her – anything was better than those endless diets – but it was taking time to get used to her new size. Of course, not that he didn't like it – if only she knew! Didn't she understand that by getting fat she was actually saving their marriage? Likely stopping him from sleeping with other women? Now, she was the perfect size for handling. Mind you, it was rather like being married to a different woman. He wondered if she had got used to it, being so big, after being so thin. She took up more space, walked differently, made more noise; it reminded him of when she'd been pregnant, how she'd hated it, carrying all that extra weight around, couldn't wait for it to be over. Look at her now – big enough to be carrying triplets! She looked a real sight, shovelling down his breakfast, as if it were her last meal. And she dressed as if she were living on benefits – from Prada to Primark – but somehow the elegance hadn't quite gone, nor the determined poise. No, that she hadn't been able to erase (by now he understood that this putting on weight was all deliberate, a way of getting back at him, making him pay); it was a different type of elegance – before, she had shimmered like a tropical fish parading in a tank, now she was like a whale heaving and humping in Antarctica. No, he hadn't asked her why – what was the point, he knew why – nor had he asked her how much bigger she was planning on getting – really, she was plenty big enough for his taste; in truth, her size was an off-limits subject. Actually, everything about her at the moment was a closed shop.

Cassandra ate his toast and marmalade – his mother's marmalade, brought back from the last trip to Yorkshire. She was watching him, watching her. "You want to say something? You don't mind me eating your marmalade?"

"*Figurati*."

"No, say it."

"I was going to say that eating's better than dieting."

"You're on a diet?"

That was funny. "Hardly. I was wearing these shorts the first time you ever saw me, remember?"

"I remember. They were too small for you then."

"I wouldn't have put it that way."

Cassandra stood up, and brought her plate to the sink.

"I'll do it," he said, coming up behind her.

"As you wish."

She turned around, and her dressing-gown cord, straining with so much poundage to keep under control, came undone, exposing all of her enormous nakedness – ripe and Rubenesque. He was right in front of her. She didn't move, waiting for him to move, was that it? He was on her in a moment – his frenzied hands on her breasts, his dry mouth clamped to her neck, her head held back, away from his lips; his rampant cock, hard inside his shorts, pressed against her stomach rolls. She didn't resist, but neither did she respond. He fumbled with his button and zip, ignoring the pain of his pubic hair catching in the metal teeth. Released, his cock sprang to rigid attention. He slammed her up against the sink, lowered his knees to gain access, penetrated her, and pushed his way in. She rocked back and forth in rhythm with him, plates and cutlery rattling on the draining board. It was all over in less than a minute, like animals rutting in the wild. He shuddered inside her, and then stood where he was, panting, his cock becoming flaccid, slipping out of her. He calmed down, stroking the folds of her belly.

"You've become so shapely."

"Is round a shape?" Cassandra pushed him away. "I have to go."

"Go where?"

"To Imogen. You remember? The fat woman who cooked for Frank and Claudia in Saint-Tropez."

He stuffed his cock and balls back into his shorts, and did up his zip and button. "I didn't know you knew her?"

"Now you do. She's teaching me how to cook. I'm sick of pasta."

"What's she teaching you?"

"Comfort food."

"My favourite."

"Yes, I know."

Comfort Food

"I WANT TO APOLOGISE before we start," said Cassandra.

"About what? We haven't started cooking yet."

"About being rude to you, the first time we met."

"Whatever it was, I've completely forgotten."

"No you haven't. I know that because I said it, and I still remember. Now look at us, it's like we've swapped places, you're me and I'm you."

"I don't think I could ever make an entrance like you."

"No? Well, size matters."

Imogen looked at Cassandra, wrong-footed by this wholly unexpected backhand volley, wondering if the fault lay with her. Had she misread the signal? Was there any malice there? But Cassandra, seeing Imogen's confusion, began to grin, at which Imogen burst out laughing.

"Anyway, I'm sorry," continued Cassandra.

Imogen stifled her laughter. "There's nothing to be sorry about. How about a drink and then some cooking? That was a long list you sent me."

"I need a lot of comforting. Yes, a drink would be lovely."

Imogen opened the first bottle of white wine that came to hand in the fridge – as long as it was white and cold. She popped the cork, poured out two glasses, and held one out to Cassandra.

"Cheers."

"Cheers. Can we make shepherd's pie?"

"*Bien sûr*. And I thought this morning we'd also have a go at cauliflower cheese, toad in the hole and Cornish pasties?"

"Fish and chips?"

"If we have some English newspaper. It's not the same wrapped in *Nice Matin*."

"My husband says exactly the same thing. The two of you would get on very well together."

"What about puddings? I thought we'd make them this afternoon."

"I still don't understand the difference between a dessert and a pudding?"

"You can't stop eating a pudding."

"That's the word for me then."

"I'm sorry, I didn't mean it like that."

"There's no need to be, is there? Look, can we get this question out of the way before we start. I don't mind being fat, it's a relief really. There was so much pressure being thin."

Imogen had known that the day would be like this – one long confessional. It seemed wrong not to big up. She was opening herself up to danger, but she felt that she owed that much to Cassandra. "I wouldn't have understood what you meant before, but now I know exactly what you mean. *En effet*, the struggle's the same no matter where the arrow hits the scales."

"Just throw them out. That's what I did."

"You really did that? You sound like a heretic."

"I am. You'd be surprised how much better you feel. Fuck men. How many do you see walking around with stomachs hanging out, who look as if they give a fuck?"

"That's because men like comfort food. Between roast potaoes and salad, the salad loses out every time."

"How about rhubarb and apple crumble? Is it very difficult?"

"*Non, c'est très facile. Et aussi, le* rice pudding, bread and butter pudding, and trifle. We'll spend all day making good old-fashioned nursery food."

"Nick calls it school food. What do we begin with? Do I need an apron? Not that it matters if I spoil these clothes. But you definitely need one. You look like I used to."

Imogen refilled the glasses. "Like I couldn't boil an egg you mean?"

"I suppose I deserved that. That really was a horrible thing I said to you. Nick went on and on about it. I bet I couldn't find anything to fit me now in Brunello Cucinelli."

"What does it matter? It was true what you said. I couldn't find anything to fit me anywhere. It seemed like the end of the world. Can you believe it, I had a breakdown in Chanel. *Basta!* Can you peel potatoes?"

"With the best of them."

The two women set to work, one teaching, the other learning. They settled into a pattern of slicing, mixing, rolling, boiling, and baking, too busy concentrating, to talk outside of the job in hand. Given the amount of wine they were knocking back, the lesson went off surprisingly well: the mashed potato for the shepherd's pie sat firmly over the meat, not slipping like an avalanche; the toad in the hole rose as it should do; the topping of the cauliflower cheese browned to a lovely crisp; and if the Cornish pasties were a little burned at the crust, they still made a good first attempt.

Imogen was rather proud of her teaching skills. *"Très bien fait!"* There you are, you see, not difficult."

Cassandra was delighted. *"Che figata!"*

"After this, the puddings will be a doddle."

For lunch, seated at the kitchen table, amongst the clutter and debris of mixing bowls, meat grinder, saucepans and spatulas, they ate what they had made, or rather, Cassandra ate, and Imogen watched as she tucked in. By this time, they were both quite sloshed.

Cassandra was relishing every mouthful. "Toad in the hole! It sounds revolting but I could eat it every day, and it tastes even better because it's *so* bad for you."

"I have a theory about comfort food: men eat it when they're happy, women eat it when they feel guilty."

Cassandra nodded vigorously, and spoke with her mouth full of sausage and batter. "Then I guess I must be guilty of something really big, only I haven't worked out what it is. Men don't feel guilty, you know that? Whatever it is they do, they think they're entitled to do it. You're not eating? You see, you don't feel guilty about anything."

"I've gone off eating. To tell you the truth I've gone off cooking as well."

Cassandra had started on a Cornish pasty. "He must have really hurt you."

Drunk though she was, Imogen was caught off guard; this was quickly becoming uncomfortable. Women can get to the heart of a situation in a single thought; men bluster and blunder their way through a fog of hints and evasions. But what did Cassandra mean? She had the knack of pickpocketing one's thoughts, spiriting them away, and leaving behind only an awful sense of shock and vulnerability. Imogen remembered how she had pole-axed the Baroness.

There was no suggestion that Cassandra was referring to Nick, or was she? What if somehow Cassandra had found out? Could it be that Andrei had spilled the beans, and today was the day of reckoning? Well, there were plenty of sharp knives lying around to do the job. No, the atmosphere was too congenial, quick and careless for revenge, which needs to be baked in a slow oven. Cassandra seemed happy to say whatever she was feeling, but that was not an option for Imogen; she could only be half honest, and what was that if not a lie? "Mary, Mother of God, hear me in my hour of need …"

She spoke at an acute angle to her true thoughts, but there was enough truth in what she said to be convincing.

"Even now, I'm not sure that I really understand what happened. That's the problem. I can't move on because I can't see properly. One moment it was good and then it wasn't." *Ça arrive comme un cheveu sur la soupe*. But it was what I'd always wanted."

"And I married a man only because I knew what I didn't want."

"What a pair we make."

Cassandra seemed quite cheerful. "It's better to talk about it than to keep it bottled up inside. And people only tell the truth in a kitchen."

"Not in the bedroom?"

"No, people can always lie there. Haven't you ever faked an orgasm? And they certainly lie around a dining-table."

Imogen instantly thought of the Baroness and Papoche. "I used to think that cooking was truth, my truth, at least. I just don't believe in it anymore. *Ce n'est pas du gâteau*."

Cassandra put down the burnt crust of her Cornish pasty, on the side of the plate. "*Che palle*. We all stop believing, don't we? First, it's Father Christmas, then … what is it?"

"That we won't make any mistakes?"

"I used to believe in being thin. More than I believed in the priest."

"Oh, I believed the same, believe you me. Thinness was the Holy Grail."

"Which nobody has ever found." Cassandra's hand was hovering over a Cornish pasty. "Can I manage another pasty, do you think?" As always, before a full confession, there is a dramatic pause. "That's what all this has been about."

Imogen knew what was coming. "Not being thin?"

"He was sleeping with somebody. *Mi fa cagare*. I couldn't carry on as I was, living with the thought of it. That's why I got fat."

Imogen confessed. "And that's why I got thin." She felt a sense of relief; she felt that she had somewhat – just ever so little – salved her conscience. She had linked her weight loss to Cassandra's gain. That was truth enough. The wine had helped them to share out the uncertain measure of experience – thinking about the same man they both didn't want. This was it, then; what it had all been leading up to, since Saint-Tropez.

"You're going to ask me how much I knew? Did I know who she was? Who she is?" Imogen was quiet. Cassandra spoke in short, painful phrases – painful to both of them – as if she were mapping out the contours of her hurt. *"Faccia di merda!* I don't know. And what does it matter? I don't care who she is. I tried to find out. I had him followed; can you believe that? I loved him so much. And I found out nothing. But I knew. I still know. You just do. They can't hide it. They don't even have to tell you any lies. They can tell the truth about where they've been, it makes no difference. They can't keep it up for every second. It's too much for them, being on stage without a break."

Imogen was silent, like a good confessor should be; and yet how awfully aware she was, of her monstrous falsity. She tried not to move, not to react in any way. Cassandra was deep inside her turmoil. "You know what it's like? It's like standing in a museum, and watching a maniac throw paint over a Rembrandt. Perhaps we were too perfect together, was that it? When it's good, you don't really listen to what they're saying because you're on the same wavelength, it all fits together. Then you wake up one morning and it's broken; all you can see is the plate falling, and you keep seeing it falling – over and over again, that horrible long moment when you know it's going to break into pieces as it hits the floor."

Imogen was not to know, but Cassandra was living in both her own pain and her mother's. "You know how much it hurts? Like a sharp kitchen knife, such a temptation, you want to cut yourself with it, to see how much you'll bleed."

Pushing away her plate, Cassandra let out an exclamation of disgust. *"Che schifo!* Look how much I've put away. I didn't touch your food in Saint-Tropez, and now there's almost nothing left." Cassandra drained her glass. She was calm again. "Did you like being like this?"

"I'd never been anything else. But no, I didn't. I wanted to be you."

This admission came as no surprise to Cassandra, but not as a cause for pride. "You're welcome to her. And you can have her husband as well if you like. *Mi infischio di lui.* I think I must hate myself as much as I hate him."

"But I thought you liked being ..." The 'F' word was now not one that Imogen could bring herself to use.

"Fat? I did it for the wrong reasons. And anyway, when you let a man out of prison he still keeps thinking about his cell."

"Oui, c'est ça. I'm still trying, but it's not easy thinking differently about your body. Claudia treats hers like a temple, but to me it feels more like a storeroom."

Cassandra smiled, lightening the gloom. "And mine's a double fridge."

"We're not so different. *Je déprime donc je chocolate."*

"You're right. *Et je raffole de chocolat."*

Both women were silent for a moment, thinking about themselves, and about each other – what they had become.

Cassandra voiced the loss first.

"Don't you miss her?"

Imogen knew exactly what the question meant, yet the answer didn't come to her as quickly as she might have imagined. But Cassandra was in no hurry, and she waited.

"I never thought I would but I do in a way ... several ways, actually. Like a twin sister who's died. Like an amputation. Like an imaginary friend you banish when you grow up."

"Yes, but whatever you've lost still exists in the back of your mind. Somewhere, the thin me is still inside, wanting to be let out."

All Imogen could think about was how much she wanted to make things right for this woman she had wronged. She had decided, late in the day, that she liked her. "Perhaps he likes the new you? Nick, I mean. Men hate it when women are always on a diet."

"If you knew my husband anything like as much as I do, you'd know that he's a selfish bastard who only thinks about himself."

"You looked very happy together."

"I think we were, before."

"You can get it back."

"Nobody loses their happiness, Imogen, they have it taken away from them. And it never comes back."

"Never?"

"Not in the way you'd ever want." Pause. "You don't agree?"

"No, I think I do agree." Another pause. "Perhaps he's unhappy? And with men it doesn't show, they hide it. They're not like us, they don't put on weight, and they don't lose weight. They keep it all inside, like mould in a jar of jam at the back of the fridge."

"Nick has this fantasy about being a gardener, and that's all it is, a fantasy. *Magnaccia*. He loves being rich."

Imogen wasn't sure where this left everything. "Then why this cooking? If he loves his comfort food ..."

Cassandra gave a lovely sweet smile. "What makes you think that this comfort food is going to be of any comfort to him?"

The Tale of a Fairy

*T*HE TALE OF *a Fairy is a fairy tale by Karl Lagerfeld. Before we dissect it, I need to point out that this is not a fairy tale in the old-fashioned sense; you know what I mean – something written by Hans Christian Andersen, that starts out all bright and shiny, and ends up dark and rotten at the core. No, Karl's fairy tale is a little bit different – you can't read it, you have to watch it; it's a video film. Karl imagined the whole thing, he wrote it, and then he filmed it.*

How you approach the film is important – for the full effect, best to go via the Chanel website, which beckons you in with the enticement to, "Enter the world of CHANEL and discover the latest in Fashion & Accessories, Eyewear, Fragrance & Beauty, Fine Jewellery & Watches." Okay, we enter.

You understand, of course, even before you press 'play,' that The Tale of a Fairy *is all part of the amazing Chanel marketing machine – focused, lovely, perfect, chic, worldly, "beautiful and elegant, like a dream" as Karl would have it. Imagine if the world were run like Chanel; looked like Chanel.*

By now, if you've read this far, you will know that this must be leading somewhere, and you'd be right – The Tale of a Fairy *is set in Villa Eilenroc. Why did Karl choose to shoot his modern-day fairy tale there? Because he understands so well the meaning and importance of myth; and Villa Eilenroc is a mythical place.*

I first went there with a member of the Monégasque royal family. I remember that day very well. I was staying at the Hôtel du Cap-Eden-Roc, not where I usually stayed – La Réserve de Beaulieu is closer to Monaco, so I preferred to stay there, but I'd driven down on the spur of the moment, and they were full. I didn't get the best of receptions at the Hôtel du Cap, which I thought was strange, because most hotels quite like young men turning up in black Ferraris. They gave me a room the size of a broom cupboard, right at the back; I didn't say anything.

I drove into Monaco, and did what I always do the first day: dropped the car in front of the Hôtel de Paris, then walked around the corner to the florists in Avenue des Beaux-Arts. I had them send up eleven red roses, with a note to say that I had arrived. Then I waited for the call, sitting in the Café de Paris. I must have been waiting an hour or so, when the concierge came over with the note; and I immediately drove up the hill. Ushered into the drawing-room, I noticed my flowers sitting on a side table, having ceded pride of place to the most enormous bouquet of red roses that I had ever seen – fucking dozens of them. I should have kept my mouth shut, but my pride was hurt.

"You got my flowers then."

I was inviting humiliation.

"Yes, thank you, they're lovely. And Karl sent these."

So I guess you could say that it's personal between me and Karl.

I don't remember why we ended up at Villa Eilenroc. We had to get out of Monaco, of course. I must have read about the gardens. I remember the avenue of palm trees leading to a classical portico – Belle Époque grandeur. That was it, the rose garden!

There isn't much to see inside the house, but I think that's why I like it so much – you can people it with your imagination, which is what Karl did.

We had dinner at the hotel, sitting outside, with that gorgeous view – only I didn't do views in those days; they were just a backdrop for me being charming. And I don't remember what we ate, but they were certainly very attentive. Then I drove us back into Monaco. When I finally returned to the hotel, I was cornered by the manager.

"Cher monsieur, I hope that you enjoyed your dinner? If you had told us before ... Et bien, I have moved you into a suite at the front of the hotel."

There was a pause.

"Forgive me, monsieur, *but we thought that you were a gigolo. De toute façon – your car, your Vuitton, your phone calls,* vous êtes beau et très charmant. *You understand?* Nous parlons de la Côte d'Azur. Enjoy your stay, monsieur."

That was not my only encounter with Villa Eilenroc. One evening, not long before he died, I had dinner with Anton Dolin, in a restaurant on the King's Road in Chelsea. What an opportunity missed! I should have grilled Patrick about Le train bleu, *about Diaghilev, about Nijinska, Picasso, and Chanel ... but Patrick had known Fitzgerald in the South of France, and that was all I wanted to hear about. Patrick said they talked about the tawdriness of glamour – at a party in Villa Eilenroc.*

I realise that I still haven't said anything about The Tale of a Fairy. *But perhaps I don't need to. Better to just watch and then read on.*

Villa Eilenroc

THERE WAS WHITE chocolate flowing from a bronze fountain at Villa Eilenroc. Life-size sculptures of wild animals – panthers, leopards and jaguars – crafted in dark chocolate by an *artiste chocolatier* flown in from Paris, guided the guests through the Art Deco rooms, and out on to the floodlit *parterre*, where a bow-tied orchestra was playing. Still reeling with the rich, bitter and fruity aromas of chocolate that filled the lovely interiors, the guests immediately stepped into another sensory experience, arising from the nearby scented garden. The perfume of espalier roses gave the balmy evening a fragrant tinge, lazily drifting amongst the dancing, the high notes and the gaiety. Minute by minute, Villa Eilenroc was coming back to life, resuscitated and revivified by the press, the smell and the noise of the rich at play.

The men came to Villa Eilenroc in white tie and tails; the women came in fabulous technicolour, except for Imogen who came to her party in black Molyneux, because she had always known that less is more – a figure-hugging crêpe evening gown, first worn by Marie-Hélène in 1938, with a plunging neckline, padded shoulders, and the skirt formed from interwoven tiers of the same soft crêpe.

Claudia, being Claudia, took the opposite approach, dazzling in a 1936 shocking pink floor-length gown by Schiaparelli, with a matching silk-velvet bolero embroidered with vivid floral motifs, and accessorised with a pair of Marie-Hélène's long black evening gloves.

The Baroness looked (but did not feel) serene in a burnt cream, silk Chanel chemise, from 1926; falling just below the knee; plain, with thin straps, a narrow leather belt girded well below the waist, and enlivened with matching flower petals bunched across the left shoulder, the silk edges left artfully frayed, and two handkerchief bows falling from the hem.

Nadia was her extravagant self in black silk georgette by Louise Boulanger, circa 1929, printed with sprigs of delicate pink, cherry red, and pale grey spring flowers; hanging just below the knee at the front, and falling to the floor at the back; with a red velvet bow, tied across the posterior, she looked like a thoroughbred being paraded about in the paddock, in the hope of winning "best turned out."

Jade shimmered in 1922 Jean Patou – a low-waisted, knee-length shift dress in gold, crafted out of metallic thread and glass that caught the light of every chandelier, and clung to her model frame like a tunic of chain mail.

Katya, with her regal ballerina's body, was draped in shades of light green diaphanous silk chiffon, by Madeleine Vionnet, from 1922, after the fashion of Ancient Greece, richly embroidered with tiny white pearls and a *sautoir* of emerald green rhinestones, and a floor-length train that slithered after her, like a peacock, over the marble, and parquet floors.

And Cassandra, what did Cassandra wear to the ball? She had come only because she had promised Imogen that she would; not to please Nick who had pleaded with her. She had agonised over what to wear – she and Imogen had talked it over, that baking afternoon, making puddings.

"What would you wear if you were me?"

"I *was* you, remember? From experience, if you can't hide, then you'd better make an entrance."

So Cassandra made an entrance in a halter neck *robe de style*, in ivory silk, modelled (because she couldn't fit into the original) after an evening gown by Lanvin, from the winter of 1922-23. The only decoration was a wide belt, in the same silk fabric, embellished with two ornate scroll forms, of metallic leather, in Lanvin blue and gold. It was a dress of wonderful simplicity that drew the viewer's eye away from the massiveness of the wearer, to the delicacy of the decoration.

The thing about having lots of money is simply this: when you need to call on all your reserves, it can carry you through absolutely anything. This evening, those millions of euro allowed Cassandra to ignore – not to even hear – the sharp intakes of breath from the people who had yet to encounter her changed appearance. To Nick's credit, the money had rubbed off on him as well, and he held his wife's arm with a determined, solicitous air, as they entered the *salon*.

"Jesus fuck," said Claudia, under her breath, to Frank and Imogen, standing on either side of her, as Nick and Cassandra sailed towards them. "Think of the damage to the floor." But she welcomed her guests with spirit. "Nick, you look like Gatsby! Cassie darling, you look absolutely divine! You look as if you belong in a Greek temple."

"And I'm the sacrificial offering," joked Nick, with good-natured bonhomie, kissing both Claudia and Imogen, and shaking hands with Frank. "That pink is really quite something, Claudia, and you look really good in black, *madame*, but what are we celebrating?"

"We're celebrating me in shocking pink, Nick, and Mo in mourning black."

Imogen felt for Nick. How was he to know that he was the

cause of all this? But perhaps he did, was that it? She had seen the double-take on his face, coming towards her. He must have understood the uncomfortable symbolism of leading his wife – unrecognisable from the woman she had been only the year before – into a party given by his ex-mistress, unrecognisable from the woman who had hidden below stairs.

"Somebody died, and you're celebrating?"

"More a sort of waving goodbye, so please drink lots of champagne! Look at all these people!"

This was a signal for Nick and Cassandra to move off, and allow the crowd of guests already standing behind them, massing in their evening finery, to greet the hosts. Claudia had been telling everyone that she wanted to see, "Lots of top hats, and white silk scarves, and canes, and flowing capes, and the biggest plumage and jewellery you have;" and that is what she got.

There was just time enough for Imogen and Cassandra to exchange the briefest of kisses.

"You look lovely."

"*Et toi aussi.*"

In a moment, Nick and Cassandra were swallowed up by the ebb and flow of midnight excitement; and Imogen, watching them go, was barely conscious of how sorry she felt for both of them.

She stood at the head of the receiving line – Claudia had insisted on this old-fashioned formality – and played her part. She looked resplendent, and she knew it. For the first time in her life, standing next to Claudia – black against pink – she was not over-shadowed; she was shining. A few hours before, at home, she had put on the dress, in front of Claudia. She had slipped it on, like a silk stocking. There had been a stunned silence, as they both looked in the mirror; stared at this unfamiliar hourglass figure; and then at each other; and together, as one, they had both burst into tears.

"Is it really me, Clod?"

"Don't be silly, of course it's you. Who else could it be?"

They had sobbed so loudly that Frank had come in to see what was the matter. "I think we'd all better have a Dry Martini," was as much as he could say.

The two women had repaired their make-up, in silence. Claudia was right; it was as if somebody had died. From Marie-Hélène's jewel box, Imogen had picked out a diamond and pearl pendant necklace, with matching drop earrings – a wedding present to her grandmother, and all that was left of the O'Rorke magnificence.

Gowned and bejewelled, Imogen sensed that, this evening, at Villa Eilenroc, she had become the woman Marie-Hélène would have loved – elegant, poised, witty; and above all, thin.

Gliding towards her, in their patent pumps and Louis heels, uniformly unable to hide their surprise, everybody said what she knew they would say – how marvellous she looked, how glowing and radiant; they asked how did she do it, what was the secret? Was it Paleo or 5:2? It was just unbelievable the difference, really, she ought to write a book ...

To hear these guests – so approving of her loss – you would think that she had won the lottery – lose some weight and get a life. Why then, if this was such a triumph, did it feel like an anti-climax? What, had it taken her too long to get here, the up and down history of her failed dieting, that the taste of victory could no longer be sweet? Or was it that she had always known how it would feel, being thin – she had practised it for so many years?

She wondered how Cassandra was faring. Oh, she knew! For while she, Imogen, might have shed the pounds, it would not be so easy to shed the remembered pain of that poundage. She knew that nobody was going to say anything to Cassandra; about how fat she had become. It would be like the awful lunch in Menton. What do you say when you see a mountain, and wish that you hadn't?

But these were only passing thoughts. Imogen quickly told herself that she was not Cassandra. She wanted to be the life and soul of the party, not just the twin centre of attention – fat and thin.

They had been standing in the entrance hall for more than an hour, gaily greeting and kissing hundreds of flushed and powdered cheeks, breathing in the wafts and draughts of many different aftershaves and perfumes; the cloying and commingling of exclusivity – Hermès, Kilian, Frédéric Malle, Serge Lutens ...; a surfeit of luxury that was really too much for the senses – imagine spending all day in the perfume hall at Harrods.

The crush of arrivals died down. Frank let out a sigh.

"Do you think that we could now, finally, enjoy this party of ours? Don't we all have something to celebrate?"

Imogen caught something in Frank's voice.

"I know what I'm celebrating, but what are you celebrating?"

"Did I say that we were celebrating?"

"Yes. Out with it. Clod, what's going on?"

"Darling, he never tells me anything. Frank's right, can we please get a drink?"

"You two go. I want to stand here and watch for a moment."

Claudia understood. "You want to see how it measures up to Marie-Hélène?"

"Something like that. I think I need to catch my breath."

Yes, that was exactly what she wanted to do. She was colouring in those black and white photographs that she had been living with, all these years – the myth reborn.

But not everything was mythical. There is no such thing as a party for rich people full of only beautiful people – money does not always equal physical beauty – but Claudia had done her best to make this last throw of the dice as beautiful as possible – if they were going bust, then they would do it in style. The waiters were dressed all in white and, rather obviously, exclusively male; Claudia had interviewed every single, young and handsome one of them – they all looked like Tommy Marr. Of course, there were also plenty of beautiful girls to go round – Claudia had ordered a big bouquet of them from an agency. You could take your pick.

Imogen watched as Bill threaded his way through the throng, keeping the moneyed guests supplied with cocktails and canapés. He was closely followed by Casimir, keeping them happy, introducing their money to whatever beauty might take their fancy – a lissome waiter for this man, a small-breasted blonde for that one; rather like selling thoroughbreds at an evening auction.

It was time to join the party. She moved in the direction of the music. A famous singer – boy band survivor, grown up – flown in from London, was crooning *Begin the Beguine*. She knew the words and the tune by heart – it was part of her DNA.

"I'm with you once more under the stars/ And down by the shore an orchestra's playing/ And even the palms seem to be swaying ..."

She stopped; the music did not. Barely a step away, Nick was standing with his back to her, talking with Papoche. She smiled as he plucked a canapé from a passing tray – always hungry. She heard everything.

"I'll give you a choice, old man: the Russians take over, and you're out, or we bring out sugar-free chocolates, and I'll make you president for life."

The song kept on coming ... *"except when that tune clutches my heart ..."*

Papoche summoned up all that he had left. *"Vaffanculo."*

Villa Eilenroc

Nick went for the kill. "Your wife got fat when you started playing around, and then she killed herself. Now look at Cassie, and ask yourself why. You've lost, old man." Nick held up a passing waiter, deftly caught a canapé, and went back to the party.

The crooner had reached the heart of the matter. *"So don't let them begin the beguine. Let the love that was once a fire remain an ember ..."*

That brassy, blaring sound – standing trumpets and sliding trombones – rattled the windows, and seemed to shake the foundations of all that was beautiful and precious about Villa Eilenroc. Pressed against a wall for support, Imogen watched, seeing how Papoche, standing amongst the throng of guests, had nothing to hold on to. She followed his gaze. His dead eyes sought out first his daughter, talking animatedly with Katya and Nadia – something obviously about ballet, which, even in his pain, struck him as a little silly. Cassandra noticed him looking at her, and returned his gaze coldly. He knew, he could see – she had that wild, abandoned look of her mother – that she would never forgive him. Then his eyes found the Baroness. She was standing by a window, by herself, looking out at the people frolicking and dancing in the garden. He willed her to look at him. She turned away from her melancholy, and found his face across the room. There was nothing she could say.

Massimo appeared in front of Imogen, bearing a glass of champagne. She noticed the ring on his finger – a simple band of brushed silver. It was a welcome distraction. She understood immediately.

"He asked you? At last!"

Imogen had never seen Massimo smile with such delight; and she understood that Claudia could never have made him this happy.

"No, I asked him. I was tired of waiting."

Suddenly (a delayed reaction maybe to what she had just seen), everything changed – her mood, her poise, her resolution. She kissed him with affection.

"Oh, I'm so happy for you! I have to go and tell him."

She was already crying as she passed Frank and Claudia talking with Charles and Nadia – something about cleaning up.

"Mo, where are you going in such a hurry!" asked Claudia. "And why are you crying?"

"To the kitchen where I belong! And I'm crying because I know where I'm going."

She pushed her way through the phalanx of guests. She passed Papoche and the Baroness, talking in the same stilted way that she had heard in Menton; and she understood that they would never overcome the hurt they had caused each other. She eased her way past Jade and Ray, talking about Casimir; and she understood that Casimir would one day become Ray. She allowed herself to be embraced by Tikhon, in full view of Katya; and she knew that they would just be good friends. She got much too close to Mat, who was smiling amiably, talking with 'the syndicate' – Oleg, Dabing, Peter, and Andy; and she understood that Mat would always lead a charmed life. She left them all behind; and they all made the same remark, in her hearing, to the effect that she was not like any woman they had ever met.

She swanned into the kitchen, brave and tearful, brandishing a bottle of Ruinart. Marcus was in a carefree mood, primping canapés. "Wow, look at you, sister! That's some dress!"

"Just an old thing I found."

Marcus noticed her tears. "Are the tears for you or for him?"

"I don't know what they're for."

Marcus came towards her, bearing a tea towel. He dabbed the tears away.

"You want to tell me all about it?"

"There's nothing left to tell."

"So then there's nothing left to cry about."

Imogen recovered. Marcus was right. "You're a fine one to talk. You might have told me!"

"Aah, he told you then. And did he also tell you that I'm opening my own restaurant?"

"About time too. But what did Frank say?"

"It was his idea."

"Where's the money coming from?"

"Frank and the people upstairs."

She felt secure in the kitchen. "Good, now let me take care of those, and you open this bottle."

"You can't work in here looking like that!"

"Yes, I can. Just watch me."

Imogen fussed over the canapés while Marcus sent the cork flying through the air, and filled two glasses. "To us, the new me and the new you. Even my spots have gone."

"I don't feel different."

"Oh, but you are, Mo. That's what makes us both special."

Marcus drained his glass. He looked past Imogen. "And here we go again," he said, with the bottle in his hand, poised for a re-pour. "Christ. They sure know how to find you, don't they?"

Turning round, Imogen knew that it would be Nick. She tried not to think how handsome he was, and what it felt like to kiss him. He had broken her heart; remember.

"I saw you running past everybody, and wanted to ask if you're all right?"

She composed herself. "I'm fine. I wanted to congratulate Marcus on his engagement. He's getting married to Massimo, and he's opening his own restaurant."

"Well, that's certainly cause for a celebration. Congratulations."

"You'd better join us," said Marcus, not very graciously. He poured out another glass, and handed it to Nick. Topping up both his glass and Imogen's, he allowed Nick to propose a toast.

"Here's to getting married, and to the restaurant, wherever it is!"

"In Cannes. I'll book you a table."

"If things work out as I think they might, I'm going to need the whole restaurant."

"Great." All the enthusiasm Marcus could muster.

Imogen said nothing. She was thinking about chocolate.

"Have you seen the rose garden?" asked Nick.

"Not this evening, no."

"It's said to be the best there is around here. Would you like to see it? You know what a rosarian I am."

"A rosarian? Is that ..." Marcus seemed quite ready to say something cutting.

Imogen cut him off. "I'd love to."

Marcus frowned. "If you want to miss the party, go through that door and up the stairs."

Nick seemed eager to escape. "See you in Cannes," he said, already opening the door.

Imogen hugged Marcus. "I'm so happy for you. I'll come back."

"Come back but never go back, darling, it's never worth it. And you're worth ten of him."

Nick was waiting for her at the top of the stairs. "I take it you know the way?"

"Over there."

They walked away from the sounds of laughter, music and mayhem. Concealed lighting below, and moonlight above, revealed the way. For a few paces, they were silent with their thoughts – but that did not mean they did not know what to say to each other. Then Nick spoke.

"Do you know that you could have any man you wanted here this evening?"

"I'll take that as a compliment."

"It was meant that way."

Both of them knew that they did not need to examine the whys and wherefores. Still, they tried.

"I almost didn't recognise you."

"That makes two of us."

Imogen wondered if he recognised anything. Apparently, he did.

"And now nobody recognises Cassie."

"Do you?"

"Hard not to."

They came to the rose garden. Imogen was all too conscious of the fact that they had been in a rose garden once before. She was not at all nervous about what he would say; she was strong enough to resist – she had learned something about herself, after all – but she kept her distance, letting him wander at will, staying just a little behind him, only occasionally coming closer as he offered up a bloom for her to smell.

Imogen knew that this was where Nick would say what he had to say.

"It is magnificent, isn't it?"

"It is."

There was still one question that she wanted to ask.

"Have you ever asked yourself why this happened?"

Nick was silent for a moment. "You mean why did I ever leave the garden?"

"No, I know why you left. I mean, why we happened."

Nick seemed to hesitate before speaking.

"Because I was powerless to resist."

If he had asked her there and then to run away with him she would have. After that confession – the unexpected baring of his soul, when at long last she understood that she had meant something to him – she would have given up everything. Part of her wanted him to clasp her in his arms, and that would be that. Part of her resisted. He was standing still, looking out at nothing, towards the sea, his perfect profile carved by the moonlight. She sensed that he was struggling exactly as she was.

But nothing more was said; and it never would be. The roses had worked a little bit of their magic, Villa Eilenroc had cast its spell, but that sprinkling of fairy dust had not been strong enough to sway either of them. It was over.

They heard voices: it was Andrei and Cassandra.

Myth-making

"I KNEW WE'D FIND you here," said Cassandra.

Imogen was finally ready to make a full confession. She wondered if Cassie would say that she already knew. Really, it would be a relief.

"I knew, the moment Andrei said 'rose garden' that this is where we'd find you. You are so predictable, Nick."

"Sorry." The only word that he could find to say.

"As if I didn't know. Did he drag you here, Imogen?"

Imogen said nothing.

Cassandra was quite cheerful. "*Magari*. It's all right, I understand."

Andrei came to the rescue. "I wouldn't have wanted to miss this moment, either."

In the moonlight, in evening tails, he looked to Imogen as if he had stepped out of Marie-Hélène's album.

A familiar voice broke into the fragrant silence.

"You can't leave your own party! So we thought we'd bring the party to you!" announced Claudia, in that voice Imogen recognised from school – she was up to no good. Frank was with her; behind them came two waiters bearing rugs, hampers and a cool box. "We're going to do something that Mo and I have always dreamed about, aren't we, Mo?"

"We are?" asked Imogen.

"We're going to walk down to the beach, and invent something."

"You mean 'be inventive,'" said Frank.

"No, that's not what I meant. Come on, I'll lead. And if anybody gets thirsty, they just have to ask." Claudia detached herself from Frank, and strode up to Imogen, pulling her away from Nick. Then, a little less loudly. "You see? I know exactly what this evening is all about."

"I'm glad you do, Clod, because now I don't."

"Well, you will. Now, you walk with Andrei, I'll walk with Cassie, and Frank can talk with Nick. The boys at the back. The one with the rugs is a dish, isn't he? He's called Tommy. Don't you just want to eat him up?"

"You're impossible. And what am I meant to say? Is there a script?"

"Oh, you can say whatever your heart desires, Mo. Makes no difference now. That's how it looks to me. Doesn't it look that way to you?"

Imogen no longer had coherent thoughts to put into words. She did as she was told. She hung back, waiting for Andrei. She could see that he wanted to make amends.

"You look as if you've been poured into that dress."

"It took a lot of getting into. You can't imagine how long."

"Oh, I think I know how long it took."

They had left the rose garden, skirted past the giant cacti, across the scrubland, and were already walking downhill, towards the coastal path. Step by step, they were leaving behind the manicured perfection of Villa Eilenroc.

Andrei held her arm, helping her negotiate the rocks and steep drops. "There's something about leaving a man-made landscape and stepping into the wilderness. Especially with a party in the background."

"I didn't think you'd come."

"Neither did I. But you invited me so I thought it meant something."

Imogen felt that she had to spell it out, for closure.

"Claudia asked me to invite you."

"Aah."

In front of them, they could hear Nick and Frank talking.

"I'm ready to make my move. I think I've got all my pieces lined up. I'm going to call a board meeting."

Frank's voice had that old easy confidence about it. "I'm afraid you're much too late to the party, Nick. We don't own any shares. None of us – not the Baroness, Jade, Ray, Charles, Tikhon, Mat, Oleg, Dabing, Peter, and even little Andy. We sold them all this morning to Nestlé. So you see, it makes no difference to us who wins this evening, you or Papoche."

Imogen and Andrei could hear the pause in the conversation. There was only the sound of footsteps on stone. A good way ahead of them, out of earshot, Cassandra and Claudia were talking about goodness knows what.

"You can't do anything without Cassie," said Nick.

"True, but she didn't need much persuading. Actually, she was the one who put it all together. Got the price up by telling them how profitable she thought your sugar-free chocolates would be. It's all gone, Nick. Take a good look at your wife. When I look at Cassie, I can see how much you hurt her; and you can't put a price on that ... or perhaps you can."

So much was happening so fast that Imogen was finding it hard to take it all in.

Andrei had worked it out immediately. "Sounds like we've both lost, he and I. Quite an evening."

There was a tune playing in Imogen's head that would not leave; she let it out a little.

"*And down by the shore an orchestra's playing/And even the palms seem to be swaying/When they begin the beguine ...*"

"Cole Porter."

"He's partly what this evening is all about."

"Partly? What else is it about?"

"Recreating a myth to see what it feels like. Fitzgerald's myth, Chanel's myth, my grandmother's myth."

"And how does it compare?"

"That's just it. It doesn't."

"Careful, it's steep here. That's because you have to make your own myth."

They had reached the beach. The sea was calm. The night was quiet. The world looked beautiful. A night for myth-making.

"You're right. There isn't anything mythical about it. It's just human."

Epilogue

Epilogue

Sur la plage

THE BEAUTIFUL WAITERS laid out the blankets. From the hampers they brought out champagne flutes and plates of canapés. The Ruinart came out of the cool box, was popped and poured. Everybody clinked glasses.

"This is it, Mo," said Claudia. "This is what that photograph feels like. Now, could one of you two boys – Tommy, be a dear, won't you – take a picture of us all looking impossibly elegant, and then we can go on living. And don't forget, all of you, that this is one for the album, so think about how you want to be remembered."

The picture was taken. There was a little bit of desultory conversation, but mostly, people looked out at the waves, and thought about what had brought them here – Imogen, Nick, Cassandra, Frank, Claudia, Andrei – weighing up their successes and their failures, their losses and their gains.

Imogen was thinking about what had happened to all of them since that lunch in Saint-Tropez – was that really only a year ago? They had changed so much. Well, perhaps Frank and Claudia hadn't changed, they never would. They would always be spending the proceeds of the last big deal, and planning the next. They seemed never to question the life that they were living. It was rich and straightforward. Imogen didn't envy them the money, she envied the fact that they lived without self-doubt.

Nick was sitting a little apart from the group, not looking at anybody; intently picking up handfuls of sand and letting it fall through his fingers. It was not hard to guess what he was thinking about – how come he'd lost? What had brought him here? How does the man who has everything, lose it? Imogen thought she knew the answer. He was probably thinking that he should have stayed in the garden. No, it wasn't that, although perhaps that was what he would tell himself. No, the garden was an excuse, not a reason. The reason for his failure was that no man can have that much talent, beauty and charm without having a weakness somewhere – the classic fatal flaw. Imogen – fat Imogen – had been his weakness, and he had given in to it. He had dared the weakness to bring him down, and it had.

There was no way of knowing how well Andrei was taking his loss – losing Imogen. Was he a man who cut his losses and moved on, or did he let them entangle him and stop him from moving forward? Imogen had rejected him, he had tried to repair the damage, she had rebuffed him. She was sure that he had more self-knowledge than Nick who, she sensed, would never recover from his fall. Andrei would keep fighting, but it might be a lonely fight.

Cassandra was looking at her husband as he measured his failure in handfuls of sand. It was not her enormous size that most struck Imogen, it was the enormity of what she had done. She had all but knifed him in the back, in an act of calculated revenge. There were no half measures with Cassandra: in Saint-Tropez, loving her husband, she had starved herself; in Menton, hating him, she had pigged out on *daube* and chocolate pudding. She had been a loyal and faithful wife, and then, with a stone-cold heart, plotted against the man she had formerly worshipped. She had broken him into little pieces. That was what she wished her mother had done to her father. In a way, it had been a double revenge: in destroying her husband, she had destroyed her father.

Imogen understood now what it was about the Baroness and her tortured life that had been so fascinating to her – she, Imogen, was a younger version of the Baroness; maybe not so thin but the parallels were there, all the same. There was such a horrible symmetry about the earlier relationship between the Baroness, Papoche and Cassandra's mother, and Imogen, Nick and Cassandra – adultery and gaining weight in both. It was as if Cassandra had deliberately planned the whole destructive process, acting out a revenge drama.

Imogen's life in the past year had moved in reverse to Cassandra's. Nick had been the reason for both the weight loss and the weight gain – the man in the middle. Imogen only wished that he might have left her because he wanted to go back to his wife, but she was certain that it was more about not wanting to lose what he had – an easy life. He had tried to have his cake and eat it – they all had.

All these years she had wanted to lose weight, and now she had. She looked like the woman she had always wanted to be. It should have been a liberating experience; well, it wasn't, her life had become corseted. Fitting into this dress had brought with it a lot of heartache, a failed relationship, a non-starter, and a broken marriage.

Most of all, Imogen was thinking about her grandmother. Was this how it had been for Marie-Hélène? What had she talked about all those years ago, on this beach? What had she been thinking?

There had been glamour, yes; yet it had stopped – or she had stopped it – abruptly, in 1939. Why? Because she must have thought that there was nothing more to look forward to, only a life of looking back. And the more exiled her grandmother had become from the old days, the more glamorous they had grown.

But what was glamour? Marie-Hélène had understood what it was – she had certainly lived it; and so had Chanel, who had dressed it; and Callas also, who had first lost weight and then her voice, for it.

This morning, *sur la plage*, looking at the cast of characters seated around her, white-tied and begowned, with a life of thinness to look forward to, one thought weighed heavy on Imogen's mind as the primary colours of Provence emerged from out of the thinned watercolour of dawn: now she understood what they had all come to know – that glamour is a losing game.

END

ACKNOWLEDGEMENTS

People ask what you are writing; when I tell them what *Villa Eilenroc* is about, almost without exception, women exclaim, "OMG, but that's my story!" which is what made me think I might be on to something.

Firstly, then, I should say thank you to all of the women I have known whose experience of the relationship between weight, food, and sex, gave me an insight into something that men used not to think about.

Above all, with more than thanks to: Nicole Petschek, for the original big idea, slimmed down; Sheila Thompson, my editor, for taking a scalpel to my prose; Felicity Cave, for her catholic taste; and to all of my friends and lovers, lost and found, who have contributed in ways they perhaps never would have suspected. All men make faults, and writing is a way to make amends for, and to make sense of, them.

Jeremy
Noble
Discover more

www.jeremynoble.com

facebook.com/jeremynoble

@jeremynoble